WENDY
MACGOWN

Megabyte Rush

Outskirts Press, Inc.
Denver, Colorado

Megabyte Rush

V3.0

Outskirts Press, Inc.
http://www.outskirtspress.com

ISBN: 978-1-4327-3240-0

Library of Congress Control Number: 2008936104

PRINTED IN THE UNITED STATES OF AMERICA

With love and fond memories to my favorite
Wang support analysts.
We may have been lower than the fallen leaves,
but we got the job done.

CHAPTER 1
SEPTEMBER 1980

A stand of pines shuddered and swayed at the far end of the parking lot, the asphalt already dark from icy rain. Even an idiot could see that the coming storm would be a bad one. Yet Megan gazed out her living room window, ticking off the things she had to do: pick up a suit at the dry-cleaners, stop at the drug store, and pop into her office to grab a datascope, manual and notebook. Chelmsford Center was a pain to drive through even on a normal day; and this weather would only make it worse. She touched the glass, wishing for the hundredth time that she had the nerve to leave, just grab her coat and walk out the door. The temperature was dropping fast and she had a plane to catch.

"Are you done yet?" she shouted, glancing

through the bedroom door, her stomach in knots. Being a good tenant, she'd called the landlord, thinking the leak from her baseboards would eventually drip down on Mrs. Goff, who'd have a fit and probably call the police. And now Stanley Zambinsky was kneeling on her bedroom floor, whistling through his teeth while he tightened the damn pipes.

It was asinine, really, and mortifying—ignoring the weather in case he might actually talk to her—as one adult to another. And then what was she supposed to do—invite him for dinner?

Stan wasn't much to look at with close-cropped, thinning brown hair, tanned skin, a prominent nose and bushy eyebrows set over pale blue eyes. He had to be a hairs breadth away from downright ugly. Yet for some ridiculous reason she'd never been able to fathom, he'd been the star of her girlhood daydreams. Blue collar, no-nonsense Stan was probably having a good laugh at her four-poster, with its frilly, flowered bedspread; and a living room straight out of the latest *Victorian* magazine.

How was she supposed to think straight with him in her bedroom of all places? Not that he'd ever notice her in that particular way. His tastes ran to cheap, painted and blonde—like Christy Connors, his supposed fiancé. Back in junior high, when girls were trading knee socks for panty hose, Christy had bleached her hair, gooped on makeup and sported a lacy black merry widow beneath her gym clothes. She'd seen the thing one hot spring day when she'd waltzed in early to gym class; with Christy in the class before hers. She'd never been early again.

She dragged her attention back to the rain-swollen clouds, shoving away the conflicting images of Christy's skinny butt and Stan sprawled across her virginal bed. It just wouldn't work.

"Hurry up!" she shouted, though the man didn't seem to hear a damn thing. If he didn't get going, she'd miss her ride to Logan. Then she'd be in huge trouble with Irene Snowdon, one of Wright Patterson's office managers, who hated inconveniencing her precious colonels.

The whistling from the other room intensified—off key.

She tapped on the window, thinking there was no time for this foolishness; but for some reason, couldn't leave him alone in her apartment. Afraid he'd steal something? No, that wasn't it. He was one of the most honest men she knew. It was more likely the novelty of being alone with him, though she'd been seeing him a lot lately. In the past week alone, she'd bumped into him at the grocery store three times, at the dry cleaners and the liquor store. It was as if he were stalking her. But that didn't make sense.

She laughed harshly. To Stan, she was just a kid; though he was only a few years older. He hung with Tom Whitfield, her sister, Val's husband, and Roswell's head mechanic. He'd been a regular at Rosswell's Garage for years—was good friends with some of the mechanics. He and Tom played baseball in a local amateur league. According to

Tom, Stan was a veritable saint, always helping his friends whenever they needed something. A few years ago, he'd worked on Tom and Val's fixer-upper, turning it into their dream house.

"If only he were Baptist," Pa had said, sending her a significant look over Sunday dinner at Val's house last weekend. She'd kept her mouth shut, grateful that arranged marriages were out of favor, and she of legal age. Marriage to a devout Catholic was about as attractive as moving back in with Pa—though she suspected Stan wasn't as devout as Pa imagined—given his choice of women.

The first time she'd noticed Stan above the din of air guns and male laughter, she'd been all of fourteen and about to commit patricide. She'd wanted to go to a stupid dance—to pretend for a few hours that she was like the other kids. Of course, Pa had refused. Stan had been leaning against the wall, laughing his fool head off—at her expense, probably—while she'd begged Pa one last time, crying of all things.

She'd never forget that hopeless, empty feeling that had settled in the middle of her chest when she'd stormed out. She'd wanted to slap Stan for witnessing her defeat. No one saw her cry. Ever.

Then an incredible thing had happened a few nights later. She'd started thinking about Stan at odd moments . . . and wondering. Even now she had to wonder—what was it about him that made her insides squeeze together and her hands shake as if he were some kind of celebrity?

She sneaked a quick look through her bedroom door and shook her head. His blue-collar façade had to be a fraud. There was intelligence and humor in his eyes made her pulse race—as did, for some odd reason, the sight of his work-hardened hands. Whenever he spoke, everyone listened; and he wasted no time getting to the point.

"You have to be done, already," she said sharply, moving to the doorway, thinking she should have taken that home repair class and done the work herself. The course application was still sitting on her desk—had been for a month. "A leaky pipe can't be rocket science. Can you fix it or what?"

"It's all set," Stan said, and rocked back on his heels with a wry half-smile. She resisted the urge to back away as he rose and came toward her. He stopped a few feet away, his eyes blazing with annoyance, amusement and something that looked too much like interest. She sucked in her breath.

"I'll just check the faucet in the bathroom," he said. "Not that you even knew it had a problem." He looked down his nose at her.

"Yeah. Right." She crossed an arm in front of her, her heart pounding. "It's through there." She waved to a door on the left. "If you can find it."

ଔଔଔଔଔ

"So polite, as always," he sneered, unable to believe he was alone with Megan Rosswell, in her apartment, in her bedroom. She looked flustered, aggravated and scrumptious. And he was getting hard just looking at her. Fred always called one of the other guys to tackle the plumbing jobs. Today however, they'd all been busy. Lucky for him.

He could hardly stand looking at her: the wanting was intense. Her cheap shots meant nothing. She'd always been prickly; and who could blame her with a mother in and out of mental institutions before offing herself; and a father half-nuts with worry, trying to keep his girls safe from the world. And now look at her—career woman, college grad, big success—looking like she wanted to slug him.

He chuckled as he took in her beautiful apartment. Funny, he would have pegged her for the modern look: chrome and glass, black leather with red accents, sleek and pricey. But she was a romantic, preferring solid, old-fashioned furniture and muted, mood softening colors. Looking down at her oval face, her narrowed eyes and pointy nose, her lips curled down in scorn, he couldn't shake the image of her in a flowing lace dress that begged for nimble fingers. How he ached to touch her hair. Soft and wild, it draped strong, yet slender shoulders, smelling faintly of citrus and herbs. If he could only bury his hands in it as he plundered those expressive lips.

He gazed steadily into her eyes, thinking this had to be the right moment. For almost a month now he'd trailed her like a lovesick moose, praying she'd want him, wishing she were anyone but Gordon's Rosswell's lovely, educated, successful daughter; and him no better than dumb Pollock nail-whacker. Yet here she was, right in front of him, and he couldn't think of single word to say.

"Maybe you should hold my hand," he said softly and leaned closer. Panic lit her eyes. And desire? Brown and warm, her eyes were like rich milk chocolate. He could lose himself in those eyes. Did she feel it too? He took another step.

The telephone shrilled and Megan reached for it, her face quickly averted. Angrily, she jerked her head in the direction of the bathroom. "Get going," she hissed, then barked into the receiver. By the time he finished, she was gone.

ଓଓଓଓଓ

Smoke plumed above the shirt-sleeved, beer-bellied bartender as he slapped drinks onto the gleaming bar. A few feet away, Megan nursed her drink, watching him through lowered lashes. His face reflected the sparkle of spout-tipped bottles set in tiers above a massive, ornate mirror. His swarthy skin suggested a heavy beard; his slicked-back hair screamed of Italy, Greece or some other warm place. There was a gold band on his meaty left hand. His name was Barry or Brad. He slipped her a sideways grin, acknowledging her look.

As if she'd know what to do with him.

She sighed as she glanced at the wall-hung TV at the far side of the room, on which an overexcited reporter announced the state of emergency. Few other patrons even acknowledged it. It was just another noise in the smoky, hotel barroom, battling the clink of glass, roar of laughter and rowdy conversation. The place was packed with pilots, flight attendants and several unlucky passengers. Voices shouted above voices. Everyone seemed to know someone else—everyone except her.

She sipped her margarita, relishing the salty rim and heat of alcohol as it trickled down her throat. Better a little liquid courage in a dimly lit barroom than the loneliness of a cookie-cutter room, she told herself. At least here, she could pretend she wasn't alone. Men didn't usually bother her when she traveled. Something about her seemed to kill conversation. Maybe she was too smart, too sure of herself. Though, unless the topic was computers, she could barely string three words together.

Unless she had a drink in her hand. The thought came unbidden, reminding her of last Friday night's fiasco. She'd had one too many in the presence of her boss—a huge career no-no. She crossed her legs, shoving away the image of Wayne's broad face, graying hair, well-trimmed beard and avid blue eyes. Had she really thought him attractive?

She shivered, thinking she'd been smart to pack a heavy sweater. The storm had bloomed into a late fall nor'easter; and was grinding its way up the coast, ripping up trees by the roots. She was stuck in Boston when she should have stayed home, listening to Stan's insults.

She looked down at her drink, wishing she had.

She was a coward really—too afraid of what he'd been about to say. For a moment, it seemed as if he were actually interested. In her? It had to be her imagination. With her experience, or lack thereof, she wouldn't know interest from insult.

She eyed a mini-skirted waitress: Dora was the name on her nametag. How did she make it look so easy—this sparring between the sexes? She looked like a human-size feather duster: her platinum hair pulled up in a huge pink bow, her makeup thick and colorful. She had to be in her late thirties—a crone in this crowd. Her frilly apron pockets were stuffed with bills—evidence that alcohol and dim lighting did wonders for a woman's appeal. With quick small hands, she added a cherry here, an olive there, then scooped ice into a glass, the diamond on her left hand glittering. She laughed with the bartender as she set the drinks on a tray, spilled a few shots, then hefted it all onto one sturdy arm.

"Damn hurricane," Megan muttered, then held her breath, her gaze snagged by what appeared to be a young pilot—one of a trio in the corner. He had a full head of wavy, sandy-blond hair and a heart-stopping face. He was looking right at her.

ଔଔଔଔଔ

Donald's gut twisted as he spied the slender brunette. She was a curly-haired Cher look-alike—until she moved. Then she was innocence afraid, scanning the room for wolves. She cradled her drink like it was her only friend; her legs tightly crossed, her slacks expensive and well pressed, her sky-blue sweater thick and fuzzy. She looked practical, yet feminine and elegant. He wanted to touch her.

Laughter burst from his two friends; but he ignored them. He nodded slightly and smiled, liking the way the girl narrowed her eyes as she scanned his friend, Steve—obviously a woman of discrimination.

"You know her," Donald asked out of the side of his mouth.

"Naw," Steven said with an abrupt laugh. "I tried, though." He scratched the back of his neck. "Seems she doesn't like tall, dark and handsome. You think an all-American boy like you is more to her tastes?"

"What'd she say?" Donald took a swig of beer.

"She wouldn't tell me her sun sign." Steve shrugged. "A little too uptight for me—too serious. What does she expect in a hotel barroom?"

"Call yourself a pilot?" Donald said with a tight grin as he stood and clasped Steve's shoulder. "You can't even find the runway, bucko, much less land. That line's so old and trite; my father must have used it."

Loud guffaws followed him to the bar.

ଓଓଓଓଓ

"This seat taken?" asked a husky voice.

Megan looked up into golden eyes rimmed with

sable lashes. They were cat's eyes, predatory, yet filled with humor. A golden-eyed playboy. Could he see in the dark?

"Have a seat," she said with an expansive gesture, as if she were playing a part in some old-time movie. He was the gorgeous pilot, one of the laughing trio. His friend was an idiot. Through a slight alcohol haze, she placed him as the archetypical handsome stranger, about to change her life forever.

"Name's Donald." He set his business card on the bar.

"Hello, Captain Donald Thomas Alexander," she said, smirking as she read the card. She looked him over, admiring his uniform. "So you're an Airlius pilot, homeport Chicago." She held out a hand. "Megan Rosswell." She flashed a warm smile. "I'm sure I've flown with you a time or two, Captain."

"Hi ho, the Ice Queen," he said, and took her hand, sending tingles up her arm. "Just as I thought," he said, leaning closer, his hand deliciously warm. "You need a little fire."

"Slow down, space cadet," she whispered and breathed deeply of beer and spicy cologne, blood pounding in her ears. She smiled as she pulled her hand away. "Alcohol makes us all look good. Like that one." She lifted her chin at Dora, who was flirting with Donald's friends. "You just missed her."

He laughed, his lips inches from hers; and she couldn't help but notice that his teeth were movie-star perfect.

"You know you're the best looking girl here,"

he said, eying her mouth, causing an ache deep inside her.

"Girl?" she gasped, the word registering. The man was a Neanderthal.

"At first glance, you look like a starched Yankee, desperate for a good time. But I—"

"Whoa! Girl? Yankee? Desperate! I don't think so." She moved away from him, reminded of Stan; then shook her head, getting annoyed. Why had *he* come to mind? Because he wouldn't like her sitting at a bar, talking to a stranger? No, that wasn't it. He wouldn't care what she did. It was the chauvinism that ran clear through both of them, and every other man she'd ever known, including Pa, who'd love to lock her in her room and throw away the key.

She took in Donald's puzzled expression, the muscle twitching at the side of his face. Here was a prime young male—good looking, smart and funny—and all she could do was argue with him. At this rate, she'd never have a boyfriend.

"What about you, Captain Alexander?" She took a sip of her drink, noting his expensive haircut and professionally manicured nails. Something about him wasn't quite real. "Can't be much going on tonight for a high-roller like you. You didn't exactly have to sit here, you know." She lowered her lashes in apology and smiled sweetly.

He chuckled, his eyes bright with teasing. "Yeah. You got me there, Meggie, sweet. I don't have to sit here. However, I want to, and you said yes."

Meggie, sweet. He'd said it softly, warming her insides.

"When did you get into Boston?" she asked, observing the blush that crept up his neck. The sight was endearing, pushing him into the little brother category; somehow reminding her of Kevin, her once best friend, who'd dumped her at twelve—another male she'd rather not consider.

"About noon," he said, eying her over his drink. "Mine was the first flight cancelled. I can fly with instruments, but the wind's too strong, the runway's too slick. I'll be out of here as soon as the weather clears, probably at daybreak."

"So how does one become a pilot?" she asked. A dozen other questions popped into her head. She imagined herself as a lead reporter on the scent of a good scoop, a headliner that would ignite her career. She chuckled, his face blurring as she took another sip of her drink.

"Long story," he said. He cradled his glass in both hands and smiled as the bartender placed a basket of pretzels on the bar between them. He grabbed a pretzel and tossed it into his mouth.

"It not like we're going anywhere," she said, glancing at the TV and shaking her head as he held out the basket. "Let me guess. She tilted her head slightly. "You're poor white trash made good, a preacher's kid gone bad, or a farmer's son sick of the toil."

He laughed loudly, leaning away from the bar. "No," he said, shaking his head. "I'm an army brat who pissed off my colonel daddy by enlisting in the Air Force. I refused to go to West Point, unlike two of my more obedient brothers." His hand shook slightly as he reached for another pretzel. "Then I failed to reenlist. Naughty me, the black sheep who went commercial."

"So, where'd you grow up?" she asked.

"I didn't." He snickered, his mouth full of pretzel; and she couldn't help but laugh. When he started to choke, she slapped him on the back, then rubbed his shoulders until he stopped coughing.

"No, really?" she said, grinning, her hand falling away. "Where'd you grow up, Donald. I need to picture it for some reason?"

"Oh . . . let's see," he said, smiling into her eyes. "There was Germany, South Carolina, the Philippines, D.C., Ohio—pack and unpack, fight a new bunch of kids, and stick by my brothers. Dad came home and we saluted. 'Course my mother's a social maven, who can pack and move on a day's notice—the perfect colonel's wife."

Was he gritting his teeth? There had to be more that he wasn't saying—maybe couldn't say. "What's Chicago to you?" she asked, and gasped as he placed a warm hand just above her knee. Momentarily startled, she blinked to focus, then looked down into an empty glass. In a blur of motion, it disappeared and the bartender slapped down another. She smiled at both men, blissfully grateful.

"My parents retired to Chicago," Donald said, moving slightly closer. She strained to hear over a burst of laughter from the other end of the bar. "I don't know if you'd call it retirement." He shot her a meaningful look. "He's in Intelligence and still gets a call now and then. Then he's gone for months." He shrugged. "I don't see them all that often. It's been a year or so. You close to your family?"

"Maybe too close," she said, the image of Pa checking her car's oil in the parking lot coming to mind. It didn't matter that she followed her car's recommended service plan, albeit with the dealership: Pa simply didn't trust her. "They're only a few miles away," she said. "About twenty miles north of here. My father owns a garage."

"Auto mechanic?"

She nodded.

"You must have grease monkeys hanging all over you," he said with a smirk.

"Not really," she said with an abrupt laugh. "My father's a Baptist. He wouldn't let me date anyone interesting. And my big sister, Val's a hard act to follow. You know, married the right guy, produced the requisite grandchildren, stays home where she belongs. Like you, Captain, I failed to conform." She laughed lightly.

"So, let me guess," he said, rubbing his chin, "you're in marketing or sales—something showy—maybe a secretary meeting her boss." He raised a brow.

"Not exactly," she said, annoyed by his negative stereotyping. But, hadn't she done the same? When his hand fell away from her knee and he reached for a pretzel, she moved away slightly. “I work for CompuLink as a customer support analyst.” She looked at him squarely. “I research software problems, help customers, travel a lot. We call them fly and fight missions.”

“Sound’s important,” he said, then threw a pretzel at his mouth and missed, making her laugh.

Her breath caught. There in his eyes was a bold little question. Would she? Could she? It would be so easy.

Then Stan came to mind, and one of his scathing remarks that had left her wondering why she’d even bothered to crawl out of bed in the morning. She could hardly focus; and yet it seemed as if the Captain’s odd golden eyes bathed her with approval. She couldn’t help but smile back, struck by his classic good looks. He was smart and educated. He lived the life of which she’d always dreamed. So he was a chauvinist—weren’t most men?

She found herself telling him about Irene and the other trips she’d made in recent months; and was barely coherent as they bantered about her job, his time in the Air Force and the marvels of various cities. She was vaguely aware of leaving the bar, stumbling to her room and taking off her shoes. Her skin seemed especially tingly and hot; and she made no protest as he, somehow naked, helped her remove her sweater and bra, then laid her on the bed. She closed her eyes, floating gently as her slacks and panties disappeared.

Then his hands were everywhere. She tipped back her head and moaned as sensations too exquisite to articulate sent her over the edge of reason. She imagined she was his captive slave, schooled in the ways of love, honor-bound to submit. Sighing, she offered her breasts to him, and then her mouth, eager for all of it.

She imagined that he was Stan.

Her eyes flew open and she was suddenly wide-awake. Now where had that come from? And what the hell was she doing, panting beneath some pilot named Captain Donald Thomas Alexander, whom she'd just met? She gasped as he laved her nipple, his tongue rough. It should have been Stan. The thought was like the lash of a whip.

She held her breath, unable to take her eyes off him as he moved lower. Barely audible sounds of protest came from her throat as he did things to her that she could never have imagined. It was as if he were playing her, his fingers and lips sure and practiced. Even falling-down drunk, Captain Donald appeared to know exactly what he was doing.

"Please," she begged, beyond desperation in the darkened room. It was as dark as sin—a cover for degradation—what Pa would say—yet he'd never know. And Stan . . ..

"Please," she whispered, struggling to wipe the image of Stan from her mind. When Donald's tongue invaded her mouth, she opened to him, barely able to breathe, telling herself that she'd asked for this, that it was too late to back out, that this was what drink had brought her to.

"Now?" he asked; and she nodded, then held her breath as he entered her, a little at first. She averted her eyes, and closed them as the pain knifed in.

"God, you're tight," he said with a grunt.

She bit her lip and stifled a sob as he pushed in deeper. It hurt. Oh, God it hurt.

"It's your first time," he said flatly. He didn't move.

Keeping her eyes closed, she hoped he'd continue, she prayed he'd stop. It wasn't his fault she'd practically thrown herself at him. It would never hurt again, she told herself. It was what she'd wanted, wasn't it?

"Are you sure?" he asked softly.

"Does it look like I'm resisting?" she asked, peering at him out of one eye, rage filling her at the unaccountable kindness in his. "Just do it," she hissed, then bit her lip as he gripped her hips and tore in all the way.

Pain exploded. She held her legs stiffly, hating the invasion, the endless thrusting, until finally, thankfully, he tensed and collapsed against her. She counted to sixty, hoping it was enough time to satisfy some ridiculous post-coital etiquette—if such a thing existed.

"That was lovely," she murmured, wanting him off her. Now. He reeked of beer; and was that gas he was expelling? Shuddering, she pushed and prodded until she managed to slip out from under him, then rose from the bed, her knees buckling.

Her head spun as she lurched toward the bathroom.

"A virgin," he said. She turned, seeing him shaking his head, looking bemused.

"I'm not anymore," she growled, and in a few practiced moves, flipped her suitcase open on the dresser. Why wasn't he taking the hint?

"How can it be?" he said, sitting up, clasping his knees. "I've never had a virgin."

"You're an idiot," she said, and laughed dryly as she pulled a wad of tissues from a nearby box, then swiped at the trickle of blood rolling down her inner thigh. Spying blood on the sheets, she held her stomach, feeling slightly queasy. What a mistake. What a big freaking mistake.

"Now get out." She pointed at the door.

He swung his legs over the side of the bed and rubbed his forehead. "Get out? Gee, I don't think so, Miss Meggie." He looked up at her. "You have to marry me now. I can't live without you."

"Don't be ridiculous." She wanted to slap him.

"I've . . . I've never felt this way before." He spoke in falsetto. "And to be your very first, my darling . . .." He held his onto stomach and moaned, imitating her, his mouth working, holding back a smile.

"Get a grip, fly boy." She whacked him with a pillow. "I'm not interested."

"I'll get a grip," he said, his expression hardening. He spanned the distance between them, pulled her to him and kissed her hard on the mouth. Against her better judgment, she kissed him back.

"All right. All right," she said, her heart pounding as she shoved him away. "That's quite enough." She returned to her suitcase. "You're just a one-nighter, Captain, and don't you forget it." She grabbed a bottle of shampoo, beyond furious. "I don't know you. I don't want to know you."

"Ah, that cuts me to the quick." He placed a hand over his heart. "You will," he said, his expression sober. "Trust me on that one."

"I don't think so." Pain filled her as Stan came to mind once again. Would he have been as gentle, as persistent? Now that she knew what happened between men and women, she wished she'd never left her apartment. Had she only imagined Stan's interest? Her head was starting to throb and she was sick of making conversation. She wanted peace, quiet and most of all, sleep.

"Come on Meggie, you have to admit you liked some of it," he said softly. "There's something special about you . . . something warm and giving . . . something I need."

She rolled her eyes. "When exactly are you leaving?"

"Just a little promise?" he pleaded, his eyes twinkling. "You must feel something towards me. Otherwise . . .?" He nodded at the bed.

"Yeah, and we were both drunk," she said, then stretched her arms over her head, trying to straighten a kink in her back. In the throes of passion, her body had done some strange and testy things.

"So you won't marry me? Or can't?" he asked, his eyes crossing as he ogled her breasts. "You got someone else?"

"Nope." She took a step back, trying not to think about Stan, though it was impossible. "Look Captain, it's late and I'm tired." She jerked her chin at the door. "I need a shower. When I come out, you'd best be gone."

"I need to see you again," he said. "I want to call you."

"I said get out!" she cried, wanting to scream and cry and throw up all at once. Her whole body shook as she fled to the bathroom and locked the door.

ଓଓଓଓଓ

Air traffic resumed early the next day, as Donald had predicted. Elbowing aside other equally desperate travelers, Megan managed to catch a flight to Dayton. At Wright Patterson Air Force Base, she blocked out what had happened the night before and solved Irene's problem in time to catch the red-eye back to Boston.

Late Friday night found her still at work, wishing she were home. She glanced at her watch, noting the time. Everyone else had already left for the weekend. She sighed heavily, scanning the battered metal desks arranged four-to-a-cubicle. It was her first job out of college, for which she was duly grateful. But it wouldn't be her last.

CompuLink was the pits; their corporate office an ugly two-story building in North Billerica, Massachusetts. Inside, the place smelled faintly of cigarette smoke, burned coffee and copy machine toner. It was a gray and gloomy cave, a place of false smiles and tense rivalries, where a careless woman could easily ruin her reputation. She'd learned that the hard way.

The latest issue of *Victorian* magazine peeked from her bag on the floor. She itched to read it, but her trip report came first. Val claimed she was obsessed with Victoriana: wedding cake-like houses, delicate laces and long flowing dresses of organdy and taffeta. That she managed to attend the open house of nearly every Queen Ann Victorian that came on the market, and knew the antique dealers in Essex by name didn't necessarily mean she was obsessed. Fascinated would be a better word—while being grateful for modern conveniences such as indoor plumbing, refrigeration and women's rights.

"Yeah, like the right to screw up," she moaned, closing her eyes, vowing never again to drink with a man. Her recent experience with the Captain was just another manifestation of her obvious allergy to alcohol.

"Stupid. Stupid. Stupid," she muttered, touching her forehead with cold fingers and closing her eyes. What was supposed to have been a few quick drinks with co-workers last Friday had turned into a bottomless drunk. Somehow, her glass had never been empty—just like with Donald. She vaguely recalled staggering to the dance floor with Wayne, where he'd groped her while whispering what he wanted to do to her—not that she'd understood half of it. But when his wife, Joyce had joined them, she'd made a speedy exit. Girl on girl was something she would not do. Wayne had the day off; but eventually, she'd have to face him. Being young and subordinate, no one would take her word over his. With her reputation in shreds, she had no future at CompuLink.

She sighed as she sat back in her chair, a badly stained number that was as comfortable as a rock. Maybe it was time to call that recruiter Pa had told her about—Pa once again coming to her rescue. She'd never live it down.

She scanned the thick stack of green and white listings in front of her, the pile of pink message notes, only half of which she'd addressed; and the mountain of service manual at her elbow, all of which she'd practically memorized. She'd have the last laugh. She wasn't dependant on father or boss for her sustenance. The job market was hot. With her experience, she'd land a great job—one that paid a whole lot better. A fresh start was all she needed. And it would be *her* success alone; not Pa's or any other man's.

For some reason, Donald came to mind; and she grimaced. His image was already fading into the abstract—what had happened with him becoming a valuable lesson in alcohol avoidance. She'd probably never see him again. At a new company, she'd meet other men just like him and would be more careful—men very different from Stan. The thought came with a sinking sadness.

It was obvious that Stan, a typical working stiff, needed a wife to do his laundry, cook supper, make babies and stock the fridge with beer. Someone like Donald would be a better choice. Sophisticated and worldly, he was an educated woman's dream. She choked out a laugh, thinking of his ridiculous marriage proposal. If she had half a brain, she'd stay as far away from him as possible.

The telephone shrilled and she grabbed the receiver. "CompuLink," she said, hoping it wasn't Irene with yet another complaint.

"Meggie, sweet."

"How did you get this number?" She pushed away from the desk, fear spiraling in her gut, her mind racing.

"Aw, come on, Megan. And after I proposed to you . . . twice." There was a smile in his voice.

"Don't play with me, Captain." She gripped the receiver and crossed her legs tightly, thinking of the way his golden eyes sparkled when he smiled.

"All right. All right," he said, slurring slightly. "I took a damn business card from your purse, so don't get flustered, princess. You know I'm harmless. I just wanted to see you again. What's wrong with that?"

"No prime female at the bar tonight, Donald?" she asked softly, pressing two fingers to her temple. "Come on now, surely a good-looking guy like you can find someone to snuggle. How about a waitress?" She held her breath, hating to admit that she didn't want to picture him with another woman; that the sound of his voice evoked urgent needs. Her face burned, her groin ached and her heart pounded—all because of what . . . a damn one-night stand? She glared at the receiver, wondering why the hell she'd picked it up.

"Meet me tonight," he said; and before she could stop herself, she was giving him directions to the Town House, a tavern near her apartment where her co-workers were unlikely to appear.

ଔଔଔଔଔ

The Town House was a sprawling, whitewashed carriage house that had served the City of Lowell for over a hundred years. It boasted a quaint restaurant, eighty guest rooms, several meeting rooms and a single noisy bar, which on Friday nights was packed with revelers, mostly from Smith Labs, one of her company's biggest rivals. The bar was a study in browns and whites, its walls adorned with framed equestrian prints and blue-gingham curtains. Small tables shoved together accommodated groups of suits and jeans-clad patrons. Middle-aged waitresses passed rounds of drinks, while several people milled around a banquet table at the back that held what looked like taco fixings—a legal concession to the happy hour.

Megan's stomach rumbled as she stood in the

doorway. She'd skipped lunch. A drink would hit her like rocket fuel. She spied Donald at once, sitting mid-bar, an empty stool beside him. Around him, business-suited men talked shop while awaiting their drinks, smoking their brains out. Her whole body screamed in protest as she moved toward him.

"Hello there," she said, nudging his shoulder as she slid onto the barstool.

"You look fantastic," he said, his gaze devouring her cream cashmere sweater and pressed black slacks. "It's great to see you again."

His words were inane, his look leering. He was expecting sex. She looked at the margarita in front of her—the frosted glass, the salty rim—just the way she liked it. "You, too," she said, smiling coolly, disliking the breathless, out of control way he made her feel. He looked delicious, reminding her of what she had done with him in bed—what she wanted to do again.

She took a gulp of the drink. It was liquid fire. She pushed it away. In the shadowy bar, Captain Alexander was just another stranger, watching her over his drink. "Survived your flight, I see." She held his gaze, mortified by the heat that rushed to her face. Damn, but she wanted to kiss him.

"You look tired." He brushed a stray lock from her face, his touch unimaginably gentle. His fingers grazed her neck, his movements slow, deliberate, as if he had all the time in the world.

"Long day," she mumbled, pulling away

slightly, telling herself that it was lust alone that drew him—though a tiny voice cried out that it wasn't quite that simple. In a single, loveless act, had he staked a claim?

"The Ice Queen returnith," he said, and laughed into his drink. "And it's only been . . . what . . . all of two days?"

"So, what's new in Chicago?" she asked, ignoring his jibe, her expression bland. He'd probably booked a room already—or worse—planned to use her apartment. Agreeing to see him had been stupid. Leaning closer, she tried to concentrate on what he was saying.

"I've been flying pretty much straight since I last saw you." His eyes were heavy with fatigue. "I needed a break. Sometime I forget what direction the plane's heading. Boston. Chicago. Boston. Chicago. It's like driving a lousy bus."

She scanned his face, hoping that not all pilots echoed his sentiment. She'd never liked flying; and it wouldn't help to know that pilots were bored. Or hung-over.

"Oh no!" He looked around anxiously and sloshed his drink on the bar. The man beside him sent him a nasty look.

"What is it?" she asked.

"I just remembered something," he said, and put a hand on her leg, making her flinch. "I have to make a phone call. I was supposed to meet someone and forgot to cancel. I'll be just a minute." He was looking toward the door.

Myriad feelings crowded her mind: relief, anxiety and fear not the least of them. She swallowed against dry heaves, hating herself, grateful.

"Save my seat, sweetheart. I'll be right back," he whispered in her ear as he rose.

She watched him weave through the crowd, then followed, holding her breath, shielding herself among a group of business people on their way out. She passed within a yard of him as he spoke in urgent and hushed tones to a desk clerk in the lobby, his back to her. Seconds passed. Her heart pounded. Then she pushed through the door and was gone.

On Monday morning, she made several furtive phone calls to Skip Davis, the headhunter her father had suggested. He was supposed to be the best; and she was desperate to snag a new job. Donald had her work number, but her home phone number was unlisted. A job change would end his pursuit, along with her career's stagnation. Or so she thought until the flowers began to arrive.

The first delivery came at nine o'clock when the guard at the security desk handed her the most exotic and exquisite arrangement she had ever seen. Word spread fast. Within the hour, workers from other floors—strangers—started passing her cubicle to catch a glimpse. She grimaced as she brushed a fingertip over a deep purple iris. There were several of them, like velvet jewels dripping with dew. Fresh and vivid, their stark beauty was stunning—as were the clusters of pink and white carnations and the luscious cream roses. The arrangement took up half her desk. She lifted the card.

Please see me, it read.

"Please yourself," she muttered, carefully screening the card from Dave Griffen, her office-mate, before she tore it in half and threw it in the trash.

"New boyfriend?" Dave asked, flicking fine brown hair off thick glasses, as he craned his neck to see. He was a fellow support analyst, a geek and company know-it-all. If the rumors rang true, he'd soon be her group leader—another fine reason to change jobs.

"Not really," she said tiredly, and pushed away from her desk. "Just someone I met on a trip." She grabbed a user manual and pretended to read.

"Wright Patterson?" he asked.

"No," she said, focusing on the manual, daring him to press further.

He turned away with a nervous snicker.

It was just the beginning of an irksome day. Whispers pursued her as she strode from her cubicle to the lab and back. A few of her bolder coworkers asked direct questions that she refused to answer. Clutching her throbbing head, she'd left for an early lunch and took the flowers home. In their absence, gossip seemed to abate. Yet, with the arrival of another, equally stunning arrangement the following day, the rumors started up all over again. Then, each subsequent day for the remainder of the week, another gorgeous arrangement arrived, sending the gossipmongers into overdrive. By Friday afternoon, she couldn't move from her desk without hitting a wall of whispers.

"How am I supposed to do my damn job?" she snarled at Wayne, who stood outside her cubicle, not meeting her eyes. He'd just rescinded her machine time for the next two weeks, effectively canceling her job. She had nothing to do now but look busy at her desk.

"You'll do it just fine," he said huskily, then laughed as he walked away, making her want to strangle him—though strangulation was decidedly too humane. In the cafeteria that morning, in front of a large group of people, he'd insinuated that he'd been sending her the damn flowers—for services rendered.

She grabbed her phone, punched in the number she'd read on Donald's business card, and listened to a recording. "Great," she muttered and slammed down the receiver; then looked up to see Wayne standing at the end of her cubicle row, laughing with a group of managers, probably at her expense. To her left, Dave was eyeing her speculatively. He lived with his mother and had the annoying habit of chewing wads of computer paper and leaving little piles behind her chair. By this time of day, he was usually gone to his miserable home life. The hungry gleam in his eyes made her stomach lurch.

"Just what I need," she said, turning away, shuddering at the thought of having to look at him across a dinner table.

When the telephone rang, she pounced on it.

"Hello?"

"Please, Meggie. Please don't hang up."

"Donald," she said, letting out a long breath, the ice around her heart starting to melt. "Sorry about last week—"

"But?"

She winced. "But, I didn't think it was such a great idea—seeing you again. The flowers—"

"Did you like them?" His tone was intimate, making her shiver. She pulled at the collar of her turtleneck sweater.

"Like them?" She smiled. "How could I not like them? They're gorgeous. But I—"

"I'm glad, sweetheart," he said firmly. "Now tell me, what could you possibly be doing at work on a late Friday afternoon?"

"I'm . . .." She swallowed hard and closed her eyes. Channel Two was showing a special on antiques at nine. That and a pizza delivery—what more could she want? She glanced at Dave, who was watching her closely.

"Come to Boston for the time of your life," Donald said softly. "I'm staying at the Park Plaza. We'll see a show, go shopping—you name it. Please, Meggie. I've been thinking that this must be new to you . . . you being an innocent and all. You just need a little coaxing, a little tender loving care."

It was like water to the parched. Anything was better than another lonely night in her apartment; and it wasn't as if she hadn't already done the deed with him. "Okay," she said, barely above a whisper; then gave him her address.

An hour later, she slid into the back seat of the Boston-bound limousine he'd sent for her, took a glass of champagne from the uniformed chauffeur, then sat back with a sigh, vowing to enjoy every minute.

ഗ്രഗ്രഗ്രഗ്രഗ്ര

Late Sunday night, she stood pressed against Donald outside the Park Plaza, her hands in his coat pockets, wondering at her sanity. His black limo sent plumes of white into the frosty air, while the chauffeur waited discretely inside. Lights from the surrounding buildings glittered in sharp contrast to the navy sky. Traffic zoomed past, part of the back-drop. A few hardy pedestrians hurried along, hats lowered over foreheads against the cold. The sights, sounds and smells pressed into her brain in slow motion, memories she'd never forget.

Like in a movie, they'd ordered room service in Donald's suite. They'd soaked in his Jacuzzi, then made passionate love in his king-sized bed. She had been his concubine, his gangster moll, his treasured virgin wife. He'd been eager to feed her fantasies and create a few new ones. In the morning, they'd devoured bagels and coffee before traipsing through the Back Bay, throwing hundred dollar bills at bold jewelry, pastel silk shirts and a pair of cute platform shoes. They'd laughed and pointed at teens sporting

Mohawks, girls in combat fatigues and black matrons holding cherubs under tight control. Saturday night they'd attended a play, then shared a plate of pasta and a bottle of wine at a rowdy North End bistro. As the weekend passed, she found herself liking his careless touch, his infectious laugh and happy golden eyes.

"What am I to do with you?" she asked, looking up at him, wishing she could drag him back to his room. He'd already checked out, and in minutes, she'd be heading home. He'd be gone for several weeks.

"Promise you'll see me again?" he asked, then kissed her softly on the side of her neck.

"Of course," she said, closing her eyes, melting into his magic. Then she lifted her chin and smiled. In all honesty, she barely knew him; but leaving him now was like a jail sentence. It was back to her regulated life, her role as daughter, sister, aunt and dedicated support analyst. She had to believe there'd be other men, other times, other places. It didn't pay to get too close to any one person. But when his arms went around her, she uttered a soft cry and met his kiss, tasting excitement and danger.

All too soon, the limo's horn sounded. Tears filled her eyes as she pulled away.

"Don't," he said, and kissed her forehead. "Keep it light. Keep it fun. I'll see you again. I have to. I need to."

"All right," she said, and straightened her spine as he opened her door, then helped her inside. The door closed firmly, locking out the city sounds, the smell of gasoline fumes and the cold. She forced a smile and waved as the limo pulled away.

ଔଔଔଔଔ

Rain splattered against the window. Megan moaned softly and peered at her clock radio, wondering for a hazy moment what time it was—what day it was.

Saturday.

The thought came with relief and she snuggled beneath the covers. There'd be no work, no appointments, no hassles, no schedules to meet, and it was raining. She closed her eyes, replaying the past week: the blur of job interviews and the long drive to and from Hartford, Connecticut, for a customer presentation that had lasted all of fifteen minutes. She'd called Donald each day, but left no message. Friday night had come with its usual drinking invitation from nosy coworkers, which she'd declined, using her nephew, Tommy's tenth birthday as a convenient excuse.

She shivered as she donned her fluffy cotton bathrobe, then padded to the window and shoved it open, the cold, damp air like a balm. Val was probably throwing her windows open, too; and pulling back the bed covers to air them, as they'd done when they were kids. She was probably at her window even now, studying the wash of blue that filled the eastern sky, praying the sun would shine on her eldest child's birthday.

Ten was a milestone age—the first two-digit number. Her own tenth had come during one of her mother's bad spells, when guests had not been welcome. Back then, now that she thought of it, guests had rarely been welcome; and even now, her family would not welcome Donald. She could hear Pa, calling him an army brat or a fly-boy, right to his face. Behind his back, he'd rub it in that Donald wasn't a keeper; that eventually, he'd move on to someone else—as if she were too stupid or naïve to figure it out for herself.

She backed away from the window, imagining Val's shock if she should ever learn of last weekend. She'd never tell her.

"It's my life," she said, without much conviction, as she moved to the center of the room, trying to relish the quiet, the solitude. Her little apartment was all she had. She'd fought hard to get it.

She smiled appreciatively at the sunlight slanting across her living room, illuminating her beige wingback sofa and the magazine-strewn solid cherry coffee table before it. "It's my life," she murmured as she collected a food-encrusted plate, a half-empty wine glass—evidence of a solitary meal—then dumped the dirty dishes into the dishwasher.

Pa and Val would have their hurtful say; so she'd tell them nothing. Donald was just a friend. It had been a long time since she'd had one of those. She grimaced, picturing Kevin O'Connor's blue-black hair and mischievous bright eyes. He'd been a friend since Kindergarten—until he'd dumped her at twelve for the company of boys. The second of nine kids from a devout Irish Catholic family, he'd been small and wiry, like a leprechaun. Elf-boy she'd called him. She smiled, thinking of his mother, Mary, a solid, pleasant-faced woman, who'd been as generous with hugs as she'd been with her food. As often as she'd dared, she'd tried to blend in, scrub-faced and solemn amidst Mary's kids, thankful for a mouth-watering, wholesome meal—until Val had dragged her back to a too-quiet house, where Pa had always been grouchy, tired and quick with a slap.

Once puberty hit, she'd watched Kevin from a lonely, angry distance—until he and his family had moved away. Last year, Pa had let it slip that Kevin was gay and living in Florida. So much for her luck with men. Since Kevin, she'd trusted no one, living like an ice queen, just as Donald had said. And for what?

Her gaze lit on the plastic cake box on the kitchen table, reminded of Tommy's birthday. At least Val's kids were having a happy childhood. They had a mother who loved them, who was actually home. She had a few good memories of her own mother, Helen holding her hand as they crossed a busy intersection and sitting in church as a family. She had memories, too, of sopping wet pants and fighting the straps of her high chair while Helen had stared at the refrigerator—until Val had returned from school.

These days, Helen would have been diagnosed as bi-polar. Given the proper medicine, she'd probably still be alive. Back then, however, most families believed that time and patience would cure all ills; or they'd lock their loved one away. It had been a shameful thing, whispered behind hands, with eyes quickly averted. She'd been almost ten when her mother's episodes had intensified. She remembered it clearly. Strange men had taken her mother away. Val had been sobbing, wringing her hands. Then Aunt Sarah, her mother's younger sister, had appeared like an avenging queen in a severe navy dress, her blonde hair elegantly styled. She'd stood in the kitchen accusing Pa of worsening Helen's condition, saying that children were too much for her. Against Pa's gruff protest, she'd said he was a monster for making her give birth to a second.

She remembered standing in the shadows, feeling the hatred between them like a load of dark soil heaped upon her head. Three days later, the day after her tenth birthday, Aunt Sarah had returned, dressed in black, saying that Helen was dead—suicide. With wild eyes and a grief-roughened voice, she'd stood in the front doorway yelling that Val was damaged—a child of incest and not Pa's at all. "She needs institutionalization," she'd cried, educating the neighbors.

Later, she'd looked up the words in the dictionary; but at the time, she'd clung to her sister, afraid that if she let her go, even for a second, Aunt Sarah would take away the only mother she'd ever known.

In a flurry of noise, movement and lights, the police arrived to help Aunt Sarah out to her car. Then Pa had escaped to Rosswell's and Val to her room, sobbing for hours, forgetting to make dinner.

Megan's hands trembled as she poured a glass of orange juice, then sat at the table. From her first breath, Val and Pa had tried to manage, control and contain her; as if by doing so, they could erase the pain of Helen's demise. Yet according to Aunt Sarah, it was Val who needed watching, Val who came up short. Even now, the subject of Helen's death was taboo; as were Aunt Sarah's accusations. But she'd never forget; and someday she would learn the truth.

She looked around her apartment, considering her victories. Renting an apartment and buying a car had been major. How could Pa and Val not be proud of her? Yet they seemed to enjoy tearing her down, as if testing her, seeing if she was worthy. Of what? Was she supposed to live with Val like a sheltered child, or with Pa as an unmarried daughter, praying for a wedding day? As if anyone would want to marry her. As if she'd ever let anyone get that close.

"There's always Donald," she said with a laugh, and ran her finger around the rim of her juice glass. He was a fling, an exotic drink for a thirsty soul—not exactly husband material. He was the first of many, by her reckoning. If it wasn't for Tommy's birthday, she'd be with him in Boston right now. She glanced at her watch and grimaced. It was time to leave.

ଓଓଓଓଓ

Val's oversized white cape was set back on a good acre-and-a-half, the back quarter part of a forest, the trees ancient, massive. A colorful birthday banner waved from a flagpole attached to the doorframe. It was the American dream—for Val and Tom, anyway.

With cake box in hand, Megan stood at the door, vowing to keep her mouth shut. She'd made the cake herself—from scratch—though she'd taken great pains over the years to hide her culinary skills. In high school, boys had wanted the wild girls who drove too fast, drank from bottles and passed joints around at parties. Susie-homemaker types like her reminded them of their mothers.

But it was time to brush aside that old hurt. So she'd never been popular. It was Tommy's day; why spoil it? Her hand hovered over the doorbell; then she took a shuddering breath. It was too easy to slip into her accustomed roles, letting Pa and Val pounce on every word she said until she was defensive, or worse, verbally paralyzed, second-guessing her every thought. She snickered, thinking of Donald, who'd taught her that polite silence could be painfully unnerving—a cute little trick he'd learned from his mother.

She looked up at the massive oak that marked the property's border with a farmer's hay field in quiet appreciation. Its naked silhouette rose majestic against the cloud-filled sky, bringing back memories of climbing trees with Kevin and spitting cherries down at the neighborhood boys. A crow called from atop a stone border, reminding her of hot summer days, dripping red popsicles and running barefoot across spiky cool grass.

Children's laughter bubbled, then Tommy rounded the side of the house, his face bright with exertion. He wore Red Sox pajamas. His sneakers flapped untied. The back of his hair spiked in odd directions. Sturdily built, with sandy hair and determined blue eyes, he was the image of his dad.

"Auntie!" he cried, eyeing the cake box and licking his lips. "Just in time for a second breakfast."

"Why aren't you dressed?" she asked with a laugh; and with one arm hugged him and then kissed him, forgetting for a moment that at ten, he was too old for such foolishness.

"Yuck!" he cried, though his eyes sparkled with joy as he backed away, swiping an arm across his lips. His eyes widened. "Gotta go," he shouted over his shoulder, and began to run. "Roger's being a pain in the you-know-what."

Her chuckle died as five-year-old Roger came into view, his mop of corn-yellow hair matted and snarled. Like Tommy, he wore pajamas, but with a black and red triangle pattern with a green stain down the front of one leg. Head down, his mouth in a grimace, he was about to race past.

"Don't I get a hug?" she asked, forcing a smile. Val's youngest was an odd child, often appearing out of nowhere, making smart-ass comments like a cranky old man. For some reason, he reminded her of Pa. He squinted through his glasses, his expression dour.

She turned at a sound and smiled, seeing her niece framed in the doorway. "Letty," she breathed, taking in her blue knit dress, white tights and black Mary Jane's. At seven, she looked like an exquisite French pastry. With Tom's chiseled cheekbones, Val's blue eyes and blond hair, she promised to become a stunning woman.

"Auntie!" Letty's smile faded as she spied Roger. "Roger Whitfield, you get in here right now! Mom's been looking for you. You're supposed to be dressed."

Roger stumbled up the steps, his thick glasses glinting in the sun. "Hi Auntie," he mumbled and bumped into her, jostling the cake. He was clutching his privates, in obvious need of the bathroom. He gaped at the cake box, his glasses falling down to the tip of his nose.

"Can I . . . ha . . . have some?"

"You need the bathroom right now," Megan said through gritted teeth, taking his arm, helping him through the doorway. He stared at her, his eyes huge behind his glasses.

"When you're done, you and Tommy can come

back out and get the bags I left in my car," she said, thinking of the countless times he'd waited too long, then bawled his eyes out after wetting his pants. For a smart little boy, he could be a pain.

"Okay, Auntie," he said, his gaze too knowing, too grown-up. There was hurt in his eyes; and she looked away quickly, guilt and shame washing over her. Then the moment passed. A child once again, he skipped through the house, making racecar sounds.

"Is that chocolate?" Letty asked, her gaze encompassing Megan and the cake.

"Of course," Megan said, laughing as she kissed her upturned face. "No way, Missy," she said, and snatched the cake from her playful, grasping hands. They headed toward the kitchen at the back of the house, which overlooked Val's gardens.

She set the cake on the calico covered table, then with an arm around Letty, looked out the bay window at her sister, who stood at the edge of her autumn-browned plot, probably planning the next year's harvest. She seemed distant and fragile, a lovely pensive statue in a powder blue parka, faded jeans and green rubber boots. Slowly, she turned to the house, then smiled and waved.

Megan tensed. What would she find fault with today: smudged makeup, too infrequent phone calls or a recent snippy reply to Pa's questions? Tom's footsteps joined Val's at the door, and it was flung open, in time to glimpse them kissing, their faces flushed from the cool morning air. Still holding hands, they scraped their feet on the doormat.

Her heart twisted with envy. Through hard times, babies and sickness, Tom and Val were still deeply in love; her Boston hiatus nothing but a cheap thrill in comparison.

"Megan! Welcome!" Tom grinned as he closed the door. He was a big man—solid muscle, from what she could tell.

"Hi Tom." She smiled faintly, then hugged him and backed away, wary of the possessive warning in Val's eyes. Even Val had her insecurities. She looked closer, seeing the lines of worry and exhaustion on her sister's face, the purple shadows beneath her eyes.

"How's CompuLink these days?" Tom asked, drawing her attention.

As if he'd even want me, she wanted to scream at Val, painfully aware of Tom's natural virility as he leaned negligently against the door. "As sorry as ever, Tom," she said, her pulse racing, unable to look him in the eye, now that she knew what a man's body could do. "How's the garage?" she managed to ask.

"Great," he said, and stuffed his hands into his jeans pockets. "New cars came in this week. Parts we've only seen in print. Might prove interesting." He raised an eyebrow; hinting at conversations they'd had in the past about the automotive industry's rapid computerization, and Pa's aversion to the new technology. Pa left such concerns to him and the other young mechanics.

"You'll figure it out," she said, her gaze narrowing as she turned to Val. "You okay?" she asked, then hugged her. "You look tired."

"Roger's been having nightmares," Val said with a sigh. "Something about a crash and being the only one left. Poor baby." She smiled at Tom, who was heading to the bathroom where Roger cried out for help.

"Still?" Megan asked, rolling her eyes. "He's been dreaming that one for weeks."

"He'll grow out of it," Val said, tightlipped; and Megan looked away. No one disparaged her baby.

"You look good," Val said, eyeing her critically, touching her sweater almost reverently. It was lemon yellow, cashmere and new—sure to raise her ire if she knew its cost. "Where did you get it?" Val asked.

"A discount store in New York," Megan said, raising her chin. She'd bought the damn thing in Boston, a Back Bay boutique; but Val didn't have to know everything. In fact, she'd bought her a blue one just like it for Christmas.

"You weren't home last night," Val said sweetly, her eyes shards of winter sky.

"I was out." Megan held her gaze.

"Anyone I know?"

"Friends from work. No one in particular." Megan shook her head, wishing she were home reading the historical romance novel she'd started last night. "Just an after-work thing. You know." So she'd ignored the phone. Was there a law against it?

"Where'd you go?" Val persisted.

"The Town House," Megan said, then folded her arms across chest, feeling the rage build.

"I don't mean to pry," Val said softly and backed away with that viperous innocent wounded look she'd long perfected. "I just—"

"Yeah right," Megan choked out, hating that Letty looked about to cry. "I'm not your kid, Valerie."

"Ladies, ladies." Tom stood in the doorway, smiling brightly. In a few quick steps, he had them both around the shoulders. "Come on now, don't start. It's proving to be a gorgeous day, and Tommy's expecting a party."

Megan shook him off, her stomach churning. She closed her eyes briefly, then glared at her sister. "I'm not your irritating baby sister any more. You know . . . the one who stole your childhood."

"Megan, please." Val glanced nervously at Letty, her face ashen.

Megan sighed, suddenly deflated, seeing the closed look on Letty's face. "I don't know," she mumbled. "Maybe I should go. I don't want to spoil your day." She took a step back.

"Auntie, please." Letty took her hand; her tear-filled eyes making her feel even more like an idiot.

Then Roger bounded in, grabbed Tom's hand and pulled him over to the cake. He bounced as he spoke. "Dad, can we lick the frosting now? Can we, huh? Can we? Please." He tipped his head to one side, his grin impish, his glasses hanging precariously from the tip of his nose.

Megan burst out laughing, and for a fleeting second, experienced a warm connection with her youngest nephew. Her breath caught as she recognized the courage and intelligence in his eyes. He'd interrupted on purpose; and it wasn't the first time.

"No subtlety with him," Tom said, shaking his head and laughing. Val's gaze was tender.

Megan winked at Roger, wondering why she'd never seen this side of him before. Behind thick glasses, he was a master manipulator.

"No cake, Roger. You know better," Tom said gently and patted his head. "We'll have it after lunch, after Tommy opens his presents. Like always."

"Awwww," Roger groaned, his shoulders slumping.

Like always. Megan closed her eyes, trying to capture the moment. This time with Val was precious. Despite their differences, her sister would always love her.

Then reality hit. Later, like always, Pa would appear for lunch as if from on high, the omnipotent patriarch, come to perform his inspection. How could she stand it?

Roger ran shrieking from the room, sounding like a police car in hot pursuit. Tom and Letty followed him laughing. The front door slammed, announcing Tommy's arrival.

"Come on," Val said, her look an apology. "Come help me close the windows, just like the old days, Meg. Things weren't always so bad. We had some good times, too."

Megan followed her up the stairs, inordinately glad to be asked. It was Val who'd checked her temperature whenever she'd had a fever; who'd sewn buttons on her shirts or a fallen-down hem; who'd made sure she'd had a hot meal every night and breakfast every morning.

Val paused at the top, then turned, her hair and face bathed in the muted colors streaming in from an octagonal stained-glass window at the head of the stairs. Megan sucked in her breath. No one was as beautiful as her sister was.

"I'm sorry," Val whispered, looking like a fairy princess under a spell, or an angel, her worry lines and shadows magically erased, the image of their mother. "Sometimes I forget you're grown and gone," she said softly, her eyes brimming with love. "It must be the mother in me. I just can't help it, Meg."

"I know," Megan said, and smiled as she took her hand, grateful that Aunt Sarah hadn't prevailed.

CHAPTER 2
NOVEMBER

In November, Megan started a new job at Smith Laboratories, an up and coming minicomputer manufacturer founded by Gordon Smith from Singapore. Half-British, half-Chinese, he'd earned a Harvard Ph.D. at twenty-five. Tall and gangly, he always wore a navy suit, white shirt and red striped tie, his speckled brown eyes bright with intelligence. Though a gregarious man, his English was measured and precise—the product of a British education.

Excitement hummed through the company's corporate complex—a new twelve-story tower connected via hallways and tunnels to other assorted buildings. Touted as Lowell's latest economic savior, the company had plans for three more towers, and was already constructing a gorgeous, fully equipped Education Center in downtown Lowell. The recent recession was officially over. Smith Labs' management bragged of three-percent attrition, well below the industry average.

Smith Labs' premier product was the DataStorage-7, a minicomputer that was revolutionizing Fortune 500 Companies and military organizations on a worldwide scale. Department managers, fed up with the slow, paperwork-intensive requirements for even the smallest change to mainframe software, were flocking to minicomputer manufacturers like Digital Equipment Corporation, Burroughs, Wang and Smith Labs for easy solutions at reasonable prices. When it came to speed and flexibility, the DataStorage-7 was years ahead of its competition, providing state-of-the-art communications software that linked hundreds of users to existing mainframes.

Megan's first day was a flurry of meetings, jammed into a room with more than thirty other excited new hires. Her salary was extravagant, the benefits phenomenal. As days passed, she threw herself into the job, immersing herself in the new technology, canceling family events as often as she dared. Mondays zoomed into Fridays, punctuated by rounds of hasty errands to stock her apartment, maintain her closet and squeeze in dentist, doctor and hairdresser appointments; then trips in and out of Logan, flying to customer sites.

Then there was Donald.

As November rains stripped trees bare, she became increasingly brittle and manic, snipping at coworkers, yelling at the boy behind the drug store counter, packing in ten-hour-plus workdays. The week before Thanksgiving, with need bordering on desperation, she met Donald in Boston to gorge on the treats he offered: shopping in luxury boutiques, dining on the best and partying in flashy, expensive clothing with people who liked to laugh and be seen.

She managed to keep her mouth shut during Thanksgiving dinner, leaving Val's house early, claiming a headache. Then Christmas came and went, a frantic time during which she struggled to balance the two worlds, yet keep them carefully apart. While Donald introduced her to caviar, champagne and wild, uninhibited parties; Val criticized her Christmas gifts as too expensive and Pa blasted her for neglecting her car's maintenance. Work became her salve; her justified escape from her family's incessant prying and the relentless exhaustion of short days, long night and the inevitable hangovers and forgotten business appointments. Thankfully, the New Year brought an end to revelry and the lull of ordinary days.

ଔଔଔଔଔ

Megan looked across the lab, seeing rows of sturdy benches, upon which were several drone-like, flickering green monitors. Buff-toned DataStorage-7 systems stood on either side of the door. Against the back wall was a huge communications matrix: a jumble of cables, outlets, wires and modems. She exhaled slowly, resting her head on one arm, then slumped in her seat before the smallest DataStorage-7 model, her personal test system. Her test didn't work and she needed to ask Bob Cartright a few questions. Where could he be?

Bob was her officemate and the Communication Support Group's lead analyst. With a wife and new baby to support, while attending grad school at night, he was the most stable man she knew. Too bad, he was unavailable. Considering that his wife, Rosie was Barbie-doll perfect, he probably always would be.

She raised an arm, stretching her aching shoulders, then rose, wondering where he'd gone. He'd been at the matrix the last time she'd looked up. She rubbed her burning eyes, vowing that someday, she'd be able to isolate and replicate any communications problem without his help. His kind of knowledge took months to acquire, if at all. Fortunately, he was generous, actually liked women and didn't mind her endless questions.

"Damn," she muttered, glancing at her watch. It was two-thirty and Donald was supposed to be in Boston already. There was also supposed to be a snowstorm raging outside—a bad one according to the morning weather report. She had no time for storms—not with Hercules threatening to send back the equipment and Chase Manhattan pulling strings with upper management. Both customers had snagged the ear of Steve Grant, Smith Labs' Vice President of Customer Service. No way did she want to explain to him her lack of answers.

Grant was a towering, heavy-set man with piercing hazel eyes—a guy from the old school of hardware maintenance, who hated women, though he allegedly had two grown daughters. It was clear from his innuendoes and sarcasm, and from conversations overheard and passed on, that he viewed women employees as girls on a lark, and female managers as alien creatures to be slapped back into the kitchen where they belonged.

Her stomach growled, reminding her that she'd skipped lunch. The thought of coffee had her lips quivering; and maybe there was a slice of pie left over. The cafeteria closed at three-thirty.

She shut the lab door softly on her way out her, then headed down the row of cubicles to her own, hoping to find Bob. Glancing around, she couldn't help but compare her old job to this one. Unlike the gloomy gray of CompuLink's drab offices, there were no offices along two outer walls, allowing sunlight to stream across all the cubicles. There were no battered metal desks, either; but cubicles from Herman Miller, with smart bookcases and modern work surfaces.

She glanced over the cubicle wall and saw that Bob's monitor was off and his coat-hook empty. Clearly, he'd left for the day. She continued toward the windows and pressed both hands to the glass.

Wind-whipped snow had buried the parking lot. Last time she'd looked, the snow had been light. That had been hours ago.

She listened carefully, hearing the dull drone of the air filtration system and the hum of the overhead lights. Around eleven, Bob had said that Human Resources asked everyone to leave at their discretion—whatever that meant. Entombed in the lab, she'd lost track of time. Fear gnawed at her throat. It looked bad outside. How was she supposed to get home?

Back in her cubicle, she pulled on her coat, shoved her feet into boots and searched for her gloves, finding them in her coat pockets. Then she stuffed manuals in her bag and shut off her monitor. There was no telling how long the storm would last; and she couldn't afford even a day off the job.

Her breath puffed white in the outside air. Her boots made soft, plodding sounds. Snow was dropping in heavy, blinding sheets. The air was still, with an expectancy that made her hurry as she brushed off her car, scraped the windows and drove away.

Keeping panic at bay, she white-knuckled it through Chelmsford Center, grateful for a lumbering snowplow just a few yards ahead. Snow grazed the car's undercarriage as she skidded into her apartment building's back lot. Except for two peepholes, the windshield was coated with ice. With trembling hands, she shut off the engine, grabbed her things and set out, telling herself that she could whine when she was safe and warm inside.

Something moved at the edge of her vision, but she kept going. The wind howled around her. Snow battered her exposed face, stinging her eyes. Cold stabbed through her down parka. The indentations from her boots filled quickly. Shuddering, she pulled her hood around her face and focused on her apartment building just yards ahead.

She gasped, grabbed from behind, then turned, her arms flying out in defense.

"Donald!" She barreled into his arms and kissed him. His face was impossibly cold. "What are you doing here? When did you get in? How—"

"Come on," he said, laughing; then threw his hood back in contempt of the storm, slung an arm over her shoulder and moved with her toward the building.

"Logan's closed and will be for while," he said as he stamped his feet in the lobby. She couldn't take her eyes off him. "I grabbed a rental car and was hoping we'd get snowed in." He grinned, his golden eyes gleaming. "You don't mind, do you?"

"No, why would I mind." She shook her head, grinning, then laughed as snow billowed in, scouring the already wet floor. "I can't believe you're here."

The door flapped open like a piece of ripped cardboard; and they pulled it closed as one, using all of their strength.

"That was fun," she said, collapsing against him laughing.

He pulled off his gloves and shoved them in his pockets, his gaze softening. "Ah, Meggie, I missed you." His hands were warm as they cupped her face, his kiss gentle at first. Then the kiss deepened. She couldn't think straight as she held onto him and kissed him back. He'd braved the storm. For her?

More. She wanted . . . more. Seeking warmth, his warmth, she found the inside of his parka; and for a delirious moment, forgot all but him.

A loud clang sounded from beyond the locked wrought-iron door, making her jump. Far down the hallway, a door closed and a figure emerged. She peered closely, then grimaced. It was Stan Zambinsky, of all people. She sucked in her breath as he headed toward them, and for an awful moment, caught the disapproval and disappointment in his eyes. Her cheeks flamed. Her heart pounded—in shame, she realized. Her shame grew as he took a good long look at her and Donald, standing together. Then he left through a side door.

"Swell," she muttered, pulling away from Donald, picturing Pa's face once he'd spoken with Tom. "Just swell." Word was bound to get back. Then Pa would never let her hear the end of it. "It figures he'd show up the first time I have a man over."

"What's going on?" Donald asked, looking annoyed. "Who is he, anyway?"

"A friend of the family," she said. "No one special." She shook her head, thinking of last week. Stan had been laughing with one of the mechanics when she'd picked her car up at Rosswell's, giving in to Pa's nagging about checking out a thumping noise. It had been bad enough having to listen to Pa's usual tirade; but seeing the two men clam up had really irked her. Obviously, they'd been talking about her.

"He's just some maintenance man," Donald said, leaning closer, his arm coming down on her shoulder, trying to claim her attention. "What do you care what he thinks?"

"Maybe this wasn't such a good idea," she said. With jerked motions, she searched her coat pocket for the key, snagged it, then shoved it into the lock. Her right temple was starting to throb. She should have taken that lunch break.

Donald spun her around. "You owe him or something? You got the hots for him? Something going on I don't know about?"

"That's ludicrous," she said, and made a huffing sound. Then she pushed through the door and motioned him to silence. Stan wasn't the only nosey person in the building. The Merit's, a middle-aged couple in the apartment nearest the door, made everyone's life their business.

She climbed the stairs with him close behind, half-wishing she'd stayed at work, and he'd stayed in Boston. He'd probably want to drink and have sex—a great agenda if she was up for it. But the fact was—she wasn't. She was tired, hungry and had a headache coming on. Usually, she went along with him, no matter how she felt; but in the split second that it took to open her door, she decided she'd known him long enough. It was time for brutal honesty.

She set her things on the small, marble-topped table by the door and flipped on the light. "I have a headache," she whispered. "I'm sorry. I'm not the greatest company right now."

"Tell Uncle Donald," he said, and helped her out of her coat, his hands lingering. She slid away from him, hoping he'd take the hint.

"I did too much today, was in the lab too long, didn't stop to eat." She closed her eyes as he nuzzled her neck, wishing he'd stop. "Then the drive from work—the snow and the wind. I should have come home sooner. It's my own fault." She slipped out of her shoes and moved toward the bathroom.

He grabbed her hand, restraining her. "Why don't you lie down for a while?" His grin was wolfish as he dropped their coats to the floor. She looked down, thinking of the mess they made. She looked from the coats back to him, baffled. The closet was mere yards away. What would it take for him to lift the damn things onto some hangers?

Then his hands were working on her back; and she forgot all about the coats, the storm outside and the horrific commute home.

"Relax a little, Meggie," he whispered in her ear. "You just need my special back rub, guaranteed to make you feel better. We've nowhere to go. About time we got to know each other. I'd like to advance from hotel rooms to something a bit more permanent, wouldn't you?" He toyed with her blouse's top button, his face glowing with health and joyful optimism, sending a jolt through her.

"More permanent?" She laughed nervously. "Why?" She moved closer, unable to help herself, thinking him insane; then caught her breath as his hand dipped into her blouse.

"Because I want to," he breathed, his lips trailing moisture as they traversed the side of her neck. "Because I need to."

"All right, Captain." Her breath was ragged. "You win for now." Smiling, she turned and locked the door.

ꟹꟹꟹꟹꟹ

The wind howled, the snow piled and drifted against the lower windows; but Megan was oblivious. She had no recollection of when they lost electricity until hours later, upon emerging from her bed to an ice-cold room. Traipsing around in the cold and dark, she managed to light several candles, locate the small, portable radio she kept for emergencies, then slip back into bed.

"I don't suppose you have any food," Donald said, his gaze appreciative. "Though I could feast on you for several more hours."

She warmed her hands against his chest as he pulled her close.

"Yes," she said, and sent a silent thanks heavenward. "I have a natural gas stove with an old-fashioned pilot light, as a matter of fact. We can have a hot meal and heat, too."

"You have food?" He looked surprised.

"Of course," she said, smiling. "I've got plenty of staples and perishables, too—as long as we don't open the fridge too much."

"That's you," he said, and kissed the top of her head. "Ever the girl scout."

"I'll show you a girl scout." She pressed her body against him and opened her mouth for a kiss, relishing the crisp scent of his skin, the rasp of beard stubble and the tangy taste of his mouth. Then, in the far reaches of her mind, she detected the shrill of a telephone.

"Damn and blast!" she cried, pulling away. "Stupid. Stupid. Stupid." She slapped the side of her head.

"What is it?" He sat up.

"My family. I forgot to call them. What a pain. You don't know how they can be. Just shut up. Don't make a sound." She leaped from bed and grabbed the receiver. "Hello?" Shivering, she climbed back in.

"Megan?"

She crumbled inside, hearing relief, criticism and no small amount of fear in Pa's trembling voice. Her heart pounded as she tried to reign in her temper. Just once, she'd like to tell him to get lost. It was always a test with him—to see if she could manage on her own—as if a single wrong decision would give him the right to reel her back home.

"Yes, Pa," she said, sounding calm yet annoyed,

knowing it would irritate him. "I'm here. Where did you think I'd be?"

"You could have called," he said. "I've been worried sick. And Valerie—she's frantic. Tom said Smith Labs let out hours ago. You couldn't bother to call; or are you too independent? Maybe self-centered is a better word. You got a secret? Tom said a friend of his called. He said—"

"I've been home for a while." Her chest tightened. "Alone." She bit down on her lower lip, using all of her control to keep from hurling the receiver against the wall. Her headache had returned with a vengeance. Obviously, Stan had tattled. She'd just deny it.

"I've been stowing perishables in my car," she said, "just like you recommended." Looking at Donald, she rolled her eyes.

"Did you gas up your car and stock up on canned goods and water?" He sounded unconvinced.

"Yes, Pa." She gripped the receiver, hating him. "What's new with you?"

She saw that Donald was laughing and took a deep breath.

"Nothing," Pa spat. "Worried about you, that's all. I wish you were here, safe and sound, instead of all the way across town by yourself. In times like this, I wish you'd listen to reason and come home where you belong. It's foolish spending all that money on rent when you could be saving for when you get married."

She bit down hard on her lip.

"Well, got to go," Pa said after a long pause. "You think on being more considerate."

"Yes, Pa."

The line went dead. She replaced the receiver and the phone rang immediately.

To her horror, Donald reached for it and lifted it to his face, his mouth opening. Gasping, she snatched it from him and motioned him away. He flopped on the bed, gripping his middle, laughing soundlessly.

"Hello," she said, her voice cracking. She placed a hand over her heart and shot Donald a quelling look. He shrugged, then started to move toward her.

"Oh, hi, Val," she said, praying he'd behave. It was bad enough that Stan had tattled. One sound from Donald and she'd be toast. She tried to shrug him off as he kneaded her shoulders; but he wouldn't stop.

"I'm fine," she said. "Snow's battering the window. What else can I say?"

"Did you have trouble driving?" Val asked, as Donald's lips found the side of her neck. She closed her eyes against the exquisite pleasure.

"No, I was home before it got bad," she forced out. Donald's hand curled around her breast and squeezed gently. She sucked in her breath.

"What's going on," Val asked. "You sound out of breath."

"Breathless? Me?" She shot Donald a hot look.

Her sister wasn't the only woman snowed in with a sexy man. "I'm just winded from some exercises. I think I'm going stir crazy." She winked at Donald. "What's Letty doing?"

ଓଓଓଓଓ

Megan awoke the next morning to the sizzle and smoke of frying bacon. Spatula in hand, Donald grinned from the doorway. "Come on," he said, gesturing for her to join him.

"I'm coming," she said, and laughed as she grabbed her bathrobe.

She could only stare at her kitchen. Blessed heat poured from the open oven door. Shadows cast by several candles flickered across the room. He'd set the table with silverware and napkins. Two plates warmed at the back of the burners. A huge cheese omelet sizzled in a skillet and strips of crisp bacon lay draining on a paper towel-covered plate. He motioned her to a chair, then seated her with a flourish.

"You know how to cook?" she asked, shaking her head. He was bundled in gray sweats, with an apron around his middle. His cheeks were rosy, like a Nordic prince.

"That's only one of my surprises, babe," he said with a wink.

"Bacon and eggs are my favorite." She smiled up at him, and he kissed her upraised lips. "What a nice surprise. With all the talk about fat and cholesterol, I can't remember the last time I've had this."

"And there's more," he said, then turned and pulled a bottle of champagne from the refrigerator. He uncorked it deftly, filled two glasses and handed her one. Then he filled their plates and set them on the table. Propped in the middle of her omelet was a huge, sparkling diamond ring.

"What's this?" She looked at him and the ring in mild confusion. It was too soon, too serious. Wasn't it?

His expression hardened as he set his glass on the table, dropped to one knee and clasped her left hand.

"Megan Rosswell, will you do me the honor of becoming my wife?"

For a long moment, she could only look at him. This wasn't happening. "You're crazy," she choked out.

He plucked the ring from the omelet. "Third time's a charm," he said, grinning. "I won't ask you again." His eyes were shadowed in the flickering light.

"Third time?" she asked, shaking her head, chuckling, starting to get uneasy. "You asked me once, Donald. This is only the second time. And what difference does it make?"

"I asked you in Boston and then over the phone," he said, sounding peevish. "Come on Meggie, don't quibble. I'm serious about this." He held out the ring. "Please take it."

Anxiety rippled across her shoulders. "Marry you? I just don't know, Donald." She looked away, seeing the food growing cold. "We've had fun together, but marriage is a big step. I'm not sure I'm ready." She swallowed hard, thinking of Pa and Val and their likely reaction to Captain Donald Thomas Alexander.

"You cut me to the quick," he said. He stood and gripped her shoulders, his look intense. "Is there someone else?"

She shook her head as Stan came to mind. Steady and reliable, he'd be a better choice. Her family would readily accept him. Unfortunately, he wasn't the least bit interested. Donald, on the other hand, except at this particular moment, would never be serious. He'd probably ruin her.

His lips were compressed. There was a strange light in his eyes. He must have read something on her face. "I'll swashbuckle him!" he cried, raising his fist. "I'll challenge him to a duel, or whatever Victorian men do under such death inspiring circumstances."

"Don't be ridiculous," she said and laughed nervously. She brushed his shoulder with the tips of her fingers, hoping to convince him. "There's no one else, Donald, seriously."

"Then what is it?" He looked hurt and puzzled. "I love you and want you for my wife." He shrugged. "What else can I say? It's either yes or no, Meggie. Do you love me or not?"

"I don't know," she said, scanning his face.

She went to the sofa, putting distance between them. "So I slept with you. So what." She raked a hand through her hair. "There's more to marriage than sex and parties. Life isn't always fun and games."

"It's not just about sex." He moved closer. "I need you, Meggie."

"But that's all we have," she said and groaned, seeing the adoration in his eyes. "It would certainly be my father's conclusion."

There were fine lines of dissolution across his face, and an alcohol gleam in his eyes. The top of an empty champagne bottle stuck up from the trash bin like a warning flag. The endless drunken parties and mindless indulgences had stolen something from her. Half the time, she felt dried up, brittle and needy. She could hardly imagine him sitting at Val's dinner table without a glass in hand. Marriage involved families, and hers would detest him. He rarely spoke of his.

"You need his approval or something?" he asked softly.

"Not really." She looked at him, a little surprised. "I'm just thinking of family dinners and such. You've never met my family; nor have I met yours. I just think we need more time."

He whacked his forehead with his palm. "I know. You want the prospective groom's traditional grovel before the bride's father."

"I don't care what my father thinks," she said, getting irritated. "I'm a grown woman and it's my decision."

"Then, what is it?" he asked again, his hands

splayed as he came to her. "I adore you, Megan Rosswell. I want to spend the rest of my life with you—just you—no one else. Can't you see that?"

She sighed as he pulled her into his arms. What could she possibly say? Was it do or die with him? Would he walk away if she said no? His lips were tantalizingly, tasting of bacon and champagne as he kissed her lightly, making it hard to think straight.

"Come on Meggie," he whispered, "we're good together. I love you and you love me. Please."

Love? What was love?

"We'd have to elope," she said, her will sliding away as his fingers moved across her throat. "No parents. No relatives. We'll tell them later."

"Fine. No problem." Relief quirked the side of his mouth.

Relief?

"I won't change my name," she said, uneasy.

"Don't matter," he said, looking too pleased. He gripped her shoulders and gazed into her eyes. "Don't change your name. Don't change your job. Don't change your phone number. Don't even change your clothes ever again. We'll just roll around naked and have food delivered. Just say yes."

"I want a career and no kids." She could hardly breathe: the walls were closing in.

"Fine! Fine! Fine!" he cried. "Make money, not babies. We'll have one endless, lovingly financed, glorious love fest . . . in the Victorian style." He kissed her soundly.

"Nothing changes?" she asked, pulling away, trying to catch her breath.

"Nothing changes. Cross my heart." He made the childhood gesture. Then, in one smooth motion, he pushed her down to the floor beneath him and covered her lips with his.

"Yes or no?" he asked, breaking away, his eyes dark with passion.

"Yes," she murmured, already drowning in his kiss.

CHAPTER 3

MARCH 1981

Megan stood beside Donald at Val's front door, wishing she'd been an orphan. Lucky Donald, his parents were in Chicago; and probably as oblivious to her new role as she wished her family could remain to his. Nevertheless, he'd insisted, and here they were headed for a hellacious Sunday dinner. He held a bag containing a little something he'd picked up in Chicago. She couldn't imagine what it was.

"You sure you want to do this?" she asked, observing his pasted-on optimism with a sinking feeling.

"They can't be that bad," he said, laughing nervously as he looped the bag handle through one arm and straightened his tie for the third time. His eyes were still a little bloodshot from last night's party. They'd met several of his friends in Boston; then crashed at her apartment around three in the morning.

She bowed her head, wishing she could offer some hope of a decent welcome. Twice now, Stan had caught them kissing. In addition to the first time she'd had Donald over, he'd also seen them arrive by limo, hanging all over each other after an exhilarating Las Vegas wedding and honeymoon. Unaccountably embarrassed, she'd caught his smirking disdain; then caught herself taking a second look at the way his jeans hugged his thighs, the word beefy coming to mind, along with fresh air, strength and tenderness. Beside him, Donald looked jaded and frenetic. She'd muttered a trite greeting, uneasy with her disloyalty so soon after her wedding; before he'd sauntered away.

"We have to do this sooner or later," Donald said, interrupting her thoughts. "Just like you have to meet my family. Maybe in a month or so, we'll go. You can fly first class on one of my flights."

She forced a smile as she looked up at the massive darkening clouds that scudded across the sky. Sinister shadows seemed to cover Val's house. She shivered, apprehension tickling between her shoulder blades. Then she smiled, seeing a pair of small faces at the window. The kids laughed and pointed, their eyes filled with surprise.

"Letty and Roger," Megan said, grinning as she waved.

"Come on then," Donald said, pushing the door open. "They don't look dangerous."

She scanned his all-American good looks, praying her family would accept him.

ଓଓଓଓଓ

Small sounds filled Val's dining room: the clink of silver on china, the grandfather clock softly marking time, murmured requests to pass the mashed potatoes, roast beef or pickles. Looking up from her steaming plate, Megan scanned her sister's face; seeing no trace of emotion. Blonde and beautiful, Val looked like a Disney princess. Her nails were pink-tipped and perfect, her dress impeccably tailored to enhance her curves. Behind her, sunlight streamed through lace-curtained windows, casting a play of light and shadow across the dessert-laden sideboard.

She toyed with her fork, swirling gravy through the potatoes, wishing she'd listened to herself. She shouldn't be here; at least not with Donald. No one spoke. No one dared. She gazed across the table at her husband, who looked mighty uncomfortable between Roger and Letty.

Like a bear guarding his den, Pa had offered no welcome at the door. She should have warned Donald about the wine; though she thought she'd made it clear that her family didn't drink. Most people would have accepted Donald's ice-cold Chardonnay with some degree of civility. But Pa wasn't most people. He'd considered it an insult. Hunched over his plate, he looked intent on his meal. The silver in his hair had multiplied since the last time she'd seen him—more than a month ago. His skin was pale, almost gray, and his frame impossibly thin.

"So how did you meet?" Tom's voice boomed across the stuffy room. "Not that it's my business," he added, his smile sheepish, earning her forgiveness for backing Pa on the wine. "Just curious," he added, his gaze locking with Pa's for a second until Pa looked away.

Letty giggled nervously, and they all looked at her. Blushing furiously, she ducked her head; and Val laid a gentle hand upon her shoulder. Pa's jaw muscle worked as it always did when he was agitated. Val shot him a worried look.

"I don't mind," Megan said, shrugging, refusing to be cowed. "We met at the airport." She tilted her head slightly to smile at Donald, and he winked back. "I was late for my flight and bumped into him at the gate. Literally. I made him late by managing to strew the contents of my briefcase all over the entrance. Nice guy that he is, he helped me pick it up."

The corner of Donald's mouth lifted; he raised his chin slightly.

"That's it?" Tommy asked, squinting.

"'Fraid so," she said, and patted his knee.

"Was it love at first sight?" Letty asked softly, her blue eyes innocent. Donald choked, then grabbed his water glass. Val looked at Megan with mild concern.

"Not exactly," Megan said, and scowled at her sister. The scene at the door had been as painful as she'd imagined it would be. Val, upon seeing her wedding and engagement rings, had shrieked. Then had come Pa's unguarded expression, his self-righteous rage, the look of unadulterated hatred he'd cast in Donald's direction.

She smiled, looking down at the rings flashing on her finger. "We . . . we fell in love slowly with each flight to Chicago."

"What do you know about love?" Pa spat. He shoved away from the table, folded his arms across his chest and threw his head back in contempt as he scanned her and Donald. "How could you marry this *pilot,* this . . . this playboy? What is he . . . an army brat? I've seen his kind before."

"How dare you?" Donald said, rising from his chair. Megan could only stare, her mouth open.

"One look and you can tell he's a good-time Charlie," Pa continued. "Don't tell me you've brought him into the family without even letting us meet him? What were you thinking? Is this a sick joke, or another one of your stupid woman's lib games?"

"Who do you think you're talking to?" Donald moved toward him, his fists balled at his sides. "She's a grown woman and doesn't need your approval."

They were fighting about her, as if she weren't in the room, as if she were a possession or a child to be scolded. She rose and threw down her napkin, furious at both of them. Blood pulsed at her temples. But she could see only Pa: the pinpoints of his pupils, his trembling hands, his reddening face. This was the day she'd always dreaded. He was making her choose.

"Pa," Val warned, gripping his wrist. "Please, don't do this, Megan." Her look was imploring.

Pa shook Val off and leaned across the table. "You knew it was wrong, Megan. You knew—"

"Back off," Megan cried, fighting tears, wanting to spit, ignoring the shocked expressions around the table. "Nothing I did ever met with your approval, Pa! You never liked my job, my apartment, my clothes or the way I take care of my car. None of my friends have ever been good enough—if I ever dared have any. All you do is criticize. Criticize. Criticize."

She was shaking uncontrollably. Tom placed a hand on her shoulder, but she shook it off. "It doesn't matter that this man is my husband—that I plan to spend the rest of my life with him. Nothing matters; and there's no winning with you, Pa, now is there?"

"Don't you take that tone with me, young lady!" Pa shouted.

"Or what?" she asked, putting her hands on her hips, looking him in the eye. "I'm supposed to keep my mouth shut and be the quiet dutiful daughter with no mind of her own? Or you'll do what . . . hit me? Send me to my room? Don't be ridiculous." She held up a hand, showing her rings. "I'm married now, Pa, and there's not a damn thing you can do about it. If you don't accept Donald, you don't accept me."

Pa's mouth snapped open.

"Megan, please!" Val cried. "He doesn't know what he's saying."

Pa sent her a scowling look.

Come on," Megan said, glancing at Donald. "I've had enough."

CHAPTER 4

SEPTEMBER 1982

Megan sat in her chair by the window, gazing out at the parking lot. To the left of the lot, separated by a chain-linked fence, was the building's swimming pool, reflecting the moon's chopped up glow in the water's unnatural blue. Bright-colored deck chairs stood empty in the autumn chill. In a week or so, the maintenance crew would drain the pool and cover it for the winter; and one by one, the chairs would disappear. Sighing, she scanned the tops of nearby pines searching for an early star, trying to forget that Donald would soon be home.

The situation was impossible.

Eighteen months had passed since the last horrible family meal. In that time, she'd managed to avoid her father, but not the truth. Donald was indeed a loser; though to her way of thinking, he was more of a lost soul, someone who'd never be satisfied with life. What irked most was Pa's need to rub it in. If he ever knew.

Those exhilarating, self-indulgent post-nuptial days were long past. She was sick of forced conversations with artificial people; and dreaded the inevitable weekend hangovers and awakening in someone else's bedroom or a hotel room, or worst of all, in her car. She hated having no memory of great chunks of time. And Donald, once her eager playmate, had become her nemesis with his talent for ugly put-downs, often veiled behind loving suggestions. He didn't love her. He didn't even love himself.

Admittedly, her marriage was a farce. Sometime in the next week, she'd call a lawyer and end this regrettable charade.

"Mister playtime," she sneered, wishing she'd listened to herself from the beginning. She should have stayed in her hotel room during that lonely fall nor'easter. She shouldn't have been in such a damn hurry to shed her virginity. Donald had been pushy; and she'd taken it as keen interest. But he'd never bothered to really listen to her, to see her strength and stability. Drunk, she was a different person—and that was the person he wanted.

His pilot's schedule didn't bother her: she was often on the road. For all she knew, he was a faithful husband. What she didn't like was that he'd appear suddenly, expecting her to drop everything and match him drink for drink. Then he'd disappear for weeks at a time without even a phone call to indicate that he was alive. He'd leave the apartment a mess, with her distraught, exhausted and often with a bladder infection. It was a stick-figure marriage, the convenience of strangers, without depth or honest caring, yet well decorated with all the trappings of material success. This morning he'd called from Logan, saying that his flight had been canceled, that he'd be around for a few days.

More than anything, she just wanted to be alone. Gripping her bathrobe tightly around her, she gazed longingly at her bed. Even if she were fast asleep, he'd just awaken her, not caring that she'd had a lousy day—hell, a lousy week.

"Damn George Russo," she sputtered, waving a fist. If it hadn't been for Mr. Russo, Smith Labs' Southern Maine District Support Manager, she'd still be in Augusta, finishing off a round of highly productive customer visits. She should have figured from his wall-size poster of nude models that he was a knuckle-dragger when it came to women. He'd groped her at the entrance to the ladies' room, a place she'd thought safe until she'd spotted the ill-concealed peepholes at the back of each stall. She shuddered, remembering the way his bony hand had curled around her breast.

Come morning, she'd file a complaint with Human Resources and pin *him* to the wall.

She stared at the door, hearing footsteps, her

heart sinking. A key clinked in the lock. She bit her lip as Donald stumbled in, obviously drunk.

He'd driven from Logan like that?

She bit back harsh words, hating to think of the people he'd endangered. She turned away, tears forming in her eyes. This had to stop.

"Meggie!" He dropped his things on the floor, gathered her in his arms and kissed her.

Her half-practiced lecture dissolved into nonsense as she struggled to stay upright. She stumbled, filled with revulsion as he released her; then swiped the back of her hand across her battered lips. In numb silence, she watched him strip off his jacket on the way to the kitchen.

"It's good to be home," he said, flashing a smile, somehow looking like a dream in his navy uniform, not a crease out of place. Her knees wobbled and she sat quickly. This wasn't going to be easy.

Ice tinkled in a glass and she looked up.

"Drink?" he asked, poking his head around the kitchen partition. She shook her head.

"Why not?" he asked, and moved toward her holding a brimming glass. "Come on, it's not like you. It's time to welcome the old man, have some fun. Try one of my trademark vodka concoctions. Pink, icy and delicious, just like you." He held the glass up and smiled, his hand trembling slightly.

"No," she said, more firmly than she intended; and shuddered, imagining the drink's sour taste and the burn of alcohol as it slid down her throat. "I don't want one."

He looked hurt and a little stunned. "But I—"

"I have to work tomorrow," she said through tight lips. "I can't play with you tonight, Donald." Though she could feel her face heat, she kept going. "I'm sick of being both savior and playmate. It's burning me out," she said, waving a hand; though he'd told her countless times that it was a vulgar gesture. "What am I—a plastic doll? I have a job that requires brain capacity, so listen carefully, Captain." She took a deep breath. "I. Am. Busy. Tomorrow."

"With?" His eyes narrowed.

"Smith Labs is hosting a beta symposium," she said, sitting forward in her chair. "I've told you several times, but you obviously didn't listen. Ten of our biggest customers are reviewing our new networking products. I'm making a presentation."

"So?" He looked at her as if she were about to explode.

She exhaled loudly and folded her arms across her chest. "I suppose what I do with my career—my life—is irrelevant."

"What's that got to do with tonight?" he asked, looking puzzled. "You don't fly my planes; I don't keep track of your schedule. So what's the problem? I'm here now and I need you."

"What?" She could only stare at him.

"It's only eight o'clock, Meggie." He sidled up to her with his most winning smile. "We're wasting time arguing, babe." He shook his head. "Come on now. I haven't seen you for three whole weeks." He handed her the drink. "Just sip this, then I'll rub some soothing cream on your shoulders and we'll talk." His gaze slid away. He was hiding something.

"What happened?" she asked flatly, and set the drink on the coffee table.

He slumped on the sofa, a hand shielding his eyes, the tragic set-upon hero. She'd seen the look too many times.

"Well?" she asked, fear pricking the back of her neck. She folded her hands in her lap.

"I've been fired, dumped, ousted," he said, squinting, gauging her reaction as he threw back his arms and cradled the back of his head. "That bitch, Nancy, you know . . . the flight attendant from hell. She called security on me." Crimson mottled his face. "The other two—Flora and Candice—they'd never pull that crap."

Megan nodded, recalling the women from a party several months back. Pleasant and almost middle-aged, Nancy had stood out as the only non-drinker; while the other two had been wrapped like hot towels around a couple of married pilots.

"She claims she smelled booze on my breath." He shook his head, a small boy caught in a lie. "What the hell does she know?" He sniggered. "I've flown with a pop or two many a time. Just set the auto pilot and it flies like a damn bus." His laugh was tinged with hysteria.

Megan closed her eyes briefly as a chill washed through her. "What happened?" she asked, glad someone had finally caught him. She stopped flying with Airlius soon after she'd met him. Flying was scary enough, without hearing him tell about drinking on the job.

"Good old Larry," he said, then rummaged in his pocket and pulled out what looked like a marijuana cigarette. She stared at it, shocked. "Security came and hauled me off. . . found some other stiff to pilot the damn plane. Larry-boy comes charging into the secure room they'd stuffed me in." With a few practiced movements, he lit the roach, took a few puffs and held it out to her.

She shook her head and folded her arms across her chest, her throat constricting on a sob.

"Who does he think he is?" He took another puff and held it in, his watery eyes narrowing to slits. He exhaled a cloud of smoke. "Larry was nothing but a low life geek in flight school. Could barely get a Piper off the ground, from what I heard. Now look at him."

"What happened?" she asked, finally managing to get the words out.

His eyes widened and he smiled. "Larry started with the finger shaking and the yelling, of course. He likes to play the tough boss." He flung out an arm expansively, then cradled his neck. "I just couldn't take it—not from him." He looked down at the roach, as if studying it. "I walked out. Felt damn good, too. Had enough of their shitty rules. Who cares about their rehabilitation program? So I had a few drinks? Is that such a crime?"

"Let me get this straight," Megan said after a long moment. "You got caught drunk on the job and then rejected Airlius' rehabilitation program." She leaned forward. "You walked out. You . . . think it's okay to pilot a plane filled with people when you're drunk, not to mention drive twenty miles in a rental car in the same condition?"

"Yeah on all counts, dummy," he said, slurring slightly as he rose and patted her hair. "Now be a nice girl and do as I say. I'm dying to play Captain Hook with you, Meggie. I think about it all the time when I'm away. I need a blow job along with . . . you know . . . one of our little Victorian reenactments."

A dull weight filled her at his use of the word girl and his crudeness. She'd given up explaining to him that calling her a girl was the same as calling a black man a boy; and that a little romance got him a whole lot further. But he didn't get it, and probably never would.

"No, Donald," she said, and rose. "I don't want to play with you. I don't even want to breathe the same air as you. And I'm not drinking this." She picked up the drink, ignoring his hurt expression; then strode to the kitchen, dumped the contents in the sink and set the glass on the counter. "I don't know where you get your arrogance," she said, turning, seeing him sway toward her at the edge of the kitchen. "Were you spoiled or deprived as a child?" she asked, her fury mounting. "I've played both scenarios in my head countless times, thinking your military family story must be a lie. Your parents never replied to our wedding announcement, or to the few letters I sent afterwards. Do they even exist, Donald? For all I know, you're a farm boy from upstate New York."

"What's with you?" he asked, shaking his head. "This isn't what I planned at all. I had a rough day. I lost my job. Where's the compassion, the wifely nurturing? And my drink—you wasted my drink?"

"I am not drinking with you!" she cried, then stepped back, seeing his self-pitying expression turn to rage. Fear prickled her skin, but she ignored it. "Who do you think you are, waltzing in here whenever you damn please? I have a career, if you haven't noticed. Compassion? I have plenty of compassion; but not for someone who keeps drinking when it's already cost him his job. Now you're smoking pot? When did that start?"

"Miss high and mighty," he sneered. "As if you don't like to drink?"

"You have a drinking problem," she said firmly.

"And you don't?"

She looked away, thinking of the blackouts. "Maybe I do, but I don't put other people in jeopardy."

"I'll get another job," he said softly. "There are plenty of other airlines, plenty of other jobs. You'll see."

"I hope so, for your sake," she said, and sighed as he reached over and touched her hand. "You're wasting your life, Donald."

"Come on, Meggie," he said softly. "Do you always have to have the last word?" He pulled her into his arms.

She held herself stiffly at first, hearing in his taunt an echo of Pa when he wanted to shut her up. He reeked of pot, making her stomach churn. Or was it from the lack of food? She hadn't eaten all day—and that was getting to be a bad habit.

"Come on," he said, pressing his forehead to hers. "I don't want to fight. We don't have to drink. Let's just grab a bite, Meggie. I'm tired and hungry, just like you. It's been a long day and I have nowhere else to go."

She sighed, hating that he got to her with his dejection. As if she'd kick him out. He was still her husband. "All right," she said and nodded, noting his glassy eyes. She felt weighted down, too weary to fight. "You want pizza and salad?" she asked automatically.

"Okay."

"I'll have it delivered," she said, then moved out of his grasp and turned on the television, hoping he'd pass out to the evening news.

ଓଓଓଓଓ

Over the course of the next several weeks, Donald's optimism dimmed with each rejection. He claimed that Airlius had blacklisted him; and she suspected he was right. No employer would take a chance on a known drinker. After he'd maxed his credit cards on distant interviews at obscure airlines, he *borrowed* one of hers until a quick phone call from a suspicious credit card company shut down that source of funds.

Meanwhile, she pushed herself at work; keeping pace with product releases, traveling further and longer to solve customer problems, trying to keep out of his way. By the end of October, she'd had enough.

Clutching her garment bag and shouldering her carryon like a soldier of fortune, she trudged into her apartment, wanting to forget her recent trip to Salt Lake City, where the customer, a short balding Nazi, had screamed at her for over an hour, venting his spleen about the bumbling Los Angeles District Office. As the Home Office representative, she'd listened respectfully—or at least pretended to—then rolled up her sleeves and solved his problem; which happened to be caused by IBM's equipment, not Smith Labs. Her flight home was delayed, and then cancelled. She'd spent last night waiting for another flight, only to sit on the runway for two solid hours, listening to the engine hiccup. Finally in the air, she'd white-knuckled it to Logan, taking small comfort in the fact that she was heading home.

She dropped her bags on her apartment floor, unmindful of the noise it made to Mrs. Goff below, then slammed the door. She rubbed her eyes, wanting nothing more than a steaming shower followed by several hours of sleep.

"This is freaking unbelievable," she said, scanning the room she'd left in pristine condition just five days earlier. The place reeked of cigarette butts, pot, wine and rotten eggs. Encrusted dishes were piled in the sink and across the counters. Magazines and newspapers were strewn across the living room floor. On the table beside the window was a silver dish piled high with cigarette butts. She'd never seen it before.

Gagging, she ran to the window and shoved it open; hating to think of what she'd find in the trash bin, or the bathroom. Cold damp air gusted in as she took quick inventory.

The bathroom floor was thick with talcum powder. Several bottles of shampoo and conditioner were open; some tipped over and spilled around the sink. Donald's electric shaver stood in a pool of water. A pile of musty wet towels filled one corner.

The bedroom was in shambles, as if he'd wrestled an ape. Bedcovers and clothes were strewn about; and one of her expensive feather pillows had burst its seams. Feathers were everywhere, as were crumbs, gum wrappers, empty plates and whiskey bottles.

She reached for the note on the dresser.

Meggie,

I've started with a small company that offers something big. Call you in a few weeks.

Love, Donald.

"Fine," she whispered, and stared at the letter, recalling the hope on his face the morning she'd left for Utah.

"It'll work out," he'd told her. "I can feel my luck turning." He'd smiled oddly; and she'd asked no questions, not wanting to spoil their last few moments before her trip. Now she wished she'd asked those questions—like where the hell was he?

She sank heavily on the bed. No matter what he'd done or where he'd gone, she wanted him home.

ଓଓଓଓଓ

Christmas was days away when her phone rang at work. Grimacing, she ignored it, and glared instead at the IBM manual she'd been studying. For the past fifteen minutes, she'd been trying to parse Allied Chemical's data stream, and almost had it. Glancing across her cubicle, she caught Bob Cartright's worried frown as he punched in a code and answered the phone. He'd become a friend of sorts, but not close enough for confidences. He was simply too happy with his gorgeous wife and sweet baby son. He had it all, knew it and was touchingly grateful. Why couldn't she have found someone just like him?

She blinked hard, trying to focus. Bob would be able to identify Allied's puzzle in minutes, maybe seconds. Without practice, however, she'd never approach his skill.

"It's for you," he said, holding out the receiver, looking concerned. "It's Donald."

Fighting anger, she took the phone. Minutes

later, she was racing out the door.

ଓଓଓଓଓ

"What is it?" she asked, ready to spit nails as she slammed into her apartment. Donald sat in a chair by the window in a haze of smoke, his feet up on her new coffee table. She glared at his feet, but he didn't take the hint.

"I came to get you." His tone was matter of fact. He took a long drag on his cigarette.

"Just like that?" she said with a laugh. "I haven't seen or heard from you in two friggin' months, and you want me to go with you." She laughed harshly as she shut the door. "Get serious, Captain. I'm not going anywhere."

"Oh, you're coming with me." His feet touched the floor and she backed away, scanning his wrinkled clothes, bloodshot eyes, trembling fingers and red-rimmed nostrils with mild distaste and a blooming fright.

"No more woman's lib crap," he said slowly, his expression hardening. "No more working late or traveling for days on end. I want a wife, a willing supportive wife, to help me with *my* career for a change."

"Your career?" She laughed and put her hands on her hips. "So where exactly are you taking me?"

"Ah," he said, his smile grim as he moved closer. He stopped a yard away and rubbed his chin. "Look, maybe I started this off wrong. I don't want to argue. It's just that my job's going great, and I need you with me in Miami." His eyes held a glimmer of panic and fear. He glanced at the door.

"Miami," she said softly and backed away, thinking of sun, sand, skyscrapers and the pushy customer last year who'd asked her to fly with him to a small, secluded island off the coast. Smith Labs' office in Miami boasted of many such well-heeled customers. "What's the new job?" she asked, and tried not to flinch as his arm came around her waist. He stumbled as he moved, pushing her toward the kitchen; and leaned on her heavily, probably stoned out of his mind.

"Come on, Meggie." He pulled her hard against him, grinding her hips. "You owe me, damn it. I shouldn't have to beg."

With one quick move, she dug in her heels and shoved him to the floor, sending his cigarette flying. She stared at him and then her hands in awe. She'd done that?

He laughed up at her. "You been taking self-defense lessons or something?"

"What's going on?' she asked. Spying his cigarette beneath the kitchen table, she leaned over to retrieve it. A fire in her kitchen was the last thing she needed.

"I'm smuggling," he slurred, his expression beatific as he looked up at her.

She froze in the act of picking up the butt. "Smuggling?"

"Yeah," he whispered, looking around as if

someone could overhear. "For some rich dudes, Columbian drug lords." He laughed. "You should see their Miami estates—swimming pools, a dozen servants, champagne flowing like water, not to mention the cocaine—on little silver platters, no less. We'll have a house like that. You'll see. Just a few more runs and we'll never have to worry. But meanwhile . . .." He closed his eyes, looking about to pass out.

Flames filled her vision. "I'll give you something to worry about!" she shrieked. Using all of her strength, she pulled him up by the arms. Groggily, he stood, looking confused.

"I'm not going anywhere with you," she said, a cold strength filling her veins. "Being a drunk is bad enough; but now you're doing drugs—hell, transporting them? There's no future in that, you stupid dumb ass. You actually think I'm going with you? I have a career, if you hadn't noticed; and I'm not about to give it up for a loser like you."

"Been talking with your Pa?" he sneered as he swayed. "You look just like him when you talk like that. Mighty ugly."

"Get out!" she shouted and pointed at the door. "If you aren't gone in five minutes, I'm calling the police."

ᴄᴃᴄᴃᴄᴃᴄᴃᴄᴃ

Stan heard a woman yell and then a door slam. Megan. The thought hit like a punch in the gut.

He'd been heading in the direction of her apartment, anyway; but now he ran. He hadn't seen the pilot's car for a few months now—yet to hear from Tom; the newlyweds were doing just great. He laughed, picking up speed. Except for the first time he'd seen the stiff kissing her, pissing him off royally, he'd never seen the man sober. He was half way up the main stairs when he spied him—the flyboy who'd stolen his girl—lying in a heap on the floor.

If he were smart, he'd mind his own business. Megan wouldn't thank him for interfering; and she definitely was not his girl.

He stepped closer, his curiosity overwhelming, eying the man who'd gotten under Gordon Rosswell's skin. The old buck had never been so depressed, or angry. Mr. Rosswell had tried to protect Megan all of her life; yet he'd overprotected and neglected her in so many ways. She'd been a tough kid, a strong one; yet her father was always second-guessing her, as if she were a brainless female, which was definitely not the case. With a mother in and out of the Tewksbury State Hospital, and a father who hit to make the smallest point, she'd grown up hard. When he'd first met her, she'd been a scraped-knee, loud-mouthed brat. Even then, he'd seen the sweetness and purity beneath all that bravado. Then at fourteen, she'd gone and bloomed into vixen shaped jailbait.

"Megan," he breathed, thinking of those long legs, fluffy hair and big dark eyes just beyond the apartment door. She was a natural beauty, and didn't even know it. She should have been his; but he'd blown his sole chance and then she'd met the pilot. He winced, remembering the shock of seeing her kissing the guy; and the time they'd shown up in a limo like a pair of movie stars: her with a glittery new rock on her finger and a gold band to match; and him a loud drunk with a fancy haircut.

He shook his head sadly. Even if she never looked in his direction, she deserved a whole lot better than this idiot; and by the looks of his pale face against the dark carpet, he was a druggie to boot. She had integrity and stamina; and was miles out of her league with this joker, who had to be somebody's poor little rich boy, this asshole who couldn't possibly appreciate the jewel that she was, judging by the fact that she'd thrown him out.

He smiled as he took in every detail—the messed up hair, puffy eyes, wrinkled uniform, scuffed shoes and the acrid-sweet smell of whisky.

He may have blown his single chance with her, but regret was a nasty beast; and maybe she was too fine for him, anyway. A sinking feeling filled gut. He was better off with a girl like Christy, who could sling a beer with the best of them. She was easy on the eyes and didn't make him tongue-tied—unlike Megan, a college girl and career woman, who needed a man she could look up to.

He laughed harshly, eying the honorable said husband, who was lying on the floor like a landed bluefish, his eyes closed, his hands waving as if he were taking to someone. No one would be looking up at him anytime soon.

"You all right there, buddy?" He nudged him with a foot.

The pilot's head bobbed. Then he managed to sit up, groaning and holding his head. "That's just about all I have here," he said, slurring slightly, waving an arm in the direction of his luggage. "S'like I don't even live with the damn girl, and she's my wife, goddamnit. All my stuff's in Chicago—a big mistake. Should have moved in here like she said, changed my mailing address, taken a little more control of the situation, have her meet the folks." He started to rise, fell on his ass, then righted himself.

Stan gripped him by the elbow and helped him up. "She kick you out?" he asked, suppressing a smile. Megan's so-called marriage was hopeless.

"Yeah, she sure did." The pilot rubbed his eyes, then grabbed his luggage and lurched toward the stairs. "She'll change her mind," he muttered over his shoulder. "But right now I've got to get moving. Things are happening. Big things. Don't have time for this bullshit." He paused, then looked back. "Do I know you?" he asked.

"No." Stan shook his head, his smile grim.

The pilot was already halfway down the stairs.

CHAPTER 5
MAY 1983

The Chicago-bound 727 was tightly packed for the morning commute. Megan took a deep breath, then let it out slowly. The smallest deviation from her focused attention would surely send the plane into a death spiral. With each dip, rise and shudder, a shriek rose in her throat and she prayed the flight would soon end. Glancing around, she saw only glazed, disinterested stares and closed eyes. No one looked the least bit frightened. The flight attendant at the head of the cabin sat with her legs crossed, her top leg bouncing, as she flipped through a magazine. The cabin bell chimed and she stowed the magazine in a drawer, then clipped on her seat belt.

Swirls of colors whipped past the windows.

Megan forced herself upright, to keep from assuming the crash position. Sweat pooled beneath her arms and trickled down her back. Lights flamed behind her lids as she closed them in prayer. She stifled a scream as the plane touched down, first one set of wheels, then the other. Her chest heaving, she let out one long breath. The flight was finally over.

She looked down, seeing white knuckles. She'd been foolish to take Donald's old flight—the drunk flight, she called it—though she had no way of knowing if this pilot and his co-pilot, both strangers, had been drinking. The plane's engines roared in reverse, first squealing high-pitched and then softly humming. After a few stops and starts, the plane lumbered to the gangway. She glanced at the fat, sweating businessman sitting beside her. His breath could knock over a horse. He was fingering the dog-eared detective novel he'd prattled about at the start of the flight—until her silence had stopped him.

Her thoughts turned to Donald, who was probably airborne, or God knew where in the steamy tropics. Or dead. She glanced out the window at the dreary Chicago sky. It was already spring, and she still hadn't heard from him. Even on their worst days, she hadn't considered life without him; and here she was, half-widowed, half-divorced, wanting him no matter what he'd done. Tears filled her eyes and she closed them. Now that she was actually in Chicago, she'd call his parents and finally meet them. Maybe they'd know where he was.

The ceiling lights blinked and the cabin bell

sounded. She grabbed her things and pushed out with the throng, using the overhead signs to locate the baggage claim area at the far end of the concourse. The place was already packed with other passengers, jockeying for position beside the whirling belt that pumped steadily from a covered hole in the wall. Spying her garment bag, she slipped past two gangly teens and a multi-generational black family to grab it. She was walking away when someone called her name.

"Megan!"

She turned and froze. Five months without a man; and the sight of this one unnerved her.

"Adam," she said under her breath. Supposedly married, with rumors of hot tub parties and drug-fueled orgies abounding, Adam Clark, Smith Labs' Vice President of Marketing, was the epitome of danger. Looking deceptively wholesome in worn jeans, with a navy cashmere sweater slung over his button-down denim shirt, he waved from the far end of the baggage claim area. His hair had been carefully highlighted. He had a long, thin face, strong jaw and an intense look that made her suck in her breath,

"Great," she muttered, noting his decisive stride and the effortless way he carried his luggage.

"Adam," she said with a brisk nod, breaking eye contact quickly.

"Good to see you," he said, looking her over. "How are you getting to the hotel?" His voice was smooth and clipped, what Charlie Maxwell, one of the software engineers, called his crisp-speak. Charlie joked that he could sell sand at the beach.

"I'm taking the shuttle," she said, her heart racing. "It's just up the stairs and to the left." She lifted her chin in the direction of the escalator that rose in the middle of the floor. Then she looked at him fully, noting his predatory smile.

"No need for that," he said softly, somehow reminding her of Donald. There was kindness in his eyes and desire, as if he understood everything—her loneliness, her insecurities—and how badly she wanted someone to hold her.

"I've got a rental car," he said, and touched her arm companionably. "You just come with me." He winked and took her bag. "Come on," he said and cocked his head in the apparent direction of his car. "That plane food was awful and I'm starving. A couple of glasses of wine and a good meal will do wonders. You'll see. The hotel restaurant is supposed to be great."

"All right," she said, returning his smile.

ଓଓଓଓଓ

She took a hard look at the face in her hotel room mirror. She'd shed a few pounds since Donald's departure. Her cheekbones looked gaunt, something he would have noticed right away—if he'd been around. In the midst of his job search, he'd taken to criticizing her weight, comparing her unfavorably with the waifish, half-starved flight attendants he liked to hang around with.

She happened to like food, and actually ate it when she remembered to—though nothing tasted good these days—and she hated grocery shopping and cleaning up a mess in the kitchen. Eating solo was the pits, along with admitting that her husband was gone for good and her marriage a complete failure.

She sighed. The good days with Donald had been few; and she'd wanted more—more home cooked meals together, more lazy Sunday mornings, more shopping sprees in Boston, not to mention traveling with him around the world. She'd actually looked forward to meeting his parents. She backed away from the mirror, shaking her head. It wasn't as if life had passed her by. She was only twenty-seven, with plenty of time to find someone else, maybe settle down and raise a family. She stared at her image in shock, and balled her fists on either side of her face.

Marriage and family? Now where had that come from?

"No way," she hissed, and then fled.

ଓଓଓଓଓ

Megan scanned the smoky barroom, her eyes adjusting to the dim lights, seeing the hunting prints, the gleaming oak bar, brass wall sconces against the far wall, fake trees in each corner hung with tiny white lights. It was typical of many four-star hotels, ubiquitous and comforting, second home to business travelers finding themselves in Boston, San Francisco or Chicago.

The room was packed with marketing, sales and technical support staff from the world's leading computer manufacturers. The clamor was deafening—a jumble of jocular laughter, clinking glasses, silver striking china, the tinkle of a piano—sounds thick with hope and the exhilaration of money to be made. Bodies pressed against bodies as colleagues postured and boasted, studying rivals, capturing details for future gossip. Cigarette smoke hung in the cool dark air. The biggest computer show of the year was just two days away.

She spied Adam at the bar. He smiled a welcome as she slid onto the empty stool beside him. His gaze held hers as he handed her a glass of wine.

"Thanks," she said and smiled as she took it, determined to enjoy herself, his languorous perusal sending warmth to her cheeks.

"Who else is here?" she shouted over the din, her expression carefully neutral. He was obviously playing a game; and she wanted to play along.

"No one, yet." He leaned closer. She breathed his expensive cologne and minty toothpaste, her excitement building. "Charlie and Ming will be here tomorrow morning," he continued, "and Scott's flying in late tonight. Something about his kid's birthday."

She nodded and took a sip of wine. It was dry, perfectly chilled and delicious.

"Clark, party of two?" the bartender called out. Adam raised a hand.

"That was quick," she said, and smiled inanely as he directed her with a hand to her back toward a black-gowned hostess who stood at the entrance, holding thick, leather-clad menus. She had sleek, dark hair and a sparkling chain around her neck. "Follow me," she said, eying Adam appreciatively.

They followed her down a small hallway that led to a quiet restaurant—a showcase of china, crystal and silver. A trio of candles lit each linen draped table, most of them occupied. Talk was subdued, the smells delicious. Efficient-looking wait staff scurried across the thickly carpeted floor with well-laden trays.

During the meal she let him talk, stroking his ego, steering the conversation carefully away from herself. Like most men she'd met, he was a walking resume and talked at length about his family. He and his wife, Kathy had four kids: Andrea, a willful high school junior, Nicholas and Noah, twin twelve-year-old baseball addicts, and Bethany, a bossy Kindergartener. She pelted him with questions throughout the delicious prime rib dinner, refusing to answer any of his. Dessert and Irish coffee followed the meal.

"That was superb," she said, as she rose from the table and dropped her napkin onto her plate. He rose, too, and stuffed his wallet back into his pocket and nodded at the waiter who was walking away with the signed and credited check. She joined

Adam and they moved companionably toward the exit.

"Enough about my family." His glance was speculative as he took her arm. "You've said nothing about yours."

"What do you want to know?" she asked, leaning on him, dizzy from the drinks and stuffed with delicious food.

"Ah, a question for a question from the best support analyst in the company." He smiled slyly as he patted her hand. "That's exactly what makes you so good at what you do, Megan. Such a professional."

"So ask." She shrugged as they stepped through the door.

"There must be a husband?" He glanced at her rings, then nodded at a well-dressed Asian couple, who passed them in the hallway.

"Of course," she said, and looked up at him, forcing a smile, unable to recall the image of Donald's face.

"What does *Mr*. Rosswell do for a living?" he asked.

Her smile faded. He was steering her toward the elevators, toward their rooms.

"Mr. Alexander, actually," she said with a tight laugh, wanting to cry. "Donald's a pilot. He used to fly for Airlius, but works for a private company now." She shook her head slightly, as sadness engulfed her. She wanted a husband just like Adam, who bragged about their wonderful life together.

She raised her chin slightly, refusing to be mired in such negative emotions. She was drunk, that was all. The sadness would pass. "What does Kathy do?" she asked.

"She takes care of me and our kids, looks decorative and keeps a nice house." He chuckled. "There you go again, changing the subject. You're good at it, too—did it all through dinner."

They stopped in front of the elevators. There was no one else around. In a quick movement, he took her hand, turned it over and kissed the underside of her wrist, sending shivers along her arm. The tight aching knot that had started in the bar now droned in the pit of her stomach.

"Come on, Megan, give a little. It's just me, Adam. I'd like to be your friend. What can it hurt to have a friend in high places?" His look was appealing.

"All right," she said, smiling as she leaned toward him. "I met Donald on a business trip about two years ago. He's tall, with blondish hair and light brown eyes—almost golden. He's away a lot." She shrugged a shoulder.

"Oh really," he said. "You could be describing your brother." He looked at her intently. "So where is he right now? This pilot of yours?"

"I don't have a brother." She swallowed hard, the odd glint in Adam's eyes bothering her for some reason. She looked away. "Let's talk about something else," she said, then ran her fingers through her hair, pulling it back from her hot face, wondering at her sudden confusion.

"Sounds like you're . . .." He turned away, then pressed the up button. "Dissatisfied?"

She looked at him sharply, seeing the tense little question in his eyes. "Perhaps," she said after a long pause, then smiled brightly, desperate to change the subject. "But I'm here now and glad to be at the show. I've never been to Chicago. It looks like a fun place." She ran her tongue along her lower lip, and looked sideways at him as the elevator doors opened, feeling like a chatterbox.

"Yeah." He nodded and they stepped inside. "It's definitely a fun place. I'll grant you that."

"Which floor?" she asked when the door closed, her finger hovering over the buttons. She pushed the button for hers.

"Same as yours," he mumbled. She looked at him in panic. With a deep sigh, he leaned against the chrome rail. His eyes were downcast as if he were deep in thought, his arms crossed over his chest. He looked bored. Or was he tired? Had she said the wrong thing?

The car began its ascent, the lights blinking over the doorway in an arc. When the door opened at their floor, she took a step, but he didn't move.

"Are you all right?" She stuck out an arm to stop the door from closing. It chimed in protest.

"Yeah, I'm fine," he said, and lifted his head, his grin wide. "But I guess I need some help here. Had too much to drink, probably." He chuckled as she reached for his arm; and then in a blur pressed the stop button, and was grabbing her and kissing her hard and shoving her against the wall.

"No," she managed to get out and tried to push him away. This wasn't happening.

But his lips came down again, this time softer, dragging at her senses, drugging her. He was an expert. He was delicious.

Slowly, ever so slowly, she began to relent, giving in to the pleasure, opening her mouth, her arms going around him. His grip loosened. With a gentle hand, he caressed the back of her neck and under her hair, still holding her against him. It seemed natural and delightfully sexy. She tried to catch a breath, but her knees buckled as she luxuriated in the pleasure of his masterful lips, his hands upon her. She found herself kissing him back with hunger bordering on desperation. His hands kneaded her buttocks and she moaned, making no protest as he parted her jacket and slid a hand down her blouse.

The elevator bell shrilled.

His hand shot around her and disengaged the stop button. The door opened promptly, revealing two Japanese businessmen: the elder shaking his head, the younger smirking, glancing at his superior, then masking his expression. Adam laughed as he bowed slightly in derogatory salute; then pulled her with him down the hall. She ducked her head into his shoulder, laughing, mortified.

"Adam, Adam," she whispered. He was kissing her throat as she fumbled for her key. "Adam, this isn't right." She pushed on his arm, but he kept squeezing her breasts, pushing her forward. "You have a wife, a family."

"Oh, no you don't," he said with a laugh, and pulled her to the room next door. "You can't escape that easily." He pushed in his key and yanked her into what she realized was his room. Right beside hers?

She giggled as she backed away from him and her calves struck something solid. She fell laughing, thinking what a ridiculous coincidence it was to have adjacent rooms; and smiled up at him as she sprawled across his exquisitely comfortable bed. It was massive compared to hers and right next door. He must have asked for it special.

"We shouldn't." She laughed as she looked around in panic. He was stripping off his jacket, taking off his shoes and socks, removing his pants.

"Why not?" He dove on top of her, knocking the wind out of her. It was like Donald all over again—the drinks, the hotel bed, the anonymity. But this time, she wasn't a virgin. She knew exactly what she was doing. Didn't she?

His kisses softened. She touched his face, seeing his hunger; and her stomach twisted in an incredible yearning. He's a good man, she told herself, a lonely man. And she was lonely, too. No one had to know.

With hands and mouth, he urged her to take; and yet it was he who took control, ruthlessly claiming her surrender. Her breath came hard as he moved over her, stripping away her pride along with her clothes. Under his tutelage, she became a panting, writhing whipcord. He devoured every inch of her, causing her to cry out several times, begging him to stop as pleasure cascaded to wretched agony and then back to pleasure; until finally, he went rigid and collapsed against her. She couldn't move. Her body had turned to jelly.

He grunted as he pushed off her, then sat on the edge of the bed and raked a hand through his tousled hair.

"You're a sly one," he said, glancing over his shoulder with a soft smile. "All that passion going to waste. Glad I had some. Let's get dressed and go out. I feel energized, don't you?"

Glad he had some?

She pulled the sheet up over her breasts, stunned. Granted sex had been wonderful and spontaneous and they were both married and all that; but it had been degrading, too; and something essential was missing. She wanted him to hold her or at least say something.

"What's you wife going to think?" she asked, then immediately regretted it.

"Same as what Donald's going to think?" he said with a harsh laugh. "As if you care." He rose and stretched, his long pale frame gleaming in the dim light. "I'm here." He shrugged. "You're here. And the downtown's a sight to see after dark. You said you've never been to Chicago. So let's go explore it. Do some shopping. Don't tell me you're a romantic. Don't tell me you want empty promises about some bright future after that." He gestured at the bed.

"Of course not," she said, trying to sound composed. Admittedly, she *was* a romantic, but her feelings would change nothing. The man was an operator, a sexual mechanic. She'd known it all along. "Let's go," she said, putting a purr in her voice and a smile on her face. "I'd love to see Chicago at night."

ଔଔଔଔଔ

"Tomorrow's coming early," Adam said at his door much later that evening. His arm barred her entrance. There was a definite chill in his eyes.

"Yeah, tomorrow," she said with a tight laugh. She peered over his shoulder into his room, the place of their debauchery.

"Don't be like that," he said, raking a hand through his hair. "We had a good time. It's just—"

The phone rang in his room and he sprinted to grab it, not bothering with the door.

"Yeah, a good time," she muttered, starting to move away, hating to appear so needy. But she was needy; and for some odd reason, Stanley came to mind. What would he think of her now? By her own volition, she'd become the cheap thrill he seemed to prefer. So why did that make her feel dirty, when it should have given her comfort?

She paused, hearing Adam speak in rapid-fire Spanish. She heard her name and Donald's. Dredging up four years of high school Spanish, she recognized the words *querida*, love and *te quiero*, I love you. Was he already pursuing his next mark? No, that wasn't it. His tone was conciliatory, as if to a wife. But as far as she knew, Kathy wasn't Spanish.

"Night Adam," she said softly; then froze when she heard him say Miami.

Was there a connection to Donald? Was that why he'd been grilling her? Adam looked at her over his shoulder, his eyes blazing, and waved her away. She bolted for her room, chilled.

In the bathroom, she stripped off her clothes and stepped into the tub. She'd been a fool again, and this time with a co-worker—a powerful man with powerful connections, whose intentions had been clear all along. But hadn't hers been, too? Hadn't she wanted some anonymous sex, a little on-the-road delight?

She hugged herself as water beat down on tender shoulders, and sagged against the tiles.

ଔଔଔଔଔ

A shrill sound sliced through the heavy gloom. Megan batted at the invasion, sending the hotel alarm clock crashing to the floor. She burrowed deeper into the blankets, only to sit up at the telephone's incessant ring.

"Thanks," she croaked into the receiver at the perky wake-up caller; then flung it down and leaped from bed. Room service wouldn't be far behind.

She sighed as she headed to the bathroom, recalling the previous night. Drinks and a persuasive man were a fatal combination—at least for her. Adam had best keep what had happened to himself.

Or what?

She examined her puffy, bloodshot eyes in the mirror, glad she'd brought Visine. She could hardly stand against the man if he decided to kiss and tell. He was a friend of Steve Grant's, for God's sake, who'd once told her that she couldn't possibly be as good at her job as customers claimed, that they just liked seeing a pretty girl's smile. The man was just aching to put her in her place,

Pretty, all right. She growled at her image. Not with a nose like hers and hair that refused to cooperate. Grant was obviously nearsighted. It was her brain that mattered, her experience and skill. Logic ruled her world, as did patience—not only with irate customers, but also with herself. She'd worked hard to acquire her knowledge, and no one could take it from her. Adam may own the Smith Labs booth, but she owned the demos. Without her, he'd have nothing to show. He'd make damn sure their booth was a success—which meant staying on her good side.

With a sinking feeling, she thought of the rumors: his infidelities, the harassment cases, and the striper in his office. Adam Clark was no gentleman.

She was combing her hair when room service arrived with coffee and pastry. Still half-asleep, she directed the deferential young black man to the table by the window, signed the check, then locked the door behind him. With coffee cup in hand, she leafed through the thick phone book she'd found in the dresser.

"Well, what do you know," she murmured, setting the cup down, her finger marking the place. "James and Marybeth Alexander." She grabbed the phone and punched in the number.

"Hello." It was a woman's voice—an annoyed, sleepy, hated to be awoken voice.

"Is this Marybeth Alexander?" Megan's breath hitched as she glanced at her watch. It was six in the morning. Most people were still asleep.

"Yes."

"This is Megan, Donald's wife."

"Excuse me?"

"Megan Rosswell," she said, a little more firmly. "I'm married to your son, Donald. You *are* Donald Alexander's mother?"

"Look, young lady." came the crisp, well-educated voice "I don't think this is amusing in the least. Donald is certainly not married to you. And do you have any idea what time it is?"

Megan closed her eyes. "I sent you our wedding announcement . . . and wrote to you . . . twice." She gazed at the window, where sheers fluttered in the blustery breeze, thinking back to the times she'd handed Donald the envelopes. He'd written the address, licked the stamp, then stuck it on. It was the same address as in the phone book. Each time, he'd slipped the envelope into his coat pocket. Her heart sank. "Apparently, you never received my letters."

"This is a ridiculous conversation," Marybeth said shrilly. "Utterly ridiculous. And I can't imagine your motivation."

"I'll send you a copy of our marriage certificate," Megan said, trying to sound calm, though her heart raced and she gripped the receiver like a cudgel. "We were married in January 1982, in Las Vegas."

"You are not Donald's wife," Marybeth said. "You simply can't be. His wife's name is Victoria and they live in Florida. I shouldn't even be telling you this. Do you need money or something? What exactly do you want from me?"

"Victoria?" Megan ran a mental inventory of all the flight attendants she'd met through Donald. There was no Victoria. But there had to be an explanation. "Have you ever met her?" she asked, thinking of Donald's dream house in Miami and of her own Victorian obsession.

"Not yet." There was worry in her voice.

"I see." Megan clasped the receiver even more tightly, her hand now shaking. "Have you heard from him lately, Mrs. Alexander? Do you know where he is?"

The dial tone sounded.

She set down the receiver, her mind racing. Her mother-in-law—for that was whom she'd spoken to—was afraid of something. It sounded like she loved her son and wanted to protect him.

"But from whom?" she whispered, then glanced at her watch. The show wouldn't wait.

ʗʆʗʆʗʆʗʆʗʆ

The cavernous auditorium was a warehouse of unfinished walls, unassembled kiosks, stacked crates, piles of carpeting in various hues, armies of potted plants, many with brilliant flowers, and foam packaging strewn about the cold cement floor. A chill wind blew in from the open cargo bays. The place reeked of sawdust, new plastic and gasoline. Burley men drove forklifts, carting crates and boxes, beeping as they went. Shivering, Megan scanned the floor map, then peered up at the overhead row signs, noting her destination.

The Smith Labs booth lay at the center of the sprawling maze. Within hours, order would win over chaos, and the place would dazzle the eyes, showcasing the best computers in the world. She nodded a terse greeting at a few other early-risers—support staff like her, judging by disk packs and battered briefcases. She took a breath and headed into the maze, calculating that she had to finish by three—four at the latest. The show would open promptly at six.

She looked down at her copy of the booth plan. There was to be a registration table, a small stage, complete with a black velvet curtain that flanked a ten-foot high video wall, several rows of folding chairs and three tubular demonstration kiosks. She nodded at a worker who was placing the last kiosk in the Smith Labs area. Pale peach squares of carpet, bordered with aqua and black, rose in stacks beside potted palms that would flank the stage. Potted flowers in a wild profusion of colors, intended to line the front of the stage, surrounded the registration table, now hidden beneath several boxes.

She plucked a pair of eight-inch disks from her briefcase. Light and flexible, they were easier to carry through airports than a bulky hard disk pack; and attracted a lot less attention. Each disk contained a product demo: one showing the DataStorage-7's ease of use, and the other a Hawaiian insurance carrier's application with links to their mainframe—the reason for the booth's colorful theme.

The Chicago District was sending Naomi Wickam, nicknamed Tootsie by some of Megan's colleagues, with the third demo—if she bothered to show up. Tootsie had a reputation for promising things she couldn't deliver.

She quickened her pace, seeing Scott Hibbard, Smith Labs' show manager and Adam's right-hand man, heading her way. He was a bundle of optimism, a pleasure to work with. Tall and gangly, he had three cute kids and a devoted wife. He was deep in conversation with the DataStorage-7 hardware crew. One of the engineers was giving hand signals to a forklift operator, who was carting a load of boxes containing the DataStorage-7s. Scott waved to her as he and another engineer began unloading the boxes.

"Morning, Scott." She smiled at him, then exchanged curt nods with the engineers. She didn't like them; just as they detested her. In weekly support meetings, their jokes were often at her expense. She turned to Scott. "What can I do to help?"

"Morning to you, too, Megan." Scott moved away from the box and took her extended hand. "If you have to ask that, we're in deep yogurt. I was about to ask you the same." He turned his head slightly, his glasses glinting, his smile playful. "Time for some music, eh?"

"Of course," she said and laughed. "What's a computer show without some tunes?"

It was Scott's way of kicking off each show. Along with square dancing with his wife and potluck suppers at his local church, country western music was his passion. He reached into the wiring cabinet and in seconds, Crystal Gayle resounded on the speakers. He flashed a toothy grin.

"Thanks," she said, and laughed at the thumbs-up signals from three coffee-toting workers at the adjacent Digital Equipment booth. Humming along, she moved to the first kiosk, and reached into a box to grab a cable. The hardware engineers had installed and booted each system, but left the communications connections to her. She spent the next hour running cables through the patch panel inside the wiring cabinet and rebooting each system—a touchy process due to the buggy, pre-release software she'd brought with her.

After typing in the same command for the fifth time, she crossed her fingers and watched the screen she'd been hoping for finally appear. She exhaled slowly, and prayed that Charlie Maxwell wouldn't be bringing his latest software. Untested and filled with allegedly fabulous new features, it could destroy the demos she'd carefully crafted.

By mid-morning, the Smith Labs booth looked magnificent, as did most of the booths around it. She'd just finished connecting the Aloha Insurance demo to the mainframe when Charlie Maxwell and Ming Yen, another developer, arrived at the booth.

Charlie's pale blue eyes glinted behind thick glasses. His blue jeans were threadbare, with a hole in one knee. His flannel shirt was rumpled, yet clean, and his work shoes scuffed. Pudgy with a bite-me attitude, he'd once made a fledgling tech writer burst into tears with a single scathing remark. He was lugging a disk pack.

Megan moved quickly, nodding at Ming, recently his girl friend. Ming's jeans were carefully pressed and topped with a tan velour sweatshirt. Dressing flashy was not her style.

"I'll take that." Megan grabbed the pack before Charlie could blink.

"Don't you. But I—" Charlie turned brilliant red as Ming grappled with his arm.

"Chill, honey." Ming steered him away, her eyes adoring. "Megan knows what she's doing. You shouldn't mess with her stuff. Remember the last time?"

"But I . . . I have some new features . . . some . . .."

Ming hustled him toward Scott, who was stacking brochures on the registration table. With a spill of slippery black hair and narrow brown eyes, Ming gave the impression of Asian female subservience—until one dared look closer. She was tough and smart, with an earthiness and honesty that, in the world of fast deals and brush-off answers, Megan found refreshing. Despite Ming's intelligence, she was assigned maintenance work, never the innovative projects craved by engineers of her caliber. Her elder brother, Eric, one of Smith Labs' development directors and a member of the inner circle, made sure of it. Ming was an oddity—not quite accepted by her peers—yet obviously one of them through family connections. With the percentage of female software engineers hovering at twelve, Ming was a prime example of high tech's endemic misogyny. In Ming's case, however, her brother had more to do with her low employment status than her gender. He was big into power, especially over her. She'd set her sites on Charlie from the beginning of her employment, angering him even more.

Before Ming, Charlie had often worked twenty-four-by-seven, sleeping on the sofa in his office, grabbing pizza on the way home to a dank room in his parents' basement. Ming's love had transformed him into a man who cared about the world around him, who discovered in his late twenties the joys of hiking in the deep woods and sipping coffee with a donut on a stool at Dunkin Donuts. Practical, nonverbal Ming had also benefited from Charlie's subtle workplace maneuvering. Before Charlie, she'd never have gone to a tradeshow.

She winked at Megan over her shoulder. With a few quick movements, Megan stowed the disk pack deep inside the stage's wiring cabinet; then returned to her task. A half-hour later, she looked up at Ming's approach.

"How's it going?" Ming asked. Her hair hung over one eye.

"Great. Just one more try with this connection." She bit her lip as she entered the final command, then pressed the Enter button.

"Scott's got him sorting T-shirts." Ming tossed her head on the direction of the registration table and sighed. "Of course, he forgot all about last quarter's fiasco." She leaned closer. "Did you hide the pack good?"

"I hope so," Megan said, then pushed away from the kiosk as the Aloha Insurance byline appeared on the screen. "And now everything's working," she said with a wide grin, then turned slightly, seeing other people approach.

"Look who the cat dragged it," she said softly, shooting Ming an arch look.

"Tootsie," Ming breathed.

Naomi Wickam was a chesty, long-legged blonde. She trotted beside Adam in a beige designer suit, clutching a disk pack with one hand and an expensive-looking leather bag with the other. A few months back, Naomi and Ming had dueled over a nasty finger-pointing memo that had escalated to management. Though in the right, Ming had been ordered to apologize.

"The goddess worshipping the god." Megan folded her arms across her chest.

"More like a wolf with a snake," Ming said, and they both laughed.

"Megan, how the hell are ya?" Naomi dropped her case on the kiosk and held out a hand. Adam touched her slender waist, steering her around a potted plant. Naomi smiled up at him, and then grimaced in Ming's direction.

"Naomi." Megan nodded, ignoring her hand. "That your demo?" She glanced at disk pack, wanting to scream at Ming, who'd lowered her lashes and backed away like a deferential servant. She looked from Naomi to Adam, seeing the threads of lust already tangled between them. The man was a predator and the woman an idiot. She wanted to kill them both.

"Adam." She said and nodded pleasantly, meeting his gaze. He looked particularly fetching in a pale gray suit and red power tie—the bastard. He wouldn't fool her again.

"Megan." Adam turned away, his fake smile like a slap. "Good flight, Ming?"

"Fine." Ming shrugged, her eyes wary. She backed toward the registration table, with Adam following.

"I saw him first," Naomi whispered as she handed Megan the disk pack.

Megan coughed, practically gagging under noxious cloud of heavy perfume Naomi must have poured on herself that morning. “Good for you,” she said, then strode to the nearest kiosk, Naomi on her heels. “No need to worry.” She smiled as she loaded the disk pack into the third DataStorage-7, and scanned Naomi from her golden blond hair to her pretty red shoes, trying to make her feel uncomfortable. “I’ve no luck with men, Naomi. Adam’s all yours. Why don’t you show me your little demo?”

Tootsie, she almost added. The girl had no clue she was just a bright little doodad men liked to play with when they needed to feel adequate.

ഗ്ഗഗ്ഗഗ

Minutes before show time, Megan raced through doors, duly impressed by the auditorium guards, who’d taken on the patina of wary, stone-faced warriors in black uniforms with shiny silver badges. A few hours ago, they’d been joking and laughing, scarfing down donuts and sipping coffee brought to them by one of the Digital Equipment guys. The first evening was by invitation-only, for media and corporate executives, who could make or break a company’s image. Every detail counted.

She fumed as she slowed to a walk. It wasn’t her fault that Charlie had sneaked back from lunch early to load his disk pack. It had taken an hour to reinstall that one DataStorage-7; and thankfully, Ming had stopped him from wrecking the others. Damn Adam for his arrogance. So she’d had to use the bathroom. What was she supposed to do—hold it for the next three hours?

She'd gotten the demo running again—by the skin of her teeth, for which Adam owed her big time. During lunch—a quick feed back at the hotel—she'd been forced to witness his sexual predation, this time sober and upon someone else. He'd slobbered all over Tootsie, charmed the hostess, the waitress and practically every woman in the room—except Ming, who'd been attached at the hip to Charlie—and herself, who knew better. And it wasn't just women he attracted—Scott hung on his every word.

The scent of flowers was overwhelming as she approached the booth. She had to hand it to Adam: he was a superb actor. At center stage practicing his speech, he nodded in her direction. She ignored him and joined Charlie, Ming and Naomi in front of the kiosks, then waved at Scott who stood at the registration table, ready to collect business cards, imprint show badges and hand out brochures. She caught Ming's slight nod, then Charlie's. A nervous giggle burst from Naomi's crimson-painted lips. Megan smiled vacantly, not bother to hide her loathing.

Seconds later came the sound of a popping cork. The vibrations of many feet reverberated through the walls. Then came the resonance of talk and laughter; and faintly at first, the sound of a marching band. Footsteps rumbled closer and closer. Then a crowd of business suits burst around the corner. Cameras flashed. Adam flipped the video wall switch and began his presentation.

ᴕᴕᴕᴕᴕ

The show spanned four hype-filled days and nights, during which Megan pasted on her most fetching smile and spoke her charming best to customers, vendors and colleagues; then threw back beers each night with the team, eager to drown her despair. Her smile remained intact while watching Ming and Charlie share a plate of barbequed ribs like a long-married couple, while seeing Adam fondle Tootsie in the darkened alcove of a French restaurant, and then in the morning, waiting in the hotel lobby while Scott spoke quietly to his wife. Everyone had someone—except her.

By the time her plane touched down at Logan on Thursday night, she was ready for a full tissue box, gut-wrenching, floor-banging howl. She held it in during the stop-and-go traffic out of Logan, and then on 93 north and 495, and finally, her drop off at the Town House. She even managed to hold it in during the teeth jarring, pothole avoiding drive through Chelmsford to her apartment. It was seeing Donald's car in the parking lot that finally broke her. By the time she plugged her key into the door, she was bawling.

The door swung open.

"Meggie." Donald pulled her in and took her bag, his hands wondrously gentle. "What happened?" His arms came around her. Unable to think straight, she found herself kissing him back. In his arms, she felt safe and loved—at last.

Dorothy from "The Wizard of Oz," came to mind, saying over and over, "There's no place like home." It didn't matter that he'd left her. He was here now, holding her, wanting her. And best of all, he was her husband—not some lousy, humiliating one-nightstand in a freaking hotel room. In seconds, she'd stripped off her clothes and was giving him the welcome of his life.

"Great to see you, too," Donald said, brushing the hair away from her face an hour later. He leaned over her on the bed and kissed her nose. She laughed, seeing the bare mattress beneath her, the sheets and blankets heaped on the floor and the framed prints now hung at odd angles.

"I thought for sure you'd be pissed," he said huskily. "Some of those tricks you used . . .whew."

She blushed, thinking of the things Adam had done to her; then brushed those memories aside, telling herself that what really mattered was here and now. She was finally with own man, and not a stranger posing as a friend. She reached up and caressed his razor stubble, wanting to bask in the acceptance in his eyes. He'd just sandpapered her face and she was blissfully happy.

"I missed you so much," she sighed. "I really missed you."

"It's only been five months." His eyes glinted with amusement.

"Almost six," she said, pouting. She touched his

gilt hair wondering why she'd ever even looked at another man. "Almost six friggin' months," she repeated, and yanked on a strand. "Don't ever do that again."

He laughed and then rose, scratching his head. "A welcome like that and I'll leave every other day. Speaking of which . . .." He moved into the living room, the sound of his voice fading. She got up and followed, and was immediately struck by the room's tidiness. Aside from her luggage by the door, not an item had been moved since her trip. He was opening the window when she saw the gun on the kitchen table.

"You just got here?" she asked, finding it hard to breathe. He nodded. "So what's going on?" she asked, trying to sound casual. "What have you been doing?"

"Questions, questions," he said, and laughed as he waved a hand in front of his face. "Let's get reacquainted first, maybe get something to eat. I'm starved. Especially after the workout." He gestured toward the bedroom.

"All right," she said, hating that the tender mood of their reconciliation had already shifted. The thought nagged that he wanted something and that nothing had changed. "Why don't you call for pizza while I shower?"

"I know. I know—pepperoni and mushroom with a Greek salad." He grinned as he took her in his arms and kissed the top of her head.

"I'm glad you're home, Donald." Tears welled

in her eyes. “I’ve been so worried about you. It’s been hard, wondering where you are, if you’re okay.”

His gaze slid away, but not before she caught what looked like remorse. Something was wrong. She hugged him again, her heart sinking. “I won’t be long,” she said, her voice soft as she grabbed her luggage and fled to the bathroom.

ଓଓଓଓଓ

Water, almost scalding, streamed over her body. She tried not to think about the gun as she closed her eyes, her shoulders drooping. It was hopeless. He was mired in something bad—otherwise she would have heard from him a whole lot sooner.

The bathroom door opened. She felt a breeze.

“Is that you?” she called out.

“Can you explain this?” Donald’s voice rumbled over the rush of water. She turned off the water and opened the curtain.

“Excuse me?”

His expression was hard. In his hand was her diaphragm case. Open.

“It’s a diaphragm,” she said, stunned. She’d forgotten to use just now . . . and earlier that week. She counted back, dread mounting. Her cycle was dead center.

“Oh,” she said. It came out as a squeak. “It’s not—”

“I know what it is,” he said. “I thought you were

on the pill."

"I was but . . . you were gone so long . . . and I had some bad side effects . . . so—"

"So who is he?" He snapped the lid shut, looking wounded and furious.

Denial, confession and excuses streamed through her mind. But they were mere words, meaningless sounds that obviated the truth. Sorry would never work. She was most sorry for herself, for yielding to Adam's predation and for believing that Donald, her husband, truly loved and cherished her. As for their marriage, promises on both sides had been flouted. Raw anger rose within her.

"I don't want to talk about it." She ripped the shower curtain closed. He tore it open. She gasped and covered her breasts with both hands.

"I'm talking to you," he said, holding the curtain out of her reach. "Don't ever shut me out, Megan. Don't ever forget who I am."

"And just who are you, Captain Donald Thomas Alexander?" she asked. "You've shut me out of your life for half a year, and months before that. I know next to nothing about you, having never even met your alleged family. And why is there a gun on my kitchen table?"

He stared at her for a long, measuring moment. "Let's tell the whole damn building," he said, his voice barely audible. "My lovely wife." He looked her over as if taking inventory.

She ripped the curtain away from him and across her body. "We'll talk when I'm dressed," she said, then waited until he'd stomped away.

He was sitting at the kitchen table, sipping a tall iced drink. He set the glass beside a flat ceramic dish, upon which was a line of fine white powder. Her breath caught as he picked up a straw and inhaled the entire line. Then he grinned lazily, his eyes almost closing. "I was waiting to show you," he said sweetly. "I've plenty more, if you want to try it. Probably do you some good—take off a little of that New England starch. It's easy to come by in Miami."

The walls seemed to close in on her. She swayed for a moment and then regained her composure. "Stronger medicine than the last time," she said, and folded her arms across her bathrobe. "Getting in deeper, I see."

"Like you're an angel." He pressed a nostril closed, then sniffed with the other. "Who's the guy?" he asked, and pushed the plate aside. Then he rose with his drink and took a step toward her.

"No one you know." She stepped back.

"It's a million a flight," he said, looking away. "I've flown five times. Another flight and we'll be set for life. Can he promise you that?"

"What are you doing?" she asked quietly.

He laughed. "Drugs, you cheating tramp; if you haven't already guessed. I fly drugs out of the jungle—pot mostly. It's a hoot. Those Columbians, you should see 'em. So damn serious. Though maybe they'd lighten up after a round or two with you. Ernesto says I should smack you around a little. Said he'd be glad to help. Maybe I should think of this new boyfriend of yours as a skills investment."

"Get out," she said, pointing at the door.

In a flash, he grabbed her face, his nails digging in, drawing blood. His other arm pulled her to him, his mouth inches from her neck. His breath was putrid. She whimpered and struggled. His grip tightened.

"You listen to me, Meggie," he rasped, "I'm your husband, and until the law says otherwise, I'll come and go from this dump as I please, when I please. My place in Miami makes this look like a shit hole; so don't go telling me what to do. You're mine. You'll do as I say."

Not likely, she wanted to shout as he released her, more shocked by the emptiness in his eyes, than by the burn of her cheeks where he'd griped. Death moved in his eyes. Whom had he killed . . . or was she the target?

"Tell me about your place," she said, keeping the panic from her voice as she backed toward the windows.

"It's on the edge of a Laguna," he said and sighed heavily, misreading her demeanor as acquiescence. He rubbed his face as he moved through the living room; then sat on the sofa and set his drink on the coffee table. "It's got a private dock with a forty-five foot boat that can really fly. It's not ours yet. I've put down a deposit and expect to hear in a few days. There's some details yet to iron out."

"How many rooms?" she asked, noting his glassy eyes, and the compulsive way he toyed with his shirt's top button. She sat beside him.

"Twenty," he said, and flung back his head and shook it, his sun-kissed hair falling effortlessly into place. He reached an arm across the back of the sofa and touched her cheek. She looked down at her lap, suppressing a shudder of revulsion. "It's no good without you," he said. "I'm no good without you, Meggie. I've no one at the end of a run. No one who loves me."

She looked away, her heart aching. "So you told your mother my name's Victoria." She turned back with a slight smile.

For a moment he looked confused. Then he dropped his hand and chuckled. "Yeah," he said, "couldn't have them connecting you and me, Meggie. You'd be a lever, a tool. I needed to earn the Columbian's trust, make a few bucks, without that threat hanging over my head. Though, ..." His eyes clouded over. "I suspect they've known all along."

"Who are they?" she asked.

"The Columbians?" He laughed. "Haven't you been listening? You'll meet them soon enough. No a bad bunch, really. They've got families like everyone else." He took a swallow of his drink, then closed his eyes, his expression like melted wax. Then he turned to her, his eyes wild and desperate.

"Look, I came to get you, Meggie, even if I

have to haul you back. You can toss that career bullshit most men don't buy anyway. It's always getting in the way of things—an excuse for you to ignore me. Soon I'll have enough money for us to retire, and then we can be together always. My next run will be the last. I promise."

She folded her hands on her lap, her rage simmering. "Tell me more about this house in Miami."

He flashed her a grateful smile, then went on to describe his living room's floor to ceiling windows, the commercial kitchen, private movie theater, recreation room, ten guest rooms, Olympic-size swimming pool, fully stocked cabana and library. She nodded occasionally, urging him to continue, somehow needing to visualize the entire nasty, blood-moneyed picture. He went on and on, extolling the property's attributes. She watched dispassionately as his face began to twitch; and counted each time he had to stop to blow his bleeding nose. It came to her that he thought he could buy her, that money would solve everything.

"Stop." She held up a hand. His gaze was unfocused, his lips slack.

Lips she'd kissed?

"I'm not going with you, Donald," she said quietly. "Not now. Not ever."

"Oh, Meggie, but you have to." He was beside her in an instant, clutching her hand, his breath acrid.

She tried to shake him off, but he clung to her like wet cellophane.

"I like my career," she said, hoping that this time he would actually listen to her. "I've worked hard for it, Donald; and you'd know that if you'd been paying attention. You can't buy me, just like you can't tell me what to do. It just doesn't work with me and you need to respect that."

"It'll be great—a life we've dreamed of." He smiled vaguely.

"You're not listening," she said, shaking her head, wanting to shriek. "You never once asked me what I wanted. You're too busy drinking. And taking drugs . . .."

"How many times do I have to say that I need you?" he slurred. "This other guy . . .." He waved a hand expansively. "He doesn't even know you—not like I do."

"You do? Well, that's a joke." She puffed out a breath, wishing she were somewhere, anywhere else.

"Yeah, yeah," he said, looking taken aback. "You're the one fooling around on me, but it's my damn fault for staying away too long? So I'm back now and things will get better. Lots better. We just need to spend more time together."

"You don't get it, Donald," she said sharply, beyond frustration. "I'm not interested—not in the least. And furthermore, you don't love me. You can't. You're asking me to give up my family, my career, my morality?" She jerked her chin at the table. "And now you're carrying a gun? What the hell for?"

"Ernesto said you'd be a bitch," he said, moving fast. his hand coming down. She dodged the blow.

"No!" she cried out as he snagged her hair. In one quick movement, he shoved her to the floor. Effortlessly, he grabbed her wrists, then raised them above her head, his well-muscled thighs pinning her down. He kissed her savagely, trying to force her obedience. "You're my wife, damn it," he sobbed, his spittle searing her face. "I love you, Meggie. You *have* to come with me."

"I. Do. Not!" she cried, and with a huge groan, shoved him off her. Then she rose to her knees, her whole body shaking.

Head down, breathing heavily, he came at her like a viper, this time grabbing her by the throat. The room spun as he hauled her into the bedroom and threw her onto the bed.

"Why are you doing this?" she cried, going to her knees, sucking in great drafts of air. "You're nuts, Donald. You can make me go with you!"

She tried to lurch away, but once again, he grabbed her by the neck; and she clawed at it, getting desperate, fading in and out, seeing haunted eyes and mossy places, tasting metal.

"You'll do as I say," he whispered, opening her bathrobe with his free hand. "I paid for this fucking place with hard-earned cash and gave you everything you wanted. Now you're going with me and play the dutiful wife."

"You paid for nothing!" she screamed.

His fist crashed down and she awoke in a pool

of blood.

ଓଓଓଓଓ

"Val, please come," she whispered into the receiver, holding her aching head, hoping the Tylenol would kick in soon. Somehow, she'd managed to throw the bloodied sheets and blankets into a trash bag, and pulled on sweats and warm socks. She was cold . . . so cold, even after jacking up the heat. Wakes of pain and nausea swamped her and she choked back a sob.

She glanced at the wall clock, deflated. There was no way she could go to work today. "No, don't bring Roger," she urged. "Get a babysitter. Please, Val, I need you. Just you."

She bowed her head as she set down the receiver, then looked around. Not a trace of Donald remained—not even the framed photo of his squadron—ten smiling young men, filled with promise. Sadly, there were only two filled trash bags outside her door—testament to a marriage that had never really happened.

The telephone shrilled. She picked it up, barked a few words into the receiver, then grabbed a package of peas from the freezer and put it on her face.

ଓଓଓଓଓ

"Well, what is it?" Val burst into the apartment, looking annoyed, toting a bag of groceries. "Oh my

Lord!" She froze in the doorway. "Your face. Oh my Lord, what happened to your face?"

Megan burst into sobs as she stepped behind her and closed the door.

Val moved quickly, shoving the bag onto the counter, then holding her arms out. Megan ran to her, her sides aching from muscles overused, her throat parched from crying, glad for the comfort.

"Who did this?" Val asked; and Megan cried even harder, unable to think past the hurt, of both body and soul. She cried for a long time, reminded of all the times Val had held her when she was small, crooning to her, loving her. Safe in her arms, she wanted to stop seeing Donald's hand coming down and his face—with that evil-gremlin grin—just before he hit. She wanted to stop thinking of what he'd done to her body—the bruises on her thighs, the raw sore of her bottom. How could he have derived pleasure from hurting her so badly, when she'd run into his arms just hours before, when she'd trusted and loved him. He'd hurt her in the most elemental and destructive way that a man could hurt a woman. And worst of all, he'd considered her his property all along, a mere appendage, a punching bag. Why had she been so stupid, so blind?

Gradually, she became aware of her surroundings. Her stomach was in knots. Her eyes stung as she pushed Val away; and then took a wad of tissues from her.

"Thanks," she said, putting them to good use.

"Lovely, eh," she gestured at her face. "He broke my nose, hence the blood and blackened eye. He grabbed my neck, hence the bruises. You don't want to know what else he did." Avoiding Val's eyes, she turned and stuffed the tissues into the trash bin. Then she sat at the table, her legs suddenly weak.

"Donald did this?" Val asked, sitting across from her.

"Who else." She was so tired, could barely get the words out.

Val lowered her eyes for a few seconds, and then looked up. "Do you remember Richie Thompson from church youth group?"

Megan nodded, vaguely recalling a dark-haired boy.

"Charming on the surface," Val said, her gaze thoughtful, "Like Donald in many ways."

"Okay?"

"Remember the time we bumped into him at the drug store?" Val asked. "He was with his girlfriend of the week—Rachel, I think her name was."

"Yes, Rachael Phillips. Her face was—" Megan took a deep breath, then touched her throbbing cheek.

"Yeah." Val nodded and laid a hand on her arm. "She dumped him right after that. He spread rumors about her—nasty stories about her and other boys. He was lying, of course, considering that her barracuda of a mother was tons worse than Pa."

"Come to think of it," Megan said, "I was kind

of glad for her when her family moved away. But within days he was dating some other poor girl."

"Exactly."

"Well, it seems Donald's a drug smuggler," Megan said, not missing her sister's shocked expression, telling herself that she might as well tell all of it. "First it was booze, then pot and now it's cocaine. He lost his job months ago; and he's been flying for drug dealers out of Miami."

"He was fired from Airlius?" Val stared at her. "But I thought—"

"Drinking on the job," Megan said; and went on to describe Donald's roller-coaster unemployment, long absences and home in Miami.

"This," she said, touching her face, "is because I wouldn't go with him. Some of his new friends have been coaching him on wifely obedience. But he went too far, probably freaked when he saw all the blood and went running. He never could stand the sight of it."

"What else did he do?" Val asked softly.

Megan looked away. There was deep ache in the pit of her stomach. "Pa was . . . he would . . .." She bit down on her bottom lip.

"Pa, nothing," Val spat. "He really hurt you? Do you need to go to the hospital?" She placed a hand on her shoulder. "Aw, Meg, I'll take you there right now."

"No." Megan stood quickly, trying to regain her composure. She crossed her arms beneath her breasts, feeling her energy return. "Pa was right. I was in over my head. But not any more." She touched Val's shoulder. "Look, can I offer you coffee or something? That's about all I have. I just got back from Chicago." She glanced at the clock above her table and shrugged. "Yesterday."

"It'll be okay, sis." Val stood and slung an arm around her shoulder. Megan clasped her arm, glad she'd come.

"I'll make you some breakfast," Val said. "I brought eggs, milk, cheese and . . .." She looked at her expectantly, "coconut donuts."

"You're the best," Megan said with a laugh, then reached for the grocery bag.

While she brewed coffee and arranged the donuts on a plate, Val cooked scrambled eggs. Then they sat at the table, side by side—for the first time, Megan realized. Why hadn't she thought to invite her before? Because, came the answer—because they'd been too busy fighting, too busy rehashing old business when they could have been friends.

Humming a tune from her childhood, Megan loaded salsa onto her eggs and sprinkled it with shredded cheddar, a concoction she'd made with Donald, one of the few good things she'd gained from their relationship.

"That's disgusting," Val said, and grimaced as she raised a forkful of plain eggs to her mouth. "I don't know how you can eat that stuff."

"Deliciamo," Megan said with a laugh, then took a huge bite and washed it down with a swig of coffee, heavily laced with cream and sugar. "Goes perfect with these donuts."

"You should have told me, Meg." Val placed a hand on her wrist. "All this time, we thought he was pulling long flights with Airlius . . . you know . . . maybe saving for a house. And you—we thought you were just traveling a lot. That was a heavy load to bear all by yourself."

"Well, now you know." Megan set her mug down. "I guess you and Pa can say I told you so." A tear pooled at the corner of her eye and she swiped at it with her sleeve.

"Don't think that, sweetie." Val shook her head. "We just want you to be happy." She scanned her face, her eyes kind. "You can't go to work looking like that. You want me to get you some makeup? And you need to call a locksmith."

"Makeup would help," Megan said, a smile tugging at her mouth. "I've already called a locksmith . . . and a lawyer." She held Val's gaze, awaiting her judgment. "A divorce lawyer . . . I can't let this happen again. I haven't seen him in almost six months—not even a word. Then he waltzes in and does this? I don't think so."

She averted her eyes as she reached for her coffee, already hearing Val's condemnation. To Baptists, marriage was for life, no matter what.

"Make two more calls," Val said, her expression grave.

"To whom?" Megan asked, looking at her sharply.

"What he's doing's against the law," Val said.

"You need to consider your reputation. You need to distance yourself from him in the eyes of the IRS. Think about all that money he's made, and not a penny claimed. He's drawing a lot of attention with that new house, boat and servants. Then there's the CIA to consider. Smuggling's a federal issue. You've got to call both agencies right away, or they'll think you're involved."

Megan rubbed her face, slightly dazed. Once again, Val had surprised her. "You're right," she said. "I didn't think about that. What a mess."

"We're here for you." Val squeezed her arm. "I'm here for you."

"Thanks." Megan placed a hand over hers, wishing she could stop crying. It wasn't getting her anywhere. She swiped at her eyes with her sleeve. "Can you snap a few pictures?" She pointed to her face. "Not that I'd ever win any beauty contests."

"For evidence." Val nodded. "And you *are* a pretty girl," she said out of the side of her mouth. "Because you're such a brain, you never paid much attention to your looks—not that it matters. Unlike me, who's barely average when it comes to school."

"What are you talking about?" Megan asked. "You're smart." She couldn't believe Val was saying this.

"Not like you, getting straight As all through school," Val said, looking at her over her mug. "And what about winning all those scholarships. I could never have done that."

"Not that you wanted to," Megan said, embarrassed. "More coffee?" She reached for the pot, filled both mugs, then settled back in her chair, eying the plate of donuts. "We each went our own way: one's not better than the other."

"Sometimes," Val said, looking wistful.

"Sometimes what?" Megan asked. "You don't want my life, no more than I want yours. It's not supposed to be easy, no matter what you choose."

"And we don't get out of it alive," they said together with a laugh. It had been one of their mother's favorite expressions.

"I can't believe you remembered that," Val said, the laughter still in her voice.

"Oh, I remember lots of things," Megan said, then smiled softly. "Most of all, how you were always there for me."

"Sometimes you look just like Aunt Jo," Val said, grinning, leaning closer, touching her hand. "She loved coconut donuts and also happened to be very pretty—and hated it."

Megan swatted her hand and they both laughed.

"Did I ever tell you about her husband, Uncle Ivan?" Val asked.

"Of course," Megan said, waving a donut she'd snagged, relieved at the change of subject. The old photo of Ivan and Jo from Pa's living room wall came to mind. "He was from Russia—after World War I, as I recall. Aunt Jo took in Pa after his parents died in the influenza epidemic. She asked Ivan to help raise him."

"I didn't tell you everything," Val said, her eyes

alight with mischief. "Don't ever repeat this. It's supposed to be a secret."

"Too many of those." Megan smiled, liking the banter. For once, they were acting like sisters.

"Promise?"

"All right." Megan took a swallow of coffee.

"Ivan made moonshine during the Prohibition," Val said, leaning closer.

"No!" Megan almost spit out her coffee. "Moonshine? Pa?"

Val nodded. "One snowy winter night when he was a boy—about ten or so—Pa watched from a grove of trees when he was supposed to be home. He followed Ivan and saw him open an old tool shed. Inside was a still and stacks of jars filled with the stuff. Ivan took some jars, closed the shed, locked it, then headed home. Being a smart boy, Pa surmised what it meant and struggled with what to tell his aunt, who was a staunch teetotaler."

"He must have been torn," Megan said, "considering his loyalties. So what did he do?" She took another bite of the donut.

"He said it was tough," Val said, "because he adored Uncle Ivan, who was like a father to him." She sat back in her chair. "On his way home, he ran into Ivan again. But this time Ivan was alone in a clearing, surrounded by four of Chelmsford's richest men. He wore an old oiled sailcloth coat and was toting a shotgun. In front of him on the ground were the jars, the tension ugly. Fearing for Ivan, Pa ducked behind an old log. One of the men, in a thick beaver coat, handed Ivan wad of bills. When Ivan backed away, heading for Pa's hiding place, Pa burrowed deeper, expecting to be discovered at any moment." Val bit into her donut, then sipped her coffee.

"What did he do?" Megan asked, wishing Val had told her sooner. It would have put Pa's eccentricities in a more human light.

"He stayed there, shaking with cold," Val said, "his lips turning blue until long after Ivan and the men had left."

"Did he tell her?" Megan took another bite.

Val shook her head. "No. Aunt Jo never knew. Without the booze money, they would have starved. Uncle Ivan saw Pa come in later, and knew he'd watched. He made Pa promise on his honor to provide for his women. You know how Pa is about that."

"Sure do." Megan rested her chin in her hand. "But Donald's not Ivan," she said. "Uncle Ivan didn't drink; and he never hit."

"That's true," Val said, looking her over sadly. "He never hit Aunt Joe and he never drank. Couldn't abide the stuff—said he'd seen too many Russians drink themselves into an early grave. He was just meeting a demand; and at the same time, making a living."

"I made a bad choice," Megan said, tossing her head. "But, I'll live."

"You certainly will," Val said, touching her arm with affection.

They both reached for the last donut, but Megan got it first. Carefully, she broke it in two, examined the pieces, then handed the larger to Val.

ଓଓଓଓଓ

Don lay on his side, snuggled up warm and cozy beneath a soft blanket in the middle of a king-size bed. The room lay in thick darkness; and he relished the silence. It was a nice room, as hotel rooms went, its thick walls and windows cocooning him from the noise of adjacent rooms and the city sounds below. He exhaled deeply of the chilly air and pulled the blanket higher, covering his ear. The room was cold—perfect for sleeping, as his mother had always insisted—though her motive had probably been thrift, not pleasure. He'd turned the heat down automatically upon retiring, hoping for a good night's sleep. Thankfully, the room had a Jacuzzi, which he'd put to good use the previous night, washing off the blood, massaging tight muscles and places where Megan had hit.

He rolled over and groaned, the image of her white and helpless body as he'd risen above her filling him with disgust. He grabbed hands full of hair and pulled. What had he done?

The lights blazed. "What!"

He sat up squinting, rubbing his eyes; and scanned the room, seeing dark shapes, hearing an odd popping sound—someone cracking his knuckles.

His vision cleared and he sucked in his breath.

"Morning, Don."

Agent Ted Graham lounged against the door, dressed all in black from turtleneck to tennis shoes. Even his leather jacket was black. Slender, with a close-trimmed beard and faded gray eyes, he could have been thirty or forty. He smiled pleasantly.

About to reply, Don cried out as another shape hurtled toward him, smacking him hard. Pain erupted. He lay sprawled on the floor, naked and shivering, holding his throbbing head, looking up through narrowed eyes at Agent Arden McClelland, a bastard of the first-degree.

He lunged for his blanket, but McClelland snatched it away.

"What do you want?" he asked, glaring at McClelland, whose bloodshot eyes held a yellow caste. He shuddered, seeing massive hands, rough and battered; and the face of a bulldog that had somehow leached out of his worst nightmare. McClelland's open trench coat hadn't seen a dry cleaner in years. Beneath it was a wrinkled plaid shirt, torn jeans and scuffed Dockers. He reeked of cigarettes.

The last time he'd seen these guys, they'd talked nice, said he had potential as an agent. Obviously, things had changed.

"Hurting your wife's not part of the deal," Graham said softly. "I thought you wanted her protected from the Columbians. And then you go and beat the crap out of her?"

"Do what?" Don's eyes narrowed. His breath quickened. Was she in the hospital? Had he killed her? His mind reeled. He couldn't remember.

At Graham's nod, McClelland pulled a small cassette player from his coat pocket and pushed a button. As the tape played, Don sat up on his heels and pressed a fist to his mouth, his tears dripping on the thick carpet. He shook with sobs, hearing his own cruel words, Megan's brave defense and her last futile argument.

"Enough!" he cried, hearing the unmistakable slap of skin on skin.

There was a click and the room went silent.

McClelland cleared his tobacco-coated throat. "Though we appreciate your endeavor, Mr. Alexander," he said softly, "we think you're in too deep. We advise you to back off for a while, perhaps take a little vacation."

Don rose, grabbed the terry bathrobe away from him and put it on, belting it tightly. "Yeah, well." He stood with his hands in his pockets, looking at the floor, feeling like the biggest fool. Of course, they'd bugged her apartment. And Megan couldn't be dead. She just couldn't.

"I didn't mean to hurt her," he said, and looked up into Graham's flinty eyes. "I just wanted her to come with me; and she wouldn't. Is it too much for a husband to ask?"

"You've been using again, Don." Graham eyed him coldly. "Using and dealing. We saw you pass money and drugs. Cocaine is nothing to play with.

Pretty soon it'll be heroin at the rate you're going. Didn't your father explain the rules of engagement?"

"Leave him out of this," Don said, hating the reminder that his father had pulled strings to get him this job—that he was following in the old man's footsteps. He swiped at his burning nose. "I've got to fit in, get cozy with the players. That's what they stressed in training. That's what I was told."

"Following the Columbian's marital advice?" McClelland asked, tut-tutting and shaking his head. "Not a recommended strategy when it comes to someone as intelligent as Ms. Rosswell. You should have known better."

"If you'd wanted a brainless bimbo," Graham said, "you should have married one."

Don closed his eyes tightly, picturing Megan the time he'd surprised her during the blizzard. Even then, she'd been too strong, too independent. She'd resisted marriage, saying she wanted just friendship. Hadn't it been a ploy? Didn't all women play hard to get? "But Ernesto said—"

"You don't listen," Graham said, his fist connecting with Don's midsection. Don gasped, unable to breathe. Then he felt his arm yanked behind his back, almost to the point of snapping, making him rise on tiptoes, gasping at the fine point of pain that held him.

"We don't pay you to break laws, Donny-boy," Graham muttered. "And if you push it too far, we can't protect you—nor can your old man. And your friend in high places is a wild card. His motive's still a mystery."

"Friend?" Donald managed to get out. He looked from Graham to McClelland.

"Mr. Clark." McClelland's bushy eyebrows rose slightly.

Donald's shoulders slumped. There was no use lying about it. Of course, they'd been watching him. He'd met Adam Clark at the Hermosa's family home just outside Miami. He was Ernesto's future brother-in-law and a prized connection to the affluent Lowell drug market. But if it hadn't been Clark, it would have been someone else. Smith Labs was only one of the many high tech firms employing the twenty and thirty-something age group that was eager for Columbia's premier export. Like many of his well-heeled peers throughout the industry, Clark had a fondness for the product.

Graham moved closer and jabbed him in the chest. "Your job is to fly high, land safe, smile pretty and name names. That's what you signed up for—nothing more, nothing less."

Donald swallowed. One more flight and he'd have it all—excitement, money, the good life. As a bonified CIA agent, he was supposed to have a dream job, like in a James Bond movie. So why wasn't he having fun? Why did he feel scared shitless half the time? His life was like his parents' all over again: Dad flying off without a word, Mom holding them together any way she could for months at a time, stumbling though life, blitzed from cocktails or prescription drugs, crying her eyes out every night. And then the wild celebration when Dad returned. Why had he thought Megan would stand for it?

He looked down at his hands, hands that had hurt the only person he'd ever loved. If only he could have been straight with her from the start. But it had been too dangerous—for himself, he realized. And now, she was lost to him forever.

He raised his head and peered at Graham, his throat tight, the place deep in his chest, in the vicinity of his heart, like an aching boil.

"Yeah, that's what I signed up for."

ଓଓଓଓଓ

Afternoon shadows wrapped the maze of cubicles like an eerie cloak. It was a ghost town of drab and gray. Megan shivered in the chill made by droning air conditioners. She glanced into the double-size cubicle belonging to her boss, Jeff, spying the huge ceramic dish mounded with cigarette butts, a monument to bad health; and the Styrofoam cups strewn around haphazardly, some half-filled; and the stacks of green and white program listings rimming the space like gravestones.

"As if he knows how to read them," she said, and hurried past; glad he was home and not sitting behind his desk like a sneering taskmaster. His absence was the only good thing about being called in on a Saturday. His message had been insulting at best, but his orders clear. She was to collect trouble-shooting equipment for her and Bob before a Sunday afternoon flight to San Francisco. Transshipping had gone critical. Bob lived in out Marlboro; so it was up to her to collect their tools.

"Piss on his arrogance," she muttered, pausing at her cubicle door. Aside from Friday, she'd never called in sick. Unfortunately, Jeff was one of those bosses who thought all employees were slackers, and liked her on the defensive. With his wife in and out of the hospital with breast cancer, she wanted to feel sorry for him.

When she'd first joined the company, he'd seemed fair and easy-going, though during the interview, there'd been no mistaking his leering perusal. She'd taken no offense, having learned from the CompuLink fiasco to hide her assets behind conservative suits and high-necked blouses.

Three months ago, Jeff had changed with his wife's diagnosis. He'd taken to hiding in his office, issuing cryptic commands, using her as a liaison to the other analysts, who couldn't stand him. She'd tried hard to please him, though she was probably the lowest paid person in the department. Recently, she'd been compiling the section's monthly reports and performing most of Jeff's less-than-interesting managerial duties; while he dangled a management position, saying she had potential. He was such a liar.

Yesterday she'd spent the day at Val's, nurtured

like a wounded lamb; and should have refused this trip. Bob could handle it, though the customer had insisted on both of them making an appearance. With Jeff's needling, she couldn't refuse.

"Freaking asshole," she sputtered, as she set the datascope, a five by twelve-by-twelve-inch box loaded with electronics, onto her chair. It was a marvel of technology, with a tiny three-inch screen, tape recorder and numerous dials, switches and lights for recording a mainframe's data stream for later analysis. She tossed four tapes in her bag, followed by the latest manuals, a memo pad and some pens. In spite of Jeff, she adored her job. It was her salvation, her escape.

Without thinking, she brushed at her face, and her hand came away with a gob of makeup. "Shit," she said, the sound of her voice falling like dead weight in the metallic silence. She grabbed a tissue and a mirror from her purse and made quick repairs.

The telephone shrilled and she picked up the receiver. "Hello?"

There was no sound on the other end and she strained to hear. There was a slight noise, barely audible. Then came a click and she replaced receiver, her heart pounding. She sighed as she leaned over her work surface, flipped on a monitor and entered a few words.

It was Donald, came the frightening thought. Was he checking up on her? She glanced at the soiled tissue in the wastebasket and shuddered. She should call the police, but with the CIA involved, it was probably a waste of time. Transshipping was threatening to return their equipment: she had better things to do.

ᴓᴓᴓᴓᴓ

Logan International was unusually quiet, even for a Sunday morning. There were few travelers, and the conversation subdued. In the waiting area, Megan selected a seat facing the windows, staring at the Airlius DC10, already attached to the gangway. She scowled, seeing two Airlius flight attendants comparing notes and joking behind the check-in desk, their uniforms a grim reminder of Donald's failure. They looked vaguely familiar—but from another life, another time that she refused to consider. Seeing no sign of Bob, she opened a romance novel and pretended to read.

Other passengers straggled in as flight time approached. A curly-haired man in shorts, T-shirt and flip-flops, toting a large, tattered bag sat two aisles over, giving her the creeps with his goofy smile. Then a family appeared—a bookend set of rotund parents with four loud, tumbling brats. They filled the row behind her. For some reason, the oldest child reminded her of Roger, and she smiled, thinking of the way he'd sidled up to her yesterday to give her a hug.

Slowly, the seats began to fill, and she shifted in her seat, wondering if Bob was stuck in traffic. Then someone touched her shoulder and she turned.

"Oh. Hi," she said, and smiled into Bob's worried eyes. She removed her coat from the seat beside her.

"Lost the power last night," he said with a tight smile, looking exhausted and somewhat irritated. He opened his briefcase on the floor and riffled through it. "Damn alarm clock was flashing when I woke up. Ethan had the sniffles again last night."

"Is he okay?" Megan asked, picturing his round little baby and Rosalie, his wife, a serene smile on her face as if nothing fazed her.

He nodded. "I don't now how Rosie does it, day in and day out. She has such patience with the kid. Never even raises her voice. She was sleeping when I left."

Megan heard her name paged.

"Did you hear that?" she asked, looking toward the check-in desk.

"Yes," Bob said, looking puzzled. "Ask over there."

Three women stood behind the desk, and judging by their brisk movements, were about to start boarding the flight. Megan hurried over.

"I was just paged," she said to a cool blonde with dagger-sharp nails. "Name's Megan Rosswell."

"Let me find out for you," she said with a friendly smile, then punched some numbers into her phone. She spoke a few words, nodded, then handed Megan the receiver, averting her eyes.

"Hello?"

"Megan, is that you?"

For a second she couldn't think straight. "Pa?" Her whole body went on alert. She was on her way to the west coast and Pa was calling her at the airport?

"Megan, there's been a terrible accident," he said. "It's Val. She's gone, Meg. All of them. Gone."

The sound of his sobs was unreal. What was he saying?

"Gone? Gone where, Pa? All of them? What are you talking about?" She turned from the desk, pressed her finger over her opposite ear and closed her eyes, trying to block out the conversation of passersby, the clicks and slaps of luggage opening and closing and her flight being called. "Pa, what happened?" Her heart was pounding.

"They were on their way to church," he said, then moaned. "It was an elderly man, Meg. His wife had just passed away. He left the scene and then came back. He's taking it real hard. Said there was another car involved. Two men. They veered into him; and he turned to avoid them."

For some reason, Donald came to mind; but she focused on Pa, who was starting to wheeze. "Pa, what else?" Panic filled her. This was just a bad dream, she told herself, and rubbed her forehead. It couldn't be happening.

"It was a head on, Megan," he rasped. "They were killed instantly. All of them—all except Roger. He's with me now. Hasn't said a word. Please, Megan. We need you. I need you."

She wanted to scream. Tears rolled down her face. Val dead? And Tom, too? Pa wouldn't be lying about this. He wouldn't be calling her. She shook her head, seeing the image of her sister's family as she'd left them just yesterday. The kids had fallen asleep on the sofa in front of the TV. Val and Tom, holding hands, had escorted her to the door, looking grateful for a little time alone.

"No!" Her knees started buckle, but she caught herself and managed to hold herself erect. "Val, Tom, Tommie, and Letty?" She whispered each name, hearing Pa sob, imagining each dear face. Only Roger was alive? It couldn't be true.

"I'll be there within forty-five minutes," she said, hating to imagine what Roger had seen. At Pa's choked acknowledgement, she replaced the receiver.

She looked up to see Bob at her elbow. As if in slow motion, he handed her a tissue. He waited for her to speak, his eyes impossibly kind.

"My sister and her family have been killed in a head-on." Her shoulders shook. "All except Roger, the youngest. It was an elderly man and possibly another car. They were going to church, goddamn it!" She pounded Bob chest with her fist, then crumpled in his arms as they came around her.

"Aw, Megan," he whispered into her hair as she cried.

All she could think was that another pair of arms was holding her; and she missed her sister desperately. Val! she wanted to scream, thinking of the shared donuts. There should have been other times, countless other times. What was she supposed to do without her sister?

Bob held her away from him and passed her a handkerchief from his pocket. “I’m so sorry, Megan.” He looked toward the gangway as the last call came for their flight. “I hate to leave you like this, but I really have to go. I’ll call Jeff for you, so don’t worry about him.”

“Give my regrets,” was all she could manage.

“And what about this?” he asked, and brushed her cheek with his finger.

Reaching up, she realized that tears had washed away most of her makeup. Blood rushed to her face, and she took a step back. “I . . .”

“I don’t mean to pry,” he said, his eyes filled with concern. “It just looks like you’ve taken a sucker punch.”

She nodded, unable to meet his eye. “Yeah well, Donald was back in town. But he left. For good this time, I hope.”

“If you need anything . . ..” He grabbed the datascope with one hand and his briefcase with the other.

“Thanks, but no,” she said, shaking her head tiredly. “Here.” She handed him the bag containing the tapes, manuals and the problem reports.

“Thanks,” he said and went off at a trot.

She watched him enter the gangway, her life dissolving before her eyes. Duty called; and now she knew what the phrase really meant. Considering the fastest route to Chelmsford, she headed for the exit.

ଓଓଓଓଓ

"He hasn't spoken yet?" Megan whispered, glancing at Pa. In his reddened eyes were hours of tears. They stood in her old room, which lay in the semi-darkness of late afternoon. She scanned her old Monkeys posters, the polished pine furniture, the yellow dotted Swiss at the windows, gripped by an old churning pain. A child lay bereft in her bed; and this time it was someone else who'd lost a mother. The window was open a crack, letting in a finger of chill air; and the shades were drawn. Roger sighed in his sleep, looking like a tired old man.

"No, he hasn't," her father said, shaking his head sadly. "Poor kid. He's all we have left of them." He griped Megan's arm, then turned and hurried from the room, his shoulders bowed with grief.

She looked down at Roger, wondering who would care for him now. At seven and a half, he was a handful. She hated to think of him living with her father; or worse, in foster care. She had asked for and gotten, much to her surprise, a two-week leave of absence. During that time, she'd have to sort things out, make some important decisions. With a heavy heart, she turned away.

"Ready?" she asked her father. He was sitting in

front of the television, staring at the screen. The babysitter, a fleshy middle-aged woman who lived up the street, sat in the stuffed chair beside him, her eyes already glazed over.

"I suppose," he said, then lurched out of his chair and tottered a few unsteady steps. "I'll drive," he said weakly.

"No, I will," she said, and grabbed his keys from the wooden dish on the kitchen counter where he'd kept them for as long as she could remember. No way would she put her life in the hands of a distraught elderly man, when another had created enough pain for a lifetime.

Pa nodded sadly, and followed her outside.

Their first stop was Lowell General's morgue, a sterile room tucked beneath the sprawling hospital complex. She held Pa's hand as they identified the bodies, coming finally to Letty's, whereupon they both broke down, then stumbled out into the painfully bright day. They drove in silence to the funeral parlor for a surreal conversation with a soft-spoken man about caskets, hymns, burial plots and payment plans. After a quick lunch at Skip's, where they barely spoke, they met with Pa's minister, Pastor Thomas, a kindly man with free-flowing tears, who'd baptized Val and Megan, and presided over Val's wedding. Megan was quick to forgive his well-oiled words, which brought little comfort. His grief was real enough.

Roger slept in Megan's old room that night, while she slept in Val's. A churchwoman came early the next day to watch Roger, though he ate nothing and did little more than stare at the television or sleep. He still refused to speak.

The wake and funeral went on for most of the day, with four draped caskets telling of lives cut short, an unconscionable tragedy. Dry-eyed through it all, Megan stayed close to Pa, who looked ready to collapse. In the afternoon came the reading of the wills, where she learned that she was Roger's sole guardian and the trustee of his parents' estate.

That evening, she sat in Pa's gloomy kitchen, nursing a cup of chamomile tea, grateful that Roger lay sleeping. It was too much, this guardianship business. How was she supposed to care for a child—a grieving one at that—when she could hardly think straight with all that she had to do? More than anything, she hated seeing the pinched look on his sad little face, the hopelessness in his eyes. She wanted to reach out to him, hold him close and whisper that everything would be okay. But would it?

She sipped her tea, noting that her hands shook. They were bound to. She couldn't sleep, and was drained beyond any morning hangover she'd ever suffered. She pondered the weeks and years ahead. Val had made it look easy. But it wasn't. Raising a child was the last thing she'd imagined herself doing.

Her beautiful, hard-earned apartment would have to go. It was for adults only; and moving back home was not an option. She was a married woman now—though soon to be divorced—with a career that involved travel, late nights and extended commitments. The rebellious daughter, striving for independence, was gone forever.

"Poor Pa," she whispered, thinking of the countless times that day he'd reached for her hand, his eyes filled with tears, his head bowed. Something had shifted between them in that moment at the airport when he'd begged for her help, becoming the supplicant, almost childlike in his plea, no longer the imperious patriarch. Now, both man and boy were in her charge. Exactly what was she supposed to do with them?

She looked up into Pa's intent gaze. "What are you going to do?" he asked, as if reading her mind. He sat opposite her at the table, looking ragged. "I thought your apartment was for adults only. How do you propose to rearrange your life so suddenly?" His expression was kind.

"Can you can keep Roger for a few weeks?" she asked with a heavy sigh. "I need time to get things straightened out, sell the house and cars. Please, Pa, just two weeks. I think the churchwomen will help."

"All right," he said, and echoed her sigh. "You're taking on a lot more than you think, Meg. But at my age . . . I just can't." He shook his head sadly.

"I know, Pa." She laid a hand on his wrist and he looked down at it.

"The sooner he gets into a routine, the better," he said gruffly, looking up at her. "I know you don't want to live here." He waved a hand at the kitchen, his eyes narrowing. "You sure you don't want to move into Val's house?"

"No," she said, shaking her head. "Too many memories. I can't handle that and Roger . . . I don't know about him. I'll save some things, store what I can." The image of Val and Letty swam behind her eyes.

Pa looked away quickly, his eyes bright with tears. "You're a good girl," he muttered and patted her hand, then rose stiffly and shuffled away.

A week later, she'd sold Val's house along with most of its contents. With the help of a local mover, she put Roger's things in storage, along with several mementoes and a sizeable collection of photo albums and videos. The following Monday, she returned to work; and Roger to school, to finish second grade. He still hadn't spoken.

☙☙☙☙☙

Just after three in the morning, Megan sat at her desk, letting the quiet office fill her senses. It was good to be back. The drone of air conditioners lent soothing white noise to her jumble of thoughts: the image of Val's house, empty and silent, the bare gardens, the plants in her greenhouse dying for lack of water. She shuddered, seeing Roger's slightly questioning stare each night as she sat beside him at her father's kitchen table. She rubbed her eyes and scanned the pink phone messages strewn across her desk. They held familiar names, like old friends reappearing after a long absence. Had it been only a few weeks?

Her computer screen flashed with problem reports, indicating more than three screens full of new problems awaited her scrutiny. She wanted to bury herself in it, to exhaust her confused mind so she could sleep at night without dreaming of Val and Letty torn and bloody, and Tom lying cold in some ditch, and Tommy . . .

"Stop it." She tapped a key to view the next screen. "They're gone," she whispered, "and I am not."

She had to earn a living for someone else now, someone she'd just started to care for, who'd burrowed deep inside himself, who needed her as much as she needed him. It wasn't supposed to be this way; but by the end of the week, Roger would be all hers. That meant planning his summer camp, buying his clothes, feeding him and learning how to live with him amicably.

She ripped the top off the extra large coffee she'd brought with her, leaned toward the terminal and began to enter a response.

Several hours later, deep into writing a memo to the UK office, she happened to look up and gasped. "What the hell!" she cried.

Ed Veasey's head hung over her cubicle partition, his eyes dark with malice.

"Transshipping causing a little trouble?" he said, his laugh harsh. Thin to the point of emaciation, he had a sharp chin and a head of unruly light brown curls. His eyes made a single line of a perpetual squint. His primary job seemed to be taking credit for other people's work—typically hers.

"Don't startle me like that!" She let out a sigh. "Do you have any idea how annoying you are?"

"Tut, tut, sweetie," he said, shaking his finger. "Hope you keep the nasties for us friendlies; and not the dear, check-paying customer. I suppose you're looking for special treatment, now that you're *bereaved*." He rolled his eyes.

"Not that I'd ever get *your* sympathy," she said. "You're just a snake," she muttered, "Why don't you find some rock to crawl under."

"Nasty. Nasty," he said, his tone mockingly effeminate, "How you can say such a dreadful thing? And of course I'm sympathetic, el boss-woman." He eyed her suggestively. "You want some after-hours consolation? I'd be happy to provide it. Of course, then you'd just be taking advantage of me and well I just couldn't." He put his wrist up to his forehead, then dropped it.

"Get over yourself," she said, thinking there had to be a way to fire his ass. Always the joker, he rarely did his share of the work. He was slippery and arrogant. Even Jeff, mister slippery himself, considered him a liability and wanted nothing to do with him. There was a rumor that Ed had the ear of someone higher up, or knew a secret. He seemed untouchable, dangerous, a lawsuit waiting to happen. One day, he'd annoy the wrong person, and then he'd be toast.

"Don't sneak up on me like that, okay Ed. I've been here since three," she said quietly.

"Can't sleep?" he asked, his face oddly serious.

She shook her head, and for some reason wanted to laugh.

"Yeah, it was like that when my dog died." He raised his chin and howled softly, like a baying wolf.

"Go away," she said and chuckled, unable to help herself. He strode away laughing; and she had to hand it to him—a lot of people had expressed their condolences, but he'd made her laugh. Glancing at her watch, she saw that it was almost time for her meeting with Jeff. She set aside her work and sprinted to the bathroom.

When she returned, Bob Cartright smiled and waved from his side of the cubical. He spoke calmly and slowly into the mouthpiece of a thin headset while he tapped on his keyboard, following the customer through the login process. She made a mental note to ask him about home buying, then grabbed her notebook and a few pens and headed to Jeff's office.

"Come in," Jeff said, glancing up from his paperwork. The overhead light had burned out. He was backlit by a floor lamp from home. He held a steaming mug of black coffee, on which was the picture of a buxom woman bent over, holding her breasts. A thin trail of smoke wafted from a cigarette atop an overflowing metal ashtray at his elbow. Behind him was his massive ceramic ashtray, still full to overflowing, smelling like a toxic waste dump. He hadn't bothered to deal with the Styrofoam cups either; some nearly full, forgotten in a crisis. The stacks of green-bar paper had doubled since the last time she'd been in his office. Many had toppled over.

She peered at the brass-framed photos of his wife and two boys, taken when his boys were smaller and his wife healthy; then reminded herself of the countless times he'd taken advantage of her work ethic, made empty promises, then backstabbed her to Steve Grant.

Sympathy for Jeff was a waste of emotion.

"What's shaking?" he asked, shoving away the papers. He gestured for her to sit, then lit a fresh cigarette, flicked ash onto the overflowing ashtray and took a hard drag. A spiral of smoke rose from the forgotten cigarette on the edge of the ashtray. He grinned at her across his desk, his beady washed-out blue eyes glinting as she took her seat.

"The travel's got to end," she said, looking him in the eye. "My nephew's living with me starting Friday. I've got to make a home for him. Then there's his school and doctor's appointments. It's gonna get complicated."

"So now you get to play mommy," he said. Something like sympathy softened his expression.

"It's a tough break, kid, what happened to your family."

She shook her head, not wanting to go down that path. No way would she bawl in front of this man. "I may not be the greatest thing that ever happened to my nephew, but I'm all he's got," she said. "What if I don't get him into a camp for the summer? I don't know the first thing about this stuff." She winced; thinking she was babbling.

"You'll handle it," he said. His eyes narrowed as he took a puff. "So what else do you want?" He looked her in the eye; and she saw his distance, as if she were an adversary. "You seem to have friends in high places, Ms. Rosswell."

"What do you mean?" Blood drained from her face. Had Adam betrayed her? She'd deny it. "You got a complaint?"

He took a breath, as if conceding. "I mean, I'm moving on to another job—Operations Manager," he said. "My job's open and you're it."

"You're kidding?" She sat back in her chair.

"No." He shook his head slowly. "Seems Adam Clark thinks you're the best support analyst this side of the digital world. He's spoken to Grant, who's put the word down like law. You are it. The job won't even be posted."

Steve Grant was no friend of hers. But Adam?

"When?" she asked, thinking of the team's upcoming performance appraisals, each of which was at least fifteen pages long. She'd thought all along that Jeff would try to pawn them off on her. Now *she'd* have to deal with Ed's incompetence.

She took quick inventory of the other analysts. Ralph Stevens, a quiet, slim little nerd of man who spoke softly on the phone to customers, would demand a big raise. Already a senior analyst, he'd performed miracles at five customer sites over the last month, winning an Employee of the Month award. Yet he was never around when she needed him, and his aversion to women was annoying. Then there was Shirley Giakakis, a tiny Greek girl from Peabody, a fashion plate who was popular with the men and treated her like an ugly elder sister. It wasn't surprising that Jeff had the hots for her. And not to lose sight of the best analyst of them all—Bob Cartright—who also happened to be a friend. How was she supposed to manage him?

"You start today," Jeff said, his grin wide.

"What about performance appraisals?" she asked, trying not to think of all the work she had ahead of her.

"All yours, kid." He raised his mug in salute.

"I guess congratulations are in order for both of us, then." She smiled brightly, wanting to spit his glee back at him.

"Yeah, I'll buy you a drink sometime." He looked down at his work, a clear dismissal. When she rose to leave, he made a small gesture. "There's something else." His tone was hushed. He looked her in the eye.

"What is it?" she asked, getting a sick feeling.

"Stevo's asked that I pass on a special project. He wants you to help with the new problem resolution system design—you know—merging the software and hardware problem escalation systems into one."

"All right." Her stomach tightened at the thought of dealing with Steve Grant on a day-to-day basis, as the project would warrant. She'd heard rumors about his Friday noontime predilections, his drug habit and the women who rose to special appointment on his approval.

She moved closer. "You have any documentation?"

He smiled lightly, removed a thick file folder from his desk drawer and dumped it on the desk between them. She leafed through it, scanning the specifications. On top was single sheet, with Jeff's writing on it.

"These are the passwords and systems you need to take a look at," he said softly. "Steve asked specially for your help." He winked suggestively. "I'm sure you can handle it."

She looked at him intently. "What did he say?"

His eyes narrowed to slits. "You might want to watch your buddy in marketing." He crossed his arms over his chest. "I understand Mr. Adam has his hands on a lot of things these days." He eyed her chest.

"I'll take it under advisement," she said, scowling as she turned and walked away. The man was an ass, a complete ass.

ଔଔଔଔଔ

Megan flipped on the kitchen table lamp, set the bag of groceries and her purse on the counter, then strode through the living room and closed the drapes. With the workweek finally over, it struck her that she'd probably never celebrate Friday night happy hour with coworkers again. It was no great loss.

"Come in, Roger," she said, not even bothering to keep the irritation from her voice. He stood outside the doorway, his expression sullen.

"So where's my room?" he asked. "And why do I have to live here?"

She sighed, unable to look past his thick smudged glasses and unkempt hair. He needed a mother's touch, and she was a poor substitute.

"I already told you we have to live here for a while," she said, keeping her tone even, though she wanted to throttle him. He'd refused to order at the pizza restaurant, then picked over a slice of pepperoni he would have gobbled with his family. He questioned everything she said, but at least he was talking. She reminded herself of that fact as she took his arm, propelled him in and closed the door.

"Take a seat," she said sternly, and pointed at the sofa. "That's where you'll be sleeping until we can find a decent house. I'll get your sheets and pillow in a minute."

"I want my own house," he whined, and hung his head as he shuffled to the sofa.

She closed her eyes tightly, wanting to scream, reminded of the countless times she'd seen Val deal with his obstinacy. It hadn't looked this difficult. But there he was, sitting on her sofa, his head hanging, his fists balled in his lap, a sure challenge.

"You want to watch TV?" she asked, despairing of how to reach him. At his nod, she flipped the set to a kid's channel. He sat back, his arms across his chest.

"I'm taking a shower," she said, watching him closely, trying to decide whether to go or stay. "You'll be okay?" He nodded again.

She looked at him for a long while, wanting to shake him, wanting to hug him, wanting her life back—the way it had been before the accident. With a big sigh, she headed to the bathroom.

Silence met her when she emerged. In a glance, she saw that he'd turned off the television. He was on his back snoring softly; his glasses perched on the end of his nose. Beneath him on the sofa was a large dark stain.

"Roger." She prodded his shoulder, unable to take her eyes off the stain as the reek of urine hit her nostrils. She touched his jeans, and her heart sank as she felt the wet. "Roger?" Tears stung her eyes. She hadn't once asked if he'd needed to use the bathroom; and she'd picked him up at school more than five hours ago. A hard place deep inside began to soften. He acted like an old man, but he was just a little boy.

"Oh, Roger." She knelt on the floor beside him

and began to cry. As gently as she could, she lifted his glasses from his face and set them on a table.

"Mommy," he cried out, his eyes wide with fright. Then he touched his jeans, and curled up and began to sob.

Megan brushed his hair lightly with her fingertips, unsure of what to do. This is it, she told herself. Her nephew, her sister's baby, was now all hers.

"I'm so sorry," she said, and pulled him into her arms, not caring that he soaked her. "It's okay," she murmured, patting his back as he tried to pull away. "It's okay," she repeated, then pulled him even closer and rocked him gently, as he sagged against her.

She was such an idiot, taking him back to her office so she could finish a few calls. What had she been thinking, especially their first night together? Then she'd dragged him through the grocery store, as if his need for food was a major inconvenience? No wonder he was angry. Granted, she was trying to staunch her own grief with meaningless errands; but he was just a kid, and an emotionally wounded one at that. It was her job to help him feel safe and wanted.

She rocked him and sobbed with him until they both stopped crying.

"I'm sorry," he said at last, indicating his jeans and her sofa and now her slacks.

"It's not your fault," she said, looking deep in his eyes. "I should have paid more attention. I should have taken better care of you, Roger. I'm the one who should be sorry—not you."

He closed his eyes, tears welling again. "I really miss them," he said, his voice catching. "I miss my mom the most."

"Me too," she said, and rested her forehead against his. "I can't believe they're gone. It seems like a bad dream; and I just want to wake up."

A long silence stretched comfortably between them.

"You know what?" she asked with a soft smile.

"What?" he asked, his eyes mildly curious.

"You and I really need each other, Roger. So you have to tell me what you're thinking, what you need, even if it hurts, even if you think it might hurt me, or make me mad." She caressed his cheek.

"But you don't really like me," he said, his look half-plea, half-challenge. She thought back to the way she'd treated him over the years. Even that last day at Val's house, she'd favored Letty.

She sighed and pulled him closer. "Yeah, I know," she said, refusing to lie to him. "And for that, I'm sorry, Roger. You sister is . . . was … the kind of kid I always wanted to be. I guess I ignored both of you boys; but especially you." She looked into his eyes. "I can't change the past, but I want you to know that I always thought you were a good kid, a smart kid. You and your Grandpa are all I have now." She ruffled his hair. "So I guess we're stuck with each other."

"Yeah, I suppose." There was the hint of a smile.

She smoothed his hair, hating to think what it would cost to replace her sofa.

CHAPTER 6
JUNE

Two weeks later, after numerous drive-bys, three over-eager real estate agents and five false leads, Megan and Roger found themselves standing before a massive, dilapidated Queen Anne Victorian. The sky was a brilliant blue. Ancient oaks, lining the side of the property, swayed under the burden of newly sprouted leaves. A few straggly tulips poked through the jagged grass on the front lawn. The neighborhood was tight with similar Victorians; all in various stages of decay, built for a time of long dresses, foot traffic and horse drawn carriages.

Megan gaped at the house in awe.

It was two houses really, built by two brothers for their growing families, with a huge main door in the middle, flanked by matching bay windows. Above them on the second floor were another pair of bays. A row of smaller windows spanned the third floor; and perched on either side of them, a pair of magnificent conical turrets.

She'd learned of the house from a cryptic ad in the Lowell Sun, placed by its current owner, Harriet Spenser who, according to the ad, had been born in the house and could no longer care for it properly. The ad stated that the house had character and charm and needed repair. Roger had insisted she call.

"What do you think?" She looked down at him, a little breathless. "Think it's too big for us?"

"Kinda spooky," he said, looking at her out of the corner of his eye. "It'll be cool for Halloween, though; and I really like the cones on top." He grinned, his glasses glinting in the sun. "We're supposed to be here, Auntie. I can feel it."

"They're turrets," she said and laughed. "And why are we supposed to be here?"

He shrugged and laughed with her. In the past few days, her respect for him had grown. Though not quite eight, he had the uncanny ability to spot both winners and losers in the real estate listings. The winners had been few. Yielding to his relentless pestering, she'd told him the details of his trust fund and her plans for the money: to invest most of it for college, and use a small portion for the down payment on a multi-family house where they would live. Rental units were becoming scarce, as apartment buildings were being converted into condos, driving up the remaining rents. With rental income, she'd be able to pay off the mortgage and save her salary for living expenses. In the end, she and Roger would share a valuable asset. Tears came to her eyes as she thought of how he'd researched mortgage interest rates. The kid was a genius.

The front door opened and laughter drained from her face. She took Roger's hand.

"Yes?" asked a gray-haired, bent old woman. She stared at them, looking about to keel over. She breathed heavily, as if she'd walked a long distance. A splash of red dotted each papery cheek. Thin silver hair lay coiled atop her head. She wore a voluminous belted aqua dress that matched her eyes.

"I'm Megan Rosswell and this is my nephew, Roger," Megan said, and glanced at Roger, who, unbelievably, was smirking. Time stretched as the woman stared at the boy as if trying to place him.

"We're here about your house," Roger said, his smile deepening as he held out a hand. The woman took it, her expression softening, her once startling beauty becoming apparent.

"We saw your ad," Megan said, and looked at the woman closely, sensing a kindred spirit. For some reason a wave of relief hit her.

This is home, came the inexplicable thought.

"Yes, of course," the woman said, with a chortling laugh. "Excuse my manners, dear. I'm Hattie Spencer." She took Megan's hand. "Too many strangers have been coming to my door. Crazies and riffraff, I'd say. But you fellas . . .." She smiled and shook her head slightly. "You're a different crop of strawberries, now aren't you, my young man?" She patted Roger's hand. "You must come in," she said, and straightened slightly as she gestured for them to enter. "It isn't every day that I sell my house."

Roger winked as he slipped past Megan into a vast lobby, at the far end of which stood two doors on either side of an enormous fieldstone fireplace. The doors sagged—propped up by carefully placed two-by-fours.

"This of course, is the lobby," Hattie said, gesturing broadly. "My father and his twin brother wanted shared space for their growing families; though they couldn't abide each other's personal habits. Each door leads to a separate and complete house. Father's—now mine—is on the left. Long ago, this place was just filled with sound and activity." Her expression seemed to melt and she shook her head sadly. "They're all dead now—except me that is. I suppose one could say it was all for naught. But, this house . . .." Joy suffused her face. "Just look at it."

Light streamed through the bay windows, illuminating the lobby. Megan could hardly believe her eyes. It was a room straight out of a *Victorian* magazine. Priceless antiques had been arranged in comfortable grouping before the windows and around the fireplace. There were two silk-covered mahogany sofas in the Sheraton style, a neoclassical armchair with splats in the form of a lyre, a

Victorian burr walnut davenport and a mahogany long-case clock that looked to be in working condition. She turned, seeing not one, but several Queen Ann walnut wing armchairs with matching ottomans; upholstered in tweed and pale blue damask. Gilt-framed pictures, probably original oils, decorated the muted walls. There were a myriad of gorgeous tables: solid rosewood, cherry and mahogany, some topped with polished marble, most holding potted plants.

The smell of beeswax and lemon polish filled the air, not quite masking the more acrid odors of mold and mildew. Stains marred the yellow-patterned wallpaper. Strips of wall molding hung down from the ceiling. Tattered sun-bleached brocade drapes framed the windows. A shabby tan carpet, showing distinct wear patterns, covered the oak floor.

"It was once quite beautiful," Hattie said, as if reading Megan's mind. "Come along dear. I have a lot to show you."

Still reeling, Megan traipsed after her, trying to absorb her running commentary on the people and events that had once imbued the twin houses with life. Ghosts of the past—a weary mother bathing her child, a stern-face father reading a newspaper, smoking a cigar, and an elderly parent taking her medicine—seemed to flit at the edges of her vision. Looking across Hattie's broad kitchen table, she could almost see a Thanksgiving feast, with heads bowed around it in prayer.

Not a room had been spared the ravages of time. Crumbling plaster, disconnected radiators, mouse droppings, peeling wallpaper and extensive water damage competed with the odor of damp and decay. In one of the second floor bedrooms, something in the wall must have died. They backed out, choking on the noxious smell.

It would be an expensive proposition, she told herself. But what if she did most of the work herself? She'd finished her second carpentry class; and was proficient with basic tools. What if she hired someone to help her—someone who understood plumbing, electricity, furnaces and roofs—someone who actually liked women? Did such a man exist?

Her thoughts turned to Stan Zambinsky; but she quickly rejected the idea. He'd come to the funeral with Christy Connors, who was probably his wife by now. Christy, with her bleached blonde hair, red-tipped fingers and well-rounded breasts in a skin-tight black dress had hung all over Stan—when she hadn't been hanging on other men's arms. Stan had looked like a fool, bouncing around the room, trying to keep track of her. Shaking Christy's hand had been like touching a dead fish; and her eyes had been too busy scanning the room for interested males, to show even an ounce of sympathy—not that she'd been looking for it.

"The twin houses were for twin sons," Hattie said, interrupting her thoughts as they descended the servant's stairway at the back of the house. "I had such a perfect, joyful childhood."

At the bottom, Megan glanced out a slim window beside the back door, seeing an overgrown apple orchard and a lawn that could have been baled into hay. Off to the side was a good-sized carriage shed that was peeling badly.

"And this is the apartment where my aunt cared for her sick mother," Hattie continued as they rounded a corner that led to small suite of rooms. Megan's excitement grew. There was yet another apartment? She took quick inventory as she peeked into the surprisingly spacious rooms. There were two bedrooms, a moderate-sized sitting room, a bathroom and an eat-in kitchen, all wreathed in golden sunlight.

"Auntie Agnes was well-cared for here," Hattie said. "When we visited, her eyes would light up. I guess she'd had several strokes and couldn't walk or talk."

Aside from a library that Hattie's father had added to his house and the suite of rooms tacked onto the back, each house was a mirror image, containing a living room, kitchen, pantry and half-bath on the first floor; and another bathroom and four huge bedrooms on the second. The combined third floor was a warren of what had once been servant's room, and a circular room for each of the turrets. The back staircase connected all the floors.

She forced herself to look past the suite's restful timelessness. The plumbing and wiring needed replacement, the kitchen and bathroom should be gutted, and replacement windows and insulation were a must. It was in no better condition than the rest of the house; but a third apartment would double the rental income.

"Look!" Roger shrieked. He pointed out the window,

She laughed, seeing an old tire swing hung from an apple tree. It swayed slightly in the breeze. "It's certainly a place for kids," she said, smiling down at him.

"Lots of children have used it," Hattie said slyly, "including me."

"I believe it," Roger said, grinning. "I can't wait to try it. Auntie, can I." He tugged on her arm.

"May I," she corrected, his lopsided grin warming her heart. Then she took a deep breath, seeing the fatigue on Hattie's face. Admittedly, the house had once been gorgeous; but was it wise to take on something of this magnitude, considering the money and effort involved? It was a handyman's dream, sandwiched between a roof that needed replacement and a furnace that looked in danger of exploding. If only Pa had come with them. If only for once, she could lean on him for advice, knowing that he had her best interests at heart. Instead, he'd come up with all sorts of reasons not to buy the house, simply because he wanted them to move back in with him.

"There's a lot to do, I'm sure," Hattie prattled on, "But with a little effort, you'll have the place back to it's old self. As you can see . . .."

Megan turned her thoughts inward, trying to

gauge the pros and cons. She studied Roger, who'd become unusually quiet, wondering how to proceed. He rubbed his face and leaned against her for comfort, very much a little boy. Her little boy. She cupped his head and kissed the top of it, grateful for his presence.

Hattie was silent by the time they reached her library. Looking ready to drop, she gasped as she shuffled though the door.

"Roger, what do you think?" Megan whispered, taking him by the hand and pulling him back. "This place needs a lot of work."

"We've got to buy it," he said, with a solemn nod. "I'll help you fix it up, Auntie. I can get some books from the library."

"What a kid," she said, and smoothed his hair. "Are you sure?"

"I'm telling you, Auntie, we're supposed to be here." He pulled on her hand. "Come on," he said, his faith in her shining in his eyes as they entered the room.

Her jaw dropped. Hundreds if not thousands of books filled the floor-to-ceiling shelves on either side of the door. At the room's far end, tall mullioned windows sparkled in the bright spring light. Oaks waved outside, casting liquid shadows against a worn Oriental rug. In the room's center, a quartet of comfortable armchairs circled a low, square table. Behind the armchairs ranged several other tables of various sizes, holding an assortment of book, lamps and delicate figurines.

They quickly settled in.

"Tea?" Hattie asked, smiling through her fatigue.

"That would be nice," Meagan replied. "Thanks so much."

Hattie pressed a large round button on the wall. Within minutes, a middle-aged black woman appeared bearing a tray. Megan tried to catch her eye, to give her thanks, but she remained impassive as she set the tray down and left.

"Velma doesn't like chit chat," Hattie whispered as the door swung closed behind her. "She has strong views on the subject. Came highly recommended more than twenty years ago. Always threatening to quit. I can't do without her, though she doesn't like to hear it. After the house sells, she plans to take her retirement and live with her son in Brookline. Getting that much from her was like pulling teeth."

House sells. The words sang in Megan's head. She tried to catch Roger's eye, but he was busy eying the chocolate frosted cookies on the tray.

"Help yourself, dear," Hattie said, and handed Roger a glass of milk and a small plate, which he quickly loaded with cookies.

"Take it easy," Megan said, eyeing his plate. "You haven't had lunch." He looked at her sheepishly and was about to put some back when Hattie's hand whipped out.

"Please humor this childless old maid," she said, and smiled as she passed Megan a full teacup. "He can brush his teeth and eat his fruits and vegetables later, dear. My siblings' children were ever so sweet, but they all died young or never married. Same with my cousins. It was no one's fault. War and disease simply had its way with us, as nature intended."

"I'm sorry," Megan said, unsure of how to respond; though for some reason, found Hattie's gentle outlook mildly comforting. She took a cookie from the tray, bit into it, then closed her eyes against the sinfully fudge-like taste that filled her mouth. "This is . . .." She could barely breathe.

"Velma's a dream," Hattie said with the ghost a smile, her own cookie already half-gone. "I'm going to miss her; and she won't part with this particular recipe. Family secret, she claims."

Roger's face was already smeared with chocolate. He made little squeaky noises with each bite.

"Sip your milk," Megan said gently, and touched his hand. Behind his glasses, his eyes were slightly gazed; yet he quickly complied. Reluctantly, she raised the teacup to her lips.

"What are you asking for the property?" she said, trying to keep the excitement from her voice. "The newspaper ad was vague."

Hattie set down her teacup. She sat back and crossed her legs, then crossed her arms, her wrists on opposite knees, appearing deep in thought. A bird twittered outside. Roger coughed and reached for his milk, then took several gulps.

Hattie looked up, her eyes as sharp as nails, pinning Megan to the wall. "Let's be done with the silliness," she said. "You and I both know that you belong in this house. It just feels right, almost like a gift—to both of us. You'll find a way to make the repairs. Maybe some nice young man will help you. If you can't find one, I happen to know of a good boy. At least I did." Furrows appeared on her brow. "He's a grown man now, I suppose—a handyman and a talented one—rare these days. His name is Stanley something, from a broken home. His father, a widower, remarried; and the stepmother was a bit of a problem, as I recall. When my brother, Chad was a high school math teacher, he took an interest in him. The boy was always here, studying usually. But, often they played chess; or was it checkers? I don't remember exactly. It was so long ago." She bit her lip. "In the seventies. Or was it the sixties?" Her eyes glazed over and she stared at her hands clasped in her lap for a seemingly long time.

Megan rubbed her face, wondering what to do. Was she having a stoke, or some kind of seizure? Should she prod her, maybe check her pulse?

Then Hattie snapped back to life. "Hire a team of men, if you like," she said, her smile sly. "You're young, strong and beautiful—though you don't make much of that fact. You can help with the repairs. You have a strong back. It'll probably do you good. With the rent from two apartments, you'll be set financially." She turned to Roger. "How much can she afford?"

Before Megan could protest, he'd chirped out

the answer. Megan placed her hand over her mouth, wanting to scream, wanting to cry. Child and old woman looked at each other as if they were alone in the room. Hattie's eyes suddenly filled with tears.

"You look just like Wilbur Brownly," she whispered. Roger slipped beside her, half-sitting on her lap. She slipped an arm around him and pulled him close. "Will lived at his parents' farm, you see," she said softly, looking in his eyes, speaking just to him. "Most people were farmers in those days—not like today." She smiled faintly. "He was young, handsome and strong and I was so much in love with him, I could hardly stand it. He'd just gotten up the courage to kiss me when the war came—the First World War, they call it now. Foolishly, we thought it would be the last—as if people would ever stop killing each other. Well, Will died a week shy of shipping out. Stubbed his toe on a rusty nail and got lockjaw, of all things. He looked at me with those big blue eyes of his, unable to speak as he drew his last breath." She fondled Roger's hair. "You never know, do you?"

"I lost my family, too," Roger said, his innocent, chubby-cheeked face at odds with the grown-up despair in his eyes. "All of them—my mom and dad, my sister and brother—all gone." He took Hattie's hand.

"I read something like that in the paper," Hattie said softly and looked at Megan in mild confusion. "There was a boy left." She looked at Roger. "Are you Roger Whitfield?"

"He is," Megan said, watching Roger closely. He'd hardly spoken of the accident, worrying both her and Pa with his grim silence on the subject.

"Your sister's family?" Hattie asked, looking up, wincing at Megan's nod.

"I saw them die," Roger said, his eyes wide, his jaw clenched.

Megan leaned closer, clutching her stomach, remembering the morgue, the absence of life on those well-loved faces, the way Pa had crumpled outside the door.

"It was an old guy," Roger whispered. Megan sucked in her breath, wishing desperately that he'd stop. Only his need to speak made her keep her silent.

"I saw his mouth open like a big old fish," Roger said, his eyes closed tight. "He was really scared. He knew he would hit us. Another car hit him first—two guys, like on purpose. Then the jolt came. We flopped around like dolls. Bibles flew. And glass. When it stopped, my Dad called out, but I wouldn't answer. I was mad, 'cause Letty's hand was on my neck and she wouldn't take it off." He took a long, shuddering breath. "I didn't know she was dead. I really didn't." He began to sob.

Murmuring soft endearments, Hattie pulled him close.

"They were upside down," he cried. "I didn't know my Dad would never talk to me again."

Eyes filling with tears, Megan moved to him; but held back at Hattie's gentle belaying gesture.

For a long while Hattie let him cry as she rocked and murmured, telling him that he was a brave and special boy; until finally, he stopped.

"Bad things happen," Hattie said with a tear-roughened voice. Roger looked at her through smudged glasses like a trusting puppy.

Jealousy, furious and painful, rose unbidden in Megan's throat. Unable to stop herself, she plucked Roger's glasses from his face and kissed the wet spot between his eyes. On her knees, she clung to his hand, daring Hattie to push her away. He was her child now, to comfort, correct and shower with affection.

"It's not your fault, Roger." Hattie smiled at Megan fondly, ignoring her anger, though she must have felt it. "You didn't understand what happened. It was a horrible tragedy; and now your family's gone and you have to get on with your life. You have to make your nice auntie proud of you." She took his face in her hands. "Do you hear what I'm saying?"

Sniffling sadly, he nodded. She handed him a tissue she'd pulled from her sleeve.

"Now let's sign some papers, young woman," she said, turning to Megan. "I need to move on with my life, too. I've already put a deposit on one of those expensive retirement community condos. Though I'll be back to visit from time to time, probably on holidays, I'm sick and tired of living alone. Maybe I'll find an old buck whose wife is too sick to have fun anymore. Maybe I'll dance on the tables, scare them all." She grinned as she patted the side of her hair, a sweet reminder that age had nothing to do with vitality.

"You'll . . . you'll take our offer?" Megan asked, choking out a laugh, the implications of Hattie's words screaming in her head. Could she find a handyman, or even a team of them to help? And this Stanley she'd spoken of—who exactly was he?

"Of course," Hattie said, chortling. "I don't need your money, dear. I would give you the house for free, except you probably need the write-off. I'm as rich as fudge and twice as lonely. When my family died, I got all their money. Now, I've finally found someone who'll love my house as much as I do. Hey, you can even keep the furniture."

"The furniture?" Megan whimpered. She looked around at the priceless antiques, then backed up to a chair and sat, unable to speak.

ఆఆఆఆఆ

Stan whistled as he climbed the stairs to his apartment in the old brick building beside Chelmsford's newest Dunkin Donuts. The place was a dump, its rugs stained, the reek of cat piss from a neighbor's menagerie made his eyes sting. The hum of tires from the 495-access ramp just a few yards away made the windows vibrate. But it was a home of sorts—his home.

His landlord, Jay Worth was a friendly guy, always saying he'd get right on a leaky pipe or a cracked window or mow the lawn—eventually. So Stan did the work himself, then sent Jay the bill; which he always paid, months later. The other tenants were like family—hell, even better than family. There was Mrs. Franklin, an elderly widow with a soft spot for stray cats, who lived on the first floor. She was always making an extra casserole or a batch of cookies, and was an excellent cook. Her two kids, long grown and gone, lived in California. She'd adopted him; and he looked out for her.

Mr. Danielson and Mr. Savage, a middle-aged gay couple, both in finance, shared the other first-floor apartment. Their investment advice had been rock solid. Then there was Syd Harris, a Vietnam Vet, and his wife, Nora, a tiny Vietnamese woman, who lived on his floor.

The smells coming from Nora's kitchen made his mouth water; making him wonder if Christy had gotten out of bed yet. She'd worked the late shift again, after promising to give up Sunday nights and start being a family with him, in light of the fact that they were getting married in a week. He'd left the bar at ten, and had awoken briefly when she'd stumbled in at three. She'd been dead to the world when he'd left for work at seven that morning.

He shook his head, thinking of her dismal failure at cooking and cleaning. Good thing he knew how to cook—if that was what you called throwing pasta in a pot of boiling water and dousing the results with microwaved sauce. At least she knew how to do laundry and was great in bed. He was getting hard just thinking about the things she could do with her mouth.

At the top of the stairs, he jammed his key in the lock, carefully balancing both bags of groceries, anticipating the evening to come. In a week, they'd be on their way to Cozumel, for a lazy, sun-drenched honeymoon—two weeks exploring Mayan ruins—if they managed to get out of bed. He'd always dreamed of seeing Chicken Itza.

His smiled drained as he turned the key and shoved the door open. Last night he'd heard Christy bragging again about her trio of string bikinis. If only her listeners hadn't been Lowell Hilton customers, where she was the head bartender. If only he hadn't walked in on her suggestive description, seeing the men watching her, their eyes narrowed with lust, their grins sly. He shook his head, annoyed. She knew exactly what she was doing. Lately, the only time he ever saw her was at her damn job.

The apartment was dark, the living room window open a few inches. The dusty frayed curtains, that Christy had yet to replace, blew in a slight breeze. He set the groceries on the bar between the kitchen and living room and turned. Sounds were coming from the bedroom.

"Christy!" he called out, his hackles on alert. Then he heard a thump and "oh shit," whispered softly. It was a man's voice. Fists raised, he headed toward the door, his blood pounding, his breath controlled. He took a step back as the door flew open.

"Buddy . . .." Butch stood in his boxer shorts, pants in one hand, shirt in the other, his face red.

Stan barely moved, barely breathed. Butch Sawicki had been his best friend since the first grade. Their grandfathers had come from Poland on the same boat. Behind him, Christy lay in bed—his bed—pulling the sheets over her pale nude body.

"I can explain," Butch said, his eyes pleading, almost desperate, as he struggled with his pants, then fumbled with the buttons on his shirt, then gave up altogether. "It's not what you think."

"Get out." Stan jerked a thumb at the door, refusing to look at him. His gaze was riveted on Christy: her puff of platinum hair, silky and fine, and her blue-green eyes, now filled with tears.

"But . . . I didn't mean." Butch reached out a hand.

Stan knocked it away. Then he grabbed Butch's arm and propelled him out the door.

"Out. Now."

He slammed the door and then advanced on Christy, his rage cooling. He'd been a damn fool. He should have seen the signs: his best friend staying on after he'd left last night, his grin foolish and slightly guilty. There'd been other incidents for a week or more. He'd just refused to see.

Christy sighed as she rose from bed on the side furthest from him. She trembled visibly. Was she afraid . . . or stimulated? It didn't matter. The sight her lovely body, lightly tanned, perfectly toned, as exquisite as her perfect heart-shape face, left him as cold as a slab of ice. He sat heavily on the bed, suddenly drained, his face in his hands.

"When were you going to tell me?" he asked.

"About Butch and me?" she began with a pout. "It's not important, Stan. You know that." She shrugged a slender shoulder, then donned a fragile garment that hid nothing, a reverse striptease, her graceful movements belying the sly calculation in her eyes, and the practiced way she caressed the silky fabric over her breasts. It hit him that she was in love with herself, that she couldn't possibly love him or any other man. Preening like one of Mrs. Franklin's cats, she straightened her spine and slinked toward him.

"They'll be no wedding," he said, eying her, wondering how long she'd try to change his mind. "At least not with me."

"Oh, come on now, Stan." Her smile was dazzling as she moved closer, her hips swaying hypnotically. Her hand came down on his hair in a soft caress. "We had some good times, honey—you have to admit. And Butch has been your friend for years. You can't throw that away."

He rose swiftly to put some distance between them. Even now, with the truth slapping him in the face, he wanted her. He folded his arms across his chest, the pain rising in his throat in choking waves.

"First Trisha and now this," he muttered. "I have no luck with woman, that's for damn sure." He swallowed heavily. "Walt said you'd never settle for one man; and I guess he was right. I was the fool to think otherwise." He raised his chin and looked at her fully. "It was the trip, wasn't it? That and my paycheck, most likely." He shook his head and laughed. "Classic soap opera—me finding you in bed with my best friend. Right up your alley with the theatrics, hey Christy?"

"Your life's a damn soap opera," she said, then stooped over and with a delicate hand, began picking up her clothes. "The sorry thing is, Stan, you don't even know how ridiculous you are. Always so serious. Like you were actually going to relax in Mexico. You'd probably pull a tool kit out of your luggage and set about fixing the hotel's plumbing. Chicken Itza my ass—who wants to see some old ruins anyway? The night life and the beach are where the action is."

"I want you out of here," he said and headed for the door, glancing at his groceries, which were about to topple. They could rot for all he cared. "I'll give you a day," he shot over his shoulder.

"Stan?"

He paused outside the door and looked back. "What?"

She was eating grapes from one of the bags, now tipped on its side.

"Can I at least keep the Mexico tickets and the hotel? It's all booked and paid for." Her eyes were bright, her mouth a half smile. "I really wanted to go and . . . well . . . Butch can get time off from his car dealership and I . . . I just hate to think of all my lovely new clothes going to waste."

He eyed her for a long moment, wanting to laugh. She was serious.

"Go for it, girl," he said softly. "Butch'll find out soon enough that he can't keep tabs on you night and day." He chuckled as he let himself out, then took two steps at a time on his way down the stairs, his heart unaccountably light.

ઙઙઙઙઙ

"Get out!" Megan screamed at Henry Crossley, who stood in the main doorway of her soon-to-be home. Her skin crawled at the sight of his mustache. Perched above two fleshy lips, it looked like twin caterpillars on his sweat-shiny face. His long brown hair was lank and greasy, there was dirt beneath his fingernails, and his clothes were stained and torn. About her age, he leered at her over his clipboard. He had to be stoned.

"I don't think so," he said, his bloodshot eyes blinking fast. "You need me, baby, you really do—and with more than just construction."

"I said get out—or I'm calling the police."

"Aw, come on now, honey," he whined, waving a meaty hand. "Can't you take a joke? I didn't mean nothing—"

"Joke! Groping me's no joke, pal." She balled a fist, ready for him to try it again. "Who the hell do you think you are . . . you fat brained low life slug!"

"You gotta admit your job's a little unusual," he

said, his eyes glassy as he gave her the once-over. "Tutor you in construction? Who are you kidding, sweetheart? Female brain's too puny. You'd end up in the sack with half my crew. I'll show you construction that would make your crotch ache for a month."

He made an obscene gesture and laughed as he stomped through the open front door, shoving past a burley man who had the nerve to look familiar.

She folded her arms across her chest, wishing, not for the first time, that she'd never bought this house. The smells of decay filled her nostrils, the peeling paint a reminder of what she and Roger had lost. Val came to mind, and tears choked her parched throat.

"What do you want?" she asked and fingered the dust on the ornate fireplace mantle. The men who'd responded to her ad had been without exception, sexist, insulting pigs. The old ones treated her like a stupid wayward daughter, and the young ones were like Henry—hormone buckets. Never in her career had she encountered such ignorance. Pa had warned her; but of course, she hadn't listened.

"You had an ad in the paper," an irritated, familiar voice insisted. "We had an appointment."

She looked up, disconcerted, half-expecting to be alone, then glanced at her black spiral-bound calendar, which, in her fury, she'd rolled into a tube.

"Stan," she said. All the hair on her body stood on end. She just looked at him, the waves of longing crashing over her. He seemed different somehow—sadder, like a light had dimmed inside him. In younger, more innocent times, she would have wanted to know why. But he was married, Catholic and her divorce wasn't final. Not that it mattered. She had no time for such foolishness.

"Stanley Zambinsky?" She took a quick in-drawn breath, seeing close-cropped, thinning brown hair, earnest blue eyes and muscles that had seen many a hard day's work. In the space of a breath, she recalled each painful encounter she'd ever had with him. "You?"

"Yeah," he said, his face like stone, the blue of his eyes intense against tanned skin. He stood with both legs planted as if he owned the world, a prime example of what she hated most about men.

"Sorry about your family," he said. She took a second look. There was kindness in his eyes. His voice was soft, well modulated and slightly musical. "I was at the funeral," he said with a slight shrug, "but didn't get a chance to speak with you."

He was a baritone, she decided, and then remembered Christy. There was no ring on his finger.

"Tom was good people," he said, "and Val a sweetheart. She used to bring cinnamon coffee cake to the garage. It was like a miracle—and eaten in minutes. I still can't believe they're gone. Tom and I . . . you know." He looked at her closely. "How's the kid doing?"

"He's fine," she said, raising her chin slightly. He'd once made her life with Donald his business;

and for that, she'd never forgive him. "Shit happens," she said, looking him in the eye. "I don't have to tell you that. You have an appointment—I'll show you the house—see if you want the job."

"Seems to me you don't have a lot of choices," he said, his expression thunderous as his glance slid over her T-shirt and jeans. Her breath quickened and she resisted the urge to cross her arms over her chest. "Maybe Henry there could show you a thing or two," he sneered. "He seemed pretty eager."

She eyed him coldly, gratified by the slight twitch along his jaw. "Seems to me you like to stick your nose where it doesn't belong," she said, wanting to grab his thick, peasant neck and shake it hard. "What gives you the right to talk to me like that?"

"Stan Z!" a voice cried out.

Megan stepped back as Roger flew past her and threw himself into Stan's arms. Stan's arms came around him.

"Oh, Stanley Z," Roger said, "I can't believe it's really you. I haven't seen you in such a long time. I missed you. I'm so glad you're here." He was crying and laughing all at once.

Megan moved forward, wanting to snatch him back. How dare he lean on Stan when she'd been caring for him all these months? She bit her lip, wanting to scream. So they liked each other? What did that have to do with her?

"It's okay, buddy," Stan said, patting his back, sending Megan a warm look that stopped her cold. "I would have found you sooner or later, kiddo. It was only a matter of time."

"Let's get this over with," Megan said through tight lips, hating that she sounded like a shrew, hating that for some odd reason, she wanted to fling her arms around the both of them.

"You're gonna work on our house?" Roger asked, his eyes wide. "Please, please, please, Auntie," he begged, reaching out for Megan. "He'll help you and he's a good teacher. The best, Dad always said. He'll even give you a ride on his motorcycle, if you ask him nicely."

Hands on her hips, Megan shook her head, and tried not to laugh. Ask him nicely? It was unfreaking-believable. "There's no winning with you, Roger Whitfield," she said sternly. "Come on, *Mr.* Zambinsky. I guess I can show you the house." She waved a finger. "But this is the deal: you teach me and we work side-by-side. No coddling. No chauvinism. Otherwise, forget it. I can't afford the big bucks you guys try to charge ignorant females."

"Yeah, and I have a rule, too." Stan's eyes narrowed as he set Roger down.

"Which is?" She took Roger's hand, ignoring his squawk of protest, and pulled him to her side.

"No personal questions." Stan made cutting motion with his hand. "Not now, not ever. You get nosy . . . I walk." His expression softened as he glanced at Roger. "Understand?"

"Whatever," she said, rolling her eyes, trying to ignore the prickle of curiosity—especially about Christy.

"I mean it," he said, then turned as if to leave.

"Auntie!" Roger wailed. "Don't let him go. We need him. We really need him."

"Oh, all right," Megan said, waving a hand in front of her face. "So we'll keep it strictly business, *Mr*. Zambinsky." Shrugging, she headed toward the right-hand apartment. "Let's get this over with."

"Wait," Stan said.

She stopped and turned, hearing the reverence in his tone. Excitement shone in his eyes as he scanned the lobby.

"What is it?" she asked.

"I'd like to take my time," he said, his eyes disconcertingly intent. "I'd like to look at all of it, draw some diagrams and prioritize. It's a substantial project. Do you have a budget?"

She mentioned a number and he nodded. Then he pulled a small notebook from his back pocket and began to write.

"Can we do it or not?" she asked, trying, yet not quite succeeding to quell her anxiety.

He continued to study the ceiling and write, ignoring her; and she wanted to hit him. How like a man to clam up when asked a perfectly reasonable question.

"Do you know what dialog is?" she asked, then stepped back when he looked at her vaguely and returned to his notebook. She sighed and turned away, frustration mounting.

"Look, I know it's a lot work," she said, hating the way she babbled, yet unable to stop. Just the sight of him made her nervous. How could she work with him, day after day? Donald would soon be history—the divorce a few months away. And here was Stan, as sarcastic as ever, filling the space around him. "Maybe we should just forget it; maybe it's too much."

He kept writing.

"Everything seems to be falling apart at once," she continued. "Maybe the house can't survive without Hattie. Maybe I should wait for more replies to my ad. Just look at the roof, for instance."

"And the furnace," Roger added gleefully.

"Roger!" She shot him a dark look.

"Let's see the rest," Stan said sternly. "And by the way, Harriet Spencer will be around for a good many years."

"You know Hattie?" A numb haze washed over her. Of course, he knew Hattie. He was the boy she'd talked about. What was it she'd said about his stepmother?

"Sure," he said. "Her brother, Chad was my friend." His expression clouded, warding off further questions.

"You like Victorians?" she asked, cocking her head to one side. "You don't look the type."

"What type is that?" he asked coolly. "Just because I work for Harden Construction doesn't mean I don't appreciate fine architecture? I've worked on big commercial projects for years, Ms. Rosswell. But that doesn't make me like it."

She narrowed her eyes, irritated by his formality. "So?"

"I'm tired of the bullshit," he said, "tired of cutting corners, implementing decisions that have dangerous consequences—like inadequate ventilation. While, this . . .." He waved a hand, his expression lightening. "This is a historical landmark."

"I can't argue with that," she said, and smiled bleakly. Though a roar of protest filled her head, she gestured for him to precede her through the door. Once again, she was probably making a huge mistake. She eyed the cobwebs and the rubble, thinking that if she were smart, she'd sell the house and move into a condo. But there was Hattie to consider, and Roger, who trailed after Stan like a gangly puppy, his smile enormous.

CHAPTER 7
JULY

The conference room was packed, every chair around the long rectangular table occupied; as were the chairs lining the sides of the room. The door was closed, the air inside oppressive. Shirt-sleeved developers mingled with tech writers, support and QA analysts and business-suited product managers, reviewing schedules, bug reports and customer complaints. A secretary passed the glassed-in Herman Miller wall, her eyes averted. Aside from the rustle of papers, the room was absolutely quiet, all eyes on Eric Yen, the Director of Communications Development. He sat at the head of the table, focused on the reports in front of him. He was about thirty, with a shock of thick black hair and a heart shaped face that would have better graced a lovely young woman. But there was no beauty in his hard expression, or mercy. Ming sat at the far end of the room against the wall, head down, her hair across her face, trying to look invisible; while Charlie sat at the table between two product managers, his lips compressed. No one smiled. No one had even brought coffee.

"Transshipping satisfied?" Eric barked, barely glancing in Megan's direction.

"Yes," she replied, knowing better than to give him more than he asked. He spoke English with a heavy Chinese accent and hated chitchat. He seemed to hate most everything.

"Bank of Boston?" he asked, looking at her fully, his mouth a grimace.

"Ralph Stevens is on site. I expect a report by noon," she replied. "He thinks it's an IBM problem, but we need proof. He'll get it."

Eric nodded, then moved on to his next agenda item and potential victim.

Megan released her breath slowly and tried to focus on the meeting. At any moment, he could train his sights on her and blast her with another question. She'd seen him in the elevator a few times lately, deep in conversation with Dr. Smith. He was the favorite de jour, in hot pursuit of a coveted Vice President's title, his Chinese heritage a huge advantage. He liked to badger people, to seek out weakness and exploit it. She couldn't imagine living with him. Her sympathy for Ming grew with each encounter. It boggled her mind that a kind person like

Ming could have such a jerk for a brother.

An hour later, she was nursing a sick headache, shoulders tense as she filed out of the room with the other drowsy participants, determined to complain once more to the facilities manager about the lack of oxygen in that conference room. She turned, about to head through the maze of cubicles to the elevators; and saw Eric pulling his sister back into the room. Ming looked dazed, her last glance a quiet plea.

Megan paused for a few seconds, not quite knowing what to do; then continued on her way. She had tons of work back at her office; and another meeting in fifteen minutes for which she needed to prepare. She shook her head as she pushed the elevator button. Whatever it was, Ming knew where to find her.

ଓଓଓଓଓ

Megan sat at her desk, scanning the latest problem report. “There,” she whispered, pointing at an item, identifying another resolved issue. She entered the requisite information into her system’s word processor. Tonight’s report deadline was fast approaching, and she had to pick Roger up from camp in a few hours. Sighing, she looked around her office. It was double the size of her previous cubicle and hers alone. Without the benefit of Bob’s orderliness, it was a jumble of manuals, listings and equipment. Off to the left, was a circular table, around which stood several chairs. A cut glass candy disk took the place of honor at the table's center, filled with Hershey's kisses. Though she stocked the dish regularly, she paid scant attention to the dirty coffee mugs, left from yesterday's staff meeting, and the three straggly plants perched on the windowsill. She couldn't remember when she'd watered them last.

She sat back and chuckled at something Stan had said the night before—something about eating wallpaper paste. Though talk of his personal life was strictly forbidden, he'd seeped into her life like a quiet river, filling her head with possibilities. In the last month, they'd worked together two or three nights a week, and Saturdays, too, gaining an understanding of sorts. His silence was unnerving, but his commitment to the job solid. She cringed, thinking of the time she'd asked one tiny question about his family. He'd been out the door and driving away before she'd caught her breath.

It had taken five phone calls to reel him back. Now she only asked about construction. But it warmed her heart that he liked her taco salad; and never refused a glass of iced tea, or a cookie, which he'd eat standing up. He shared Roger's passion for pepperoni pizza; and in the kid's cheerful presence, kept arguments under wraps. It was hard to bash the man in front of an adoring child.

Subcontractors had already replaced the roof and furnace and updated the wiring and plumbing; during which time she and Stan had ripped down wallboard and plaster, carted away old fixtures and started the reconstruction. After three more weeks of appliance, fixture, and replacement window installations, paper and paint applications and floor sanding, she and Roger would be moving into Hattie's old apartment; with the back suite next on the agenda. Roger's money was going fast. By the first of the year, they needed the rent from both apartments.

"Do you have a minute?"

She looked up from her terminal and blinked. Ming stood back from the doorway, twirling a strand of hair between two fingers, her face a map of worry.

"Come in," she said, studying her for clues. "What's wrong?" she asked, thinking of Eric. "You don't look so great." She set aside her report, refusing to think about the mountain of work yet to be tackled. Ming's visit wasn't exactly unexpected. "You want to go for a coffee, or something? I'll just be a minute."

"Sure." Ming sighed as she sat at the table and helped herself to a chocolate. "Take your time."

The cafeteria at the base of the Tower One was empty. The room lay in shadows, the late afternoon sun on the far side of the building. The low-ceilinged room with its tall glass outer wall was a study of order: rows of banquet tables, chairs pushed around them, another glass wall on the left, overlooking a small courtyard. To the right was the food service area, sectioned off by industrial-size refrigerators and soft drink dispensers.

The choices were pitiful: a few stale donuts and a dried up slice of carrot cake. Megan wrinkled her nose as she poured coffee into two paper cups, nauseated by the lingering odors of overcooked food and disinfectant.

They prepared their coffee in silence, moved to a table beside the courtyard window, and sat across from each other. Outside, a bird lit on one of three small picnic tables. Another bird joined it, dropping down from a small flowering crabapple tree.

"What's going on?" Megan asked, turning her attention to Ming.

"I hear you have an apartment to rent." Ming looked at her shyly. "I understand it's not finished, but I'd like you to consider me for a tenant."

Megan repressed a smile, picturing Ming and Charlie in her back apartment. Eric was a pill. As one of Smith Labs' Development Directors, he could have made Ming's life a whole lot easier. But he was always discounting her, finding flaws. One look from his pissed-off face was enough to wring the joy out of anyone's life. Generally, office romance was a bad idea; but Ming and Charlie were meant for each other.

"It'll be ready in about a month," she said, eying her. "You want to see the apartment? You and Charlie?" She took a sip of coffee, then set it aside, her stomach roiling.

Ming studied her cup, a slight tinge of pink blooming up her neck. "Not with Charlie," she said, shaking her head slightly. "Not yet anyway." She looked around anxiously. "You can't repeat this," she whispered, and clasped Megan's wrist. "Already, I have lost much face."

"All right." Megan leaned closer.

"You have to promise not to tell," Ming said, her eyes pleading. "In America it's not so bad; but in my family, my country, it's a huge shame. You see, I have a little girl. Lydia is eight. I need a place where I can live with her in peace. I promise, she'll be very quiet. You'll never know she's around."

"You have an eight-year-old?" Megan shook her head and looked her over. "You can't be more than . . . you don't look—"

"It's true." Ming sighed, then bowed her head, her hands gripping the edge of the table. "I need a place of my own, away from my family. They don't like Lydia because she's a love child; her father's long gone. Of course, Charlie knows all of this."

"I don't think—"

"It's a family secret," Ming whispered, backing away from the table, her hands out. "I have no money. I give it all to Eric." Her eyes glistened with tears. "His stupid wife gives me an allowance when she feels like it. She hates Lydia because her own daughters are such ugly cows." She leaned forward. "Please, Megan. I can pay in a month or so; once I get my checks straightened out. Lydia won't be a problem; and I can help with construction. I'm strong. I'll be useful. Please. I promise."

Megan looked at her quietly, considering her alternatives. Ming was one of the smartest developers in the company. Her computer science degree must have come easy, the way she solved problems so effortlessly. Yet her group leader, one of her brother's cronies, assigned her the most trivial projects. She, of all people, needed a chance to live on her own.

"Of course you can have it," Megan said, patting her hand. "You'll be a fine tenant. It'll be great having another mom in the house. Who needs male relatives anyway?" she snorted. "They just try to take over. As if they have a serious clue about what's important. Speaking of males, maybe you can help crack my new handyman. He defies curiosity."

"You mean it?" Ming wiped at her tears.

"Come by tonight." Megan said, smiling, her heart warming at the prospect of renting to a friend. "I'll show you around. And bring Lydia. My nephew can keep her company while we talk. And you'll get to meet Stan, my handyman." She clamped her lips shut, seeing the speculation in Ming's eyes.

Ming's smile softened as she sipped her coffee. "You like this Stan?" she asked, looking out of the corner of her eye. "You think you need *my* help?"

Megan pushed her chair back, and studied the depth of her cup. "I think he's beyond help."

"Really?" Ming's eyes glinted with challenge.

ଓଓଓଓଓ

Apartment three's living room was a shambles of plaster, sawdust, old newspapers and mouse droppings. Dust filled the air as the last piece of plaster fell with a bang. Perched atop a stepladder, Ming had just ripped the final corner from the wall, her expression gleeful. Megan flashed the thumbs up signal. In the past few weeks, Ming had been by every night and Saturday; performing whatever task Stan assigned them, without a hint of complaint. Today was the second Saturday of the project.

The air in the room was stifling. Megan gasped as she lurched to the window, practically gulping the faint moist breeze. She wiped at the sweat on her brow with a heavy hand, then glanced at her watch. It was well past noon and time for a break. She was ravenous.

She waved at Roger and Lydia, who shared the tire swing outside, talking animatedly, their faces alight with laughter. Lydia's exquisite, fragile beauty did not faze Roger in the least. The two fought like siblings, long accustomed to fighting; and had become instant friends, relieving both parents of worry while they completed Ming's apartment.

"That was a hoot," she said, turning to Ming, who was climbing down the ladder. Ming had had the sense to pull her hair into a ponytail. Her own unruly mop hung down her back in a filthy sheet. She glanced at Stan, who stood at the room's far end looking ferocious. He'd had them carting antiques into the attic since early morning. And now this. The man was a freaking slave driver.

"A barrel of laughs," Ming said, and then coughed. "Can't wait to move in. Should be any day." She laughed as she surveyed the wreckage on the floor."

"Whose brilliant idea was this anyway?" Megan said, placing fists to hips. "I don't know about you, but I can barely breathe. And I'm starving."

"Yeah, but another room bites the dust," Ming said, and giggled as she picked up a chunk of plaster and dropped it into a large trash bin. Dust filled the top of the bin like a small explosion. Ming's face was coated with grime and sweat, as if a load of gray powder had been dumped on her head. "One down: just a few more to go. And what about you, mister strong but silent John Wayne type?" She punched Stan's arm playfully. "Enough of a workout for you?"

"We ain't even begun," he said softly, and pulled up his T-shirt, exposing well-tanned, well-sculpted abs as he mopped his streaming face.

Megan tried not to gawk, her mouth dry.

"If we push, we can finish ripping out *all* the walls in this suite today," he said with a scowl. "So let's get going, ladies; if you want to move in this month." He looked pointedly at Ming.

"Lunch first," Megan said, her eyes narrowing. "We aren't damn machines, Mr. Zambinsky, though I know you'd like to think so. We need food and we need it now." All of a sudden, she ached with hunger.

He looked at her closely. His face was starting to blur.

"Come on," she said and blinked, not caring what he thought. "Ming brought lunch today." She stumbled across the room to Ming's cooler. "Let's see what's inside."

She was reaching into the cooler when all of a sudden, the world spun. She fell slowly, her arms hitting first. They buckled beneath her and all went black.

She was fading in and out, trying to make sense of a series of jumbled images. Stan's face was impossibly close. He smelled of . . . tomatoes; and for some odd reason, he was carrying her, his unintelligible words strangely soothing.

ଓଓଓଓଓ

She found herself flat on her back, the lights above painfully bright. Fighting panic, she opened her eyes a crack. Peering down at her was a strange woman in a white smock over a navy pantsuit. Her face was masked, her eyes smallish and hazel, her short hair a non-descript brown.

She was in some sort of hospital room with three empty beds, a bay of closets and a bathroom, its door wide open. Mauve and green seemed the predominant colors—aside from white.

"Who the hell are you?' she asked, her words coming out garbled. She wanted to scream.

The woman ripped off her mask, exposing a thin

face with a long tapered nose. “Hello Mrs. Rosswell,” she said with a wry smile. “It’s good to see you awake. I’m Doctor Ames. It takes a while to get used to the hormonal changes. However, given time, you’ll be just fine. I assume you’ve chosen an obstetrician?”

“Obstetrician? Why?” Megan rose abruptly, then held her swimming head.

“Oh, I see,” the doctor said, and crossed her arms, her smile dissolving.

Megan looked her in the eye, her throat constricting as realization hit. “You’re kidding,” she said and twisted the edge of her sheet, her knuckles white.

“You’re pregnant, Mrs. Rosswell,” the doctor said softly. “About two months along, I’d say; although you’ll need to consult with an obstetrician. Meanwhile, please get some rest. Your husband described all the work you’ve been doing today.” She shook her head. “You need to take it a lot easier. You could harm your child and yourself.”

“He’s not my husband,” Megan said and dropped the sheet. “He’s my employee—my soon to be ex-employee if he indicated otherwise.”

“Oh, no.” The doctor held up her hand. “He didn’t say that. We only assumed it by the way he treated you.”

“I don’t have time for this,” Megan said and swung her legs over the side of the bed. “How can I be pregnant?” She let a dizzy wave recede, then rose to her feet, her mind latching onto the image of

Donald leaning over her, his face twisted with rage.

"I'll get a second opinion," she said, and moved slowly to the nearest closet, keeping a careful hand on her flapping jonnie. The closet was empty.

"No way am I pregnant," she said, turning to the baffled doctor. "Now where the hell are my clothes?"

ଓଓଓଓଓ

Billowing thunderheads filled the northwest sky. Heat streamed off the rooftop of the elegant old Victorian. Rain-swollen wind battered the oaks that stood like sentinels beside the lovely old house. Leaves, sticks and crumpled newspaper skittered across the driveway that tracked around the house to the carriage shed.

Stan sat in his truck craving a smoke, sweat pooling between his shoulder blades and under his arms. He should be heading up the driveway to see her, something about a spigot she needed, something that, in his mind was just a ploy to get him to come. And somehow, damn fool that he was, he couldn't say no. She'd get that puppy-dog look that made his insides ache, and he'd do anything she asked.

He scanned the brand new black Cadillac idling a few blocks up the street. Inside was Floyd Mello with his hat pulled down to his eyes, slouched over, trying to blend in—for the third time that week.

He chuckled, thinking back to a similar hot

summer night when he, Butch and Floyd had been about ten. It was one of those golden days before Ma died. He and Butch had jumped out from behind a tree—scared Floyd so bad he'd pissed his pants. They'd laughed their heads off dousing each other with the garden hose; until Pop had come out in his skivvies to yell at them, making twice the racket.

Floyd had started his own detective agency several years ago, shortly after Clovis, his high school sweetheart, had married Walt, Stan's older brother. What a fiasco that had been. Judging by Floyd's wheels, Clovis had made a horrible choice. But she was family now and he had his loyalties to bear—Walt being his only sibling.

He snickered, seeing the humor in Floyd's hunched-over posture. Few people recognized Floyd's goofy appearance as the front that it was. He had a memory like a computer and missed nothing. Whatever he was up to, it bore watching.

Stan jumped from his truck and spanned the distance, laughing as Floyd tried to slump down even further. He slid into the passenger seat a heartbeat after Floyd unlocked the passenger side door.

"Stan!" Floyd said, feigning surprise, his hands fluttering bird-like and settling on his skinny thighs.

"It's a goddamn refrigerator in here," Stan said, rubbing his hands together and blowing on them. The AC blasted.

"So, I run hot," Floyd said with a shrug, looking for a second like the skinny kid of long ago, his mother chasing after him, holding his coat out, screeching about pneumonia. Floyd extended a bony hand and Stan shook it warmly. "How's it going, buddy? Long time no see. What's it been . . . a couple a years?"

"Great. Great," Stan replied. "More like six months."

Floyd grinned, showing all of his stubby little teeth. Stan looked closely, seeing beyond the narrow blue eyes, coifed dark hair and expensive designer casuals. Floyd's face was heavily lined and bore acne scars—testament to bad food and late nights in bars. A cigarette burned in the ashtray. A pack lay on the seat between them. Stan fought the urge to snatch one, salivating when Floyd brought one to his lips and took a long drag. At thirty, Floyd could pass for forty. And it wasn't all because of Clovis' rejection.

"Why you watching the Rosswell house?" Stan asked and took a cigarette from the pack. "Anything I should know?" He dangled it between his lips, but waved off Floyd's lighter. "I quit," he said, liking too well the way it felt in his mouth.

"You know I can't talk about business," Floyd said, a smooth façade slipping across his narrow face.

"Yeah." Stan nodded, remembering how tight-lipped he could be.

"I see you going in and out, helping Ms. Rosswell," Floyd said, looking at him out of the corner of his eye. "It's real sad what happened to her people. Tom was the salt of the earth and Val a knockout. I heard there were kids in the car—only one of them lived."

"Yeah," Stan repeated, and looked down at his hands. No way was he talking about Roger, or the grief that had dulled Megan's beautiful dark eyes.

"The place looks great," Floyd said, waving a hand in front of his face as if caressing the majestic old house. "Miss Spenser . . . she did well to sell it to Ms. Rosswell. She'll make it a show place. Smart cookie I hear. Got one of those computer jobs at Smith Labs—a good job. You sweet on her or something?" He looked down his skinny nose.

"You know I have no luck with women." Stan shook his head, something close to pain filling his head. "Trisha . . . you know . . . and Christy."

"Yeah, Trisha." Floyd flicked his cigarette at the ashtray, sending a shower of ash onto the floor. "Shit!" he stuck the cigarette in his mouth and stooped over, wiping ineffectually at the mess. "I saw her the other day," he said, the cigarette clenched in his teeth. He lowered his window a few inches, tossed out the ash he'd managed to collect and in the process, bumped his cigarette against the glass, scattering more ash across his shoulders and onto his hair.

Stan resisted the urge to laugh.

"She was trotting alongside your Pa like a proper wife," Floyd said with a shrug. He lowered the cigarette to the ashtray, ignoring another spray of ash. "Her boobs were wiggling all over the place. You should a seen her—like a banana split on a hot day." He gestured wildly with his hands. "She asked for you, kiddo. Been avoiding your old man again?" He eyed him gravely.

Stan raked a hand through his hair; reminded of the last time he'd seen his stepmother. The bitch, he liked to call her, though he hated casting aspersions on poor defenseless canines.

His eyes narrowed as he watched Ming drive past in a Chevy-2 Nova, her latest contraption. Charlie was with her, probably moving in this time. The guy was a nut job, a computer geek who thought he was God's gift. His eyes were always bloodshot and he was constantly sniffing, sure signs of a cocaine habit. Ming turned her head away as she headed up the driveway, pretending she hadn't seen him. Another bitch.

"Let it go, Stan," Floyd said and patted his shoulder. "No woman will ever take your ma's place. She was a saint—even at the end. She loved you and Walt like the sun and the moon. Trisha was just a man-hungry skirt, who needed a home, a stray dog, really. Your Pa can handle her. She's actually a very nice lady."

"Right." Stan looked away, hating the dark helpless anger that flooded his head at the thought of Trisha. She'd been a young boy's dream and worst nightmare. Thank God, those awkward days were over; and he a grown man.

Floyd punched the radio buttons, searching for a station. A country western blared—one of Stan's favorites. He flashed Floyd a smile, then watched him sit back, his face beaming. Music was something they had in common.

"Now Christy's another story," Floyd said, eying him, shaking his head. "She's got the body of an angel and the mind of a viper. I saw her brand of trouble coming two miles away. I warned you, but you didn't listen. I hear she's giving Butch the run for his money."

"That's the only kind that wants me," Stan muttered. He stared out the window at Megan's Victorian, the haven of his lonely teens. Back then, Chad and Hattie Spenser, brother and sister, had enjoyed their solitude from adjoining apartments. Chad had been his favorite math teacher. Skinny, heavily wrinkled and close to retirement, he'd opened his mind to literature, art and logic—once a week welcoming him in to study; then later, playing chess or scrabble until Hattie served a spectacular tea. His mouth watered, thinking of the pastries and sandwiches she'd served. Chad had always encouraged him to become an architect, had even promised to help fund his education. But he'd declined. Pop hated even a hint of charity; and he'd rather work with his hands, anyway. Hell, he needed to work with his hands like he needed to breathe.

For some reason Megan came to mind and her recently acquired cooking skills. She was a natural, her abilities rivaling those of her late sister's. It was nothing short of amazing what she could do with a simple pan of brownies.

"Don't kid yourself about Christy," Floyd said.

Stan looked at him sharply. It took a second to redirect his thoughts. Floyd shot him a knowing look as he stubbed out a butt in the ashtray. "Butch got the raw end of that deal. He did you a favor by taking her off your hands. Ms. Rosswell is miles above her in both class and intelligence. You picked right for once, boyo. So don't blow it."

"What makes you think I'm interested?" Stan asked glumly, and glanced at his watch. He was already five minutes late. Megan would be pissed.

"How's Clovis?" Floyd asked, his hand trembling as he took another cigarette and lit it, trying to look nonchalant. "I mean, really. How is she?" His voice trailed off.

"She's fine, Floyd," Stan said, wishing he could say more. It wasn't his fault that Clovis had picked the wrong man. Walt was his brother, for crying out loud. He wasn't a bad guy. He was just dense. Once a high school football defensive tackle, he'd let himself go. Beer, food and sports had consumed him—in that order. Last time he'd seen Clovis, she was guzzling wine, ignoring her three kids who were glued to the TV. Walt ignored Clovis and Clovis ignored the kids—the story of most American families. End of case. It was nothing Floyd could fix.

Stan opened the door and stepped out, welcoming the blast of heat. "I got a meeting, Floyd. See you around." He shoved the cigarette into his pocket—for later. Then he closed the door and strode away, rejecting the sting of tears beneath his lids. He had nothing to be ashamed of. His family was no different than most.

He set his jaw, a shield against the edgy tightening fear that women seemed to induce. Megan was waiting for him. Pissed as a wet cat, Megan. His Megan. He saw her shadow, saw the folded arms and the tapping foot, and smiled. She sure was something.

He kicked at the leaves as he strode toward the carriage hose. Its propped-open doors crashed against their stakes, the wind blowing fierce. Inside, however, was an oasis of calm, a shadowy space built to house a half-dozen horses and an assortment of carts and carriages. The stalls had been removed years ago. Megan's small blue Honda was parked dead center. To its left was Ming's Chevy; and to its right, a riding lawn mower, a pair of bicycles and a soggy pile of boxes. The dirt floor smelled of gasoline, fertilizer and oily rags.

Megan stood inside in the shadows. The wind had whipped color into her cheeks. Her tousled brown hair looked soft and touchable. One of these days, she'd swallow him up with those huge dark eyes of hers. She eyed him warily, holding his gaze for a long time before she looked away. She was definitely pissed.

"What's up?" he asked, and smiled, seeing her lips curl in annoyance. She hated that phrase. His heart raced as he looked in her eyes, pleased that he'd made her mad. At least she was starting to feel something; and it was a fine game, baiting her, just to see her reaction. One of these days, if she behaved herself, he'd tell her about Floyd's surveillance.

"You're late," she shrilled.

"So?" He stuffed his hands into his jeans pockets.

ଔଔଔଔଔ

She watched him saunter toward her, getting madder by the second. Leaning against the doorpost, half-exhausted after spending the morning at the toilet bowl, she barely listened while he explained, as if to a child, why the plumber had been detained.

"I just want to draw water from a spigot behind the garage," she said weakly, though she was trying her hardest to sound reasonable. "If it isn't the plumber, Stan, it's some other down and out friend of yours who needs a second chance." The glint in his eyes annoyed her, as did the way he held his hands behind his back, looking too much like the quintessential servant.

"He just can't come this week," he said and shrugged, his arms now hanging down. "His wife had a nervous breakdown. His kids are out of school for the summer. His mother's trying to help, but she's not well either."

"Tell him to send the kids to camp," she said, resisting the urge to walk away, hating the way her body responded to his gaze. His eyes were kind, yet stern. He was obviously holding back his temper. Since her trip to the hospital, he'd been looking at her as if she were fragile, as if he cared. It had to stop. She pushed away from the shed and moved toward the orchard. The trees shook and waved above her, a fury of wind and sky.

"He's called all the camps," he said, keeping in step beside her, "but it seems they're booked. I understand most camps are booked by the end of March." He looked at her quizzically.

"Yeah, I suppose," she said and sneaked a look at him, admiring the way his eyes matched his jade green T-shirt. They were chameleon-eyes, turning blue, gray or green, matching his shirts. But he wasn't a chameleon like Donald. He was as steady as the earth—as steady as Pa. She looked away quickly; not liking the way her pulse raced. She was just lonely. She hadn't been with a man for far too long. Anyone would feel the same.

There was a crack overhead, and before she could look up, he'd grabbed her arm and pulled her away. "No!" she cried, his touch burning her skin. She sucked in great drafts of air as she shook him off, then watched in horror as a massive branch fell with a loud crash just where she'd been standing.

The urge to leap into his arms came out of nowhere. She ached with it, wanting to claw and kiss her way into his very soul. A sob escaped as she registered the confusion on his face, and then the pity. Unable to bear it, she turned and ran to the carriage shed, arriving out of breath, hating that her face was ten shades of red, hating the truth he must have seen in her eyes. She leaned over, hands on knees, gasping for breath.

"Megan?"

She coughed to cover her embarrassment; sensing him behind her, hovering like a concerned older brother. He and Pa must have discussed her fainting spell—reason enough to keep her condition a secret. She'd made Pa promise not to tell; then he'd jabbed her about the house; saying it was too much for her to handle, that she needed a husband, especially now. Last night, he'd had the nerve to suggest that Stan would be perfect. Yeah, like that was going to happen.

She winced, seeing the distance in his eyes.

"Come on Megan, I was just trying to help," he said softly, holding an arm out in appeal; then throwing it down, indicating that he was backing off. "You don't have to bite my damn head off. I know you're under a lot of pressure. Whatever I did wrong, I'm sorry. All right?"

Rain burst from the sky with a rumble of thunder. It beat against the carriage house roof in sheets. Stan turned away, clearly frustrated. For some reason, the sight of his thinning hair, now flattened and dark with rain, deflated her rage. She grabbed his wrist, pulled him inside the shed, then backed away.

"I know you're just being a friend," she said. A bolt of lightening rent the sky; followed by a deep-toned clap of thunder. "Stan?"

He was leaning against the inner wall, his arms folded across his chest, his eyes closed. “What?” he snarled. There was hurt behind it.

“Oh, don’t mind me,” she said, fighting back tears. “I’m sorry. I haven’t been well lately. It’s been getting me down.” She turned her head away. “Just do what you want with the plumber. From what I’ve seen of his work, he’s good; and he’ll be back soon enough.”

His lips tilted up and for some idiotic reason she took a step toward him, craving his arms around her. She stepped back; but it was too late.

“I’ll let you know,” he mumbled. His neck was red.

She smiled softly, emboldened by his shyness. “Whatever happened to Christy?” she asked, then could have bitten her lip. She held her breath as he scanned her for a long moment, his expression unreadable. “I’m sorry,” she whispered, and winced. “You warned me not to do that.”

She gasped as he spanned the distance between them, his breath warm and smelling of fresh air. She couldn’t think straight, seeing the silver flecks in his eyes, feeling the heat of him, his rage. Rain pelted the carriage shed, which enclosed them like a tent. Her stomach ached as he eyed her lips, looking about to kiss her. She couldn’t help but move closer as his hand, calloused and warm, brushed against her cheek.

“True love,” he said softly. “Is that what you want me to talk about, Ms. Rosswell? Hmm? Or maybe a romance gone bad?" She shook her head, seeing the steel in his eyes. "You know Christy. You went to school with her. I caught her in bed with my best friend, Butch Sawicki. Imagine that? It was a just week before our wedding. Not that it mattered to her. She went on our honeymoon anyway—with Butch."

She opened her mouth, but her throat constricted.

"I suppose it doesn't mean much to you," he said, his eyes narrowing. "Living life in the fast lane with that pilot—Captain Donald Alexander. Fancy name. Fancy dinners. Shopping in Boston. Maybe you like to screw around. Maybe he's real busy right now, giving you time for a lowly blue collar like me."

"I've filed for divorce," she said, shaking her head. Tears filled her eyes.

"You don't listen," he said and backed away, his hair instantly flattened by the deluge. "My personal life's none of your concern. I don't want a woman. I don't need one. I've no luck with them and there's no changing my mind." He turned and began to walk away.

"Well, I'm pregnant!" she shrieked; and he turned, looking surprised. Then something in his eyes hardened and died.

"Not by me," he said, then walked away, becoming a gray blur amidst the driving rain.

"As if I'd want you," she whispered, then closed her eyes and balled a fist against her trembling lips.

ꙮꙮꙮꙮꙮ

Saturday dawned hot and sunny. Stan had dragged his heels all morning—getting up late, grabbing breakfast at the donut shop and tinkering with his truck. He sat in his truck now, parked at the curb of his father's white triple-decker, a few blocks north of the Merrimack River. Built by his late great-grandfather, an immigrant mill worker, it was tucked in tight with a string of houses just like it.

He scanned the street, noting the vinyl siding amidst peeling white clapboard. The vehicles, most parked on the street, were older models. Toys sprinkled across small front yards showed evidence of young families. It was a lazy morning, with the soft sounds of rock music and classical intermingling with the squeal of truck brakes from down near the bridge. Pots of bright geraniums and impatiens adorned window boxes and porches. Lace curtains hung from most windows. Wind chimes tinkled on a neighboring porch, promising a slight northern breeze.

He stepped from his truck slowly, almost paralyzed by the familiar feeling of defeat. He'd left this place the last few times in disgust. If only Pop would let him fix the house. Peeling paint hung from it in sheets. The windowsills were dark with mildew. The front porch sagged from rot and carpenter ants. In a few months, he could have it looking like new. If only Pop would let him.

If only Trisha would leave.

The thought of her made his stomach churn; yet he moved toward the house deliberately. Never let it be said that he was afraid of his stepmother. He headed down the rutted dirt path to the right of the house, toward a pile of rubble that had once been a rickety garage, brought down by a nor'easter. He steeled himself as he turned behind the house into the small grassy yard, surrounded on two sides by a six-foot weather-beaten stockade fence, the back of which was propped up by large round posts. Pop considered the yard a family treasure—a postage stamp of earth, the working poor's version of prosperity.

Randy, Kate and Ellie, his brother's kids, sat around the picnic table, bare legs dangling, munching on potato chips. His brother, Walt fussed over a grill, swearing under his breath. After two years in Vietnam as a helicopter gunner, he'd come home mean, his bark promising a bite. Thus, his kids were silent and his wife a drunk. Alcohol had been a big part of their whirlwind courtship.

He imagined Megan viewing the scene: pots of thirsty geraniums, a small, withered vegetable garden, three green and white striped lawn chairs, the picnic table, a rickety gas grill and his silent nieces and nephew. Then there was Walt's faithful battered blue cooler—probably packed with beer—a beverage not allowed in Gordon Rosswell's vicinity.

However, Megan wouldn't begrudge him. Hell, she probably missed the cookouts at her sister's house. He took a hard look at his family, wondering at her strength. Not only had she lost Val, Tom and the kids, but she'd lost her husband, inherited a kid and was pregnant.

Then it hit him. She'd been afraid when he'd touched her. But of what? Had someone hurt her? Donald? He thought back to the time he'd seen him on the floor in front of her apartment; and the times he'd seen his father, dead drunk, raising a fist to Trisha. Pop had never really hit, as far as he knew . . .but Donald . . .?

He sucked in his breath, wishing he'd paid more attention. Carl Spenser had once told him he was his own worst enemy. In the beginning, he'd lashed out at Carl; who'd responded with sympathy, concrete advice and a place to escape his miserable life. He'd lashed out at Megan, too, come to think of it—because he couldn't handle the attraction. Then there was his wounded pride—that she'd come to him last, after squandering herself on the pilot. In fact, she was a good woman—too good for him. He had no business even looking in her direction.

He studied Walt, wishing he could talk to him man to man. Good solid Walt, no matter their differences, he was still his brother. They shared a common history. But, unfortunately, Walt didn't know squat about women either. His beer gut had bloomed since last summer, packing the cheap polyester shirt that sported sweat rings beneath each armpit. His temples and mustache were streaked with gray. Approaching middle age, he was the most sought after plumber at Dracut Plumbing and Heating.

Walt turned and grinned, his mustache rising slightly, looking like feral old wildcat.

"Stanley, my boy. 'Bout time you showed up."

"Hey, Walt. Kids." Stan extended a hand and found himself pulled into a bear hug and the top of his head rubbed hard with massive knuckles. It was as if they were boys again, with Mom shouting from the kitchen for them to cut it out. The kids watched with wide eyes, shifting in their seats.

"Baby bro," Walt said with a laugh as he let him go. "What's happening, kiddo?" He danced from one foot to the other, looking Stan over, making him smile. "Looks like you need some meat on ya."

"Speak for yourself." Stan feinted a punch to his gut.

Walt laughed. "Have a cold one" He reached into the cooler and handed him a beer. "Take the load off." He winked at his kids, and they released their breath as one.

"Uncle Stan!" The kids ran to him, breaking his heart with their eagerness.

"Randy," He hugged the boy, saddened by his sullen expression. Randy had his mother's dark eyes and ginger hair; but his barrel chest and hard jaw were pure Zambinsky. He should have a kid like this, he realized with a jolt—with Megan. He shook his head slightly, trying to erase the thought; then released Randy and ruffled his hair, gratified by the new light in his eyes.

"Look at you, Katie," he said, turning to the

oldest girl, who'd just turned seven. With light brown hair and blue eyes, she looked just like him, proving the power of genetics. He hugged her gently, seeing the approval in Walt's eyes. Walt made no secret that she was his favorite.

"You're growing like a tadpole," Stan said, tickling her chin, making her giggle. Her eyes sparkled with delight. Then she looked down, as if embarrassed, as if she'd overheard something about him, most likely.

Stan released her.

"Ellie." He picked up the little one and spun her around. At four, Ellie was all beauty and innocence—a picture-perfect darling with huge dark eyes and ginger curls. She looked like Clovis had before drink had drowned her hopes.

Walt cleared his throat. Three pairs of eyes looked up in fear, hurting Stan in an oddly familiar way. Walt exerted control as Pa had, with the threat of a slap lurking behind the easy laughter.

"Go play," Walt said, and the kids scattered like leaves: Randy running to the house, Kate sprinting up the path and Ellie flying to the other side of the picnic table where she grabbed more chips and began stuffing them into her mouth.

Clovis staggered off the back porch and landed flat-footed, though wobbly, clasping a plate heaped with hot-dog rolls. Her hair was frowzy, her face heavily made-up, her orange striped shorts clashed with her purple floral tank top. Neither item hid her flabby midriff. Her feet were bare, drawing Stan's attention. Her perfect feet matched her perfect hands, each nail pink and pearly.

"Stanley!" she slurred, already drunk.

"Good to see you, Clovis," he said, resisting the urge to check his watch. Drunk by noon was her usual state. He took the plate from her, set it on the table, then hugged and kissed her. She'd been a good kid, the girl next door, who'd traipsed after him and Walt like a little shadow—until Floyd had moved into the neighborhood. He couldn't help but feel sorry for her. She'd had dreams and expectation like everyone else.

"Saw Floyd the other day," he said, trying not to eye her cleavage, though it probably would have given her a thrill, if she'd been half-aware. "He's got his own PI agency."

"Lucky Floyd," Clovis said and batted her lashes. She leaned heavily against him. He slung an arm around her and helped her to the table.

"Slut," Walt said, shaking his head. He poked at the coals, sending sparks flying across the sparse grass.

Ellie looked up, her frightened face smeared with chips and soda. Stan sighed as he sat beside her, opposite Clovis, and placed a calming hand on her little leg. She leaned against him, a soft trusting weight, and started to hum. He wanted to shake his brother, to make him appreciate what he had.

"Floyd asked for you," he said through clenched teeth, feeling like a jerk, yet unable to help himself. His brother and sister-in-law had some serious problems; and here he was, adding fuel to the fire.

"Oh?" Clovis said airily. Her smile sagged as she glanced at Walt, who was watching Randy sneak back to the table like a snake trained on a mouse.

"Yeah, he looked good, all dressed up in a three-piece suit," Stan continued, ignoring Walt's set lips and rigid back, hating the way he watched his kid, looking for flaws. "I hear he's the best in Lowell."

"Well goody for him," Walt sneered. He pointed his spatula at Stan. "With three ex-wives he'd better be damn good. He always was a sly bastard, showing off with the girls like he was some kind of stud. He's nothing but a filthy little weasel!"

Clovis frowned, opened her mouth and then closed it again, her face gone pale.

Stan followed her line of view, seeing the shadow that filled the yard. Pop stood on the top step, surveying them. His insides began to ache.

Pop had grown enormous. His pitted face was bright red. He tipped back a can of beer and guzzled it, dribbling it down his shirt. Silence filled the yard as he tossed the can to the ground. All legs, Randy flew to grab it, then threw it into the trash barrel.

"So, the prodigal son's returned," Pop drawled as he stepped down. A dog snarled in a neighbor's yard. A cat screeched. Then there was silence.

"Hello, Pop," Stan said quietly. He crushed his beer can and threw it into the barrel, recognizing the shame and longing in Pop's sad eyes. Instead of Pop being proud of his accomplishments, he'd always seemed diminished by them.

"Hello Stan," Trisha said as she poked her head around Pop's bulk. She prodded Pop down the last step and toward the table, then minced toward Stan on high-heeled sandals. She was an aging Betty Boop, with sultry brown eyes. She puffed on a slender cigarette with tight red lips. His mother had smoked, too; but there the resemblance ended.

"Trisha." Stan nodded, holding her gaze. In cut-off jeans and a blue tube top, she was hanging out all over the place. "How's tricks?" he asked, ignoring the warning in Pop's glare.

"Oh, Stan." She waved a heavily ringed hand, looking annoyed. "We're fine, though it probably wouldn't kill you to come and see for yourself. Your father hasn't been feeling too good lately and you know—"

"Quiet," Pop hissed. He gripped Trisha's arm, silencing her, causing her breasts to jiggle, and her mouth to screw up in a tight resentful line.

"What's new, Stanley?" Pop mopped at the sweat on his face with a large white handkerchief. "Walt said you were bringing a girl." He scanned the yard. "I don't see her, boy; so what's the matter? We ain't good enough for her, or maybe you just don't like girls? Is that it?"

"I didn't come here to fight," Stan said softly, every muscle tensed for flight. He grabbed another beer from Walt's cooler, crossed his legs and scratched his neck, hating the way Trisha glanced from Pop to him and back like a worried terrier. It was hard to believe that Pop had been to college, had planned to be an architect—before the Korean War.

"No?" Pop hung his head as if in defeat, one of his well-used ploys. "Don't mind me. I'm just making conversation." He headed toward the back fence, his grief souring the air.

Stan clutched his beer, filled with a helpless fury. Should he go to Pop, yell or walk away? Gordon Rosswell's words came to mind—that Pop was his father, that he owed him respect.

"Just leave him be," Walt murmured, his eyes kind. Stan nodded.

"Stanley, can you help me bring the food out from the kitchen?" Trisha asked, looking concerned, her high-pitched voice slicing through his head. He followed her inside.

In Ma's kitchen, memories flooded his senses. Nothing had changed. The room was still gold and blue—her favorite combination. His knees shook as he spied her lace curtains, their bottoms frayed. Dust covered her angel collection, set on little shelves on either side of the window. Her treasured gold-rimmed china was stacked in a food-encrusted heap in the enamel sink. Cigarette butts filled the Blue Willow plate Pop had bought at an antique store the year before she died.

Blindly, he tore through the house, wallowing in the evidence of Trisha's disrespect.

"The bathroom's on the left," she called out

from the kitchen, making his insides clench. As if he didn't know the layout of his own damn house.

Magazines were piled along the hallway and in both bedrooms; along with a jumble of costume jewelry, clothing, broken furniture, trashy novels, pizza boxes and broken lamps. The beds were bare, the bedclothes heaped on the floor. Someone had punched several holes in Pa's bedroom wall, oddly spaced.

The bathroom, however, was an oasis of order and cleanliness. The floor, toilet and sink were spotlessly white. A wicker table, pushed against the near wall, held a small flowering plant, its leaves deep green and glossy, the flowers a bright pink. Pink towels hung beside the sink and on the long bar across the sliding shower door.

Why? He shook his head. Why just one damn room, with all the rest in shambles?

He stumbled down the hallway, shaking his head, seeing an army of dust bunnies in every corner, reminded of his mother's relentless scrubbing. Her prized cross-stitching hung tilted in grimy frames. The carpet looked worn and stained.

Ma had been loud and funny at times; but she'd kept Pa calm, pacified and out of the local barrooms. She'd cleaned the house with a passion bordering on obsession; and she'd known how to cook.

"Trisha!" He shouted, his fury mounting as she minced toward him, her face alight.

"What is it, Stan, honey?" Her look was pure innocence.

"Look at this house." He shrugged, palms out. "What the hell do you do all day? My mother kept this place spotless; but you just clean the bathroom? There's more to being married than sex, you know. Or is that all you're capable of?"

Her face flamed. "How dare you." She put her hands to her hips. "Maybe I'm not the saint your mother was, but I do the best I can, considering the way I'm not allowed to touch anything. And besides, your father's been sick and I've—"

"You've been hitting on anything with pants, that's what you've been doing," he said, wishing she'd cover her cleavage for once. Did her breasts have to look so smooth and white?

Her mouth made an O. Then she caught her breath and came at him with arms flailing. "Just because I made one teensy mistake . . . you impossible, pig-headed, arrogant bastard. I've had to work two jobs to fight off the bill collectors. You have no idea!"

He grabbed her wrist, but not fast enough. She slapped him hard.

He put a hand to his burning face. "Shit!" He backed into the kitchen, and whacked his hip on the counter. The back door opened and Clovis stumbled in. He rubbed his face, resisting the urge to rub his hip.

Trisha had fled.

"She after you again?" Clovis asked with a wan smile. She swayed before the refrigerator, clutching a bowl of chips. Clovis made no secret that she hated her stepmother; who treated her like a brainless drunk.

"She never gives up," Stan said, wishing life had been kinder to Clovis. She was barely five feet tall, a fairy child like Ellie would someday be, and easily overlooked. "If it weren't for you, Walt and the kids, I wouldn't be here," he said, then moved to the window, seeing Pop at the picnic table, his arms around Kate and Ellie. "Do you remember the way he was before Ma died?"

"Yeah. He was a peach," Clovis slurred. Her legs wobbled and she sat at the table. "It was a huge loss for all of us."

He'd forgotten how sweet she could be. "As sweet as vanilla ice cream and twice as rich," Floyd had once said; and indeed, the rapt expression in her wide, dark eyes begged a man's confidence. He was about to speak; but her lids closed ever so slowly and then her head bobbed.

"Things aren't always as they seem," Trisha said softly from the hallway. She pointed at the refrigerator. "The salads are in there, if you've a mind to help." She seemed sad, defeated.

"In what way," Stan asked, seeing the lines beside her mouth and the dark circles beneath her eyes. Time had not been good to her.

"We all have hopes and dreams." she replied. "But maybe no one gets what they really want; or maybe only a few of us are so lucky." Her eyes glimmered, tears ready to fall, reminding him of the way she'd looked after he'd refused her drunken advances that night long ago. Pop had lay snoring in his room after a night of drinking and dancing—probably killing his grief. She'd practically stripped him that night, then clutched his pajama top like a barrier, all horrified and angry, as if she'd wanted to curl up and die, as if it had been his fault. Back then, he'd only been able to think of the wild, out-of-control way she'd made him feel. She'd been in her early twenties then, soft and feminine, fresh out of beauty school, too young and good-looking to be his mother's replacement.

He sat back in his chair, eying Clovis, who was asleep, her head on the table, her lips slack. "Not that I particularly care; but what did you want?" he asked softly.

"I was way too young when your father married me." She smiled lightly. "As if you didn't notice." She leaned on the counter and clasped her hands together. "I wanted a few kids, too; and a family who loved me. Did you ever stop to think about that?"

He took in the practiced pout, the keen speculation in her eyes. He knew little about her background, what she did all day. He'd never thought to ask.

"So where's my adoring daughter-in-law?" She jerked her chin at Clovis. "And where's the husband to provide for me?" Her eyes narrowed. "As if you care what goes on in your father's sorry life."

"What's going on?"

She looked away sharply, shook her head, then

looked at him directly. "I think you should ask him yourself."

"Cat and mouse games again?" he asked. Refusing to look at her, he grabbed three bowls from the fridge and spoons from the drawer. Then he looked down at Clovis.

"She'll wake up in a while," Trisha said with a shrug. "She always does."

"Then make yourself useful," Stan said, glaring at her. "Help her to a bed, maybe put a sheet on it first. That is . . . if you have a clean one in this house."

He ripped open the door and stepped out. Pop, Walt and the kids all looked up as the door slammed behind him.

"How's things at Princeville?" Stan asked as he set the bowls on the table and peeled off their cellophane covers. He looked up sharply at the uncomfortable silence.

"Shows how much you keep in touch." Pop's expression was bitter. "They let me go six months ago." He looked at Stan out of the corner of his eye, as if pained by the sight of him. He set a burger and hotdog on Ellie's plate then helped her to condiments. "Come on. Come on. Help yourselves," he said softly, urging Katie and Randy to refill their plates, too.

"You got fired?" Stan asked, then took a plate of burgers from Walt and set it on the table. "But you've been there for decades."

"No, no. Early retirement they called it," Pop

said, waving a hand. "They gave me a send-off—you know—the party and the gold watch. Three other guys got the same. Seems management's relocating . . . to Mexico or Puerto Rico, some low-wage place . . . just like with the production. I don't understand it. They say Prince can't compete by paying Union wages. The Union's just pricing us out of jobs. You still in the Union, boy?" He peered at Stan. "Hear that the Smith Labs' Ed Center will be opening soon."

"Yeah, Pop. Harden's is still all Union," he replied stiffly, thinking of Harden's latest series of fiascos. "You know how it is with business—management pushing to be done." He shook his head, seeing electricians poking holes in finished walls, AC installers failing to connect key areas and plumbers unable to get joint compound. Sloppy workmanship, sub-standard supplies and poor planning were adding hours and days as tempers flared. Then there was Megan, needing his help, and more than just for construction.

"You don't look too happy about it," Pop said. He shoved a forkful of potato salad into his mouth. The salad looked good; but between Trisha's filthy kitchen and Clovis' daily drunk, it looked risky. He stuffed a burger in a roll and took a bite, refusing Pop's offer of condiments. The meat, at least, had been seared on the grill.

"It's a job," Stan replied. To Pop's way of thinking, a steady paycheck was priceless. "So what are you doing with all this time on your hands?" he asked, adroitly changing the subject.

"He plays with me," Trisha said, coming down the steps, her smile hard. She'd brushed her hair, refreshed her make-up and reeked of perfume. Laughing, she threw an arm around Pop's shoulders and kissed the side of his face with a loud smack.

Pop's eyes opened wide. He squeezed his beer can, causing beer to gush over his hand, anger and embarrassment warring on his face. Anger won.

"What I do with my time is none of your damn business!" he shouted, flailing the air with a fist. "You've had it in for Trisha from day one. She's your stepmother, goddamnit. I'll teach you about respect." He lunged for Stan; but Stan jumped up, spilling beer down the front of his jeans. He gasped at the icy cold hit, and looked down. "Shit!" he hissed, seeing the dark stain, like he'd pissed his pants.

"Come on, guys," Walt said, hurrying over. Ignoring Stan, he set a hand on Pop's back. Pop was sobbing, bent over.

"Pop, please," Stan said, and swallowed hard. "I meant no disrespect. I don't even want to look at her." He sucked in his breath. His words were coming out all wrong.

"Why you!" Pop lunged for him again.

Walt grabbed at Pop, tipping a bench over, sending Randy flying.

"Come on guys," Walt begged. "Can't we get along for one day, for Christ's sake?" He picked up Randy, who lay stricken on the grass. With an arm around him and a hand on Pa, he balanced the generations. “The old man’s not been himself.”

“I can’t do this,” Stan said, looking from Kate to Ellie, who were staring at him wide-eyed; and at Randy, who looked ready for a fight.

He didn’t belong there. He raked a hand through his hair, wishing he hadn’t come.

“It isn’t your fault, kids,” he said softly, refusing to acknowledge the plea in Trisha’s eyes. Carrying an ache that weighed like cement, he turned on his heels and left.

CHAPTER 8
DECEMBER

The scent of pine boughs filled the lobby. Red and green candles were clustered on several tables. Angel figurines of various sizes danced across the broad fireplace mantle. A massive Scotch pine, sparkling with tinsel, old-fashioned lights and antique glass ornaments, crowded the right bay window. It was a magical scene straight from a women's magazine, with Christmas a week away.

Megan barely gave it a glance as she traipsed through, lugging a bag of groceries, her feet making wet prints on the thick new Oriental rug. Roger trailed behind, whining about some toy he'd wanted at the store. Huffing, she passed down the hallway to the kitchen, a marvel of bluestone counter tops, glass-fronted oak cabinets, sparkling white appliances, built-in microwave and convection ovens and a commercial gas stove. Her collection of blue-patterned teacups perched on a ladder of tiny shelves on either side of a pair of windows that overlooked the back yard. A big old square farm table, surrounded by eight ladder-back chairs, took up the near end of the room. Under it was a thick braided rug in many shades of blue.

Like every Saturday morning since they'd moved in, she'd managed to pry Roger from his cartoons to endure the obstacle course of grocery shopping. For an eight-year-old kid, he had the most limited diet, with ketchup his primary consumable vegetable. Today, he'd badgered her about junk food, candy and toys from the moment they'd left the house.

"I said I'm not buying you any crap today, so stop asking." She dropped the bag onto the nearest counter; barely seeing his screwed up face, ready to howl. Her vision blurred as she backed from the counter and clasped her abdomen against a particularly vicious kick from within. If this was a preview of coming attractions, she was in big trouble. One ornery kid was bad enough—two would incite a rebellion. She wasn't up for this.

"What is it, Auntie?" Roger asked, his anxiety reaching her as nothing else did these days. She looked over her girth into huge blue eyes.

"Sorry sweetie," she said and sighed. "I'm just not myself today." She ruffled his hair, wishing she were in bed with the shades drawn. "It's not your fault, and you know it." Seeing him eye her swollen mid section, she reached into a bag, pulled out a bag of chocolate chip cookies and ripped it open.

"Take two," she said, smiling. He was, after all, a good kid who knew how to entertain himself and rarely complained.

"One for each hand," they said together and laughed. It had been one of Val's pet phrases.

"Thanks," he said with a shy smile that warmed her deep inside. She turned away first, ready to cry, reminded that he was her kid now, brattiness included. She couldn't imagine life without him.

"Pour a glass of milk while I put this food away," she said gruffly. "A lady's coming to look at the apartment any minute." Tears pricked her eyes as she reached into the grocery bag. Roger had sneaked into her heart smile by smile; but it wasn't supposed to have been this way. She was too young for this kind of responsibility. He should have his mom still; and now here she was carrying his little cousin. How was she supposed to cope?

She was stowing a carton of eggs in the refrigerator when the doorbell rang. She glanced at the clock on the wall, washed her hands, then wiped them on a towel. The prospective tenant was ten minutes early.

"Race ya," she said to Roger, who then stuffed a cookie in his mouth and sped past her through the apartment and to the main door. Laughing, she ambled as fast as she could. He grabbed the door ahead of her and struggled with it. "Let me," she said, when it wouldn't budge.

The door swung back on its well-oiled hinges and they both gasped. A woman who could have been Val's twin stood in the doorway.

"Mommy!" Roger cried and started to go to her.

"Roger, no!" Megan grabbed his arm and hauled him back. He whimpered, pressing against her side.

"Who are you?" Megan scanned the woman, holding Roger close.

She looked harried, distracted, on the verge of tears. At closer inspection, Megan noted designer clothes that Val could never have afforded. An adorable little girl, around five or six years old, clung to her leg. Behind them were two gangly boys, around eleven or so, probably twins, looking bored.

"Is he all right?" the woman asked, her voice deep. She sounded moneyed, educated and snob-bish.

"Yeah," Megan said and cupped Roger's head. "I'm Megan Rosswell." She extended a hand.

The woman took it stiffly. "Kathy Clark," she said. "I've come to look at the apartment."

"Sure," Megan said, anxiety pricking the back of her neck. Kathy Clark? She knew that name. But how? "Just a moment," she added, then turned, shielding Roger. His eyes were full of questions.

"We'll talk about it later," she whispered, seeing his closed in, stubborn expression. "You watch TV while I show the apartment."

"Do you have to?" He shot the woman a dark

look. "This is too weird."

She nodded, then opened their door.

"Why does she look like Mom?" he whispered. "And the girl. She looks like Letty, and it's freaking me out."

"I know," she said, rolling her eyes, "but we have to rent that apartment." He nodded slightly, an old man's gesture that reminded her of Pa. "I'll find out what I can," she whispered.

He moved inside, his backward glance mistrustful.

"Sorry about that," she said, turning to Kathy with a shrug. "You look like someone he knew. He'll be okay."

"Is there anything . . .?" Kathy was wringing her hands.

"No. Shall we proceed?" Megan held out a hand toward the second apartment and smiled slightly. Val's death and her relationship to Roger was none of this woman's business. She affected a calm expression; ignoring the sympathy in her eyes that told her she must have read the local papers; then began describing the lobby.

ଓଓଓଓଓ

For the next half-hour, Kathy followed Megan through the spotless apartment. The rooms were freshly painted, the oak floors gleaming, the light fixtures new. She paused at the threshold of largest bedroom, a lovely space that would make a quiet retreat, imagining her queen-sized sleigh bed against the left wall and two blue brocade chairs around a small table near the windows. She toyed with her purse strap absently, enjoying the play of light and shadow that crossed the room as clouds moved overhead.

The apartment was spacious and comfortable. It was perfect. Like all the other landlords, however, Megan would probably find some reason to dismiss her and her kids. Never in her life had she had to look for a place to live. After her wedding, she'd moved from her parents' home in the Back Bay into a sparkling Cape Cod her husband had purchased in Marlboro—just as he'd selected all the homes in which they'd lived. Her job had been to decorate, manage the servants, be decorative and produce the requisite children—in that order. She'd been watching Megan closely for clues, trying to determine what she was looking for in a tenant. This apartment was miles above the others they had traipsed through that day.

"This color's almost golden," she said, touching the wall reverently, imagining floral paintings and sheers at the windows.

"Yes, it's a soft color," Megan murmured, her gaze taking in the three children, causing Kathy to study her offspring more closely. In the past few weeks, she'd paid them scant attention; and there they were looking like angels, their blond hair ethereal in the streaming sunlight.

Her eyes watered. How could she possibly care

for them alone? They were four wounded darlings whose lives had been irrevocably changed by weak and selfish parents. Before the divorce, she'd had nannies and maids and time on her hands. Now she couldn't make ends meet, and was racing from one errand to the next. She'd be damned if she'd run begging to her mother.

"Come on children, let's keep going," she said, and gestured for them to follow her into a second, equally charming bedroom. She took Bethany by the hand, reminded that she'd told them that apartment hunting would be fun—a few hours at best. And it would have been.

She grimaced as the boys trooped past. If only Adam had paid the nanny, or if Andrea hadn't chosen this day to run off with her friends, when she needed her to baby-sit. She wanted to throttle that girl.

"Mom, we're missing our game," Noah whispered, pulling on her sleeve.

"I'm sorry," she said, glancing at her watch, seeing that he was right, wishing she could be anything but the focus of her children's frustration. Even Noah, her calm one, his dear face a copy of Adam's, was furious with her. Nicholas, his face more angular and masculine, shot her a scathing look before turning back to the window.

"Mommy," Bethany pulled on her hand. She was grabbing her privates. "I need the bathroom."

"Okay, Bethany," Kathy sighed. "Down the hall?" she asked Megan.

"I'll show her," Megan offered, her eyes filled with humor. She held out a hand and Bethany took it. The two left without a backward glance.

"Mum, we can't miss another game," Nicholas whined.

"I told you five times that it's not my fault," she snapped, hating the shrill in her voice, yet was unable to stop. "Your sister was supposed to baby-sit. She could have walked you to the game. But, as usual, she's run off with her friends."

In a totally male, devastatingly unconscious imitation of their father, the two shrugged then turned back to the window.

"Fine. Be that way," she muttered, wishing they'd go live with their father—all of them. But then Adam would win; and no way would she let him take her kids along with her home. The thought of them living happily ever after with that Columbian woman was enough to make her want to end it all, here and now.

"Mommy!" Bethany skipped into the room as if she'd been away for hours.

"Thank you so much," Kathy said, her expression softening as she hugged her little girl.

ઉઉઉઉઉ

"No problem," Megan said with a tight smile. Bethany's resemblance to Letty was like a spike in her throat. For a long moment, she just looked at Kathy, wondering how to begin. There was something familiar about her, and not just her resemblance to Val. It was her name and her kid's names. "Where do you live now?" She folded her arms across her chest and backed away, disturbed by familiarity of the twin's angry faces.

Kathy raked a hand through her hair, mussing it slightly. "Let me be frank," she said, and raised her chin. "This is the fifth apartment we've seen today, and by far the most spacious. I have no idea what you want for rent, but it's tough being a single mother with four children. One look at us and suddenly every decent apartment is spoken for. Do we stand a chance?"

Four? For some reason Megan imagined the forth was a teenage girl. Then Adam Clark came to mind and her breath caught. Of course. The twins looked just like him.

"Do you have any references?" she asked, wishing she had more tenants from which to choose. The other prospect was a pair of male college students—a definite bad risk.

"I'm the ex-wife of a Smith Labs Vice President and a once-active member of the Green Knoll Tennis Club in Andover," Kathy said, standing a little taller. "I graduated second in my class from Leslie College. I . . . I've never been questioned about my character in my life."

She was Adam's *ex*-wife. That ought to be interesting.

"You're a mom," Kathy pleaded, misreading her look as rejection. "You obviously want what's best for your child. I've seen tenements today that shouldn't house a cat. I've seen—"

"So what's the problem?" Megan asked, taking a step forward. "Why can't you answer my questions? I need references and I need to know where you're living."

Kathy began to cry. With a few simple gestures, she gathered her children around her. Megan narrowed her gaze, saying their names in her head. Kathy. Andrea. Bethany. Noah. Nicholas. Adam had told her all about them.

"My divorce is almost final," Kathy said, swiping at her tears, her face taut with exhaustion. "Our home in Andover is under agreement. In two weeks we'll be homeless." She put her hands to her hips. "So whom should I use as a reference? My soon-to-be ex-husband, who already has a luxury condo in Wellesley; one of my ex-tennis partners, who won't return my phone calls; or my dear mother who'd like me under her thumb in Boston?"

"I work at Smith Labs," Megan said, trying to sound bland. There'd been rumors about Adam for months concerning a Hispanic woman he'd met in Miami, the sister of one of Smith Lab's biggest Miami customers.

"Do you know Adam Clark?" Kathy asked.

Megan looked away as blood rushed to her face. She rubbed her chin, struggling for words as memories of Chicago came flooding back.

"As a matter of fact, I do," she said, her stomach churning as she looked at Kathy directly. "My sympathies," she said, eying her kids. It was wrong to cast aspersions on their father, but what else could she say—that she'd slept with him? And here she was about to make another big mistake.

"How could I turn you away?" she asked softly, wanting to weep with her. She clasped her hands before her, knowing that they were tied. "Of course I'll rent to you, Kathy. You'll make a fabulous tenant."

CHAPTER 9

JANUARY 1984

Megan stomped through the lobby, gripping her purse under her arm, pulling a sobbing Roger by the hand. Her breath came in gasps. She was ungainly and huge, like a Weeble toy, ready to topple at the slightest push. Muted light filtered in through the lobby's half-closed blinds, closing out the sight of snow, freshly fallen and the bright azure sky. She was supposed to be at work, sneaking peeks at nature's bounty at odd moments. But Roger's school had called, asking her to come get him. If he wasn't so cute, she'd throttle him.

She'd gone to work that morning with an inexplicable lightness of spirit. She was feeling better than she had in weeks. How naïve she'd been, thinking she'd get a break just because she was pregnant. Women—especially the pregnant ones—were treated like dog-meat in the business world.

Stan was coming that evening to check the furnace and a host of other things. She hadn't seen him for weeks—he'd called instead. Last night on the phone, she'd actually made him laugh; and he'd sneaked in a question about how she was feeling—as if he cared. She and Roger had laughed over their donuts that morning, almost giddy with Stan's impending visit. How pathetic.

Hell, it was supposed to have been be a great day, a productive day; but by ten o'clock, her rose-colored world had gone to crap. Like every Thursday, she'd arrived at the dark-paneled Boardroom early for the database project meeting, clutching her status report, grabbing a good seat at the massive conference table. The room had been packed with twenty business-suited men and three equally tough women. The meeting had been boisterous and jocular—like always. Then halfway through, her boss's secretary, Trudy had pranced in looking for her.

"It's the school nurse," she'd trilled, casting hot glances at some of the men; not having the sense God gave a horse to pass the message to her on a slip of paper. In front of everyone, she'd explained how Roger and another boy had soaked themselves in a bathroom water fight, and were suspended for the day. Steve Grant had pumped her for details, getting a good look at her cleavage, seemingly interested.

She'd known better. Her fury rising, she'd barely been able to breathe.

"Damn women; they should stay at home with the kids," Steve had whispered to Adam upon Trudy's exit, just loud enough for Megan to hear. At the beginning of the meeting, Steve had smoked a finely carved pipe that smelled suspiciously like marijuana; but at that moment it reeked of cheap tobacco.

Turning in disbelief, she'd caught Steve's gloating, self-righteous look, full of loathing, as if she were a bug needing to be squashed. She'd risen from the table, wanting to shout that Adam never visited his own children, who happened to live under her roof.

Adam had snickered; and she'd looked away, refusing to lose control in front of the other women who were busy feigning disinterest. She'd held back tears and straightened her aching spine.

"Freaking bitches," she muttered and shoved her key into the apartment door. In her absence, they'd probably nailed her to the wall. Sans husbands and kids, they were married to the job. She dropped Roger's hand, wishing he were in his room, safe from her rage. She had all she could do to keep from exploding.

Suddenly, laughter bubbled up from her throat at the image of Roger's devilish joy the day he'd bested Tommy at checkers. How could she stay mad at the kid? He was full of mischief, all she had left of her sister's family and *her* kid now—all hers.

Big eyes peered through thick, smeared glasses—filled with hurt. “You’re mad at me again, Auntie.”

“It’s not your fault,” she whispered, then sighed, her shoulders sagging. He was a little boy, after all—a very smart little boy. So he was having a little fun? Was it a crime?

“It’s okay,” she said, and laid a gentle hand on his head, acknowledging that she needed him as much as he needed her. In truth, her pregnancy was killing her career.

“You’re always mad at me,” he said, then began to cry. She knelt down, not caring that she’d never be able to get up again, and pulled him into her arms.

“I’m really sorry,” she said, wishing things were different. “I’m a god-awful mom. And now I have had another kid on the way and nary a man in sight who gives half a damn.” She turned; hearing someone call her name; then rose with all the dignity she could muster, clutching Roger for support.

“Megan?” Book in hand; Kathy rose from a seat by the window. “I’ve been meaning to speak with you.” She frowned, seeing Roger, her expression making her look too much like Val. “Maybe this is a bad time,” she said softly.

Suddenly it was all too much and Megan began to cry. She sagged against the door. Like a limp doll, she sobbed as Kathy took her key, ushered her inside and seated her at the kitchen table. Through a fog of tears, she watched Kathy hustle Roger to the living room, turn on the TV and hand him some cookies. Then, unable to contain her grief any longer, she folded her arms on the table, rested her head on her arms and sobbed.

Several minutes must have passed, for when she looked up, there was a plate of cookies before her and a steaming mug of tea at her elbow. She took the mug and sipped, drawing comfort from its sweetness and warmth.

"Eat something," Kathy said, "It'll make you feel better." She sat across from her looking smug, stirring her tea. Megan bit into a cookie, remembering the day Val had rescued her. It seemed like years ago. And Kathy wasn't Val.

"You must miss her very much," Kathy said over her mug.

"You know about my family?" Megan glanced toward the living room, not wanting Roger to hear. Hopefully, he was engrossed in his show.

Kathy nodded slowly. "After Roger's initial reaction, I did some research. The story wasn't hard to find. I'm truly sorry I look so much like Valerie. It must be painful for both of you." She leaned closer. "Why on earth did you rent to us? Bethany looks just like Letty, for heaven's sake."

"Yeah, Letty," Megan whispered, and put a hand over one eye, her other arm cradling her elbow. "I . . . I knew of Adam's reputation. I . . . just felt sorry for you. And your resemblance to Val . . .. It wasn't just one thing. I—"

"You slept with him," Kathy said, her tone flat.

Megan eyed her, warmth flooding her face. "It was during a trip, a one time thing," she said, surprised at the clarity of her words. "It meant nothing. He moved on to someone else the very next day."

"It's okay, you know," Kathy said with a shrug. "That's the way he is: incapable of being faithful to one woman. It took me years to realize it."

Megan looked at her closely. Her tone was matter-of-fact; but the way she flattened her lips and wrinkled her brow spoke of serious pain.

"He slept with half the women at the country club," Kathy said, with the hint of a smile. "Last year for about two months, a different woman called each day. Let's see . . . there was Cindy from Seattle, and then Libby from Salt Lake City and a lot of other names I don't remember." She smiled grimly. "He's an addict, really, and a predator."

"I—" Megan choked.

Kathy laughed harshly, then patted her arm. "Don't worry about it, my dear. You're lucky you didn't fall in love with him like I did. Look at you, pregnant and not liking it, renting to an ex-lover's ex-wife, trying to raise your grieving nephew while you're grieving, too." She clasped her wrist. "Your baby didn't cause these problems, though you'd love to blame her."

"Her?" Megan covered her abdomen and shook her head. "I'm not blaming anyone, and how do you know it's a girl?"

Kathy sat back in her chair, looking altogether too pleased with herself. "It was the same with

Bethany." She picked up a cookie. "I was seven months pregnant when I learned that my so-called country club friends were sampling my husband; or maybe it was the other way around. I didn't want another baby. I wanted a husband who loved me, a lover who needed me. He'd promised to be faithful so many times; and I didn't want another one of his babies."

"But you love Bethany," Megan said, picturing them hugging and laughing. Of all Kathy's kids, Andrea was the lost soul, the one who gave her the worst of it—not Bethany. "And you stayed with him."

"Until Carlotta," Kathy said, and smoothed her hair back, a seemingly nonchalant gesture that Val had affected when worried. "The others were passing attractions, but Carlotta was different from the onset. For some reason, she expected marriage."

Megan closed her eyes, wanting nothing to do with Kathy's problems. She didn't even have the strength to deal with her own. She rubbed her forehead, behind which fatigue had settled in.

"Please try to love your baby," Kathy said, and Megan looked up, seeing her earnestness. "You're all she has. Even now, she feels your distance. Don't let your husband's—"

"Ex-husband."

"Ex-husband." Kathy nodded. Tears glimmered in her eyes. "Well . . . at least you have Stanley, and he's wonderful."

"I do not *have* Stanley," Megan said, hating that

her hands trembled, hating that the man she loved had no clue how she felt about him.

"Oh, I see," Kathy said, and settled back in her chair. She played with her cookie, methodically breaking it into pieces. "So he's free as far as you're concerned?" Speculation gleamed in her eyes.

"His personal life is none of my business," Megan said, refusing to acknowledge the pain in her words. She shoved away the image of Stan's lips just inches from hers, and the ache she felt whenever he was near. God only knew why she loved him, but she did; and the worst of it was, she had all along.

"If you can crack his shell," she said, raising her mug in a salute, "then good luck to you, Kathy. So what was it you wanted to ask me?"

Kathy looked baffled. Then her face relaxed into a smile. "Oh. I just wanted to know if you could recommend a good hairdresser." She patted her hair, which did look a bit scruffy. Her roots were obvious, though she'd always thought the color was natural, as Val's had been.

Megan repressed a grin, wondering how Trish would like this latest referral. In the past several months, all of her friends and acquaintances had switched—to the absolute best hairdresser she'd ever known.

ଔଔଔଔଔ

Dawn peeked over the tops of the cookie cutter

houses, ranches most of them, lined up in straight rows, a tight grid of American dreams within commuting distance of downtown Chicago. Don paused before a deceptively modest-looking two-story, seeing the glint of sparkling windows, drawn shades, white Christmas lights tastefully draped across the hedge that bordered the front of the property—nothing too flashy. Dad's dark blue Caddy was parked in the driveway, with Mom's probably tucked away in the oversized two-car garage. A dog barked a few streets over, but otherwise, all was quiet. The air was frigid, burning his nostrils; the snow about a foot deep, crusted over, yellow at the edges. By the looks of the stuff, it hadn't snowed in at least a week.

He skirted the hedge, sprinted up the walkway and climbed the cement steps. His key still fit. He turned it in the lock.

The entryway was dark and reeked of wool and mothballs. He shined his flashlight at the neat rows of boots to the left, the filled umbrella stand, the hooks from which his parents' coats hung, and smiled faintly. There wasn't a trace of dust or grime, attesting to his mother's obsessive presence. She'd keep the peace, no matter what. He hung his parka on an empty hook, slipped off his boots and padded inside.

He climbed the stairs to his room, two at a time, catlike, toting his backpack in one hand, avoiding the steps that creaked. A glance told him that his father wasn't home—most likely on assignment. His mother's light shone beneath her door. She was terrified of sleeping alone. Only with Dad present, would she let down her guard.

His brother, Colin was sprawled across his bed, shoes still on, lips slack, looking half-baked. He was going nowhere fast, a derelict at twenty-three—a parents' worst nightmare come true. He'd flunked out of three colleges and couldn't hold a job. Drugs held him, heroin the worst of it. He'd confided once that he'd do any drug, any time; and that life couldn't get any better than getting a buzz on. There'd been a time when he tried to talk sense into him; but now, he realized, the kid had a point.

He slipped into his old room—one of five bedrooms in the sprawling house, testament to his mother's perpetual hope for a thriving family. With Brad buried somewhere in Vietnam, and Jeff gay, she was wishing for the unattainable. Sometimes life didn't follow one of her neat little quilting patterns. Not that he was complaining about a place to stay. His landlord in Miami must have auctioned off his furniture by now.

He sighed as he eased down on the wing chair by the window, surveying his little domain: his childhood bed, covered in yellow chintz, the bookcase with his Hardy Boy's collection, the Stones poster above a polished pine dresser, each item lovingly packed and unpacked with each move to Dad's latest assignment. It was as if by freezing time at 1972, Mom could bring her oldest son back from the grave.

Admittedly, Bradley Steven Alexander the third had been the best of them—a West Point Graduate, tops in his class. Fragging had done him in—his own men taking exception to his arrogance. Don laughed harshly, thinking of the rope burn scars on his shins. Brad had never taken kindly to disagreement—even when deciding who'd be the cowboy and who'd be the Indian.

Then there was good old Jeff, the best friend he'd ever had, another West Pointer, who somehow liked to poke other men, getting himself discharged for lewd and lascivious acts with his commanding officer. No wonder Dad shipped out so often.

He rubbed his face with both hands, wondering how he'd gotten so smart all of a sudden; especially with all the brain cells he'd killed in the last few months. Like Dad said, he'd turned into a big fat zero, a waste of human breath. His mission was a failure, smuggling getting him nowhere. He saw no one now except peons, at both pick up and delivery. If only he could up the stakes, connect with someone higher in the food chain. If only he could nail those bastards who were stealing the souls of America's youth. Trouble was, the government was involved, and at high levels. It would be an act of suicide to perform his job.

He moaned, seeing no out. Then he chuckled, thinking of something Megan had once said, though it wasn't especially funny—something about needing stronger medicine. That was an understatement. A night watching the tip of Ernesto's knife slice through a few innocents had cured him for good. Being in too deep was no longer an option. He had to bag that sucker and the monsters above him. If only he could stop using.

His shoulders sagged as his thoughts turned to Megan. Life had been whole lot simpler before he'd met her; though none of what had happened had been her fault. He'd had his friends, his drinking, his flights, his apartment; and Mom always waiting at the end of a flight with a cold drink and his favorite meal. Loving Megan had been like diving into a pool of butterscotch pudding, one of his favorite desserts. Sweet and mellow; she'd made him forget that he was second best, the replacement son. No one could step into Brad's damn shoes.

He heard a sound at the door and looked up.

"Home again?" his mother asked. She hung onto the doorframe, wearing a floating, pale blue number. Her short blond hair looked freshly combed. She toyed with her sash.

He nodded, seeing the worry around her eyes, the fatigue in the set of her mouth. "Dad been away long?" he asked, sitting back in his chair.

"Three weeks," she said, her lower lip trembling. "Can I fix you something to eat?" She looked at him expectantly, a Harriet Nelson look-alike.

He shook his head slowly, biting back a reply. No questions, no hassles? She continued to amaze him. He could be a murderer for all she knew—yet she wanted to feed him, as if he'd just stepped off the bus from high school. He'd been away for six friggin' months and nothing had changed.

"Any mail?" he asked. He'd had his mail forwarded to Miami at first, hopelessly optimistic. Then the real estate deal had fallen through and he'd had nowhere to light—except home.

"In your top drawer," she said, nodding at the dresser. She started to leave, a puzzled expression on her face, then turned back. "Someone called a few months ago." She wrung her hands, looking worried. "It was a woman, claiming to be your wife. She was in Chicago on business, she said. Her name was Mary or Margaret or something like that."

"Megan?" he asked, his eyes narrowing. "When was this?" He reached into the top drawer and pulled out the stack of mail. An official-looking envelope caught his attention. He ripped it open.

He glanced at his mother, his shock at what he'd read too much to take in. She was looking off to the left, trying too hard to remember, her lips screwed up. Prozac kept her passive, stupid, accepting—the perennial happy mother of four precocious boys.

"It was April or May," she replied with a nod, relief filling her face that she'd remembered. "Do you know her?"

"That was my wife, Mom; and now apparently, my ex-wife." He raked a hand through his hair, some small part of him noting the chagrin on her face. He picked up another envelope, this one from the private detective he'd hired, ripped it open and scanned the letter inside. Megan had paid dearly for her involvement with him, and was still paying. If he had an ounce of compassion, he'd leave her alone.

"I thought her name was Victoria," his mother said, her hands on her hips, anger and puzzlement marring the smooth oval contours of her face. "I thought she lived with you in Miami. Isn't that what you told me?"

"Yeah, Mom," he said softly, seeing his little brother lurch behind her toward the bathroom. "I guess I did." The door slammed closed, but his mother didn't even blink.

He re-read the letter and started to laugh. So he was about to become a dad. That changed everything. Now Megan had even more to lose. It was ironic really, with his parents aching for a grandchild.

"Well, then, what exactly is going on?" His mother stepped into the room, looked behind her, then closed the door. "Can you say?"

He shook his head, remembering from the Vietnam War days, the lengths to which she had gone to protect them from kidnappers or child molesters, her husband's secrecy weighing heavy on her mind. Embroiled in military intelligence, Dad hadn't been free to discuss any aspect of his work with her, including his location. Months would pass when they wouldn't hear from him—the longest time nine months and seven days, to be exact—a slow torture that had left her crying in bed, unable to sleep, terrified of being alone. Sometimes, she'd take one of them into bed with her—usually Brad.

It struck him that he'd inflicted the same slow torture upon Megan; and now she'd dumped him. With a twist of insight that made him gasp, he pictured that horrible moment when he'd run away, thinking he'd killed her. He'd become a monster. Of course, she'd divorced him—a smart woman like that. He smiled faintly. Somehow, he'd left her with a little part of him.

"Donny?"

He looked at his mother fully, seeing a weak woman who'd been tested beyond her endurance; seeing the mother he'd once adored. "Her name's Megan Rosswell," he said softly, wishing his mother loved him back. "Telling you that story was for her protection; though it did no good, apparently. The wrong people know all about her."

"Are you okay?"

He laughed harshly, trying to picture Megan swollen with his child. She was probably pissed as hell. She'd never wanted kids. "Depends on your definition of okay," he managed to say.

Her face fell: he couldn't bear it.

"Things are happening right now, Mom," he said quickly, then stood and stretched, the room now painfully small. He took several deep breaths, crossed his arms over his chest, suddenly desperate for air. He leaped to the window, unlatched it and threw it open, the frigid air like glass shards down his throat.

"I'm on an assignment that's a little tricky," he said over his shoulder, wishing he could tell her the truth. For all she knew, he still flew for Airlius, his home base Miami. "I was hoping to bring Megan to visit in a few weeks, maybe meet the relatives. But it just didn't work out." He smiled brightly.

"What kind of assignment?" She sat on the edge of the bed, a fragile fairy facing a dreaded dragon, her violet eyes wide and fearful. "Like your father's?" Her voice was barely audible, her smile brittle.

He could only nod. There was no use going into the sordid details. He didn't even know half of them himself. She could set a table for a banquet; but the world of war and men was as foreign to her as the pits of hell.

ଓଓଓଓଓ

Early evening softened the edges of the kitchen. The shades were drawn against winter's dark. Gilded Christmas candles set in brass holders flamed on the table. Megan stood at the stove, stirring a pot of meatballs, humming an old hymn. There was garlic bread on the counter, ready to pop in the oven, a tossed salad in the fridge and a pot of water for the spaghetti, almost at the boiling point. Crashing noises came from the next room where Roger played with his trucks. A smile tugged at her mouth at his shout of joy; and then came the low rumble of Stan's teasing. He was finally here.

Months ago, she'd given him a key to the house, so he could let in subcontractors and fix things at will. Now, with the apartments finished, he rarely stopped by. She spoke to him at least once a week by phone, asking pesky questions about toilets, air ducts and leaky pipes—mainly to hear his voice. And each month, by unspoken agreement, they shared a meal in exchange for a furnace check.

"He's here!" Roger cried and she looked up. Boy and man were framed in the doorway: the boy aloft the man's broad shoulders, his face swallowed in a grin: the man, looking like a dream.

"So I see," she said, ignoring the tug at her heart and the hopeless melting way she felt inside. Stan's blue eyes were like beacons against his swarthy skin, unaccountably tender as he looked at her. His gaze was a caress, without the trace of the shame she often caught in Pa's eyes, as if she'd done something wrong. She had, but it wasn't even close to Pa's worst suspicions. To her hopeless shame, every ounce of her disgustingly swollen body ached for this man—even now, as she approached delivery.

Sow, she cursed herself, resisting the urge to hold her abdomen as a painful twinge hit. How could he want her, carrying another man's child? She sighed heavily as she wiped her hands on her apron, then untied it and hung it on the oven handle.

"Food or furnace?" she asked, forcing a smile, wishing things were different, wishing Roger's glee could be her own, wishing her father had been wrong about both Donald and Stan.

"Furnace," he said, not taking his eyes from her.

A flicker of longing sparked and then disappeared. "It smells really good." He lifted his chin, daring her to argue. "You make the best meatballs," he said, his smile too meltingly surreal. She could only stare at him, wondering what he wanted. A strange tension had arisen between them. What business did he have holding Roger like his own child, his face expectant?

"Come on," she said gruffly, and headed toward the back stairs. Tears burned behind her lids. "I think the furnace filter needs replacing, and there's a light switch that's causing power spikes. I've had to flip the breakers twice today. Switch three." For some reason, she looked back. His eyes sparkled with amusement, and something that looked too much like admiration.

"A little bossy, don't you think," he said to Roger out of the side of his mouth.

"Are you coming or not!" She itched to stamp her foot; annoyed by the way Roger ducked his head against Stan shoulder, stifling a giggle.

"I'd like to think we're friends," Stan said, humor draining from his face. He dropped Roger gently to the floor, still holding his hand. Swallowing the lump in her throat, she couldn't look away. "I've been in and out of your house and know lots of things about you, Meg. And this guy." He held up Roger's hand. "He's like my own."

"And?" She glared at him.

"It's not like you're in any position to date," he said, scanning her abdomen.

"Touché," she said, taking a sharp breath, wanting to slap him. "So, what about it?" She planted a fist on one hip and cocked her head. "It's not like I asked for this." She nodded at her abdomen. "It's not like I had a choice. And besides, you never looked twice when I was single."

"I didn't say—"

"You never say!" she shouted, unable to stop herself. "That's the whole damn problem, Stanley Zambinsky. You're so stuck in neutral on past failures; you can't see that I'm fifty times better than Christy Connors, your *ex*-fiancé."

She blinked, ignoring the way he pulled Roger closer as another twinge hit. "You men are all the same," she said, "losers and allies. Who'd want a boring, career woman like me? Hell, Christy wore black lace corsets when I was still playing with Barbies."

"What's a corset?" Roger asked.

"Not now," Stan said, and rolled his eyes toward Roger in warning.

She blanched, seeing Roger's anxious frown. Though nine, he was still small. He was biting his fingers—a bad sign. When would she learn to keep her big mouth shut? "I'm sorry," she said and moved toward him. He buried his face in Stan's side.

"I'll help in any way I can," Stan said, holding Roger close, comforting him. "All you have to do is ask, Meg. You don't even have to do that. You can just point and grunt for all I care. I'm here for you,

Meg, and so's Roger."

Her tears fell unchecked. She held a hand out to Roger, shocked that she'd hurt him.

"Yeah, Auntie, just ask," Roger said, his eyes filled with love, mirroring Stan's.

"The two of you," she spat; then took a deep breath as a particularly painful twinge hit. She sucked in air and held up a hand, sensing the two moving closer. "I'm all right. I'm all right," she said, waving them away. "I just asked if you'd look at the damn breaker box." She gasped at another kick, this time harder. "If you're hungry, we'll eat. If you can wait, we'll look downstairs." She glared at Stan and Roger in turn. "Now, which is it?"

"I want you to sit down right now," Stan said, his eyes filled with concern. "I'll make the spaghetti."

"Please, Auntie." Roger moved quickly, took her hand and pulled her toward the table. His eyes were clear behind his glasses. "We'll serve you tonight. I can't wait for your meatballs."

She stared at them in shock. Her harsh words hadn't fazed them in the least. Nodding, she slid into a chair.

CHAPTER 10
FEBRUARY

Megan looked up into the nurse's kindly face. With a halo of soft brown curls and an impressive bosom, Mary Jones, as it said on her name pin, was an angel in disguise. She bustled around, shifting blankets and sheets, smoothing her nightgown, clucking over the baby. She was middle-aged, maybe late forties, her face barely lined, as if she lived life joyfully. At the far end of the two-bed room, Kathy pulled the floor-to-ceiling curtain closed with a dull rip, shutting out the sun.

Megan closed her eyes. She was bone tired, yet blessedly pain-free due to the wonder of painkillers. A mere three hours ago, she'd banged on Kathy's door, her pains too close, her overnight bag yet unpacked. She should have called the doctor sooner.

She should have called 911. She should have been at the hospital hours before. But she'd wanted to finish cleaning and savor the sweet memory of Stan's warm hand on her back and his lips against her forehead. Alone. In peace. Without Roger's incessant chattering. How many times had she told him that Stan wasn't the marrying kind; that he was just a friend?

"Next time don't wait so long," Kathy whispered after the nurse left with a pile of used sheets. "Next time, you won't make it."

"Next time?" Megan sneered, and then looked down, seeing her little daughter snuggled against her breast. Penny, she'd called her, for Penelope. She was a lovely, red-face screamer, with a thatch of blonde curls and her grandmother, Helen's chin. Her last name was Rosswell. No way would Donald claim any part of her.

"At least she doesn't look like my ex," she said and smiled at Kathy, who smiled back indulgently. "How the hell did you do this three freaking times?"

Kathy laughed, then shifted to the hallway, in search of her kids.

Megan studied Penny, her heart melting, seeing the deep blue eyes of a newborn, the thick pale lashes. When the baby snuffled, then closed her eyes, she let out a long, hissing sigh, exhaustion's bony fingers tightening inside her head. It barely registered when someone took the baby from her arms, and threw a blanket over her. She burrowed into her pillow.

"Rest now," she heard a voice say, then all went dark.

ઌઌઌઌઌ

Small sounds filled her head. She opened her eyes and let the room swim into focus. It came to her slowly that she was in a hospital room, the other bed vacant. She moved slightly and winced, reminded by the burn and pinch that she'd just delivered.

"Where is she?" she shouted, choking down panic until her hand gripped the bassinet that stood beside her bed. Ignoring the pull and throb of her bottom, she shifted around to look at Penny, who lay heavily swaddled, making soft grunting sounds. "Oh, there you are," she whispered, and lifted her with trembling hands. She smelled sweet and powdery; she weighed nothing. It was then that she saw the dark shape of a man against the window, his face shadowed by the window's glare. Fury filled her and she held her baby close. One hand groped for the nurse's call button.

"Donald?"

The man moved forward and she gasped, recoiling from the hurt on Stan's face. Shame fisted the pit of her stomach. She had to be crazy. It was hormones, probably. Donald was long gone, out of her life forever.

"I'm so sorry," she whispered, but it was too late. Would she ever get her timing right with Stan?

"It's okay, Meg," he said, his soul in his eyes. When he shook his head slightly, she burst into tears and hid her face in her hair.

"I'm so sorry," she kept saying, clinging to Penny's sweet weight like a lifeline. "How could I have been so stupid?" Of course it was Stan who'd come to see her, not Donald. Never Donald.

"It's okay, sweetheart," she heard him say; then his arms came around her and Penny. He was incredible warm; making her feel safe and wanted. "It's okay," he whispered as he stroked her hair. With her head tucked into the crook of his neck, she wondered how, in spite of everything, she'd kept her love for him a secret.

"What did he do that makes you so afraid?" he asked, then handed her a napkin he peeled from a wad in his pocket. It was the stiff kind from a fast-food restaurant. It scratched her face as she wiped her eyes.

"Thanks," she said and took a shuddering breath, not quite believing he cared. Had he just called her sweetheart?

"Donald's into drugs," she said, looking up quickly. "He's flying for some Columbian drug lord—smuggling, actually. He wanted me to join him, but I wouldn't and then Penny . . .." She looked down at her daughter, trying to swallow a thick immovable lump, unable to continue.

"What happened?" he asked, the pain in his eyes indicating that he already knew.

"He raped me," she whispered.

"Penny?"

She nodded, acknowledging his sigh, then hung her head and let him rub her shoulders for a good long while, until she could look at him without the urge to cry.

"May I?" He held out a hands. Not thinking twice, she passed him the baby, her heart swelling at the tenderness on his face. He cradled her, not at all the typical awkward male when it came to newborns. An image flashed of Tom holding Tommy, newborn and squalling, a man unafraid of his child.

"You have kids or something?" she asked, pain lancing her heart. His being a dad would explain a lot.

"No," he said, and smiled, making her heart beat a little faster. She wanted to laugh aloud, but hid her joy beneath stern approval.

"I have two nieces and a nephew," he said, "My brother's kids. I baby-sit from time to time. At least I used to." Sadness crossed his face.

"Then there's Roger," she said, trying to hide her confusion. What was she asking him?

"Yeah, Roger." He looked at her intently. "He's had it rough; but I can't make up for him losing Tom."

"No one asked you to." The words burst out, and she regretted them instantly, seeing his annoyance. When would she stop being so defensive?

He took a deep breath, his eyes narrowed, and then he chuckled. "Nothing's easy with you, is it, Meg?" He shook his head. "You've had chips on your shoulders since you were a kid visiting your Dad's garage."

"What do you know about it?" She stuck out her lower lip, feeling foolish.

"I was there. I saw you." He flashed a goofy, lopsided grin.

"You watched me?" Her heart was pounding.

Just then, Penny awoke with a piercing cry, her muscles tensed in the instant fury of hunger. Megan looked around, desperate for the nurse. She'd studied the videotapes and read all the books, yet nothing had prepared her for baring her breasts in Stan's presence.

"She's hungry," he said, his eyes twinkling as he eyed her breasts.

Her face burned as she held out her arms and he filled them with Penny. With a quick movement, she opened her gown and helped Penny's mouth to an engorged nipple; tensing at first as pain turned to relief and then pleasure. She looked up, surprised by Stan's expression—a mix of tenderness, lust and longing.

"What?" She laughed, wanting to kiss his sunburnished face.

They turned at the sound of tromping feet—a herd of giggling elephants—Roger preceding Kathy and her brood into the room, his face flushed with excitement.

"Where's my cousin?" he cried, eyeing Megan warily. He ran to Stan and looked up at him, his glasses badly smudged. "Well, where is she?"

Megan tried not to laugh, seeing his eyes riveting to her breast, then his face flame. Then the twins piled in, prodding Bethany, making her squeal; with Andrea bringing up the rear, looking surprisingly eager.

"Where is she? Where is she?" they all shouted; then ground to halt, as each child realized where the baby was. The boys rolled their eyes and started to leave, until Kathy corralled them.

"Are we a family now?" Roger asked, taking Stan's arm. Megan caught Kathy's wry look, her swift predatory appraisal of Stan, and his helpless shrug.

"He's just our friend, remember," Megan said wanting laugh at the way Stan folded his arms across his chest, backed away, then straightened his shoulders as if shaking off a cloud of flies.

"You want to hold your new cousin?" he asked Roger, and winked at Megan.

"Stan?" Megan's face burned. Penny's head was all that kept her breast from view. She was about to retort when her father strolled in. Then before she knew it, the nurse was shooing them all out and taking Penny for tests.

ଔଔଔଔଔ

By mid-April, Megan had interviewed fifteen potential sitters with a dizzying array of rules and settings. Then with pain bordering on trauma, she left Penny in another woman's arms, and walked away, choked with tears. But she'd done it—like plenty of women before her had since time's dawn. There was no special recipe for coping with the loss—except to cry her eyes out and do her damn job.

She stared at the computer screen in her office, grateful for the relative peace and quiet. Penny was a good sleeper; but Roger had been up all night with a bad cold. Thankfully, Pa was home with him. She'd already used up all of her sick time.

"Hi there."

Kathy stood in the doorway brandishing an employee badge.

"You work here now?" Megan asked, mildly surprised, and grateful for a friendly face. Her boss, Jeff, who'd recently made a lateral move back into the management slot above her, had been pushing her like a draft horse; and she needed a break. During her maternity leave, two of Jeff's other supervisors had transferred to field positions, leaving her with a larger crew of resentful support analysts. One had even expected the management slot; and for all she knew, Jeff had promised it. Nevertheless, she had ten more performance appraisals to complete before the weekend; and the problem calls kept rolling in.

It was her job to read each new problem report and assign it based on workload, priority and analyst ability. Hers was the front-end processing, without which the system would grind to halt; with support analysts standing around with their hands in their pockets, or leaving early or taking long, liquid lunches—all duly noted by Jeff—to her detriment. Then there was the database design project. During her absence, Steve Grant had finally realized her value, and now counted on her weekly updates.

"Got time for a quick coffee?" Kathy asked, looking cool and sophisticated in a pale gray suit with a white silk blouse.

Megan looked down at her own drab brown sweater and slacks, wondering how she'd be able to pick up the dry cleaning and do her grocery shopping after work. She had nothing to wear for the rest of the week, and avoidance was not an option. But Penny hated being shoved in and out of her car seat; and wouldn't tolerate more than one stop. Maybe she'd run out at lunchtime, and avoid the issue altogether.

"Sure," she said with a smile, then grabbed her purse and headed with Kathy through the maze of cubicles toward the main hallway. Maybe some women-talk—sans kids—would help clear her head. Kathy had become more of a friend than a tenant, sharing childcare duties and chatting over a hot cup of tea in their warm lobby. Beneath the sophisticated exterior, Kathy was surprisingly warm and accepting.

They were heading down the long ramp that led to the cafeteria when they passed Charlie. He was leaning against the corridor wall, one hand covering his face, looking distracted.

"Ming's with Bob Cartright," Megan said, in answer to the slight rise of his eyebrows. He mumbled thanks as an odd flush filled his face and trailed down his neck. He looked away, his annoyed expression focused on the opaque windows that slanted from floor to ceiling for the entire length of the ramp,.

"I'm not telepathic," she muttered; and wondered at the redness of his eyes and way his left eyelid twitched. Glancing back, she saw Ed Veasey stroll up to him, look around suspiciously, then tap his arm to prod him up the ramp.

Ed and Charlie? Their association made no sense. None of the developers liked Ed; and Charlie, his most vocal critic, called him a damn lazy bastard and worse. As they paused at the top of the ramp, Charlie handed Ed a package and took one in return.

"It's my first day," Kathy gushed, drawing Megan's attention. Her eyes were bright blue and the whites pure, as if she'd had plenty of sleep—in sharp contrast to Charlie's bloodshot pair.

"So, when did this happen?" Megan said and shuddered, thinking she should have followed Charlie to see where he went. He'd been acting strange lately, shutting his desk drawer whenever she approached his cubicle, retracing his steps when he spied her in the hallway. Ming had been avoiding her, too; and her rent was more than a week overdue. Then there was Ed, always looking for an angle. He spent more energy trying to circumvent work than actually doing it.

Kathy was looking at her expectantly.

"Last thing I knew, you were interviewing at

some place in Bedford," Megan said quickly. They turned into the cafeteria. "You said your interview in Burlington had gone badly. That was all of five days ago. So what happened?"

"Well, let me tell you." Kathy's voice dropped to a whisper as they passed a group of suits on their way out. One of them glanced back, giving Kathy the once over, ignoring Megan completely. Kathy flashed him a brilliant smile, making her seethe; though she smiled at Kathy, telling herself that she'd hate that kind of attention.

"I heard about this job from my headhunter the very next day," Kathy said as she plucked at Megan's sleeve, her smile mega-watt bright. "It was a perfect fit, because Smith Labs is forming a fabulous new graphic arts department to produce all of the company's brochures, press releases, book covers—you name it. My new boss, Betty is hot to get started and wants to make a good impression on upper management as quickly as possible. She loved my samples; and being a fellow Leslie graduate, I knew she'd take notice. After all, we've both learned from and competed with the best."

Megan stared at Kathy, stunned by the pretense in her voice and the arrogance in her stance. Her classically beautiful face was so achingly familiar—Val all over again—confidant and sure—more attractive and sophisticated than she'd ever be. She scanned her classy suit, horrified that she'd actually coached her on how to dress last weekend. Leslie College indeed—she should have seen this coming.

Then she chided herself, thinking of the first time she'd met Kathy. The poor woman had been tired, desperate and almost defeated, facing homelessness with four children, a failed marriage and a haughty mother who tried to infantilize her. Kathy had proven to be stronger than any of her challenges—and she wasn't Val.

"I'm glad it worked out for you," she managed to say as she clasped Kathy's arm.

CHAPTER 11

MAY

The elevator door swished open at the twelfth floor. Clenching her teeth, Kathy stepped out and moved across the thickly padded carpet through the open fire doors. She turned left on memory, having visited Adam's office several times before their marriage had flamed into a living hell. Like old times, his secretary, Joan was at her desk outside his office, typing away. Adam's distinctive voice hissed though the open door.

This was a bad idea—really bad. Sweat was already dampening her armpits and her head was starting to ache. It was hard enough taking Adam's weekly call, when he'd insist upon speaking to the kids to cancel yet another outing because of Carlotta. But this was business: her new job was on the line. He'd refused her phone calls; and department policy stated that she must clarify his work request in person. Moreover, Betty had insisted.

"May I help you?" Joan asked with a pleasant, up-state New York accent. Her light brown eyes were cool and aloof. She was a lovely girl, a tall willowy brunette, just out of Katie Gibbs—most unlike the chirpy little blonde, Mimi who'd worked for Adam more than a year ago. Mimi had been sweet and efficient—up until the day she filed that sexual harassment suit.

"I'm here to see Adam," Kathy said, keeping her voice carefully neutral. "I'm from the graphic arts department, working on a slide presentation for him."

"You need an appointment," Joan said, not even glancing at Adam's calendar.

"I'm Kathy Clark," she said in her best imitation of her mother's speaking-to-the-help tone. "I don't need an appointment."

Joan's eyes widened in recognition; and Kathy glared at her. Joan didn't look like the gossiping type, but rumors flew around the building. A light flashed on Joan's telephone, indicating that Adam was on the phone. Joan wrote a few words on a piece of paper, then slipped into his office.

Kathy couldn't help but notice her flattering tweed suit and violet silk blouse. With violet-tipped nails, flawless makeup and expensive perfume, Joan looked and smelled like the ultimate executive secretary. With a heavy sigh, she imagined how she looked in her own Marshall's two-piece special—protective armor over a plain white blouse. She wore no makeup, had clipped her nails short and smelled of Dove soap. She'd pulled her blond hair into a scarf, away from her face. Under Megan's tutelage, she'd vowed to minimize her femininity. It made sense that the wrong kind of attention could kill a woman's career.

Joan returned just as the light blinked out on the telephone console. "You can go in now," she said, then returned to her typing, not even glancing in her direction.

She took a deep breath and forced her legs to move.

"Kathy!" Adam cried, and smiled as he reached behind her to close the door. His overcoat hung on a hook behind it, the same one she'd lugged to the dry cleaners for the past three years. It looked clean and pressed—Carlotta's doing—not that it was any of her business.

"So nice to see you, honey," he said, eying her figure. "I always look forward seeing the greatest love of my life and the mother of my kids. And how are the little darlings?" His nose was red. He dabbed at it with a linen handkerchief, which he then stuffed in his pants pocket.

"Your eldest daughter won't speak to me, the boys look like lost sheep half the time and Bethany cries in her sleep. Not that you give a rat's ass," she said coolly.

"You should have been more discrete," he said, his smile gone. "You didn't have to wave that tennis instructor in Andrea's face. He's only a few years older than she is; and I think she might have dated him."

"We were already separated," she said, clenching her teeth. "You didn't have to highlight my relationship with him in front of the judge. It was over by then. And what about all the women you slept with while we were married? What about Carlotta? How do you think that looks to our almost-grown daughter?"

"Andrea can take care of herself," he said, and blinked fast three or four time, like he always did when he wanted to shift gears. He nodded vaguely, as if talking to himself, until he stood safely behind his desk.

"Look, I'm here about your damn slide presentation," she said and held his gaze until he looked away. "Obviously you don't return your phone calls. It's been ready for your approval for three days."

"Please have a seat," he said, and gestured at an uncomfortable-looking chair in front of his desk.

"I don't think do," she said, then moved to the floor-to-ceiling window across from the desk, knowing it would piss him off. It was clear and cold outside—a lovely spring day. Flags whipped on a flagpole below.

"I see," he said. She turned to him, recognizing one of his macho control tactics in the way he steepled his hands. "So, you're here about my slide presentation?"

"That's what I said." She strode to his desk and slapped his request, a multi-part form, on top of it. "We've defined a standard so that everything from Corporate has the same basic look." She ignored the curl of his lips and the lecherous hunger in his eyes. "The intention is to show the world that we have our act together." She pointed to the form. "I suggest you change what you have here to blue, and move the Smith Labs logo over here. Then your slides will conform. Do you concur?"

"Kathy, Kathy, Kathy," he said, shaking his head as he perused her. "That sad little suit does nothing for your lovely figure. What say you take it off, right here, right now, just for me . . . you know . . . for old times and all? You always took real good care of yourself."

She ripped the form off his desk. "Look Adam," she said, waving it in his face. "I came here to work, nothing more. I am not your damn wife anymore. Or your secretary. Or your next conquest. Unlike your children, I want nothing from you. Do you or do you not agree to the changes?"

Again, he was the first to look away. Moments ticked. His phone rang, but he was busy playing with an expensive-looking pen. Her attention caught on a pair of seagulls flying past the window. They were miles upriver from the ocean, drawn by the Merrimack River. Drawn by what? she wondered idly; and wished she were outside, too, and heading for home.

"Oh, you're no fun," he said, pouting like a child, looking too much like Noah. "Where's the sweet little Kathy who fucked me behind the dunes?" His nose dripped and he wiped at it again.

"Adam," she said softly, capping the rage that burned in her throat. "We are divorced. If you continue to play this game, I'll slap a harassment suit against you, just like Mimi did." His eyes widened almost imperceptibly. "Oh, and I know about Megan, too." She smirked. "Quite awkward, don't you think; considering she's my landlady."

"What do you know about Megan?" he asked. His hand shook as it hovered over the phone. He appeared to be sweating.

"You're little fling in Chicago?" she replied and watched him closely, wondering why he was afraid. "Naomi was right after that. Do you even remember her?"

For some reason, fear drained from his eyes and he started to smirk.

"I can make things bad," she hissed, though she sensed he'd won some edge. "You don't want me to do that, Adam. Not with your big promotion coming in a week or so."

His eyes narrowed this time—another rumor confirmed.

"And your recent engagement." She shook her head and laughed when his mouth opened. "We can work together, you and me; but this foolishness must end."

"Kathy, Kathy, Kathy," he said, his tone conciliatory. "Sure, go ahead, change the slides." He stood, signed the form, then held out his hand. She shook her head and backed away. "Come by any time," he added, his voice now syrupy. "I'll be glad to help in any way I can."

ଓଓଓଓଓ

Head down, Kathy strode to her office. Adam was insufferable, always making her pay for any concession. She was glad for the long walk. It gave her time to think. The new graphic arts department was deep in the bowels of one of the complex's oldest building, tucked under one side of the dusty boiler room. She strode past Betty's desk, refusing to look up, heading to the bank of cubicles.

"You need to take this call," Betty called out. Solid and built like a tank, Betty had once been a sergeant in the military. A person didn't think twice when she commanded.

Kathy turned in surprise, seeing Betty grab her phone, punch in some numbers and bark a few words. She handed Kathy the receiver.

"Kathy, you have to come to the hospital," said an urgent voice. It was Megan.

"Why? What's happened?" Kathy asked, taking mental inventory of her children. Was it the boys or Bethany? They'd all looked fine this morning. Irritation filled her. How was she supposed to keep a job with all these interruptions? And wasn't Megan home with Roger, who had a bad cold?

"It's Andrea," Megan said quietly.

"Andrea?" She pictured her daughter at breakfast that morning, her sullen face and clipped answers to the most innocuous questions. She'd only pretended to eat her toast.

"She's had a miscarriage," Megan said tearfully. "She's in surgery now, Kathy, having a D and C. You have to come. She needs you. She really needs you."

Miscarriage? Kathy mouthed the word. It was for grown women, married woman, not teenage girls, not her daughter. She looked at Betty, seeing her sympathy. Betty and her husband had two grown daughters, both married with small children.

"Lowell General?" she asked, and wanted to die. A knot of pain was forming in the middle of her forehead. Her first-born had been pregnant and she hadn't even known?

"Yes, and Kathy, I'm so sorry," Megan said.

"I'll be there." She slapped down the receiver and turned to Betty. "When did she call?"

"About a half-hour ago." Betty placed a hand on her shoulder. "Just go," she said, looking about to cry. "Just do what you need to do. Work can wait. No matter what, your child needs you."

Lightheaded, Kathy managed to grab her purse.

"Call me," Betty said, her broad face filled with worry.

She could only nod, tears choking her as she began to run. She was halfway to the hospital when she remembered Adam, then promptly forgot him.

ଓଓଓଓଓ

The room was small but private, tucked at the back of the old building, at the end of a long gleaming corridor, away from elated new moms. Megan stood beside the single bed, looking down at Andrea, at a loss for what to say. Engrossed in her own problems, she'd never taken more than a cursory glance at this angry girl. Since the Clark's had moved in, she'd grown used to Andrea's sullen, adult-hating expression. It was kind of the way she'd looked at the same age.

Today however, Andrea looked fragile and incredibly young, with fair porcelain skin and swollen lids. She also looked royally pissed.

"Go ahead and say it," she croaked, her voice hoarse from the breathing tube inserted during surgery. "I was a damn fool."

"So you got caught," Megan said and backed away, shaking her head. "You had sex without protection. You got pregnant. Did you honestly think you could trust him? That he knew what he was doing?" She laughed harshly. "He knew exactly what he was doing. Did you think you were exempt from biology? Do you even know about biology?"

Andrea looked up at the ceiling, her mouth pinched. A tear trickled down the side of her face. For a second, she looked like a very young Val.

"Like I'm perfect," Megan said, then turned away, rubbing her face. She'd known all about biology; yet she'd been caught just like Andrea. But she was a full-grown woman and her baby had survived. "I'm sorry," she said, unable to blame her for the skeptical look. "That was unkind."

"But true." Andrea said and started to cry.

"It's okay to cry," Megan said, moving closer, patting her shoulder. "You're just a kid, whose biggest worry should be getting into the right college. And now you have to deal with this." She sighed as she sat on the bed and pulled the sobbing girl into her arms. Within seconds, Andrea had soaked her expensive silk blouse. But it was worth it. An unexpected joy surged through her as she rubbed the girl's back, seeing her own teenage frustration played out. Finally, it was her turn to be the comforter.

"I'll listen if you want to talk about it," she said softly. "It might help you collect your thoughts before your mom gets here."

"My mom?" Andrea pushed her away and swiped at her tears. "She'll have lots to say—all of it bad."

Megan handed her some tissues from the bedside table. "That's up to you," she said with a shrug. "And maybe you need her. You haven't done such a great job on your own."

"Yeah," Andrea said, her eyes flashing. "She treats me like Bethany half the time, or ignores me, hoping I'll go away. My dad's the only one who really loves me; but he's history."

"You'll always be her kid," Megan said softly. She looked down at her hands. "I've learned a lot since Roger and Penny came into my life."

"Here comes the big speech." Andrea rolled her eyes.

"I have only a few memories of my own mother," Megan said. "She died when I was ten. I thought my father and my older sister, Val, who raised me, were stupid." She looked Andrea in the eye. "I thought they could only see what was wrong with me."

"And?"

"I was right," she said, and her eyes began to well. "They only saw what they needed to fix." She touched Andrea's wrist. "It's my job to care for Roger and Penny; to see that their hair is combed, their bodies and clothes clean, to see that they eat properly. It's not criticism—it's caring." She leaned closer. "Though you're practically an adult, your mom just can't shake the habit."

"She doesn't care!" Andrea yelled, but with a pathetic wobble at the end that reached out to her.

"What if you'd given birth to this baby?" Megan asked. "Do you understand the amount of work you'd be taking on; what you'd be forcing on your mom? Or were you making an adoption plan?"

"I swear I didn't know," Andrea whispered.

"You did know," Megan said, wanting to shake her. "Don't lie to me, Andrea. I've been there. Cool boy, cool parties. And then you wake up sick to your stomach and hope it goes away." Her tone softened. "How long did you know about the baby, Andrea? Not that it's any of my business."

Andrea bit her lip; her eyes filled with pain and panic.

"It's hard to tell the sheep from the wolves, isn't it?" Megan whispered, knowing she had her attention.

"Okay." Andrea looked away. "It was a boy in my class. His name doesn't matter. The first time was at a party, you know—smoking pot, drinking vodka. It was at his house. His parents were in Europe for a week. He said all the kids did it. But it really hurt." Tears filled her eyes.

"It usually does the first time," Megan said, nodding slightly. "But you went back for more, didn't you?" For some reason she looked up and saw Kathy framed in the doorway, her fists clenched at her sides, her look accusing.

"I went to his house every day after school," Andrea said, with a catch to her voice. "I even slept in his room." She twisted the edge of her blanket as if it was someone's arm. "What difference does it make, anyway? My parents are out of control—him sleeping with everything in skirts—her sleeping with one of my ex-boyfriends. They don't even know I exist."

"What will you tell your mother?" Megan asked gently, ignoring the rush of blood to her face—ignoring Kathy.

"Noooo!" Andrea wailed, "I can't." Megan

looked up to see tears streaming down Kathy's face. She gestured her in.

"Someone's here to see you," she said softly; and smiled at Kathy's tentative approach.

"Go away, Mom!" Andrea cried. She turned on her side. "I don't want to see you."

ଔଔଔଔଔ

Kathy looked from Megan to Andrea, accepting childhood's end. Never again would she be blind to her precious first-born, her daughter, her beloved Andrea, who was a grown woman now. She wanted to turn and run; but stopped, seeing Andrea at six, playing the Mommy-do-you-love-me game—a test of wills, a quest for nurturing and acceptance. She moved quickly, pulling her in her arms, throwing Megan what she hoped was a grateful look.

"It's all right," she whispered into her daughter's hair. "I love you no matter what, my darling."

Andrea held her body stiffly at first, and then with a loud bursting sob, nestled her head against Kathy's neck and snuggled close, once again her sweetly needy child.

ଔଔଔଔଔ

Megan stood at the lobby window with Pa, watching Kathy and her brood lugging groceries from the garage to the back door of their apartment; the boys poking each other, shouting and laughing;

Bethany whining, scuffing her black patent leather shoes in the dirt; and Andrea scolding the others to keep up. Kathy laughed as she stuck her key in the lock, her cheeks pink from the lovely spring day.

"Where does she come from?" Pa asked, looking agitated, his gaze directed at Kathy. He had never met her officially. They were always coming and going at different times.

"Boston," Megan replied. "Her mother lives in the Back Bay." She plucked at his sleeve. "What's wrong, Pa?"

He shook his head as he backed away from the window. "Doesn't seem like it could be possible," he muttered, turning to look at her. Sweat beaded his upper lip as if he'd exerted himself. "Life sure has a way of catching up with you," he said, shaking his head.

"What do you mean?" she asked; but he ignored her. He'd been doing that a lot lately—saying things that made no sense, then ignoring her questions. He headed toward her apartment door, and she followed closely, getting irritated.

"Called that chimney sweep yet?" he asked, glancing at the fireplace, the previous subject now closed.

"Yes, Pa, last month," she said, trying, but not quite succeeding, to keep the annoyance from her voice. There had been a time after Val and her family's death when he'd leaned on her and trusted her. Since Penny's birth, however, all that had changed. Having a new granddaughter had brought out his old protectiveness. He questioned her every decision.

She looked at him closely as he moved down the hallway, seeing the gray pallor, the trembling hands. He was breathing heavily. Something wasn't right. They walked past the living room where Roger lay sprawled in front of the TV, with Penny beside him, sleeping quietly in her stroller.

"Too much TV isn't good for him," Pa sputtered, as he slid into a chair at her kitchen table, looking old, exhausted.

"I know, Pa," she said, and grimaced as she turned her back on him, and reached into her cabinet for the coffee pot and cups. "It's his favorite show," she said, wishing she didn't have to explain every detail of how she was raising her kids. Yet he'd only get huffy if she tried to brush him off. He was only trying to help.

Roger came barreling into the room.

"My boy," Pa said, his face lighting up. He opened his arms and Roger flew into them.

ଓଓଓଓଓ

A small wooden boat sped across the bay toting three silent occupants, each intent on his thoughts. An old black man, his eyes like slits, his skin weathered like overcooked bacon, his hand firm on the tiller, nodded at his grandson, a small wiry boy who was bouncing off the bow seat. They wore cut off jeans, their feet and chests naked, the boy sporting a bright yellow sun visor. He reached for a plastic container floating at the bottom of the boat and proceeded to bail, his movements purposeful.

Don lay sprawled across the bottom of the boat, unmindful of the wet. He raked a hand through his hair, now stiff from saltwater, his eyes tightly closed against exhaustion. He upended the water bottle he'd been given and drained the last drop, trying to forget the horrors of the last several hours. At least he was alive.

The rickety boat veered to the left as the old man headed into the channel. Don gripped the side of the boat and shivered as the blast of hot air off the Miami coastline hit him square across the face. He took in the glittering buildings, the yachts and the loungers on the beach, wishing he could just lie down on a smooth cool bed and sleep for hours. His clothes were soaked through. He'd lost his shoes and socks; but somehow the key around his neck was still in place.

An image flashed of his plane going down, water filling the cockpit, him ripping at his seat belt, his earphones, scrambling for his backpack, grabbing at the lifejacket, being sucked down, pushing through the door and kicking for the surface. It had all happened as if in slow motion. It had taken seconds.

He rubbed his beard stubble, his face taut from sun and wind, almost relishing the pain. Seeing his lifejacket pop up had been the most beautiful sight he'd ever seen.

And now what? Ernesto would never believe him. He'd had a full gas tank before he'd left Miami—plenty for the round trip. Someone in Columbia had nicked the line. It had been a small leak—just enough to prevent him from reaching his destination. They'd jammed the gas gauge, too; leaving him without a clue until that awful moment when the engine had sputtered and died. Somehow, he'd managed to check his location, then memorized it. It was the key to everything.

The good news was that the old man had seen him go down. He'd sped away, not wanting to get sucked down with the plane, then circled back and plucked him from the water like a sack of rags. He'd get an address or something, send him some money for his kindness. It wasn't the rich people who helped a stranger.

This was supposed to have been his last flight; and it was—but not at all in the way he'd imagined. Ernesto must have planned it. Someone had.

He looked up, seeing the old man point; and followed the arc of his arm to a small dock well away from the trophy boats and club piers belonging to people like Ernesto who lived off the grief and sweat of others.

The docking was soft. The boy leaped with the line and tied it securely.

Don staggered onto the dock, stepping carefully around missing boards, seeing the water swirling below. This was the side of Miami tourists rarely saw—the underbelly of survival—the old shacks, the battered workboats with peeling paint, smelling of gasoline and fish.

"You'll be all right?" the old man asked, squinting up at him, holding up a gnarled hand. The boy swung a white bucket, loaded with fish, onto the dock as if it weighed nothing. Then he stood beside his grandfather, his head tipped back, his eyes bright with curiosity.

Don nodded quickly, the man's kindness bringing tears to his eyes. He took the old man's hand, then pulled him into an embrace. "Thank you," he managed to choke out.

"Jesus bless you," the old man said, patting his back. Then he released him. "You need a place to stay?" he asked, looking at him squarely.

"No." He shook his head, touching the key through his shirt, thinking of the cash, credit cards and change of clothes he'd find in the locker. For once, his training had come in handy. And his dad would know how best to approach things—if he were home.

"Do you have wheels?" he asked the old man. "If I can get to the airport, I'll be fine."

The old man looked him over, then nodded at a dark car, an older model, though well kept by the looks of it, parked between two of the shacks.

"We'll get you there," he said with a firm nod.

CHAPTER 12
JUNE

The sky was deep blue, the air scented with apple blossoms. The guests were already arriving in groups of threes and fours: lugging folding chairs, covered dishes, cellophane-wrapped meats, cheese platters and scrumptious looking desserts.

Megan took it all in as she struggled with a can of lighter fluid, cursing under her breath. Penny screamed in her stroller, protesting a particularly vile diaper rash. To save a few bucks, she'd used a cheap laundry detergent, and Penny had cried all night, only to quiet just before the phone rang that morning—with no one at the other end of the line—the same story for every morning for the past two weeks.

She supposed she could change her phone number, but the effort seemed monumental, considering all the people she'd have to notify. If only she could sleep for a few hours. If only she could open this damn can. And where exactly was Stan, who had promised to help her?

With a little snort, Penny finally quieted, her thumb between rosebud lips, her hair a red-gold halo in the bright sun. Megan took a deep breath and exhaled shakily as she scanned the backyard.

Charlie and Ming were tying a plastic tablecloth onto one of the picnic tables set on a patch of grass near the orchard, moving in tandem like matched bookends, sure of each other. It was a lie, of course. In January, soon after Penny's birth, Charlie had moved in, and the fights had begun. She'd heard them through the walls, louder than her screaming child.

It was none of her business.

She waved at Kathy, who was pushing a giggling Bethany on the new swing set Pa had bought Roger for Christmas; and smiled. Kathy's twins were playing catch with Roger, Lydia and some other kids the far end of the orchard. She laughed aloud, seeing Andrea, looking like a princess in a pale green halter dress, making faces at a trio of girlfriends while she fussed with the dance platform decorations. No longer a resentful teen, she glowed with a new maturity. It was a glorious day for her graduation party. Kathy had outdone herself with the preparations.

Her gaze riveted on a young couple near the

house. The woman, an older sister of one of Andrea's friends, stood passive and silent as her young husband strapped a baby carrier onto her plump, post-pregnancy body. His hands were sure, swift and decidedly proprietary, evoking in her a painful yearning that brought tears to her eyes. She'd never wanted that for herself and yet, seeing the man cup his baby's bottom as he slid him into the carrier, all of her efforts to be strong and resilient came crashing down.

She turned away, refusing to swipe at her tears; then spied Stan parking his truck down the street. He looked her way and smiled. Was it just for her? A slow ache burned low in her stomach, and she was starting to hyperventilate. She would not run to him, as much as she wanted to. Her feelings for him were too hopelessly confused. Even as a fling, she was a poor risk. Why else was he keeping his distance?

She sighed. Some things were just not meant to be. At least his presence would insulate her from Adam, who'd be coming with his new wife, Carlotta. In the past few weeks, Adam had been up to his old tricks; finding excuses to see her, trying to schedule a lunch date. As if she'd ever forget the way he'd dumped her in Chicago; or the fact that he'd been too busy to visit his own daughter in the hospital.

She glanced at her watch—it was almost noon—and rubbed a tired spot between her eyes, wishing she could sneak in a nap before Adam arrived. Maybe then, she'd be able to think clearly and avoid the confrontation he seemed to be pushing for. Whatever his game, she wanted no part of it.

ଔଔଔଔଔ

Stan grabbed the large cooler from the back of his truck and headed up the street toward Megan's driveway. He'd promised to come early and was glad he had. The street was empty now, but within an hour, cars would be lining both sides. He'd brought the biggest cooler he had, filled with sodas and juice cans, at Kathy's request. He saw her behind the carriage shed, laughing her head off, pushing Bethany on the new swing set he'd helped Mr. Rosswell assemble after the spring thaw. Kathy looked happy for once, though with her mother due any minute, her good mood would soon be down the toilet. He'd never met the old bag; but had heard enough about her to know that she wouldn't approve of a blue collar like him—not that he leaned in her daughter's direction.

Kathy was a fine woman—proud and loyal. But she wasn't Megan. He hoped she was finally starting to get the hint, though she'd indicated her interest in too many ways. She wasn't in love with him—she was just lonely—the same role he'd played with Christy. No way would he recreate that disaster.

Megan.

His heart skipped a beat when he spied her. She was holding a can of lighter fluid, a hairs breadth away from blowing herself up. She looked ready to spit, her face screwed up from exhaustion. The red highlights in her hair were already afire in the brilliant sun; and now that he looked closer, her hair had a nice cut, as if she'd just been to an expensive salon. And her body, still rounded from pregnancy, looked especially luscious. How he itched to touch that softly tanned skin; but knew better. The last thing she'd want was him pestering her; or at least that's what he told himself. By the looks of the fancy tablecloths, banners, potted plants around the dance stage, and the food already on the tables, Kathy had spent a fortune on Andrea's party; and Megan had worked all hours helping her. He approached cautiously, wishing he had the nerve to pursue his feelings. The fact was, he didn't know how to begin.

ঙঙঙঙঙ

"Are you okay?" Stan asked, touching her shoulder. She swayed slightly, wishing she had the nerve to throw herself into his arms. He looked so warm, safe and strong. She sighed, reminding herself that a friendly touch was better than nothing. He'd been standoffish since Penny's birth, though he'd offered to help at least every other day.

"Hi, you," she said and held out the can of lighter fluid. He took it and with a few expert twists, had the cover off, and was wetting the briquettes. The fire started in a flash.

"Thanks, Stan," she said, patting his arm, though she wanted to kiss him—just for existing. He smelled wonderful—some new aftershave he'd probably paid dearly for. He looked delicious in Levis. His light green T-shirt made his eyes glow.

"What else can I help you with?" he asked gently. "You look ready to drop." He filled the space around her, daring her to breathe—a small price to pay for his welcome presence. She kept telling herself that his friendship was precious; that there was no sense in getting her hopes up.

"Maybe you can help bring some of the food out later," she said, and shrugged. "I'm just a little tired right now." She explained about the cheap detergent as she scooped up the sleeping baby and stuck a practiced finger into a damp diaper. They both turned at the sound of running feet.

"Stan XYZ!" Roger cried. He came hurtling toward them, his face alight with joy. Megan laughed as he threw himself into Stan's arms.

"Keeping your eye on this guy is a full-time job," she said softly, and ruffled Roger's hair. "I'm sure he'll be hanging all over you now, asking a million question."

"No, I won't," Roger said and screwed his eyes up tight, making them laugh.

"I'll be right back," she said, shooting Stan a gratefully smile as she headed with Penny toward the house.

ଓଓଓଓଓ

The band arrived at noon; followed by Adam and his new wife, Carlotta.

"I've heard so much about you," murmured the slender beauty, who held a hand out to Megan beneath an apple tree. She looked about eighteen and had a marked Hispanic accent. Her navy shorts, flowered halter-top and straw sandals merely emphasized her perfect, almost child-like body. Her nails were pink, her hair as black as night and her skin golden. She clung to Adam's arm, her face a picture of innocence—far from his usual taste in women.

"All good, I hope," Megan said, and laughed nervously as she took Carlotta's hand. It was a practiced lady's hand—limp and cool. Adam hovered behind her, smiling broadly, the indulgent husband.

She could barely look him in the eye, thinking how his kids had raved about their stylish new stepmother, who plied them with candy and toys and talked about supposedly cool subjects. Now they clamored around her: the boys looking dumbstruck and Bethany gripping her hand, her face aglow.

"It's nice of you to come," Kathy said, appearing beside Adam, her voice faintly sarcastic. They all looked as Charlie lurched around the side of the house, made a small choking sound, then veered away. Ming grabbed at his arm, but he flung her away. He stormed to his car and sped off, while

Ming stumbled toward the house, looking about to cry.

Seconds passed as expressions smoothed. Megan resisted the urge to go to her friend. The flare of hostility on Carlotta's face had been unmistakable. At Ming?

"Adam Clark," Adam said, taking Stan's hand, distracting her. Stan had come up behind her, his face a mask. She looked away, hating the way the two men measured each other like snarling dogs. Their talk rumbled, mere background noise, as she caught and held Carlotta's gaze. Carlotta's smile didn't waver; but as her gaze drifted to Ming, a forlorn figure beside the house, an oddly calculating light appeared in her lovely gray eyes.

What's going on? Megan wanted to scream.

Then in a burst of commotion, more of Andrea's friends and their parents arrived. Ming escaped Megan's notice as the crowed swelled. From time to time, she spied her at the edge of various groups, holding a plate of food, listening attentively. Each time she tried to head in her direction, Penny demanded her attention or a guest started asking questions about the house. The party was a jumble of sounds: barefoot teens dancing to rock music; laughing kids playing tag and swinging in the orchard; adults making small talk about sports teams, restaurants, recipes and summer plans—all holding drinks and plates of the delicious food.

After the meal, the conversation and dancing mellowed. Megan caught Kathy's pleased expression across the lawn as she looked up from coaxing another spoonful of rice cereal into Penny's hungry mouth. Strapped in her stroller, her chubby face smeared with food, she smacked her spoon, spattering Megan's shirt.

Her laugh died at Carlotta's approach. She'd watched the girl-woman flit from one man to another, batting her sooty lashes. Yet always, she returned to Adam, as if unable to trust him out of her sight for more than a minute. Her expression was of such grave determination that Megan looked behind her, wondering at her objective. Then she spied Ming standing alone with Adam, her arms folded, her hair covering the side of her downcast face. When Carlotta blocked her view, all of her senses went on alert.

"Beautiful child," Carlotta said.

"Thanks." Megan craned her neck, seeing Adam take Ming by the elbow and steer her around the house. Ming paused at the corner and shook her head, looking incredibly sad, then moved out of sight.

"Lovely hair," Carlotta continued, her voice like a purr.

Megan looked at her sharply, hearing deception in the smooth and melodious tones; seeing an oddly gentle smile that didn't quite match the hard glint in her eyes.

"Where is her padre?" Carlotta asked softly, waving a hand expansively toward the other guests. "Surely he must be here. It is such an important day for your household, no, with the oldest child graduating?" Before Megan could react, Carlotta reached down and smoothed Penny's hair.

"We're divorced," Megan said, and pulled the stroller out of her reach and scooped up her daughter. In the bright sunlight, she detected the faint marks of a surgeon's scalpel on either side of Carlotta's lips and eyes.

Penny slapped at her mouth happily with one tiny hand, sending food all over Megan's already-stained T-shirt.

"Penny," she half-scolded as she wiped at her shirt. She laughed as she held her shirt away from her. "If you'll excuse me, Carlotta. I'll definitely need to get a new wardrobe—maybe when she's three."

"I heard about your divorce?" Carlotta shook her head. "So very sad. In my country, we do not allow such a thing." She backed away, eyeing Penny with unveiled longing. "And this small one . . . has her padre even seen her? Have you been in touch with him lately?"

Megan slung Penny on a hip, protectively away from her. "What's with the questions, honey?" She tried to stare her down, refusing to give in to her fear. What was this woman to Donald?

"No lo se," Carlotta said with a dainty shrug.

"You understand perfectly well," Megan hissed, remembering from high school Spanish that *no lo se* meant I don't know. She wiped Penny's face and hands with a wet cloth she'd plucked from a bin beneath the stroller, her whole body trembling. "Look," she said, glaring at Carlotta, "I don't know where he is, and I don't care. And furthermore, my marriage, or lack thereof, is none of your damn business."

Turning her back on her, she shoved Penny's bowl and spoon into a plastic bag that dangled from the stroller's handle, settled Penny in the stroller and moved away.

"Well," Carlotta said as she smoothed her hands down her shorts. "I can see you have your hands full. Perhaps we'll chat another time."

"I doubt it," Megan said, glancing back, ignoring the feeling of hairs standing up on the back of her neck.

"Megan!" Adam moved around the side of the house. "It's so good to finally have a chance to speak with you." He held out a hand, the ever-friendly salesman, his smile plastic. "Let me be the first to congratulate you on the wonderful job you've done on this house. Kathy's all praise, and I'm thrilled that my kids can experience such . . .."

"I don't mean to be rude, but I have to go." Megan brushed past him, stifling a growl, as with heavy arms and leaden feet, she moved Penny's stroller a few precious yards. Then for some reason she looked back. Carlotta, her eyes narrowed with speculation, was looking from Penny to Adam. Then she winked and nodded, her smile complicit.

Blood drained from Megan's face. She gripped the stroller handle, suddenly dizzy. Between the baby and man was a distinct resemblance. Why hadn't she noticed it before?

"Quiera," Carlotta said, and clasped Adams arm. She lifted her face for a kiss, then flashed Megan a triumphant smile as he pulled her to his side. She blew him a kiss as she disengaged, then walked away, her hips swaying. With a tinkling laugh, she blended into a crowd of jostling teens at the dessert table.

"Ah, Megan." Adam held out his hand again and Megan stepped back. His eyes were too bright, his expression too familiar. Was he Penny's father? Her pulse quickened as he stepped closer. Then he raked a hand through his hair and dropped it, looking frustrated.

"What's this about Andrea in the hospital?" he asked, looking worried. "I just got a bill in the mail last night and it scared the crap out of me. Is she all right?"

She looked at him sharply. It was the last thing she expected him to say.

"Kathy didn't tell you?" She scanned the yard. Kathy was carrying a platter of cheese and crackers to a table, trailed by Bethany, who lugged two bags of chips.

"No," he said, shaking his head. "She tells me nothing; and Andrea wants nothing to do with me." He gestured wildly. "Look at her over there. She's stunning. When did that happen? It was only yesterday that I was reading her "Hop on Pop."" Tears welled in his eyes. "She was my little girl not so long ago, and now look at her. It hurts so much, this . . . this distance. I didn't think Kathy had it in her to brainwash her."

Megan smiled at the sight of Andrea, slim and lovely as she laughed with two equally gorgeous girls near the dance floor. A trio of boys approached; they formed couples and began to dance.

"Maybe you should speak with Andrea directly," she said. "Though if it's any consolation, she's fine now. She's a resilient girl."

"You won't tell me?" He fingered the collar of his polo shirt.

"No." She shook her head. "I can't. Kathy's my tenant and friend. It's not my place."

He rubbed his forehead and looked at her ruefully. "Yeah, us divorced dads always get the bum rap—never around when the kids need us. Of course, I'm supposed to be telepathic these days; and the phone only works one way." He folded his arms across his chest and sighed.

"I'm sorry, Adam," she said, and patted his arm, surprised by his tender side. She'd doubted he had one. "I wish I could help you, but I can't."

Her expression froze and she dropped her hand. He was looking at Penny, her face rosy in sleep, her lashes long and lush against pearly skin.

"Fathers and daughters share a special relationship," he said softly. "We want to protect them from harm, share with them the wonders of the world, and enjoy watching their knowledge unfold." He looked up, his expression hardening. "So where's this little one's father, eh Megan. Where's Donald?"

"I really have to go." She grabbed the stroller handles and started to push away, hating her cowardice.

"Don't be in such a rush," he said, sounding desperate as he grabbed her arm and pulled her around to face him. There was panic in his eyes. "I thought we had something special in Chicago. I thought we worked well together. With Donald out of the picture and you back in shape . . . ." He eyed her lasciviously. "He *is* out of the picture, isn't he?"

"I'm busy right now," she said, and glanced at Penny. "She needs to go inside. She's had enough sun."

He moved closer, brushing a fingertip across her right shoulder, flicking her hair, sending it behind her back. "You're like an unlit torch until you've had a few drinks, you know." He spoke barely above a whisper.

"Stop it." She hunched her shoulders.

"Ah, but you're a wild thing, a glorious treat. I thought we'd—"

"Give it a rest, Adam." She slapped at his hand. "We had a one-night-stand, for crying out loud. Now leave me alone!"

She searched the crowd for Stan; but he was at the far side of the dance platform, talking with Kathy, an instant deflation. Both were smiling and laughing—Kathy obviously making great headway.

Then out of the corner of her eye, she spied Ming at her apartment window, hair and clothing disheveled, tears streaming down her face.

Adam snickered.

"You pig," she said, and balled her fists. Blood pounded in her ears. "What did you do to her?" She grabbed the stroller and pushed it forward another few feet. Penny snorted in protest, but didn't awaken.

Adam moved around the stroller, blocking her exit and her view of Ming. "Where's your husband?" he asked again.

"My ex-husband," she spat, her hands shaking. She could barely think. "He's long gone and you know it. What is it with you people?"

"Is he?" he asked. She took in his Eddie Bauer threads, expensive haircut, perfectly manicured nails, seeing a well-dressed man. Yet, his nostrils were inflamed and his eyes bloodshot—evidence of an inner rot.

Cocaine.

The word filled her mind; and she took a sharp breath. Like Donald. Like Charlie.

She looked around wildly, praying Stan would glance in her direction. And where was Roger when she needed an interruption?

"Well, forget about Donald, then." Adam's voice was like the hiss of a snake. "How about you and me share a line or two—you know what I mean."

"Share a line?" She looked at him dumfounded,

then pictured Donald snorting a line right in front of her. These people had lost all notion of morality.

"I don't know," she said, wishing she were safely locked in her library, "I'm not really into that sort of thing."

"But I insist," he said, and grabbed her arm, hurting her. "The baby won't mind," he said, and looked down at Penny, his expression softening. "In fact, she reminds me of Bethany at that age—a cute little dumpling, with the same reddish hair, though her eyes aren't exactly blue . . . kind of purple." He scanned Megan's hair and face, then looked at Penny. "She doesn't take after you at all."

"Let me go!" she cried and kicked his shin. He winced, but his nails dug deeper. Then shouts and screams rent the air.

Across the yard, Pa lay on the grass, his face ashen.

She jerked out of Adam's grasp, grabbed Penny's stroller and ran. "Oh my God!" she cried, seeing the children clustered around her father, while Stan knelt beside him, checking his pulse. Some of the adults were shaking their heads. One man, the dad of one of Andrea's friends, was urging people away; while a slight, middle-aged woman was bent over, picking up what must have been Pa's dessert plate, along with cookies and cake, now scattered on the grass.

"Can you take the kids inside?" she asked Andrea; who without hesitation, grabbed Penny's stroller and herded the others away.

It was then that she saw her, just yards from Pa, her arm around Kathy.

"Aunt Sarah," she whispered.

Even now, she looked regal—and sad, dreadfully sad. Kathy clung to her as if her life depended on it. Tears streamed down both of their faces. Megan could only gape at her aunt and friend, struck by how alike they looked. The images reverberated in her head—of Aunt Sarah, Kathy, Mother and Val—the identical shapes of their oval faces, their blond hair and winter blue eyes.

Sirens wailed in the distance.

"It will be all right," Aunt Sarah murmured to Kathy, her voice painfully familiar. Megan took a sharp breath, knowing by Kathy's shocked expression that Pa had said something.

"Aunt Sarah?" Megan finally found her voice.

Kathy turned away, tears in her eyes. She'd spoken of an imperious mother—a mother who, until today, had refused to visit her only child. It was a nightmare . . . but now it all made sense.

"Yes, Megan," the woman answered, looking at her gravely. "Sorry to cause all this . . . commotion." Her voice was cultured, distant. "I expect you're quite upset."

"Upset?" Megan looked from her to Kathy. "Is that all you can say?" She leaned closer, wanting to scratch her eyes out. "You're supposed to stay away from us . . . away from Pa . . . in Boston. And all this time you're Kathy's mother? You must have known who I was. So why didn't you say something? Why didn't you warn us? Pa's fragile. He can't take this kind of shock."

"Obviously," Aunt Sarah said with a heavy sigh. Then she looked down—they all did—to where Stan was administering CPR, while one of the other guests, the mom of one of Andrea's friends, whipped a stethoscope from her purse and knelt down beside him.

ଓଓଓଓଓ

His eyes stung, but he opened them anyway. The room was a blur; but apparently, he was in a narrow hospital bed, its metal sides up. Muted light filtered in through nearby windows. He needed his glasses; but when he tried to lift his hand, relentless, dull pain flooded his chest, stripping him of breath.

With a deft motion, the nurse did something to his IV line.

"Time for your Darvon, Mr. Rosswell," she chirped, like he was stupid. Her name was Cindy Treevor. She was a child really, spouting all kinds of names for what she gave him and did to him. As if he cared.

"Let's see how we are today, Mr. Rosswell." She took his wrist.

"I don't know how *we* are," he mumbled, "but I'm bloody marvelous."

She laughed dryly, and for a second met his gaze. She had cold eyes, cold and dead, like he should have been. She was merely doing her job.

While she took expert inventory of his tubes and orifices, his thoughts drifted to another place, where trees gleamed in the shining sun, where laughter and love reigned and pain had no voice. He would not give in to the shame of it, the humiliation. To this young girl, he was part of the machinery, a piece of flesh to be kept functional at the behest of some doctor. Shame washed over him as her hands touched places that were best kept private. Raised by Aunt Jo, modesty had been driven into him. Even in the RAF, during the war, he'd managed to keep to himself. Cindy was supposed to be a nice girl's name; but she couldn't be nice. He'd seen it in the war—clean wholesome girls jaded in a week. It couldn't be helped, what with the things they had to do to other human beings. She was wiping his chest with something warm and wet. A cloth perhaps.

"Doesn't that feel good," she crooned.

He closed his eyes, angered at what he'd become. Please God, take me, he screamed inside. But then Megan and her babies would be alone and unprotected. Floyd wouldn't watch them for free. He had to speak to Stan, explain things, get his promise. Today.

If only Sarah hadn't shown up, though he knew she would. She'd always raised his blood pressure, even as a girl, without saying a single word. She was just like her father: old money, snotty ways, with no room for a working class man like him. That party had been in honor of her oldest grandchild. He should have known she'd be there. Probably *he* should have stayed away—though Megan would have made a fuss.

It was the way Sarah looked at him—down the end of her aristocratic nose—that always got his goat. Because, truth be told, he'd never been good enough for Helen. Tears filled his eyes as he thought of her; and the years they'd lost for one reason or another. He'd found solace from her troubles from time to time; when her bright spirit would poke through that dreadful fog, and she'd return to him, as lovely and sweet as the day he'd met her. He could only pray that she was nestled in the arms of angels, laughing with the rest: Val, Tom, Tommy, Letty, Jo and Ivan. He pictured each of them in turn—his family, his beloveds—praying they were together.

Eyes drooping with fatigue, he watched the nurse bustle out.

ઌઌઌઌઌ

The room was a standard four-bed ward: tall windows at the far end, closets and bathroom near the door. Sunlight streamed through the windows and across the two nearest beds, only one of them occupied. Strong antiseptic couldn't quite mask the smell of urine and feces. Voices echoed down the hall from the incessant intercom. Footsteps padded by. It was early—just before visiting time. Only family was permitted.

Stan stood over the frail old man, seeing another

man, heavier and more florid, also dying of heart failure. A week had passed since he'd visited Pop in a similar four-bed ward, feeling the same hopelessness and rage. Pop was home now, in the care of his much-chastened wife; who'd finally realized that her comfortable life would end if she so much as thought of leaving him now.

He'd told the nurse he was Gordon's nephew; though she had to know the truth, considering he'd gone to high school with her. He supposed he was an almost-son-in-law, a surrogate son even. Truth was, he'd loved Gordon for years, the same way he'd loved Chad—with the desperation of a boy in need of a father to admire—a father who loved him back.

"Stanley," Gordon rasped, and reached for him.

Stan took an icy hand. It was a fragile clump of bones. The man looked frail and beaten, his face deathly pale. His mouth had that tender, almost childlike waver that often precluded death. He'd seen it with Chad and Ma.

"How's it going, Mr. Rosswell?" he asked, trying to sound upbeat.

Gordon's mouth worked, but nothing came out.

"You don't need to talk," Stan said. "Save you strength."

"I *have* saved it, Stanley Zambinsky—to speak to you," Gordon spat out, with a fierceness that reminded him of Megan. "I need to tell you something . . . before it's too late."

"Plenty of time," Stan said, and shook his head

slightly, his heart breaking for Megan, and for himself. Gordon had always been a grouch; but underneath the crust was a kind and loving heart. Gordon's loyalty, once given, was for life. How would Megan bear losing him after all she'd lost?

Gordon waved a hand in feeble protest, his mouth pruned up in disgust. His lips started to tremble, as if he were about to say something. Stan leaned closer, expecting to hear his decision about Rosswell's Garage. The mechanics had been going through the motions for the past few days, worrying about Gordon, but mostly about their jobs.

"Someone's casing Megan's house," Gordon said, his expression furious.

Stan moved back. "Who? You mean Floyd Mello?"

"No." Gordon shook his head. "Though I know all about Floyd." He gestured for Stan to sit. Stan relinquished his hand, pulled a chair closer and sat.

"It's a dark green late model Ford Thunderbird that has my attention," Gordon said. "They've been casing the house for a few weeks." He began to cough, then hunched forward, hacking and coughing and sucking in air.

"Easy, there. Easy." Stan rubbed his back until the fit subsided.

Gordon laid back, his face ashen, and gestured for a glass of water; which Stan quickly provided.

"I hired Floyd to keep an eye out," Gordon said after a few gulps. "You know Floyd Mello?"

"Yeah." Stan nodded, his admiration for the old

man raising another notch. Gordon's ability to read people and situations had always been keen. He saw nuances and changes that most men ignored. "I grew up with him. So he's working for *you*?"

"That's what I said," Gordon said with an abrupt laugh, his gaze unwavering. "He says they've been casing the place, taking pictures. He says that whatever's going down will happen soon. Floyd's a good boy—he'd never steer me wrong. He's from good people—the Mellos. I knew his old man from way back, and all his uncles."

"Who do you think it is?" Stan asked, wishing he'd dragged the truth from Floyd when he'd had the chance. Donald came to mind, and drugs. The guys at work had been talking about major deals going down with Smith Labs executives. Kenny, one of the French Canadians with a cousin at the Lawrence facility, said the rumor mill was going wild. Everyone was suspect; yet management had been slow to investigate—until recently.

Chelmsford, at the juncture of Routes 495 and 3, was an ideal place for drug deals. The growing Hispanic population had connections to the drug trade; while baby boomers reaching adulthood with post Vietnam War attitudes craved the action. There was a lot of money going around these days. More than a few of Stan's coworkers were users—though most smoked pot. Cocaine was the preference of the well heeled—those who wanted a bigger, more dangerous thrill; and heroin was gaining inroads in every social stratum because of its cheap initial price. Hell, one of Rosswell's most talented mechanics would sell his best friend for a hit—not that he'd be sharing this information with Mr. Rosswell.

"Lots of drugs floating around," he offered.

"That's an understatement," Gordon said with a shrug. "Floyd doesn't know for sure, but he thinks it's a single outfit. A new dealer from Columbia's flooding the Lowell market, drawing customers from a pretty wide circle, as far north as New Hampshire. Floyd says it the Hermosa family, a Miami insurance agency with important political ties to Columbia. They're a Smith Labs customer, but in reality, they export drugs—a highly lucrative business." He raised a brow. "And now the CIA's involved. You know that Megan reported her ex-husband."

"She did?" Stan couldn't hide his surprise.

"Yeah. Donald's one of their pilots."

"No way," Stan said, then remembered Donald's words—that things were happening . . . big things. "He'd stiff his own mother," he said, then sat back, Penny coming to mind. She'd tie Megan to Donald forever.

"You've met him?" Gordon asked quietly, his chin rising.

"Yeah," Stan said, picturing him sprawled in front of Megan's apartment.

"The newest Mrs. Clark hails from Columbia," Gordon said. "She's one smooth package, from what I understand, with lots of charming brothers and cousins who visit regularly."

"Carlotta?"

"She's a Hermosa," Gordon said with a slight nod. "Donald's on the run; ditched a shipment somewhere between Columbia and Miami. Trouble is . . . Floyd thinks they'll use Megan to lure him into the open." Gordon's lips set in a grim line. "That boy's a trouble magnet—saw it the first time I laid eyes on him. 'Course Megan would hear none of it. Always went her own way."

"Soon, you say?" Stan looked at him out of the corner of his eye, thinking of the revolver he'd purchased in Maine a few years back on the way to a fishing trip.

"Soon," Gordon said, nodding. "No one's seen him for a few weeks, heading toward a month now."

"What tipped you off?" Stan asked.

"Had a feeling." Gordon's eyes had a sad, unfocused look. "I hate to be uncharitable, but Megan was probably the brightest star in that boy's sorry life. Praise God she had the sense to see the truth when he lost his Airlius job." He closed his eyes. "I think she saw it even earlier. She was getting burned out. Too many good times." Tears welled in his eyes. "She was always *my* bright star. But even now, with the house, tenants, job and kids, she just shuts me out. So Floyd's been my eyes and ears." He looked at Stan slyly. "Course if you two weren't being so stupid about each other, I wouldn't have to worry so much."

"What do you mean?" Stan could barely look at him, his heart pounding.

"Anyone with half a brain can see that you love each other. Doesn't matter that you're a Catholic."

"But I—" He looked toward the door, wanting to run. The man saw too much for his own good.

Gordon moaned and gestured for him to move closer, and Stan did.

"I want you to promise that you'll take care of her," Gordon said, speaking just above a whisper.

"She doesn't need me," Stan asked, shaking his head. "She can take care of herself. Always has."

"If you think that, you're a first class idiot!" Gordon spat. Then his tone softened. "Look, Stan, she's not as tough as she makes out. She's an innocent, really; yet she's taken on a man's role in providing for those two kids. My other girl . . .." His face crumpled.

Stan laid a hand on his arm, struggling with tears. He handed Gordon a tissue from the bedside table and took one for himself. Losing Val had to have been the lowest of blows; but the man had to know that in mentioning her, he was hitting below the belt. Everyone loved Val.

"She had the best of it," Gordon said, and swiped at his tears. "A good husband, happy kids and a home of her own that she cherished. Not that it did her any good." He rubbed his temple and closed his eyes. "That's what women want, Stan, no matter how much they squawk about their precious independence. It's their nature to need us. Yet there's my Megan, all by herself, fighting off the world." He shook his head and sighed. "It just isn't right."

"She wants it that way," Stan said, picturing her most angry face. "She's worked hard for her career, her independence, you have to admit."

"Bullshit! Excuse my French." Gordon's face reddened and he grabbed Stan's hand. "Promise on your mother's grave, Stanley Zambinsky, that you'll take care of her; and I mean marriage, damn it. No shacking it with my little girl."

Stan sucked in his breath. He'd be stupid to breathe a word of this conversation to Megan. She'd kill him . . . slowly.

"She acts strong," Gordon said with a chuckle, "but she's still a woman in need of a loving man; and I know you love her, Stanley." His eyes began to close.

"But I—"

Gordon gripped his wrist weakly. "Promise me, Stanley."

"I promise," Stan whispered, then watched him drift off to sleep, the responsibility he'd just signed up for weighing like a granite collar around his neck. As he watched Gordon's chest rise and fall, he contemplated moving in with Megan, sharing her bed, eating her home cooked food each night—and shook his head. He just couldn't see it. Megan would never agree. She'd worked too hard for what she had to share it with anyone—especially someone like him.

He was halfway to work, pushing through heavy traffic at the end of the Lowell Connector, when he realized he'd left his lunch box back at the hospital.

"Shit!" He slammed his hand against the steering wheel. Without food, he'd have a raging headache by two—or risk ptomaine at the lunch wagon. He pulled a U-turn at the next intersection and went barreling back.

ଓଓଓଓଓ

Megan stood beside Pa's bed, holding back tears, wanting to take his hand. Aunt Sarah had stepped out for coffee; so finally, she had him to herself. The sight of his fingers—long, well shaped and idle for once—brought back memories of when she was small, when he'd clipped her nails and given her horsey rides, when he'd been everything to her.

A tube ran from his arm. Other tubes ran from lower down. He breathed softly, his mouth slack. He looked frail and gaunt, with wrinkled skin over prominent bones. He was a study in gray: gray hair and skin against the sparkling white bedclothes. Death seemed to hover in the brightly lit room. She wanted him up and out of bed. She wanted him mean, autocratic and opinionated. She wanted her Pa back. She wanted him alive.

A small sob escaped, quickly stifled. Was that a twitch she saw? Had he heard her? She stepped back and brushed at her tears. No way would she let him see her like this. Then, like a poorly oiled gear, his mouth closed and his eyes blinked open, rheumy and dull.

"Megan?" There was pain in his voice. He smiled wanly.

"Pa, when are you going to stop these heart attacks?" she asked softly, then knelt down and took his hand. He'd had at least three in the past year, though he'd never let on. The doctor said it was only a matter of time. Questions filled her as she looked down at him. Aunt Sarah had been more than happy to pass on the gory details of why she and Pa had been at odds—most of them anyway. There were still a few items she wondered about that only Pa could clarify.

"Now with Val gone, there's no sense in keeping things secret," Aunt Sarah had explained in her mild, matter-of-fact voice. Apparently, Val was Helen's love child, born when she was underage. She'd not mentioned an affair with Pa—just that he'd offered marriage when appraised of the situation. Whatever that meant. She'd said that her parents had disowned Helen. But why hadn't they just sent her away? Back then, pregnant daughters of prominent Boston families did not marry men of the serving class. There had to be more to the story.

"Pa, why didn't you tell me that Kathy was my cousin?" she whispered. "You must have known who she was. It must have bothered you when she moved into my house. But you said nothing. So what's the big secret? Was Mother involved with someone else? Is Val my half-sister? So what am I supposed to tell Roger?"

"You leave Roger out of this!" Pa shouted. Two spots burned on his face, and he took a wheezy breath. "Don't go trying to fix what ain't broke!" His gaze slid away. He began to cough and before she could move to help him, he'd pushed the button beside his bed, and a heavyset woman in her mid-twenties wearing pale blue scrubs rushed into the room.

"It's okay, Mr. Roswell, It's okay," she murmured, ignoring Megan as she handed him a glass of water.

Megan backed away, looking at anything but the feeble old man who sipped from a straw. He was dying before her eyes. How could she bear it? Why had she asked him such questions? Like always, he was probably just being protective. Must she always view him as the controlling father of her teenage years? He was a private man, with reasons for his secrets. She had no right to poke at what was obviously an old wound, especially considering her own daughter's questionable parentage.

When the coughing fit passed, she chanced a look. His eyes were watery and his expression closed, almost reproachful. It struck her that he was afraid.

"Just five more minutes," the nurse said as she set down the glass. Megan scanned her pale earnest eyes, the slight twitch at the corner of her mouth, the way her v-necked top stretched over well-fed flesh. Young and unsure of her authority, she was daring Megan to disagree. "He really needs to rest," she said, her lips narrowing slightly.

"Thank-you," Megan said and nodded, trying to look respectful. This nurse, however young and imperfect, was keeping her father alive; while she, his only living child, had made him angry, hastening his death. Tears filled her eyes as she sat on a chair beside the bed.

The nurse, her back straighter now, collected the few bits of paper from the straw's cover, then dropped them in a trash bin on her way out.

"It's not as if you've been forthright about your ex-husband's activities," Pa said. She could barely meet his eyes. "You with your fancy high-tech job, high-class travel and expensive meals in far-off places. And for what? All you do is collect and sell data—a slick name for other peoples' secrets? And your ex . . . with his drug habit and criminal friends? You think I don't know about these things? You think I haven't prayed to God every day for your deliverance?"

She clenched her fists and struggled to breathe. How dare he interfere in her life? How dare he judge her? Obviously, he had sins of his own. But seeing his wrinkled face and weak, helpless body, her anger drained away. He could be gone in a second. Fighting with him now would buy nothing but guilt.

"So you knew all along," she said, wanting to cry. She sighed as she took his hand, ignoring his attempt to pull away and the distrust in his eyes. "I'm not surprised, Pa. You always saw right through me. I guess I'm naïve or maybe a slow learner when it comes to men. Donald was definitely a mistake. But it won't be the last one I ever make."

He barked a laugh.

"But what happened between him and me is private," she said, eying him sternly, "like what happened between you and Mother. Can you accept that, Pa?" She smiled sadly, her heart touched by the softening of his expression.

"I suppose," he said and nodded. "We all have our trials. It's part of being human." His eyes filled with tears and he looked away.

"I'm sorry," she said, and griped his hand more warmly. How many times had she been mean to him in the past; when, like her, he craved acceptance and love? Maybe like her, too, he didn't know how to ask. "I've no right to pry, Pa."

A wavery smile lit his face. "That's my girl," he said, his eyes shining. "Did I ever tell you that you're just like my Aunt Jo?"

"A thousand times," she said with a soft laugh.

"Spoke her mind, Jo did, and kept her word," he said. "You even look like her." His expression darkened and she swallowed hard. His intent look meant he had more to say.

"You'd think you were still stuck on Donald," he said softly, "the way you're so skittish around Stanley Zambinsky. He's a good man, Megan, salt of the earth. And he loves you. I can see it in his eyes. He's always around when you need him." He looked at her closely. "You still pining for that pilot?"

"Donald's in the past, Pa, and Stan's just a friend," she said firmly. It was her mantra—what she told herself each time she saw Stan's face, each night alone in her bed, each time Roger was naughty and she craved a man's counsel.

"Come on now . . .."

"Stan's just not interested," she said, shutting down the pain that her words evoked. Stan would never be hers, not in a million years. "It isn't personal, Pa. He says too many women have burned him. Even Kathy's tried, without success."

"And Donald?"

"I told you, I'm through with him," she said, hating that he watched her closely and didn't believe her.

"Stan will protect you," he said firmly.

"Protect me?" she said with a tired laugh. "As if poor weak Megan can't take care of herself." As if any man offered his protection for free, she wanted to add. "I don't think so."

"Give him time," he said, then squeezed her hand slightly and closed his eyes. "He's the one for you, Meg. He reminds me of Uncle Ivan; who would have loved you."

She watched him drift off to sleep, her thoughts turning to Uncle Ivan—Ivan's Moldovich, a Russian prisoner of war who'd stayed on after the war had ended, claiming there was nothing in the old country to return to but unmarked graves. Pa had never stopped grieving for Ivan, the man who'd raised him.

Soon after Pa's birth, most of the townsfolk, including his parents and grandparents, were killed by influenza epidemic of 1918. Pa's paternal aunt, Josephine, left with a squalling nephew and no means of support, had reluctantly accepted the Russian's marriage proposal. Ivan was big and burley—so the story went—and liked the looks of the Rosswell spinster—a strong, outspoken woman who reminded him of the women in his old village. In better times, Jo would have lead a quiet life tending to her parents, eventually moving into her brother's home. But the war intervened, then the flu; and men were in short supply. Jo had looked upon Ivan as her salvation—though she'd taken great care never to tell him so to his face. In fact, she fell in love with him; and it was clear from Pa's stories that he had loved her, too. Ivan became the grateful focus of her exquisite cooking and haughty disapproval, much to his amusement. In turn, she'd counted on him until the day he died, crushed by a car in his own garage; at which time, she'd turned to her loyal young nephew for support. When she'd needed an operation, he'd traveled to Boston to find work, leaving her alone.

And now, like Aunt Jo, she was losing him, too.

She started at a sound at the door. The nurse bustled in, her expression grave. "Time to go," she said, then whisked the privacy curtain around Pa's bed.

ଔଔଔଔଔ

Megan stepped into the hallway, wishing she could stay, and promptly crashed into Stan. She leaped back, her senses reeling. He smelled of sunshine and Irish Spring soap. Her hands brushed soft plaid flannel, denim and a solid, work-hardened chest. She caught her breath as her eyes met his and for an instant, saw longing and pleasure.

He backed off, too, mumbling an apology, eyeing her warily. "I forgot my lunch." He held up an aluminum pail. "I was just here a few minutes ago. Saw your dad. Now I have to get back to work."

"Why?" she asked. Then unaccountably, she burst into tears, then felt his arms go around her.

"He's a tough son-of-a-bitch," she heard him say with a slight hitch in his voice as he patted her back. "He'll be home before you know it, Meg. Everything will be okay"

"Yeah, right," she said, unable to believe that she was clinging to Stan and crying. "You know that isn't true."

His voice was husky in her ear, murmurs of comfort. She was crying so hard she couldn't make sense of what he was saying. She let him lead her to the empty waiting room, an open area with several overstuffed chairs, a wall-mounted television with its volume on mute, soft pictures in ornate frames, magazines strewn across small tables and a long, comfortable-looking sofa. Her head was a maelstrom: fear, grief, hurt and need swallowing all thought.

"Pa's not okay," she said and grabbed the fast-food napkin he offered as she backed away. She dabbed at her eyes. "The doctor says he's run out. One flare of temper and he'll be gone."

Stan sighed. His shoulders sagged.

She looked him in the eye. "He's going to die, Stan, and there's no wishing it away."

"Yeah, I know," he said. And it seemed natural when he pulled her into his arms again and rested his chin atop her head. Tears streamed down her face and she just let them fall. She found herself craving his warmth; and then was kissing him; and he was holding her face, now slick with tears. He caressed the back of her neck, that tender place beneath her hair; and kissed the side of her face, lingering, making her insides melt.

He pulled her closer, his body hard, his grip sure, molding her body to his. It felt good. It felt right. She couldn't help reaching up and touching the side of his neck, then directing his lips back to hers.

Footsteps sounded in the hallway and they jerked apart. Then the sound receded.

She laughed nervously as she sat on the sofa. He sat beside her a foot away, rubbing his face.

"I can't believe I did that," he mumbled, looking at her out of the corner of his eye. "Are you okay?"

"Thought you didn't want a woman," she said with a tight laugh, and pulled a wad of tissue from her purse. "I'd given up on you, Stan. But I guess I shouldn't have."

He eyed her cautiously. "Yeah, well . . . things change. People change. You're not what I expected. You've gotten . . . under my skin. I've wanted to do that for a very long time."

"Ah Stan." She laid a hand on his thigh and he turned to her, his eyes filled with love. "I feel the same way. I just . . .."

She wanted his arms around her again, holding her close. There were so many things to tell him, but she could only look in his eyes, too afraid to begin.

His hand went to her face, his fingers trembling. "I'm sorry we got off to a bad start, Meg. I'm sorry about your dad, too. You've had more than your share of troubles and I could have been a whole lot nicer. I think I've gotten too comfortable watching you from afar."

She smiled brightly, then smacked him on the arm.

"Ow!" He pulled away.

"That's right, ya big goof," she said, grinning, gratified by the shocked expression on his face. "You could have been nicer, Stan. I've been waiting forever for you to figure it out—you know—you and me. Even Pa saw it." She looked down at her hands, suddenly embarrassed, reminded that they were sitting in a hospital waiting room, of all places. "Pa said I should give you a chance." She looked up at him, hoping she hadn't made an ass of herself. "I don't know Stan. Say something."

"Yeah. He said the same thing to me." He took her hands, and something inside her melted. Was she really sitting here—with Stan? "I thought we could be just friends, Meg, but I can't. I want to live with you and make love to you. I want you, Meg." The muscle on the side of his face twitched. "I don't know if I should tell you this, but your Pa made me promise to take care of you, and not as a friend."

"And?" She spoke softly, letting disappointment, like an achingly cold stream, seep into her chest. Take care of her? What about love? Was he copying Pa's typical sexist diatribe? His eyes were shifting back and forth. He looked panicked.

"He said you needed someone to help you," Stan said, "that you shouldn't be doing so much. That as a woman—"

"That as a woman, I need a man to take care of me?" She backed away slightly and scanned him from head to toe, her breathing unsteady. "Are you really saying this? To me?"

"His words, not mine," he said and looked away, a deep flush down the side of his neck, a stubborn firmness to his jaw.

"But you agree." She stared at him, the clarity of the situation crashing down. "And now you're annoyed with *me*, because I'm offended that *you* think my little career playacting can now end; because *you*, my prince charming-slash-knight-in-shining-armor, can take care of *me*." She smiled grimly, wanting to smash something. "That, although I've provided quite nicely for myself and my children these past few years, it doesn't really amount to much. It doesn't matter that I can hold my own in the business world and at the same time, make cupcakes for Roger's class; change my own oil, hammer a nail straight and wire my own laundry room. None of it matters, now does it, Stan?" She took a shuddering breath, wanting to weep. "Because, at the end of the day, I'm just someone's helpless daughter, wife, sister, passive female who has no business redefining my role as otherwise."

She glared at him, barely able to breath.

"Now, wait just a minute." He stood, looking royally peeved. "You can't just rant at me like that. I didn't take away from what you've done; and I appreciate that you've worked hard. All these years, I've watched you struggle, and can't help but admire your determination. You're an amazing girl."

"Girl?" Her eyes were brimming, as she rose to confront him. "I'm a woman, damn it—not a girl. What if I called you a boy? You watched me *all these years*, yet you buy into this crap, into my father's chauvinism . . . hell, into the entire world's misguided, cookie-cutter notion of what women were, are and forever will be?"

He held out a hand. "Aw, Meg, don't take it like that. Maybe we've both been alone too long; and I don't know how to talk to women. Give me a break. Didn't you ever want to stay home and look after the kids and the house sometimes?"

It was the worst thing he could have said. Her whole body trembled as she slipped her hands behind her back, resisting the urge to slap him. "So you feel sorry for me and think I need a rest?"

"Well . . . I didn't say—"

"How can you talk of *us* when you think of me that way?" She jabbed a finger at his chest and prodded him toward the entrance. "Obviously you have no idea what I want . . . who I am!"

"Come on, Megan." He shook his head, scowling, and flung his arms out. "I just said—"

"I heard what you said," she hissed. "You're just like Pa. You want me home, barefoot and pregnant no doubt." He shook his head wildly. "Or maybe you want some brainless play toy like Christy."

His faced blanched. "Now, look Megan—" He made a grab for her arm but she snatched it away.

"I can't believe you." She choked back tears; wishing she'd had the sense to stay away from him, from all men.

Then his hair fell across his forehead, making him look painfully vulnerable. It was the same look Roger had perfected. It was a joke—on her.

"Get off your high horse," he said, and once again, she began to cry.

He tried to pull her into his arms, but she shrugged him away, holding her arms rigid by her sides. She hung her head as thoughts of Donald came—the last time she'd seen him, hovering above her, about to strike—and of Adam, trying to draw her into his criminal activities—and of Pa's classic disparagements whenever she displeased him.

"You're all the same," she said, shaking her head slowly, wanting to die.

"What's that supposed to mean?" He raised his chin. "That women are better than men; that you don't need us; that men are just a pains in the asses with thick wallets. You and your damn career! You think you don't need me after I showed you those construction tricks. So I worded things wrong. I don't have your fancy education. But what about my intentions? I'm a good man, an honest and loyal man." He folded his arms across his chest. "I'm a person just like you; and I'm sick and tired of taking the blame for all the evils done by males against females since the beginning of time. In my experience, it's the men who get shafted, by two-timing bimbos who can't see the truth if it hit them square between the eyes. Why don't you try telling that little nephew of yours about his alleged inferiority?"

"Bye, Stan," she said, choking on a sob. Then she ran for the door.

ᘓᘓᘓᘓᘓ

The building's air conditioning hummed like an airplane about to takeoff. Several telephones shrilled in the maze of cubicles that had become

Megan's second home in Smith Labs' Home Office Customer Support Division. Voices babbled, cajoled and explained, offering help to customers who were giving the company yet another chance to retain their precious business. Footsteps passed Megan's cubicle—two support engineers, discussing a customer issue. It seemed like everyone had an engineering title these days.

Megan glanced at the pile of computer listings she'd been scrutinizing, wishing she'd never asked for a promotion. More pay meant more responsibility and more work; and the endless rounds of meetings, travel reports, training plans, budget projections and doling out poorly documented problem reports to overworked support engineers.

Then there was the mess she'd made of her love life, with Stan professing his love, and her arguing with him. What the hell was wrong with her? With the bad ones, she jumped into bed at the slightest hint of interest; but with Stan . . ..

She took a sip of coffee, thinking of the donut she'd refused a half-hour ago. Sweet and chewy, that bit of coconut delight would have taken a serious edge off her morning. She looked at her watch, thinking there was still time for a cafeteria run.

The phone rang and she grabbed the receiver.

"Hello?"

It was someone breathing—a soft sound that made her clutch her neck, her own breath coming fast and shallow. "Hello?"

There was a clicking sound, like someone clicking a pen, and the sound of cars moving and the blare of a truck horn, like at a pay phone. About to drop the receiver, she heard her name spoken—softly—by a voice that filled her with dread.

"Meggie, please?" He said it with such pathos that she almost burst into nervous laughter.

"Donald," she whispered, then crossed her legs and cradled the receiver to her ear. Pain filled her heart at the thought of Penny, and the politics and legalities of biology. "What do you want?" She flipped the edge of a computer printout, thinking of the hours of painstaking work she had ahead of her. And now this?

"Meggie, I'm so sorry." He took a shuddering breath. "I need to see you."

"Where are you?"

"I can't . . .." The dial tone sounded.

She closed her eyes as she replaced the receiver and leaned back in her chair. All day she'd weathered the usual interruptions: irate calls from three district offices, analysts asking for direction, Barry from accounting questioning an expense report, the babysitter blathering about the rash on Penny's wrist. She sighed, thinking of the mess she'd made with Stan. Her Stan. And just what would Mr. Zambinsky have advised? He wasn't answering his phone; and she wasn't about to humiliate herself further by leaving a message. She couldn't very well ask him about Donald or her suspicions about Charlie, considering their relationship, or lack thereof. And Steve Grant expected her report on the problem reporting system by the end of the day.

She pressed a palm to her forehead. If she could only just get up and leave—just get in her car and drive—to Maine or Canada. But then what?

She reached for the phone, then stopped. Stan would know exactly what to do about her suspicions. He had tons connections in the Lowell area. He could easily find out what was going on.

The phone rang and she picked up the receiver, sending her coffee cup flying.

"Megan Rosswell," she said.

"I need to see you," said a muffled voice. It took her a few seconds to realize that it was Ming.

"Now?"

"No. In about twenty minutes, in the fifth floor ladies' room, Tower One."

"All right," she muttered and set down the receiver. Quickly she mopped up the mess, then headed toward the Towers. She needed to use the bathroom anyway. Being a few minutes early shouldn't matter.

She hurried into the sparkling bathroom, with its bay of stalls on the left and floor-to-ceiling mirror on the right. A row of sinks backed against an inner partition that split the room in two, the sinks facing the stalls, the walls painted a muted white. Gray floors gleamed. She passed by the mirrors, not even bothering to look, then slipped into a stall.

The door opened again, immediately. Shadows shifted across the floor. For some reason, she stepped up on the toilet seat, crouched and held her breath, staying as still as possible.

A woman sauntered into the room, looking around suspiciously. It was Barb Fischer, a DataStorage-7 firmware engineer, one of the few females on the team. She was quiet, rarely spoke in meetings, yet rumors flew that she liked to party. Thick, bushy brown hair framed her delicate, clean-scrubbed face. She wore tight jeans, a flaming red sweatshirt and pink high top sneakers. Through the door crack, she watched her peer under the stalls, then stand stiffly, stuffing her hands deep in her pockets.

The door swung open again and Ming breezed in. She stuck a wedge beneath the door, then leaned against it. "Been waiting long?" she asked.

Barb shook her head.

"This place empty?" Ming asked, sounding impossibly calm.

"Yeah." Barb held out a white envelope.

Ming passed her a small cellophane packet; then rifled through the envelope, checking what looked like money; while Barb opened the packet, stuck in a finger and tasted.

"All right?" Ming asked.

"Yeah."

Ming retrieved the wedge and Barb left quickly. Then Ming stood with her back to the door, her face taut with worry, looking angry, ready to explode.

Megan dropped to the floor softly, then stepped from the stall. "What's going on?" she asked, her arms folded across her chest. She leaned against the partition, trying to look composed.

Ming backed away, looking horrified. "You saw that?"

"I did." Megan nodded, then dropped her arms. "Since when have you been dealing?"

Ming took a deep breath, then let it out in a long hiss. "It's not what you think," she said at last, slumping against the door.

"Then, what is it?" Megan asked gently, "Charlie's business?"

"He's lost to me," Ming said, meeting her gaze. "I tried. I really did. I paid his debt many times over. But he's an addict, just like Tien, my former lover in Taiwan. There's no satisfying that kind of craving."

"An addict?"

"Cocaine." Ming whispered. The word settled between them like a curse.

Megan sighed, thinking of Charlie's red-rimmed eyes and Ed Veasey, who'd been putting in a lot of after-hours work lately, making time with the hardware support guys from the Lawrence facility.

"This time, however, I've no new baby to show for my efforts," Ming said, shaking her head sadly. "What is it about me that attracts these people. Eric will be pissed when he finds out. Maybe I'm cursed like his wife says; and need someone like her to manage my life."

"But why are *you* dealing?" Megan asked. "And why'd you ask me to come here?"

Ming laughed harshly. "Nothing gets by you

does it, Megan?"

Megan looked at her closely, seeing the gaunt hollows of her cheeks, the shadows beneath her eyes, the stringy hair. She'd lost a noticeable amount of weight in the past few weeks.

"There's a lot at stake," Ming said, her dark eyes filling with tears. "It's a big risk, talking to you. There are ears everywhere." She lowered her lids, then opened them, her eyes glittering. "High-level people are involved, rich people who can destroy me with a phone call—who've already tried to destroy me for protesting, for trying to help Charlie." She clasped Megan's wrist, her expression earnest. "Adam does it for the thrill and for what he owes his new wife."

"He owes Carlotta?"

Ming nodded. "Her family and their money. They live like kings in Miami. Poor Columbian farmers sell to wholesalers, who sell to Carlotta's brother." Ming shuddered. "Her brother's a wealthy man, a dangerous man who's built and staffed several labs in Columbia that process coca leaves. He flies it to ships off the coast or designated islands. There's little risk—for him anyway. Charlie's his Lowell area connection—him and two Lawrence engineers."

"And Adam's role?" This was sounding worse by the minute.

"Using and dealing," Ming said softly. "Dealing mostly to executives in other companies and female connections on the road, if you get my drift."

"Like Tootsie."

Ming nodded slightly, as if to a clever student. "The Hermosas get a piece of every deal." She raked a hand through her hair, leaving a strand in front of her eyes. "Unfortunately, Charlie and his friends have developed a slight problem." She peered through her hair. "They've been sampling the supply and thought no one's the wiser." She folded her arms across her chest and threw her hair back with the toss of her head. "The brother's noticed," she sneered. "He loves the cat and mouse game. It's part of the appeal." She shrugged a slender shoulder. "Charlie hasn't been thinking too clearly these days; so I've been doing his route, trying to keep him alive. I don't know," she said, shaking her head slowly. "I never imagined I'd be doing this."

"Why are you telling me?" Megan asked, an uneasy feeling settling inside her.

"You've called the feds. You're involved, actually—though you probably didn't think so," Ming said, her eyes widening. "You need to know who the players are." She looked lost as she clasped her hands in front of her, as if she'd plead guilty and was asking for forgiveness. For what?

"I thought you'd appreciate the information," Ming said. "Who knows how much the CIA told you. I'm in with them, too . . . well . . . sort of."

"They've told me nothing," Megan said, her hair standing on end. All along, she'd thought of Ming as a victim. Was she playing both sides?

"It's hard to explain," Ming said, her expression

hardening. "They've found me cooperative; and I know some of the top players—intimately." She shot Megan a significant look.

"But, again, why are you telling *me*?" she asked, wanting to shriek. What wasn't she saying?

"I owe you." Ming's tone was hollow. She hugged her middle, as if sick to her stomach. Was it a deception?

"No, you don't." Megan grabbed at her arm.

"But I do," Ming said, flinging her hand away, her smile sly, not quite reaching her eyes. "I'm a fool for Charlie, but you've been a friend, one of the few people I really trust." Her gaze was hypnotic as she moved closer, away from the door. Another deception?

"Your ex-husband's one of their pilots, you know." It was a punch in the gut. "He's in the area right now, on the run. We need to know when he contacts you. We need to know where he is."

Megan could barely breathe. "Why?" she whispered, the image of Ming, distraught at her window, coming to mind. Had the scene been staged for her benefit? "It was Adam, wasn't it?" she asked. "Are you—?"

Ming laughed harshly, her eyes wild. Then she pushed through the door and fled.

CHAPTER 13

JULY

Stan slammed into his apartment, stripped off his clothes and dropped them on his way to the bathroom. The air conditioner blasted in the living room window, not quite keeping up with soaring heat outside. The station on his truck radio had said it was ninety-eight degrees in downtown Boston—a record high for early July.

Under the lukewarm spray of the pulsing showerhead, he placed his hands against the tile wall, trying without much success to forget about his day.

Nothing had gone right. The Ed Center construction site had been a nightmare. Two guys had gotten heat stroke and one of the water boys, an old duff with decades of Boston construction under his belt, had keeled over with a heart attack. To top it off, he'd had a loud disagreement with his boss, Frank, and walked off the job twice. Before the deal with Floyd, he would have taken a swing at the bastard; but Floyd's bill loomed like a rock-faced mountain. Somehow, he'd become just another working stiff, scrambling to pay his bills.

He'd never particularly liked working for Harden's, but eight years ago, he'd been eager and hungry for the work. A steady paycheck was hard to beat. Pop had drilled that fact into his sorry head.

There was no denying that Harden's paid the best in the area; and they'd been around for decades. In 1979, Jake Harden, the founder's grandson, had taken over after his father died from lung cancer. In his late thirties, Jake was a genius with contracts and contacts. He'd landed one commercial project after another in the months following his father's death, including the Ed Center contract with Smith Labs, the biggest money draw to Lowell since the Prince Spaghetti Company had pulled up stakes for a southern clime. Jake had grown-up expecting to take over the business; he'd worked on projects since high school. But he was a college boy, who'd never fit in with the workers.

Pop had once said that, aside from being born into the right family, Jake happened to be in the right place at the right time, with the new money from Smith Labs causing a massive ripple effect across the entire local economy. Office workers were taking business lunches, hiring lawyers and accountants and purchasing goods from the specialty stores that seemed to be cropping up every other day. Restaurants, hotels and office complexes appeared overnight—some left vacant on purpose as tax deductions. Money poured into Lowell and the surrounding communities—revitalization and renaissance becoming the latest buzzwords touted by politicians and the local media. In a heartbeat, the city had transformed from a grimy mill town into a city of some prestige. And in its midst was Smith Laboratories' sleek and modern Education Center.

He laughed harshly as he began to wash, and shook his head, thinking of another trendy new term—vast glass—a concept thrown around by Harden's architects—eggheads who'd never worked on a job site. They designed for looks, not habitability. Harden's bid had been ridiculously low, resulting in corners being cut and too many smiling politicians hovering around, looking for ways to congratulate themselves. And now, nearing the project's end, Jake Harden was desperately trying to deny the harsh reality of some educated idiot's unrealistic fantasy.

He'd told Jake months ago that the ventilation system was inadequate—back when he'd spoken his mind. Now, there was barely enough air coming in for ten people, never mind the full capacity of three hundred. The fans merely recirculated stale air. As the outside temperature rose, the building's massive glass walls absorbed even more heat, creating a dangerously toxic environment. Within days of opening, the building would become an airless tomb. He'd wanted to call OSHA. Jake, of course, had had a different opinion.

Every day for the past two weeks, he'd hefted and hammered along with the rest. He'd done what he was told and moved like a robot—a prison sentence from which there appeared to be no reprieve. The project was too vast, too complicated, with too many loose ends. It made his head hurt thinking of all the details and trying to string them together. If only he could stick with rotten old houses in need of tender loving care. Someday soon, he had to start his own business or go nuts trying.

His thoughts turned to Megan's attic as he shut off the water and opened the shower curtain. She wanted him to help build a living area for her father; complete with a small elevator and air conditioning. He puffed out his breath slowly. Gordon wasn't ever leaving the hospital—at least not alive. But he wasn't about to tell her.

He grabbed a towel and rubbed his hair briskly; then tightened his jaw as he looked down, seeing his body's reaction to the mere thought of the woman. A low moan escaped his throat as he headed into the bedroom.

They were both single. Nothing was stopping him but his own stubborn pride. He dressed quickly, shoving away thoughts of seeing her with yet another man, which would happen if he didn't do something about it. This time, he had to move fast, stake his claim and let her know how he felt, no matter the cost.

"Easier said then done," he muttered thinking of how she'd practically attacked him in the hospital waiting room. This time, he'd keep his chauvinistic comments to himself. Hell, he wanted her. He needed her. And she had to need him, too. Didn't she?

The phone rang and he grabbed the receiver

He sucked in his breath at the sound of Megan's voice, then listened closely as she described, in that insufferable, in-control tone she'd long-perfected, her father's quiet passing.

ᴥᴥᴥᴥᴥ

Stan leaned against the wall at the far right of the lobby with Roger by his side, hoping that Megan would at least glance in his direction. Aside from a few curt orders she'd barked throughout the day, he might as well have been another piece of furniture. Mourners streamed in and out of her apartment, filling her lobby to bursting as they enjoyed the spread she and Kathy had set out on tables in the middle of the room. All around him people were eating and drinking as they gossiped and laughed, sharing stories of Rosswell's garage, along with movies reviews and talk of the weather. They stood in tight groups, or sat on the padded chairs he'd pushed against the walls; or fixed coffee or tea from the sturdy oak table he'd set in front of the massive stone fireplace. They helped themselves to fruit drinks or spring water from the ice-packed coolers beneath the table. Early that morning, he'd carted most the lobby's furniture up to the attic; and in the past few hours had made three trips to the variety store around the corner for things she or Kathy had needed.

He froze.

Megan was stepping out of her doorway, her hand on someone's arm, one of the guys from her work, her expression mellow as she talked, as if she'd popped a tranquilizer or downed a few stiff shots of vodka. He knew better. She wouldn't drink as a matter of honor—she wouldn't even serve it—not at her father's funeral. For a few horrible seconds, her smile slipped and her expression crumbled. He swallowed hard, seeing the slight slump in her right shoulder that spelled exhaustion. Not today, but soon, she'd realize how much her father had done for her, how much she still needed a man in her life. Though of course, she'd never admit it.

She knew he cared about her—so why couldn't she accept the help that came with it? She was just too damn proud for her own good. If only he had the guts to drag her up the stairs to her bed and . . ..

The word Neanderthal came to mind. Wasn't that what women called traditional men these days? His chest deflated as he sighed, and he shook his head, trying to clear his thoughts. Forcible sex was good only in porno movies; and then only from the guy's perspective. She'd go for it like a bucket of fish bait. Admittedly, he was a fool when it came to Megan Rosswell, and a coward, too. It didn't matter what he wanted, when she kept him at arm's length.

He stuck his hands in the pockets of his rented suit pants and sighed again as he looked down at Roger, seeing the image of Gordon on his somber young face. Gordon would have hated the speeches today and this party in particular. He could hear him now, squawking that there were too many people, too much of a fuss. Gordon Rosswell had been a private man, a protective bear to those he'd loved. But he would have been proud of the way Megan had held up over the past few days. Reps from all the local charities had come to the funeral; along with several Lowell City Council members and the Mayor. He would have been touched to see his beloved boys—every last mechanic who'd ever worked for him—along with wives and girl friends—laughing and reminiscing about old times. He'd never seen so many cars parked in and around the cemetery where they'd laid his body to rest.

He eyed Roger, who'd been quiet all day. Though nine, he acted like a grown up half the time. He was smart—a wiz at math and chess—but still a kid. And he'd lost everyone he'd loved except Megan and Penny.

And me, came the thought.

Stan smiled grimly. He'd grown to love the boy, and vowed to be part of his life, no matter what happened between him and Megan.

"You alright, bud?" he asked, gripping his shoulder, thinking he looked like a little accountant in his dark suit and shoes, big round glasses and short blond hair. The kid was adorable.

"I'm hungry, Mr. Z," Roger said, squinting up at him. "Will you go with me to get some food? I can't ask Auntie. She keeps telling me to mingle, and I don't want to."

Megan was deep in conversation with Bob Cartright, one of her friends from Smith Labs. She was chattering fast, like a wind-up toy whose springs were running out. He fought the urge to go to her, to scream at everyone to leave her the hell alone. Couldn't they see she was at her breaking point? He rubbed his eyes, struggling for control. He wanted to help her, and not just with the damn furniture. He wanted to hold her while she cried. He wanted to build his life around her—if only she'd let him. Couldn't there be a meeting point, a compromise? She hadn't even let him touch her hand in sympathy. If he left right now, would she even notice?

"Well?" Roger asked, tugging on his suit jacket. "Aren't you hungry?"

"Yeah. In a couple minutes," he said with a tight smile as he glanced at his watch. "Can you make it?" He faked a punch to Roger's jaw. "I'm trying to catch your Auntie's eye."

Roger rolled his eyes; and then Stan's attention was riveted on the front door. His breath caught as a gangly man walked in, his head barely clearing the top of the doorframe. He scanned the room, then smiled as his gaze caught Stan's.

"Butch," Stan hissed under his breath, his first thought that he wanted to punch the bastard hard.

But this wasn't the time or place; and he'd actually missed Butch's stupid ethnic jokes and the way he could wind a story up for the biggest laugh. He and Butch went back a long way—long before Christy had ripped them apart. He looked away, fighting a chuckle, thinking of the last time he'd seen Butch, running out of his apartment, pulling up his pants.

Butch had been Rosswell's top mechanic for a few years before Tom had taken those honors, along with the boss's daughter. Rumor had it that Butch and another mechanic were negotiating with Megan to buy the garage. Butch hadn't appeared at the wake or the funeral, but here he was, his smile widening as he spanned the distance between them, mumbling apologies as he trod on feet and sent plates and cups flying. The floor shook as he made his way over.

"Good to see ya, Stan." His grinned like a horse as he extended a bony hand.

Stan gave him the once over, then sighed and took his hand in a grip that would have crushed a lesser man. Butch tilted his head down like a chicken scooping out corn kernels, his eyes pleading forgiveness and saying 'no need to make a scene,' all at the same time. Butch's Adam's apple bobbed as he swallowed.

"What's going on?" Stan asked with a curt nod, his anger spent. Floyd was right. Butch had done him a big favor by stealing Christy. Though stealing wasn't the appropriate word. Christy belonged to no one but herself. He'd bet a week's pay that Butch had already caught her in bed with another man. "How's the wife?" he asked, looking him in the eye.

"Hello, lover," Christy said, slipping around Butch's side as if she was stuck to him, her purple-painted talons flat against his lapel. She was dressed in black, like a Halloween witch, from black patent leather spiked heels to a ridiculously tiny black hat and veil, her dress shiny and form fitting, rising mid-thigh. Like a stripper, she looked, loaded with sparking gems: around her neck, on each wrist and dangling from her ear lobes. She moved forward, curling her hands around Stan's forearm, her knee nudging his thigh.

"Come on, Christy," Butch muttered, his face drooping. He backed up and looked from left to right as if in protest, his mouth working soundlessly.

"Christy." Stan nodded, then deftly placed Roger between them. He tried not to laugh, seeing the revulsion on her face. She'd once told him she hated kids, and he hadn't believed her.

One hand pressed to her chest, she backed away from Roger as if he were contagious, making him wonder once again, what he'd ever seen in her. He winked at Roger, whose face was flushed and angry; and was immediately rewarded by a mischievous glint in the kid's bright eyes. Stan nodded slightly, keeping his expression blank, figuring Roger would think of something.

"Pretty bracelet," Roger said, in obvious baby talk as he tipped his face up to peer at Christy. He grabbed her wrist and began to fiddle with her jewels with his pudgy fingers.

"Get away from me," she hissed, and slapped at his hand. As Roger stepped back, she stepped closer to Stan and grabbed his arm. "I've missed you," she cooed, and pressed his fist to her breast and leaned against him, her smile overly bright, her eyes glittering.

"How's tricks," he asked, not even mollified by the quick bloom to her cheeks. He winked at Roger, who was smirking, his genius brain working a mile a minute.

"N-now Stan," Butch said, looking from Stan to Christy, his arms crossed against his chest, his expression worried—a look he'd wear as long as he was married to her.

"I'm sure you'd like to find out," she preened, then wrapped an arm around Butch, who gripped her tightly. "What's this I hear about you working for little Miss Megan?" she asked, her gaze unblinking.

"I've worked on her house," he said, lifting his chin in Megan's direction. She stood near the fireplace, her head bowed as she filled a Styrofoam cup. He shot Christy a fond smile, hoping that Megan watched; though it was a petty move, a play for jealousy that Megan didn't deserve or even see, thank God.

"Lucky girl," Christy said, staring at Megan. "Maybe I could give her a few pointers . . . you know." She shrugged. "Seeing as how well I know what you . . . like."

"You don't give up, do you?" Stan said, shaking his head, chuckling. He turned to Butch. "The kid's hungry." He placed a proprietary hand on Roger's shoulder. "This is Roger Whitfield, Megan's nephew, by the way; which must make you feel great, considering what your wife just said in front of him."

Butch sucked in his breath, looking sick to his stomach. He had to be thinking of Val, Tom and the kids. He clasped Stan's shoulder, unable to look him in the eye, then followed Christy over to a group of mechanics.

Stan was making his way around tightly bunched groups with Roger in tow, when he looked up to see Megan studying him. She looked away quickly, but not before he saw the dismay in her eyes. A blush crept up her neck—not unlike the blush he'd just drawn from Christy—but it's meaning filled with hope and sweetness, not the ugly confirmation of a woman's depravity.

He sighed, thinking of the shouting match they'd gotten into a few days ago about Roger attending the funeral. She'd wanted him home with a babysitter; but he'd stood up for the kid, who wasn't a baby anymore, needing her protection. They'd both said a few mean things that had meant nothing; and in the end, Roger had gotten his way.

Would it always be like this, he wondered, battling for every scrap of control as if life depended on it? Did she think so little of him that his opinion counted for nothing? With a deep sigh, he took a step, not bothering to look where he trod, and plowed straight into Kathy.

"I'm so sorry," he stammered, and steadied her with both hands, not missing the leap of attraction in her eyes. Sometimes he wished he'd fallen for her instead of Megan. But love didn't work that way. He couldn't help how he felt.

She flashed him a welcoming smile, then gripped his arm and Roger's and pulled them closer. "You two haven't had a bite to eat," she said, looking from one to the other as if they were her kids. "Why don't you come with me? I'll fix you both a plate."

"Okay," Stan said, following her. He made the mistake of looking back, and then dragged her to a halt. Megan was deep conversation with Adam Clark, his arm around her shoulders. What the hell was that?

ঙঙঙঙঙ

They piled their plates with food, then slipped into Kathy apartment. Kathy, wasting no time, shooed Roger in the direction of her living room, where her kids were parked, eating and watching cartoons, with Andrea keeping an eye on them.

Feeling awkward, Stan looked around the room he'd torn down and built up, a little over a year ago. Like Megan's kitchen, it had bluestone counter tops, glass-fronted oak cabinets, white appliances, built-in microwave and convection ovens and a commercial gas stove. The table and buffet were dark, formal pieces atop an antique oriental rug. Framed art hung on the walls, probably made by Kathy's kids. A single window sported a swath of multi-colored fabric.

"The grown-ups are too much for them," Kathy said, and gestured for him to sit. "And you . . . it's been a long day and you need a break. You've been at Megan's beck and call since dawn—not that she's noticed. And Roger can be a handful—like all kids when they're tired."

"I suppose," he said, then sat, suddenly ravenous. He stuck his fork into the mountain of food he'd collected. There was lasagna, meatballs, broccoli chicken Parmesan, green salad loaded with Russian dressing, and Ming's dumplings and egg rolls. It was several minutes before he looked up from his plate, lulled by the food and the peace and solitude of Kathy's company. It had been a long time since he'd sat across the table from a woman who liked to eat. Kathy had already made deep inroads into her own heaped plate. What was it about funerals that made people hungry?

"Do you want to talk about it?" Kathy asked quietly. Her eyes were kind as she set her plate in the sink and returned to her seat, her movements graceful.

"Yah, sure," he said and tried to smile. He sighed as he moved his plate aside. She'd always been decent to him; though at first, she'd come across as just another rich broad from Andover. Pity was, she looked like Val; and at odd moments, the sight of her made his gut ache. He often wondered how Megan and Roger could stand it. She was like Val in other ways, too: quick to offer coffee and cake; and as he'd discovered in the past few weeks, a good listener. She had a way of knowing things without his saying a word—not that he wanted to take it any further.

He gasped as she moved around the table and touched his face, creating sensations too intimate to bear. Yet he couldn't look away. No one had touched him like that in a long time. He froze as she leaned in to kiss him, noticing for the first time how her black dress clung to her generous breasts. Her lips were soft and moist, her kiss delicious. He couldn't help his body's reaction as his arms went around her and the kiss deepened. He heard a door open and then close, but thought nothing of it as his hands moved around her back. She moaned as she slipped onto his lap, her arms coming around his neck. She pressed her breasts against him.

His hands stilled. It was all wrong. He didn't love this woman. Lust he'd had aplenty. Hell, he could have slipped Christy a nod and they'd being doing it right now. He broke away and placed his forehead against hers.

"I'm sorry," he said. "I can't do this."

"Dear Stan," she whispered, and moved away too, still holding his arms. Her eyes were sad. "I thought as much, but I had to try. You see, I get lonely sometimes, and I really like you. Megan said she doesn't have claims on you; but she does, doesn't she?"

He nodded, feeling like an idiot. She stood and brushed her hands down her dress. "When are you going to tell her?"

He looked at her with one eye closed. "I have."

"It's fairly certain that Adam's not for her," she said briskly, as if he hadn't spoken. She shook her head slightly. "He'll never settle for one woman, though his current wife thinks so. Megan knows better, of course—more than anyone except me, that is. The man's a pig when it comes to women, an addict really, a predator."

"More than anyone?" he asked, starting to get miffed. Why was she babbling about her ex? Hadn't they been talking about him and Megan? "What's that supposed to mean?" he asked.

Then he sucked in his breath, picturing Adam, his around Megan, getting a sick, sinking feeling. He exhaled slowly, shaking his head, thinking of Donald, another high-class user, his arm slung around Megan one snowy night. So, she'd had shit luck with men, and was too naïve for her own good half the time—just like Gordon had said. Was he any better?

"I'm no angel," was all he could manage.

Kathy slid back into her chair across from him, her eyes not quite meeting his, then took a deep breath. "She's in love with you, Stan, and it frightens her. Badly. So what are you going to do about it, Mr. Z?" Her smile was tremulous.

"Do about it?" He looked at his hands; work hardened and scarred, spread before him on the table. Looking in Kathy's clear blue eyes, he recognized her strength and was humbled by it. She and her kids must have been devastated by Adam's behavior. She had every reason to hate a woman who'd slept with her husband. But she didn't. He curled his fingers, making a fist, wanting Megan with a sudden fierce hunger. He cradled his face, elbows on the table.

"Well I . . . I think I've created my own monster by telling her the truth," he mumbled. "Maybe I could win a prize or something for being the world's biggest idiot, telling her that she needs me, that maybe she should stop working so hard."

"Not at all," she murmured and patted his hand. "She probably doesn't want to admit these things. And she *has* been working too hard. We all see it."

"I know Adam's no threat," he said, wincing. "She just won't have me—that's all. We've tried to connect; but she wants her independence, to make it on her own, without a man telling her what to do. Or so she says."

"So try again, Stan." She leaned closer, then rapped him on the head with her knuckles.

"Ouch!" He backed away, pressing his hand to the spot, then caught his plate, about to topple on the floor. His fork bounced against the wall, and he reached to retrieve it. "What'd you do that for? Why do you women keep hitting me?" He held his head, feeling like he was sitting at his mother's table.

"Isn't your happiness worth a little pain?" she asked, now laughing, though her eyes were sad. "Keep at her, Stan. You might be pleasantly surprised."

ଓଓଓଓଓ

It was after nine before the last guest left; and then the clean up began. Megan helped Ming in the kitchen, while Stan and Kathy swept though the lobby and the living room, retrieving plates, glasses and trash, wiping the tables and setting the furniture back into their places. With the exception of Penny, who slept in a port-a-crib in the library, the kids, including Roger, were sound asleep in Kathy's apartment.

The temperature dropped fast once the sun descended behind the trees and bloomed from ocher to vermilion to navy. A cooling breeze wafted in from Megan's open kitchen window; and for a moment, she paused, listening to the faint early-July chirp of young crickets. By August, the noise would intensify, mixing with the hum of June bugs and the rev of motorcycles.

She looked up from scraping a plate off into the sink, seeing the crusted plates, dirty glasses and silver piled on the counter, wishing she'd agreed to Kathy's suggestion of paper plates and plastic utensils. She was so tired; she could barely hold a thought.

When would Ming return from her apartment, she wondered; and how would she to get Penny to bed without waking her when she finally headed in that direction? She laughed harshly. As if she had the strength to climb those stairs. Her thoughts turned to the sleep sofa in the library, already spread with a sheet and blanket, and the pillows stuffed in one of the cupboards beneath the window seat. Penny's diaper bag was in the library. With the kitchen nearby when she needed to prepare a bottle, she'd stay put.

"Where do you want this?

Stan hovered in the doorway, looking tired and worried, holding a pair of stuffed trash bags. Blood rushed to her face. She shook her head numbly, unable to look at him. What had she been thinking—making an issue about Roger attending his own grandfather's funeral, and telling Stan she didn't need him—that she could take care of herself? On many levels, it was all quite true—she didn't need him or any man. But as a woman, when the sun went down and she drew her shades, when loneliness crept in like an unwelcome guest, she wanted and needed him –desperately.

But she'd seen him with Kathy and it hurt, despite the fact that she'd encouraged her to pursue him.

"Just set them in the hallway." She gestured toward the back door, and sighed as she continued scraping.

"You all right?" he asked, coming up behind

her, maintaining his distance.

Tears pricked her eyes. She'd practically ordered him to move the furniture, chase after ice and assumed he'd help with the clean up—like a damn servant. It was painful, seeing the longing in his eyes; and now . . . after seeing him with Kathy . . . just looking at him made her want to cry.

"We're almost done," he said softly. "Is there anything else you want me to do, Meg?

"No," she said dully, then made the mistake of turning, seeing his shoulders slumped, his silhouette, the shape of defeat. Had she done that . . . to him? Quickly, she averted her eyes, tears filling them. He was heading down the hallway, humming a Country Western tune.

"It's no use," she said and gripped the edge of the sink with both hands, not caring that tears dripped down her face as the pain came in crashing waves.

The back door swished open, but she was beyond identifying the sound until Ming's slender arm came around her shoulders. Sobs burst from her throat that she could no longer hold in. This is Ming, she told herself sternly, wanting to push her away. She'd judged her harshly over the past few weeks—because of Charlie. Yet over the course of this sad day, Ming had been there at every turn with a consoling hug, carefully prepared food and an extra pair of hands with Penny.

"You have to let it out, kiddo," Ming said, gripping her shoulder. "I learned that after *my* father died. Grief turned me wild for a time, almost suicidal. That's when I met Lydia's father; and you know what happened next."

"It's not just that," Megan said, moving away. She pulled a chair out from the table and sat quickly, exhaustion finally catching up with her. Ming stood behind her, massaging her shoulders. Her fingers were deft, homing in on pain points, smoothing out aches she'd only suspected.

"What then?" Ming asked softly.

Megan sighed as she looked up at her, touched by the concern in her eyes. "It's Stan," she said, then hung her head, sobs filling her throat. "I feel bad . . . I've treated him like . . . crap. I keep pushing him away, telling him I want to be alone, that I don't need him." She locked eyes with Ming. "But I do. In fact, I—"

"Love him?"

Megan nodded. Then she turned to face her. "It's funny. Your massage reminds me of my parents. I walked in on them once when I was about six or seven." She crossed her arms, hugging herself. "My mother had just come home after a long stay at the state mental hospital. She'd fixed us a chicken dinner . . . you know . . . with stuffing, mashed potato and gravy. It was like Thanksgiving; I think it was a Thanksgiving of sorts for her. She was so relieved to be back with us, to be home again." She looked down at her trembling hands. "I was supposed to be in bed, but I wanted another piece of apple pie—it was so delicious. I was sneaking into the kitchen when I saw them, then backed up, out of sight, embarrassed, feeling excluded and a little jealous. I don't think they saw me. Pa had wrenched his back that day and she was applying ointment, her eyes closed as she worked it into his shoulders. Her shirt was unbuttoned and her face flushed. His shirt was off and his eyes closed. I ran to my room, mortified. You see, in spite of the mental illness that in the end killed her, my father adored her, and she him. They shared something that was rare and lovely—something I could have had with Stan, if I could just stop being so stubborn."

She pushed away from the table and stood, unable to speak through the pain that clenched like a giant fist around her heart.

"Why don't you talk to him," Ming said, looking exasperated. "He has it for you bad, kiddo."

"But I saw him with Kathy," she said, picturing them together.

"Bullshit." Ming frowned. "It probably wasn't that at all. He's had a thing for you since the day I met him, probably long before that. You two just think about roles too much." She lifted her chin. "I'll bet twenty bucks he'll make a play for you before he leaves today. He's been looking like a wounded duck all day, tripping over himself trying to please you."

"But I saw him with Kathy," she repeated, weaker this time. The baby monitor at her hip sounded. Penny was crying.

"You go take care of her. I'll send him in your

direction." Ming nodded, her smile wicked.

After one last, hopeful glance, Megan fled to the library.

ଔଔଔଔ

She turned her key, let her out breath slowly, then stepped in and closed the door. The library was in muted darkness, a small nightlight in the far corner its sole illumination. It took a few seconds for her eyes to adjust. Then she turned to the port-a-crib, where Penny slept soundly, her long lashes soft crescents against peachy skin. At five months old, she was innocence personified, causing her heart to constrict at the sight of her. She adjusted a soft blanket around plump little shoulders, her hands lingering, relishing the homey task.

She moved slowly to the window seat; reached into the tiny refrigerator she'd tucked in a cabinet beneath it and grabbed a ginger ale. The can was icy against her hot face. After a long drink, she set it on a coaster on the table, then moved closer to the window.

What if Ming was right? What if Stan came to her tonight? She scanned the darkened room, seeing the sofa with its bedding tucked inside, the books filling the bookcases, all colors and shapes, and her restored and pared down furniture. Would he appreciate the changes she'd made? Would the room evoke memories of Hattie's teas and chess games with Chad? Would she get another chance to earn his love?

ଓଓଓଓଓ

"Put that on the table," Ming said tiredly, not turning as he entered the kitchen with the last tray of dirty dishes. He did as directed, then hefted the two large trash bags that were already tied and ready for curbside pickup in the morning, and carried them out to the back hallway.

It was cool and quiet out back. Even the wide staircase, built for servants, looked like a comfortable place to sit for a while. Yet, somehow, he resisted the urge. It was time to head home, maybe grab a six-pack and a pizza, put his feet up and watch the news—in a little while, anyway, after he took care of business with Meg. With great reluctance, he backed into the kitchen, dragging an empty trash bin.

"What's new, Stan, the man?" Ming asked. He looked up, seeing her smile, his hackles raised. Her dark eyes almost disappeared into her lids. She looked angry, probably because Charlie had vanished hours ago, after roosting in Megan's living room for a good part of the afternoon, his eyes bloodshot while he watched one old Western after another.

"Nothing," he said, wishing she'd leave him alone. Charlie wasn't his problem. He'd shut off even an ounce of sympathy for Ming, having seen too many signals pass between her and Adam, not to come to several lousy conclusions. Adam sure liked to cover his bases.

"Where's Megan?" he asked, trying to sound nonchalant. She'd looked ready to collapse a little while ago; yet another day would not pass before he talked to her, reasoned with her. That little scene with Kathy had been like a punch in the gut.

"In the library." Ming gestured with her thumb. "Better late than never," she added with a snicker.

"Whatever that means," he said, dismissing her as he strode down the hallway. She was one screwed up broad, playing with the wrong people.

He moved steadily toward the library, the one room she'd not allowed him entrance. It seemed fitting that he'd find her there, the scene of his best memories—not that he'd ever told her. She'd done all the renovations herself, and like today, kept the room locked. It was her sanctuary, she'd told him, her quiet reading place. Maybe it was time to tell her how much it meant to him.

She had to listen, he told himself. The cold war they were living had to end . . . today. She belonged to him and always did. It was about time she admitted it.

"Megan?" He knocked on the door, but there was no answer. "Megan?" He whispered this time, and rattled the doorknob, which turned smoothly. He pushed the door open, slipped inside and closed it softly.

It took several seconds for his eyes to adjust; but then he saw her, kneeling on a window seat, gazing out the tall mullioned windows, illuminated by the moonlight, a slender figure bent slightly by grief.

The bookcases gleamed, as did the parquet floor. She must have refinished them. The bookcases were filled with books of all colors and sizes, including a low shelf of children's books that looked well used. An oval Oriental rug spanned the room, looking soft and deep. A large sofa stood a few feet from the book-lined wall on the right. Well-padded chairs had been carefully placed, creating an atmosphere that was cozy and intimate. He smiled, seeing Chad's polished chess set on a small gleaming table between two opposing chairs. In Chad and Harriet's day, the room had been packed with massive wooden furniture, knick-knacks and collectibles. He liked the more spacious look. Hearing a small sound, he turned and saw Penny, snuffling in her crib, sound asleep.

"What do you want, Stan?" Megan asked, not turning. Her voice was muffled. She'd been crying.

"I've been meaning all day, for the past few days really . . .." He paused, hoping she couldn't hear the clamor of his heart. "I've been meaning to tell you again how sorry I am about your dad. You haven't had it easy, and he would have been damn proud of you." He held his breath, wishing he had a better command of the English language. Words were a poor salve for a grief like she'd experienced.

He took a step closer.

"Thanks, Stan," she said softly. "It's hard to believe he's really gone."

He went to her and laid a hand on her shoulder, unable to stop himself.

"Pa and I had our differences," she said, glancing at his hand, "but he always *tried* to be good to me. He always *meant* well." She smiled slightly. "Like you, Stan." She smiled as she turned to him.

His hands trembled and he put them behind his back. It was almost painful not to touch her. Her eyes were bloodshot and her nose red; but she'd never looked more beautiful.

"I can't say I'm sorry I promised to take care of you." He peered into her eyes, hoping to gauge her response.

Then she started to cry; and he swore softly, and pulled her into his arms. Like a rag doll she clung; and lust drained from him. He let her cry for a good long time; glad for her slender strength, her warmth, as she hugged him back. When she started to pull away, he pulled a wad of napkins from his back pocket and handed them to her, his arm around her shoulders, liking the feel of her, keeping her in the shelter of his arm. She blew her nose noisily.

"I'm here for you, Meg," he said softly, caressing her hair. "I want to hold you when you're sad. And maybe this isn't the right time, but I want to marry you." He took a deep breath. "I love you, Meg. Is there any hope?"

"Aw, Stan," she said, and with a watery smile, raised her lips and pulled him close and kissed him soundly. It was like coming home.

His hands came around her back and he was

stroking her and pulling her tight against him, making her insides ache. Then gently his hands circled lower and he was kneading her buttocks, and pulling her down with him onto the window seat. She moaned into his mouth as he caressed her neck in the sensitive place beneath her ears. Never had she felt such exquisite pleasure.

She opened her mouth to him, tasting sunshine; while he managed to find each tiny button down the front of her silky blouse, then pull it off. Her bra came next. Then he lowered his head and laved each nipple, fulfilling an urge so primal, she could barely breathe. She pressed against his erection, now hugely swollen, and opened his shirt and reached inside, craving the warmth of his skin, the feel of his bristly chest hairs, the lean hard length of him. He was her love, her man.

She forgot about her sleep sofa as he lowered her to the rug, his mouth moving in the wake of his hands as he stripped off the rest of her clothes. She forgot all about Penny in her crib, the stretch marks across her abdomen and Pa's funeral expenses, as he devoured her skin, tasting each inch, his fingers playing magic in every crevice. She touched him, too, in ways she'd long dreamed of. He was everything she'd imagined he would be; but with a surprising gentleness that melted a frozen, lonely place locked deep inside her.

She cried out as he touched her most tender places, his lips on hers, his words sweet, encouraging, filled with love. She sobbed as she climaxed, lost in an exquisite kaleidoscopic of pleasure. As the last beats pulsed, she welcomed him into her body and cried out again as he covered her mouth with his own to absorb the sounds. Then blindly, rendered helpless by pure sensation, she surrendered to the ancient dance.

Later, their breathing quieted. She lay still beneath him, her body humming, replete. He was heavy—yet she put her arms around him and pulled him even closer.

Several minutes later, she felt the wet rug beneath her; her lower back was starting to hurt, and his flaccid penis was about to fall out. She hated to think of the puddle of bodily fluids soaking into her lovely rug. But it was worth it—Stan was truly hers.

Or was he?

Penny stirred—a soft baby sound of protest, a dream perhaps, or a gas pain—then she settled back to sleep.

"Are you okay?" Stan asked, stroking her hair. He moved onto his side, his head propped up on one hand.

"I love you, Stan," she said softly. "And I'm sorry about today." She touched his lips to stop his protest. "I had no cause to treat you like that, ordering you around. I thought about what you said—what Pa said—and you're right. I do need you."

He closed his eyes briefly, his expression lightening. "I've loved you for a long time, Meg," He brushed her face with his knuckles. "I miss our dinner nights and seeing Roger and Penny, being a family. I think we're good together. I wish we could have connected sooner, but maybe we weren't ready."

"What about you and Kathy?" she asked, and watched him closely, her spirits sagging. Had she chosen wrong once again?

"Kathy?" He looked taken aback. "What do you mean?"

"I saw you kissing her." She was close to tears. "It looked pretty serious."

"Oh, that," he said, and jerked his head slightly as if remembering. "She was just testing me, seeing if I was really available, trying to shock me into doing something about you, more likely. It only lasted for a couple of seconds. It meant nothing."

"You sure?"

"Ask her," he said, then cupped her face with both hands, his expression sober. "Look Meg, I don't want anyone but you. Kathy's like a big sister to me; and she looks too much like Val; though I hate bringing *that* up at a time like this. She was rescuing me, that's all, and Roger, too. She got us some food; and when she and I were alone . . . well you know." He shrugged slightly. "She was just trying to help me. You and I weren't exactly speaking all day."

Megan looked away. "Yeah, I suppose."

"Tell me if I'm out of line," he said, drawing her gaze, "but I can picture myself living in your house, working on it on weekends, maybe adding a playroom in the attic, sleeping in your four-poster, taking you and the kids on vacations, maybe even going to church on Sunday, if that's what you want. I'm not big on religion, but I'll go if you want me to."

"Aw, Stan." She looked deep into his eyes, liking what she saw.

He grinned, his chin coming up. "Kathy's not exactly my type, Meg. She's too easy-going, too reasonable and quiet. I'd be bored in a day." He brushed her lips with the tip of his finger. "I'd much rather have someone like you who's stubborn and hard to live, someone who likes to argue."

"Stubborn and hard to live with!" She whacked him on the arm. "You're the one who's stubborn and hard to live with."

He chuckled as he rolled on top of her, pinning her down. Then, ignoring her squawking protest, he proceeded to kiss her soundly.

CHAPTER 14
2:00 AM

"Mum," came the urgent whisper.

Ming turned over in bed and glanced at the clock on her nightstand. It was only two in the morning.

Charlie lay naked beside her, snoring softly, one arm flung over his head. His face was flushed and his lips slack. He was wasted. She couldn't stand the sight of him.

Moonlight streamed in through the screen-clad windows. Not a breeze stirred. The room was stifling hot. An animal of some kind rustled outside—probably a skunk, judging by the smell.

"Mum."

Her gaze riveted to where Lydia stood shivering in the shadows of the doorway, a waif in a thin cotton nightgown. She ripped the sheet over Charlie's waist; though it wasn't the first time Lydia had seen him naked. The man had no concept of modesty, no clue when it came to little kids.

She scanned the room and sighed. The dresser drawers were spilled open, cosmetics jumbled and strewn across their tops, bedclothes rumpled on the floor, paintings askew. Charlie was a walking disaster once he got going. Last night he'd been particularly obnoxious. She didn't know how much more of this she could take.

Her heart warmed as she looked at her daughter, her precious gift. In those shameful days after she'd admitted her pregnancy to her mother, she could hardly have imagined the sweetheart she would receive. Lydia was the perfect child, the daughter she'd always longed to be—a friend really. She'd been such a helper last week at Mr. Rosswell's funeral; running errands for her back to the apartment, helping her prepare the dim sum, watching Penny. The sight of her lovely innocent face had given her the strength she'd needed to get through that horrible day.

The hairs on her arms stood on end. "What is it?" she asked, seeing Lydia's expression. The child had a way of knowing things that other people missed. The sense of danger smote her. She ran to the window, closed and locked it, then stood with her back to it, gasping.

"It's too late," Lydia said. Her face crumbled into a wrenching sob. Ming went to her, held her close and pressed her face against the top of her head, waiting for her to speak. It was always thus after she'd had one of her visions. Her maternal grandmother had been so afflicted—though, unlike Lydia, she'd been a royal bitch, if the family stories held true. Lydia had what people in the west called the sight. It was both a gift and a curse.

"Someone took Penny," Lydia whispered at last, her whole body trembling. "There were two of them. Two men." She shook her head, "I couldn't stop them, Mum. I just watched it happen, couldn't even move. It was like on TV . . . but real . . . and she was crying."

"Did it just happen?" Ming asked softly, caressing her silky hair.

Lydia nodded.

Tears stung her eyes, but she blinked them away. She'd been expecting the Columbians to do something—but not this—not with Penny. How could she possibly have warned Megan in time?

She looked down at her daughter, then gripped her by the arms. With Lydia safe, she could do what needed to be done—what she should have done weeks ago, instead of continually pandering to Charlie's ego. The man was a lost cause.

"I want you to return to bed and try to sleep. In the morning, go to Kathy's apartment. Wait until at least six-thirty. And stay away from Charlie. He won't even know you're here, or that you're gone." She smoothed back her hair.

"Where are you going?' Lydia asked, her lovely

face distorted by tears and fright.

Ming looked at her closely, considering her options. Telling her too much would put her at risk; but she deserved some information, or her imagination would engage and she'd make herself sick.

"I have to get to the Towers," she said at last. "I'll call Megan from there—and Kathy. I can't tell you why. Just trust me, okay?"

Lydia nodded, her eyes huge and liquid in the dim light. "I'm afraid, Mum. For you," she said softly.

Ming kissed her upturned face. "It will be all right," she repeated, hoping it was true, hoping it wasn't too late to untangle her life from Ernesto's ever-tightening web. He'd been the key all along. But if it hadn't been him, another dealer would have taken his place. Trying to stop the drug trade was like standing against a hurricane.

Lydia shuffled off, a tired little girl doing her mother's bidding. Ming closed her eyes tight, praying she'd live though the next few days so she could see her to adulthood. She shuddered, taking one last look at Charlie. He'd sleep until she returned, having snorted enough cocaine last night for a team of men, ignoring her pleas to stop. It was a wonder his heart hadn't seized up.

She felt cold as she looked at him, the man she'd once considered her true love. But those days were gone, as was the man she'd fallen in love with. The less Charlie knew the better.

CHAPTER 15
2:30 AM

Ming slipped past the snoring guard, purse bumping against her hip, ignoring the frigid blast of over-conditioned air, the potted plants, the muted pictures on the wall. She passed through the lobby's outer door and headed toward the elevators, her mind racing ahead of her. She'd hidden the notebook deep in Eric's file cabinet, behind a stash of old brochures and a dusty bottle of Chivas Regal.

The carpet was thick and spongy in front of the elevators. The jewel-tone velvet wallpaper looked luxuriant in the dim morning light. She punched the up arrow and in seconds, the bell sounded, a door flew open and she leaped inside, her breath coming fast. She hit the button for her floor and hummed as the car ascended; pondering the lock-picking techniques Tien had taught her. Tien had been handsome, charming, elusive and crafty. Like Charlie, he'd fallen for drugs in the end—jumping off a dilapidated Hong Kong pier in a euphoric fit, just to prove that he could. They'd never found his body. She'd cried for days, earning her mother's upraised fist, until her pregnancy had become obvious.

The bell sounded for her floor; and she was down the hall before the door swung shut. She passed through Tower One's outer door and skidded to a halt before her brother's office. She tried the door handle; but it was locked.

Breathing heavily, she looked over her shoulder at the rows of cubicles, reminded of the daily misery and humiliation of what was allegedly her job. In college, she'd been respected. She'd tutored many of the other students in her classes, a few of whom were now team leaders at Smith Labs, and on their way to management. After tonight, she'd do something about her career—either force Eric to acknowledge her or move on to another job, another company. She had to get away, to find a place where she could lick her wounds. If only Charlie would leave her alone. The trouble was, she still couldn't say no to him.

Her eyes burned as she thought of his treachery. She'd loved him with all her heart, mind and soul, damn fool that she was. Never again would she trust a man so blindly. It hurt, the way he'd set her up with Adam, selling her as if she were a prostitute.

To pay for his debts?

She crossed her arms and rubbed them, remembering the way Adam had hauled her against him at Andrea's party, forcing her to kiss him, telling her that it was payment due. Somehow, she'd managed to shove him away, and return to the party, mocking both him and Charlie with her cool, self-compose façade. Only after he'd left on the heels of Gordon's collapse had she felt safe—for a while.

If it weren't for good men like Gordon and Stan, and wonderful little boys like Roger, she'd have nothing to do with the male gender for the rest of her life. Men like Eric, bossing her around, treating her like dirt, were the bane of her existence.

Eric be damned. Who gave him the right to rule her?

In a few quick movements, she plucked the specially made shaft from her purse, twisted it into the lock and shoved open the door. A minute later, she was sitting at Eric's desk, his phone in her hand.

CHAPTER 16
3:30 AM

Megan flashed her badge at the security guard as she passed through the lobby across from the Town House. Middle-aged and portly, with a fringe of gray hair slung over a bald spot, he nodded in his seat behind a desk, barely awake, an unlikely threat to thief or saboteur. She glanced back at the floor-to-ceiling windows and shivered, seeing thick darkness beyond the street-light's reach. Dawn was hours away.

She climbed the narrow staircase, then sped down the shadowed hallway toward her office, clutching her stomach, trying to crowd out the image of Penny crying for her, needing her, being neglected or abused. Why had they taken her baby? A whimper escaped and she focused on her destination—a cubicle set in a narrow bay of cubicles in the two-story building behind the Towers.

Roger had howled when she'd pulled him out of bed. She'd tried to keep her explanation simple, her tone calm; but he'd flailed at her, furious and frightened, blaming her for Penny's abduction. "You're supposed to keep us safe," he'd accused.

She'd practically flung him into Kathy's arms; then managed to haul him back and hug him tight. He had every right to be angry. How could someone have invaded her room while she lay sleeping, and then steal her child? Penny was an innocent. Would she become a casualty?

She stuffed a fist in her mouth, stifling a sob. Her whole body shook, yet she kept moving, hearing the echo of Ming's voice in her head, unable to forget the shrilling phone, Ming's barely coherent sobs and looking across the room at Penny's empty crib.

"Penny," she moaned "Where are you?"

She slumped over, hands on her knees, trying not to retch, praying for strength. Her baby was gone—bait for Donald? He might not even be the child's father—or so she suspected—though Penny didn't look much like Donald *or* Adam; but more like Bethany and Letty, which was from Val's gene pool. It was all too confusing and she had no idea what to do about it. Ming had better help her as she'd promised.

She came to a halt at her cubicle, seeing in a blur the stack of manuals, piles of paperwork and pink phone messages, a half-eaten donut beside several empty paper coffee cups, pictures of Penny and Roger tacked on her bulletin board. It was like a foreign place she'd once occupied, with old habits and rules that no longer applied.

The phone rang and she grabbed the receiver. Her throat constricted. She couldn't utter a sound.

"Meggie, it's me."

"Donald," she breathed; then crouched down, making herself a smaller target. Images of his face, twisted by rage, came flooding back. Her hand trembled as she gripped the receiver. She wanted to fling the damn thing as far as she could. But Penny's life was at stake. Had he taken her? And how was Ming involved?

"Hello, Donald." Her nerves were frayed. One wrong word and she'd lose everything. "Where are you?" she asked.

"I saw you head into the Towers," he said evenly. "I'm across the street at the Town House, room 113. I need to see you . . . alone."

"I'll be there." She replaced the receiver and the phone rang again.

"Hello," she managed to force out.

"Senora Rosswell." The voice purred.

"Carlotta?" Megan's eyes narrowed. Her heart began to race. "What do you want?"

"So sorry for the intrusion, Senora." Carlotta spoke as if from a script. "I must speak with you concerning a package I have that is yours, in exchange for in item that belongs to my family."

"You have her?" Megan asked, trying to keep the panic from her voice.

"No questions," Carlotta hissed. "I was told to relay a message. You must meet me at the Smith Labs Education Center within the hour."

"But it's not even three in the morning." The phone clicked and the dial tone sounded.

She sat heavily at her desk, then replaced the receiver. She rubbed her aching forehead, trying to think. Ming had said to wait for her call; but was it a setup? She had to move quickly. Donald was across the street; and there was no telling how long he'd take to make his sorry explanation. And Carlotta . . ..

A small sound, like muffled footsteps, came from the cubicle bay's entrance. She ducked down behind the partition mere seconds before someone passed by. She held her breath, her ears straining, until the footsteps receded. Then she poked her head out in time to see the retreating figure of a small, well-dressed man. It wasn't the security guard.

The phone rang again and this time it was Ming, asking to meet her at the fifth floor ladies room. "You know the one," she whispered.

Megan dropped the receiver, then flew down the hall, pausing at intersections, looking around corners, listening for footsteps, wanting to shriek. Why the secrecy, the cloak and dagger charade? Why wouldn't Ming just meet her at her cubicle, or at home?

She stifled a sob as she ran down the ramp, past the darkened cafeteria, heading for the Towers. She bypassed the elevators and took the stairs two steps at a time, too frightened to pause even for the few seconds it would take to wait for an elevator.

The stairwell was empty, yet she paused at the fifth floor entrance, her nerves frazzled, listening intently. Was she being fanciful or was someone else in the stairwell, stopping as she stopped, waiting to pounce? She took a deep breath, shoved the door open, sprinted for the ladies room and slipped in quickly.

"Ming," she whispered, leaning against the door, her breath ragged.

"In here," came the reply. Ming emerged from a toilet stall, holding a large manila envelope, her expression grim. Her hair was tangled, her eyes bloodshot.

"This is for you." She patted the envelope. "I've kept a log of the drug deals: buyers, dates and amounts. You'll find some interesting names in here . . . like Steve Grant. He got you involved in that database project so he could keep an eye on you. This package was my protection . . . and now it's yours."

"Why?" Megan asked, holding her hand out and taking the envelope. Steve's involvement was no surprise. She'd suspected as much for months, considering he'd had the audacity to smoke pot during a business meeting. "Why are you giving me this? Why now?" she asked. "I thought you had information on Penny? I don't understand." She slumped against the door, cradling the envelope, shaking her head. Her head hurt and she wanted to lie down; but most of all, she wanted her daughter back.

Ming sat beside her, closing her eyes tightly, hugging her knees close to her chest. "Taking Penny changes things," she said softly. "No one touches our kids." Her eyes glittered with tears and rage as she turned to Megan. "I tried to help Charlie. I really did; but he's in over his head. After a while, he stopped caring about anything but getting high. He stopped caring about me. I've sold for him—done a few other things to settle his debts. But it's never enough. So I kept records, because you see, in the end, I have to answer to myself, and to my kid who needs me most of all."

Megan put a hand on her arm. "But what's going on, Ming? How does it all fit together? And why me?"

Ming looked at her intently. "It's Ernesto Hermosa," she said. "He knows about the CIA—that Donald's one of them."

"Ernesto? Donald?" Her mind reeled. She thought of her impending meeting, Carlotta and Adam's insistent questioning, and the hang-up phone calls. Donald was in the CIA?

"Ernesto tapped your phone right from the start," Ming said with a tight nod. "He had Donald's calls traced, called in a few favors. The feds won't touch Ernesto. He's a protected source."

"Is this the brother you told me about—

Carlotta's brother?" she asked, her mind reeling. Was it the same Ernesto who'd encouraged Donald to beat her?

"Yeah." Ming patted the envelope. "He's the one in charge, or so it seems. He's the head of a Columbian family . . . the one Adam married into . . . the Hermosas. I told you this already." She looked exasperated.

"And this?" Megan indicated the envelope.

"Your insurance policy, kiddo, in case things get rough. And if something happens to me." She looked away sadly.

"Ming!" Megan tightened her grip. "What are you planning?"

Ming threw off her hand, then turned to face her. "I want you to listen carefully. Charlie's not the only one who's in too deep. The list is long and growing. Unfortunately, I know too much, so I'm expendable. They want Donald. They'll do anything to get him. It's not just revenge for being a plant. He's dumped a load and they want it back. They want him in exchange for Penny."

Megan resisted looking at her watch. Time was slipping past. Donald was waiting . . . the man she'd married, but had never really known. She had to see his face, hear his voice, look into his eyes and see for herself how she really felt about him . . . how he felt about her. All along, he'd been on the side of the law? All along, she'd thought the worst of him.

Her eyes narrowed, and she bit down hard on her lip. Nothing could erase that last horrible scene in her apartment; just as nothing would change the love she had for Stan. Even before Donald, she'd pined for him. The game was different now—yet it had to be played.

"I suggest you hide that folder and use it as leverage," Ming said. "You need to call someone—maybe Stan—tell him where to find it." She lowered her lids. "If something happens to me, I've made you Lydia's legal guardian. Eric and his wife are not getting their hands on her." She flashed Megan a tight grin. "If you know where Donald is, you need to use that information, no matter how you feel about him, to get your kid back. Men are replaceable—children are not."

Megan looked at her sharply, seeing in her expression all the pain she'd suffered at the hands of the men who claimed to care for her. "Did you know this was going to happen," she asked, "that they'd take Penny?"

"I should have," Ming said with a tired laugh. "These people are ruthless." She folded her arms across her chest and looked away, the vein at her temple pulsing.

Megan eyed her warily. She seemed contrite; but all along, she'd been lying, skirting the truth and the law. Could she really trust her? "Donald's here," she said, barely above a whisper. "I'm seeing him in a few minutes."

"Here? In the Towers?" Ming's eyes were unfathomable. "What will you do?"

She ignored her questions. "I'm supposed to

meet Carlotta at the Ed Center in an hour, too. Seems everyone wants to see me." She held her breath.

"But the Ed Center's not open, yet." Ming's eyes narrowed.

"I know." She swallowed heavily. How would it end?

"Adam." Ming spoke through tight lips, her eyes flashing. "He must have a key card."

"Will you come with me?" Megan asked; stunned by the impulsive step she was about to take. "I don't want to be alone with either of them." She grimaced, imagining Donald's reaction upon seeing Ming. It wouldn't fit his expectations. He always had to do things his way.

"All right," Ming said, looking down; but not before Megan caught the flash of fear in her eyes.

A sound came from the hallway; and they froze.

"No, please don't do that." It sounded like Adam, his voice high-pitched, desperate. Megan pushed the door open slightly and peered out. It *was* Adam, his face red and mottled, his button-down shirt hanging sloppily out of his pants, his hair wild. He was on his knees, begging.

"Please, you don't need to hurt him," he sobbed. "He just needs a little help, that's all. I didn't agree to this, Ernesto. You can't start killing people. This is America, for Christ's sake."

"Ernesto," Megan breathed. Ming gripped her wrist. She was shaking badly. Tears were streaming down her face. Megan followed the line of her vision.

Charlie was caught in the grip of a greasy haired thug, hands behind his back, facing the same well-dressed man she'd seen in the cubicle bay. Charlie's head hung down. Slobber dripped from his mouth. He stumbled, almost falling. From what she could see, his face looked swollen, battered.

"It is the only way to ensure order," said the elegant man. He was slender, with a thin mustache and a well-groomed head of hair. His voice was soft, cultured, with a slight Spanish accent.

Adam grabbed at the thugs arm. "Please!" he begged. "I can't condone this. It just isn't right."

Then came the sound of a muffled impact. A red stain spread across Charlie chest and he slumped to the floor.

Megan turned, seeing Ming's eyes widen with horror and her mouth open. Quickly she lunged for her, closed a hand over her mouth and pulled her close. Ming shuddered as she sobbed, lost in grief. Megan counted the seconds as the elevator chimed, the men got in and the door closed. She counted to thirty, straining her ears, her mind racing with plans, all quickly discarded. Adrenaline rushed as she open the door. Still gripping Ming, she surveyed the landing. Charlie was on the floor, a pool of blood soaking the carpet around him.

Ming shrugged her off and ran to him, sobbing loudly. On her knees, she cradled him, crooning a tuneless sound, her words unintelligible as she searched for a pulse. "He'd dead," she said, her face a horrible mask. “Go see your Donald,” she said, spittle flying from her lips. “Bring this thing to an end.”

“Do you want me to call the guard?” Megan asked, her tears flowing freely. Charlie’s face was battered, his eyes swollen shut, his hand sprawled open, bloody and raw. No one deserved to die like that. She thought of his intelligence and tenacity, his kindness in the days before his addiction. He’d taken the wrong path; his brilliance wasted.

“Go,” Ming said harshly. “You’ve no time to lose. I’ll call the police and Stan. You need someone, but it won’t be me. I’ve had enough.”

Megan threw her the envelope and ran.

ଓଓଓଓଓ

Stan moved automatically through the darkened apartment, grabbing jeans and a T-shirt, stuffing on socks and shoes. He cursed softly, his big toe throbbing. He’d stubbed it on the footboard, trying to reach the phone. He dressed quickly, his mind racing, changing plans mid-thought. Meg needed him and Floyd wasn’t picking up the phone. The pilot was back, just as Floyd had said.

But who’d taken Penny? The Columbians? The CIA? Donny-boy had dumped a load. According to Floyd, both parties wanted him bad. He could understand the Columbians. The pilot had been on their payroll. But why was the U.S. Government so hot on the case?

His eyes filled and he clenched his fists. No matter whose DNA Penny shared, she was his and always would be. His stomach roiled as he imagined how Megan was dealing with all of this. Should he meet her at the Ed Center, as Ming had suggested, or get in on her discussion with the pilot? Oh, God, how could he protect her? There was danger whichever way she turned.

That's when he thought of Walt.

Despite the fights they'd had over the years, Walt was a good man to have at his back—like that time in grade school when Billy Waczewski had called him out after school. Billy and his friends had been ready to pound him to a pulp over a chance comment he'd made in math class that had made Billy look like the loser that he was. Walt had been there with friends, ensuring the fight stayed man-to-man. Billy had hit hard; but after a few go-rounds, they'd both walked away with a fine set of bruises.

Stan grabbed the receiver, punched in the numbers and uttered a few key phrases that had Walt on his feet and shoving on his clothes.

CHAPTER 17
4:00 AM

Megan raised a fist to knock on the door, then dropped it. She stared at the room number, 113, struggling with fear, unable to shake the feeling that something momentous was about to occur. Inside the room was an ugly part of her past. She needed to face it.

She gasped as the door swung open. Donald stood before her, looking like he'd aged a decade. His shirt and pants were badly creased. He was barefoot and needed a shave. She looked around the room with its quilted bedcovers, framed pictures above each of the twin beds, standard dressers at their feet, the small round table and two chairs before the windows, and a tiny bathroom equipped with the essentials—then back to Donald. She felt nothing for this man.

"Hi Meggie." He rubbed his face, then jerked his head, indicating that she should enter.

She passed warily; all of her hackles raised as she searched the room, ensuring they were alone. He stuck his head out the door and looked around. Then he closed it softly and stood with his hands in his pockets, his face expressionless.

"What's going on?" she asked, then sat on the bed and crossed her legs, every muscle tensed for flight. Her thoughts leaped to Penny, but she brushed them aside. She had to focus. She had to listen closely.

"You're looking good," he said, eyeing her. He reached for a pack of cigarettes on the dresser, lit one with a trembling hand, then took a long drag, his eyes going to slits.

"Do you have to?" she asked, waving at the smoke.

He stepped into the bathroom; the toilet sounded and he came out empty handed.

"An old habit," he said with a shrug. "Look, Meggie . . . I." He raked a hand through his hair, his eyes narrowing. He looked exasperated, like he didn't know where to begin.

"Go on," she said, not about to help him. "You called this meeting."

"Yeah, I supposed I did." He looked up at the ceiling. "Where to begin? That's the trouble."

"You can sit down, you know." She looked pointedly at a chair near the windows; and he headed toward it and sat, surprising her. Obedience had never been one of his traits.

They stared at each other for a long time, the memories coming back, not all of them bad. Raw emotions crossed his face: regret, longing, shame and sadness among them. Was he trying to appeal to her, to get her to talk? She stared back, effecting a calm expression, refusing.

He swallowed heavily, then cleared his throat. "What can I say?" He looked away, his eyes tearing. Then he clasped his hands in front of him, his elbows on his knees. "I'm a CIA agent, have been for some time. I was in too deep for a while, started using, started playing the part all too well, cozying up to the Columbians. At least, that's what I told myself. That's what the Miami house was all about. It just didn't pan out—not without you."

"It didn't pan out?" She sucked in her breath. "That's your excuse for raping me?"

His head jerked back as if she'd struck him. "Yeah, well, you could say that. I was trying to fit you into the picture somehow, but . . .." He shot her a sheepish grin. "You got something out of it, I hear."

"You are despicable," she said, rising from the bed. "You could have killed me; so don't go bringing Penny into this." She clamped her lips, refusing to cry.

"Ah, Meggie," he said, and sighed heavily. "I didn't come here to fight. You named her Penelope Rosswell? Why not Alexander?"

"Why are you here?" she asked, shoving away the image of Penny crying and needing her. There were puzzle pieces yet to fit: she dared not miss a clue.

"I need a friend . . . and a favor." He watched at her out of the corner of his eye, as if gauging her reaction. "And I don't know where else . . .."

She moved to the windows and pushed aside the sheers to look out. Was the room bugged? Was someone watching the place? "So you want a few things. Doesn't everyone?"

"They say I dumped a load," he said softly.

She turned back, letting the sheers fall. What Ming had said was true.

"But that's not the half of it," he continued. "Someone cut my gas line, broke the fuel gauge while they were at it. Yeah, the plane went down; but not because of me. Someone wanted me gone. I don't know if it was the Feds or the Columbians. Word around is that they're both looking for me. I don't want to end up dead."

"What do you want from me?" She watched him closely. Was he really the key to finding Penny?

"I understand you have local and federal connections, that maybe you can call in a few favors, find out which way the wind's blowing." He looked at her expectantly. "I want to stay in the business, if you get my drift; but I need to know what I'm up against."

"And you think I can help you?"

"The PI on your case," he said with a slight lift

of his chin. "He's a straight shooter, from what I hear. If anyone can uncover the truth, he can. And since you've been working with the CIA . . . you know . . . McClelland and Graham? They're supposed to be my contacts; but they aren't answering my calls."

"McClelland who? The Feds haven't even given me a courtesy phone call. And no one's watching me. What the hell are you talking about?" She backed away slightly.

"Floyd Mello has been. Just ask your boyfriend." He eyed her haughtily.

"Who?" Her mind reeled. She though of Stan and the foolish deal he'd made with Pa to watch over her and keep her safe. He must have hired a PI; or maybe Pa had. Realization must have shown on her face.

"I still love you," he said softly.

She looked into his eyes, seeing the truth of his words. But it was his truth—not hers.

"It's too late, Donald," she said. "It's always been too late." She smiled sadly, wanting to hug him despite all that had happened. He was like a brother more than a lover. They'd been through a lot together, but mostly drunk. "I should never have married you," she said, seeing the yearning in his eyes. "You don't want me, Donald . . . not the real me."

"So it's this Stan, is it?" He moved closer, his arms folded across his chest.

She nodded. "It's always been Stan, even before

I met you. I was just too ornery, maybe too naïve to figure it out."

"Yeah, and what about Adam?" His expression darkened. "Spread yourself a little thin there for a while, didn't you, Meggie?"

"We all make mistakes," she shot back. "And things have changed." Her heart pounded. "I have kids now, a home to care for and tenants who love me, not to mention Stan." Pain stabbed at the thought of Penny. Was *she* being cared for?

He flinched, looking as if she'd slapped him. "Yeah. Yeah. I've made a mess of my life: It wasn't easy growing up with a father away all the time, and a mother zonked out on anti-depressants, waiting for the big hero to show up, giving her kids only snippets of a life."

"Give me a break," she said, hands on her hips. "When are you going to stop blaming your parents and take some responsibility for your life? You're not a kid anymore; and you're not the only one with a less than perfect childhood."

"Miss responsible herself talking," he sneered.

"That's right. I have a lot of responsibility," she said. "And I don't abandon those who need me." She thought of her sister's family, now gone—a huge hole in her heart. Did he even know about Val? Did he care?

"I was going to ask you to join me again." He held an arm out beseechingly.

"On the run?" she laughed. "Do I get to bring my kids?"

"I'm hoping for a new life, a new name, somewhere safe, maybe California or Oregon," he said, his expression dreamy.

She stared at him, baffled. Had he been listening?

He moved closer, a strange light in his eyes. "You remember those early days, Meggie, that time in Boston, and the big snow storm when we used your gas stove for heat? What about that? What about our wedding and the crazy nights in Vegas, laughing and drinking? What about us?"

Tears welled in her eyes. He was hopeless—a lost soul grasping for salvation. She had nothing to give him—never did. "I have what I've always wanted," she said softly. He just looked at her. Was he even paying attention? "I have permanence, family and a steady job. Believe it or not, Donald, I'm not about to start over."

"I thought so," he said, looking away, hanging his head slightly, exhaling slowly through his teeth. "But it was worth a try." He looked tired and sad. "You meeting with Carlotta?"

She eyed him closely. "How did you know?"

He sniffed. "I know lots of things, just not the right ones, apparently."

"Did you know about Penny?" She looked at him squarely, wanting to cry.

"What about her," He asked, his expression closing. He clenched his fists at his sides.

"Someone took her last night," she managed to get out. "Came right in my room while we were sleeping. One of my tenants saw them take her. There were two men, she said. She didn't see their faces. Was it you?"

"No," he said, looking strangely cold. "It was probably Carlotta, wanting one of Adam's brats, since she can't have one of her own."

"What?" Megan sucked in her breath. "Adam's brat? Is that what you think?"

"Just look at the kid," he sneered. "She's obviously not mine; and the timing's about right. I'm not stupid, in case you didn't know."

"You've seen her?"

"I've been having you watched," he said with a shrug. "Just because you think you can divorce me without a fight doesn't that mean I share your disinterest. Couples live for years with one or both party traveling. I don't understand why you just dismissed me like that—especially with a kid involved—not that she's mine."

It came to her that, once again, he was deflecting responsibility, creating a smokescreen of confusion to cover his faults, by focusing on hers. It didn't seem to register with him that he'd raped and abandoned her; that their brief time together hadn't been all that great. Never again would she let his mind games hurt—or so she told herself. Her eyes were already filling with tears.

"So you won't help me find her?" she asked, trying to keep her voice even.

He laughed harshly. "Yeah, Meggie, like you won't help me by making a couple of phone calls.

I've given you your last chance."

"But Penny's your . . .." Her words died. What could she say? He might actually be right about Penny's paternity.

He moved to the door and opened it. "Adios, Chiquita," he said with a tight smile; and gestured for her leave. "You and I, babe, we're on our own. By the time you see Carlotta, I'll be gone."

She could only stare at him, furious. "Just like that?" she asked, snapping her finger in his face. "Just like that, you dismiss me as if I've failed some test? That's what I mean about you and me, Donald. There's no common ground. There's no real love, just your idea of it."

Before she could react, he grabbed her arm, flung her out the door and slammed it shut. She staggered back, not quite knowing what to do, then headed down the hall, tears streaming down her face.

ꙮꙮꙮꙮꙮ

There were tears on his face, too as he slumped against the wall. That was the hardest thing he'd ever done. He'd let her go; he'd pushed her really, wanting all the best for the only person he'd ever loved with any semblance of the true meaning of the word. Taking her on the road would have been a travesty, especially after what she'd already suffered on his behalf. Now he had his whole fucking life ahead of him; and no clue where to begin.

With trembling fingers, he pulled the wrinkled photo from his back pocket and stared at Penny, his little girl. Genetics didn't lie. The violet fairy eyes were unmistakable. On a baby, they were adorable; on a depressed woman, they were haunting. If only his mother could see this child. Maybe then, she'd think it had all been worth it.

There was a click of a key and the door swung open.

Exhausted beyond measure, he turned slowly, stuffing the photo back in his pocket. "I wondered when you two would show up." He smiled as the men entered, glad the waiting was over.

McClelland strode in on the balls of his feet, giving the place a once-over; while Graham closed the door, looking out of character in a blue and green Aloha shirt, kakis and sturdy brown Dockers. He'd shaved his beard, taking a few years off his looks. Graham smiled pleasantly as he headed for the drapes, then ripped them closed.

"In a little trouble, son?" he asked. He sat in a chair, ankle crossed over opposite knee, the chair tipped back.

McClelland stuck his head in the bathroom, then closed the door and stood with his arms crossed over his chest, scowling. "We want your report and fast, Mr. Alexander. You've been trying our patience. Standard procedure is to check in first, and then travel—if allowed."

"Which way's the wind blowing?" Don asked, glaring at McClelland, whose bloodshot eyes no longer held a yellow caste. He shuddered, seeing massive hands, rough and battered. The man had been one the best damn helicopter pilots in Vietnam—because he'd survived. He'd been in some top-secret unit, tasked with ferrying others of his kind—missions too controversial, too crucial to appear in any report. He'd always wondered what had precipitated his reassignment. Was he still flying?

Don offered him a smoke; but he shook his head. "Gave it up," he said, smiling grimly. "Dangerous for one's healthy, don't you think?"

There was a knock at the door. A signal passed between the two agents as McClelland went to the door.

"Who is it?" he asked.

"That you, Mac?" came an incredulous reply.

"Walt?" McClelland asked, his expression puzzled.

Don could only stare as the door swung open and McClelland grabbed a hefty guy in a bear hug—apparently Walt. The two filled the room, laughing and talking, long-lost helicopter buddies, Vietnam Vets.

Then another guy, looking mighty familiar, came bounding in, his eyes filled with blood lust. He was a mass of muscles, a fight ready to happen. His hands were huge, his beady eyes focused on him. Don took a step back.

"My baby brother, Stanley," Walt said, flashing a proud smile.

"Where's Megan?" Stan spat out. He came at

him fast, grabbing his shoulders, forcing him against the wall.

"Hello, Megan's Stan." Don twirled out of his grasp, his stomach lurching. For once, his timing was right. Megan was long gone, maybe even dead by now, if he knew Ernesto. Not even his proud Megan would stand for long against that monster. He shivered, recalling the bloodless way Ernesto had dealt with his cousin's sobbing wife. Women were a commodity to Ernesto—to be used, abused and disposed of entirely at his whim.

In an instant, Graham had Stan on the floor, his arm pinned behind his back, his knee shoved into his spine. "None of that," Graham said out of the corner of his mouth.

"Aw, let him go," Don said with a laugh. "He's Megan's friend, just trying to even the score. She should have married him, not me. Two fools, if you want my opinion. But I suppose you don't." He hoped he sounded light.

Graham let Stan up. He looked ready to come at him again; but Walt shot him a stern look, stopping him cold. Swearing under his breath, Stan backed to the windows, taking the chair Graham had vacated. He threw his arms behind his head, cradling his neck with clasped hands, the picture of arrogance.

"Speak," Graham commanded. "Another enemy to your name ain't good for your life expectancy, Donnie boy."

Don rubbed his eyes; then proceeded to pour out his story: his final flight, the plane going down, the cut line and broken gauge, the old man and his grandson, even his recent meeting with Megan.—though not all of it.

"She doesn't want me," he said, looking pointedly at Stan. "And I just want her to be happy."

"Yeah, right," Stan spat. "You should have thought of that a few years ago. Her life would have been a hell of a lot easier. And where is she now—on her way to Carlotta?"

"Yeah, well . . . live and learn," Donald sneered, pointedly ignoring the most important question, wanting to beat the high and almighty self-righteousness from the stiff's ugly face. The woman obviously has no taste in men.

He glanced in Graham's direction. "I know it looks bad," he said with a heavy sigh. "But it was supposed to be my last run. You promised." He shot McClelland a dark look. "Ernesto was getting too close to the truth. You said it yourself. Someone tipped him off. Was it you guys?" He scanned the agents.

"Where's the plane?" Graham asked, his face expressionless, his eyes as hard as wet steel on a rainy night. "And where's Megan?"

Don laughed, the sound close to a girlish giggle. Then he took a deep breath, his heart pounding. So this was it. Fish or cut bait. "I have to know how the wind blows," he said softly. "I'm asking nice. Am I in or out? Do I get a new life as a CPA, a new assignment, or do I get offed? Otherwise, I'm not telling you a damn thing."

McClelland and Walt exchanged looks. Walt nodded slightly, his glance including Stan.

"What?" Stan asked, his eyes like broken glass, his fists were clenched and ready.

"Wrong place, wrong time," Walt said with a shrug, as if the brothers were alone in the room. "We ain't seen nothing, Mac." He nodded solemnly at McClelland. "We gotta leave. Now." He jerked his head at the door, his gaze on Stan.

Stan passed Don on his way out, a bundle of nerves, a slam against the wall waiting to happen. It took all of his control to keep from shoving him first; from pounding on the man who'd stolen his wife. Seeing him walk out that door was harsh proof that no matter his fate—soon to be settled by Graham and McClelland—he'd never have his heart's desire—someone who truly loved him.

He turned slowly, seeing the gun leveled at his face, hearing the soft thud of the silencer, feeling the intense pain in his right leg before he collapsed.

"Where's the plane?" Graham repeated.

ఆఆఆఆఆ

"What's it gonna be?" Stan asked. He glanced at Walt sharply, then pulled out onto the empty road. In the wee hours of the morning, Lowell was a ghost town.

"Don't know and don't care," Walt said stiffly. He folded his arms across his substantial chest.

"Bullshit." Stan muttered. "You know exactly

what's happening right now."

Walt whistled through his teeth, in a pondering frame of mind. Stan said nothing. His brother was coming to a conclusion—one that he could trust. He tapped on the steering wheel, wondering if he dared turn on the music to fill the awful silence.

Then Walt stopped whistling. He sucked in through his teeth. "The man's holding back," he said. "There's something on that plane that they want—not necessarily drugs. They won't kill him. They'll just hurt him a little. That doesn't bother you, now does it?" he asked, looking over at Stan with a smirk.

"Hell, no," Stan said, with a laugh. "But why do you figure there's something on the plane?"

Walt grunted, appreciating the question. Stan headed down a side street toward the Ed Center, going by memory: he'd traveled this route many times over the past few years.

"If it was just the drugs, they wouldn't care," Walt said. "Sure, there's a lot of money involved—but they can always make another run."

"What is it then?" Stan asked.

Walt exhaled heavily. "Could be a message, electronics, weapons or money. Could even be a person—someone important."

"But the plane went down." Stan looked at him out of the corner of his eye, trying to focus on avoiding a pothole ahead.

"That's right," Walt said, sending him a significant look.

CHAPTER 18
5:00 AM

He came at her from the shadows—the same goon who'd held Charlie. She screamed as loud as she could, until he taped her mouth. Then she struggled to breathe. He gripped her wrists tightly behind her back, and shoved her in front of him into the Ed Center. He was frighteningly silent as he dragged her through the main lobby, past the elevators, down the hallway and into a pitch-dark classroom. He flung her to the thickly carpeted floor, almost knocking her head against a u-shaped configuration of tables, set up for the first class. The place was stifling hot. She could barely breathe.

All of her senses came into sharp focus as she struggled to rise. She searched around her for a way to escape.

A match scratched. Someone lit a candle on the far side of the table—and then another and another; until she could make out forms and faces. Carlotta and Adam stood at the head of the room before a white projector screen, holding hands. The goon stood near the door, his expression dark and forbidding, his gun ready. His jaw was massive, as were his arms. He looked like an indigenous Columbian, pressed into the service of his country.

The small hand on the clock above the door moved directly over the five.

"Welcome, Senora Rosswell," said the slender, well-dressed man as he moved toward her slowly. In one delicate motion, he ripped the tape off her face, his eyes gleaming with pleasure. She closed her eyes, resisting the urge to scream or rub her burning skin. Her eyes watered, but she trained them upon him.

"So glad you could join us," he murmured, a half-smile indicating his enjoyment of her pain. His soft, cultured voice, with its slight Spanish accent was like a nail in her throat.

"Ernesto," she managed to choke out, seeing the avid interest in his eyes. This man had encouraged Donald to beat her. When he reached out a hand to help her up, she took it, then spun away. Weakness would be her demise. She couldn't let him win.

He smoothed down his trim mustache, looking perplexed. "Dear Senora Rosswell." He smiled slightly. "Let's not equivocate. You appear to be a woman of intelligence. I want your ex-husband as much as you would like your lovely little daughter. Shall we come to some sort of an agreement?"

"Of course," she said, lifting her chin. "I'll tell you exactly where to find him. But I want Penny first."

"Ah, Senora." He moved toward her, his smile fading as he backed her into the wall. He reached out a hand, toying with her hair. "Such a lovely woman . . . so clever and refined. Donald had no idea of your worth, now did he?"

His hand came out of nowhere, slapping her hard across the face. Pain exploded in her head. She bent over, reeling, wanting to howl. A vessel had burst in her nose, and she tasted blood. Instinctively, she backed against the wall, then whacked her head. One arm out, she steadied herself, the room spinning.

"Please, Ernesto," Adam protested. "You don't need to do that. She's not even a player." Through a haze of pain, she saw him step forward. He looked worried and exhausted. He'd managed to tuck in his shirt, but still looked rumpled and unwashed, as if he hadn't slept or bathed in days. Last week's marketing meeting came to mind, and the clipped way he'd moved from one topic to the next, clearly in control. He wasn't now.

There was a muffled thud. Adam lurched forward, his chest awash with blood, his eyes glassy, his mouth open in surprise, and then slack. Carlotta sprang to his side, grabbing him as he fell, her shrieks filling the room.

"Waste of breath," Ernesto muttered. He waved a hand before him. "Like swatting a bug, really." He laid the gun on the table, looking confused, shaking his head. "Now where was I?"

He looked up at Megan and grinned, his eyes empty.

She slipped around the table, but he tripped her and she went sprawling. In an instant, she was moving fast, crab-like, away from him, her heart pounding. He grabbed his gun and pointed it at her.

She froze, holding her breath. Sweat dripped down her face.

"Don't you want your little girl?" he asked softly and gestured for her to come closer. "Donald's the only clue we have to that plane and we need the cargo. Twelve kilos of pure cocaine is not something we can overlook, not to mention certain documents that track my organization's movements. Your Feds are too hungry for a part of the action."

Unblinking, she moved toward him. As she rose, he gripped her face. Then he pushed her down onto the table, one hand digging into her face, the other on her knee. She moved on command, her teeth chattering. Blood dripped from her nose, but she focused all of her attention on his gleaming brown eyes.

He shrugged slightly in Adam's direction. "Women seem to crave the man. I don't understand it. Even you—the epitome of innocence—has succumbed to his slippery charm. Even Ming was willing, though not especially eager, from what I understand. Unfortunately, I gave him to my darling sister to watch." He jerked his head in Carlotta's direction. "What a wasted family connection, when all along, he was a nobody, a buffoon, an idiot. Emotion continually clouded his judgment. I should have ejected him right away."

The sound of sobs filled the room.

Carlotta.

"Now about you, my dear." Ernesto slid a hand up her leg. She clenched her thighs, using all of her control to remain still, to find the best moment to strike. "I must admit Adam had the right idea about women in some regards." His smile was bright. "As lesser mortals, females must do as they are told. They are innately fit only for producing the next generation and as playthings—whichever suits our needs. Otherwise, how can we protect them? Isn't that the mindset we all learned at our parents' knees?"

She leaned back on the table, her whole body trembling as he pushed up her skirt.

"Too bad about your sister," he whispered, his lips brushing her inner thigh.

"What do you mean?" she asked. A roar filled her head as horror dawned behind her eyes. She saw the broken bodies of Val, Tom and their kids, her father crumbling into a tired old man, Roger silent and watchful.

"We needed to prove Donald's loyalty, to observe his reaction," Ernesto said smoothly. He traced a finger behind her knee. "The accident was a little more severe than we anticipated; but it was still quite effective." He lifted her leg slightly, as if examining it.

"Accident?" She choked out the word. "You planned Val's accident? You killed my family?"

"Jose was supposed to merely brush against another car," he said softly, as if describing a movie he'd seen. "Any car would have done. However, the old man's reflexes were slow. He must have pushed on the gas pedal at that singular moment of panic. So sorry about your loss."

"You caused it?" she screamed as she rose from the table, only to be shoved back down, viciously this time. Then he was forcing her down, winding his fingers beneath her panties. She flailed at him with all of her might, managing to rip one arm loose and slash her nails across his face.

Then came a muffled jolt. Ernesto rolled off her, clutching his arm, bright with blood. His face was livid with the marks of her nails.

She leaped from the table; but he grabbed her arm and yanked her hard.

She screamed as loud as she could, closing her eyes, the sound filling her throat, her head and her chest aching.

"You bitch," he spat, pulling himself up beside her, twisting her arm, making her cry out again.

"Hermano."

It was spoken softly. They both looked up. Carlotta held a gun in one trembling hand. Tears streamed down her mascara-streaked face. She stood with her feet planted wide. The goon lay on the floor.

"You had to kill him," she screeched, shaking her head wildly. "You bastard, sucking the life out of people with your greed, your drugs ruining lives? You don't give a damn, do you, Ernesto, mi precioso hermano? It's all about money and power, isn't it. You dare hurt this woman who's the world to her children, after you've already murdered most of her family. Now you've stolen her lovely child and probably killed her, too. And you don't even care." She sobbed loudly. "You have your own family locked up tight, prisoners behind a fence in Miami, obedient to your every whim. Your wife's a brainless idiot, your kids are spoiled brats. You don't care if any of us live a normal life. You don't even know what that means."

"Now, Carlotta, dear." He held out a bloody hand.

"Mi strutting hermano," she sneered, rising up to her full height and looking down her nose at him. "You're a user like the rest of our glorious family, forcing me into marriage with el Americano."

She swiped at her nose with the back of her arm. "But you didn't count on love, now did you?" she sobbed. "I loved Adam Clark with all of my wretched heart, though it made no difference to you in the end. He was just another ripe market potential, wasn't he, Ernesto?" Spittle flew from her mouth. "Unlike you, however, he was capable of love. He adored his children, while you've never loved anyone, not even yourself."

Ernesto moved closer, dragging Megan with him, then pushed her before him like a shield.

"I've done everything you asked and more, mi hermano." Carlotta was shaking with rage as she lowered the gun. "But you had to kill Adam—the only man I ever loved. Now what exactly am I supposed to do?"

Ernesto leaped for her, but Carlotta was fast. There came a muffled sound, and he slumped against her, her dress dark with blood as he slid to the floor.

Megan backed away, not knowing if she should comfort Carlotta or run for the door.

There was a sound in the hallway; then the police burst in.

EPILOGUE

The Victorian Architectural style, named after Britain's reigning Queen Victoria, was popular from 1840 to 1900. It was a prosperous time when industrialization, coupled with extensive new railroads, transformed the American landscape via the mass production and shipment of housing components. At the same time, newly mechanized saws and lathes produced increasingly extravagant and complex architectural elements such as latticework, asymmetric roof gables, decorative roofing and siding materials, elaborate gingerbread trim and conical turrets. Massive homes, looking more like wedding cakes than shelters, with no regard for fuel conservation, sprang up like dandelions across America, gracing broad city streets where the wealthy lived, and quaint country roads where they took their rest. Among all the elements of Victorian architectural charm, however, none was as visually striking as the conical turret.

Megan loved her pair; their bases round, wooden, bumped-out structures that covered the front corners of the wide third floor. Within each tubular form was a lovely paneled room containing a custom-made bench topped by blue velvet cushions; and in the case of the turret above her apartment, a high-powered telescope. The turret roofs, with tiny steel points at their peaks, were shingled with custom-cut slate. It had cost her a small fortune to replace them.

She blew a wisp of hair off hair face for the third time; then yanked her hair up and back into a bright red scrunchie she kept on her wrist, impatient, irritated, her nerved jangled. She peered through the telescope, watching a crow flit across the roof of the house next door, joining its mate. They bounced across the steep pitch, cawing at each other, sounding like an old married couple.

On a clear day, she could see Mount Monadnock to the north and Mount Wachusett to the west. Today, however, it was overcast and hot, with only a slight breeze. She looked out over rooftops and trees, seeing cars that looked like toys, and the heat shimmering off the elementary school where Roger would go in the fall. Mrs. Bingham up the street was herding her daycare charges into her van. Little heads bobbed, bright flashes of brown, yellow and black as they climbed in; high-pitched voices chattering and shrieking, excited about their outing. Then Mrs. Bingham drove away.

It was wonderful, this view. Even picturing it when she went about her day gave her reason to pause. It was a quiet space, far above the relentless tedium of day-to-day rituals. Up here, she could think straight; she could see life from a different perspective. It was like looking at the ocean, seeing the endless horizon; but with the element of power, of being on the bridge of a vast ship, looking out at a sea of people and homes, in charge of her destiny.

She sighed, her hand falling away from the telescope. Was she really in charge? Her views had changed in countless ways over the past few years. Once an angry ex-Baptist, out to prove something to the significant people in her life; what was she now? She pictured Val and Tom frozen in time; never imagining that their lives would be cut short by a criminal, never thinking beyond the day, the week, the year of their love-filled lives. And poor Pa, his body worn out, exhausted with worry. He'd been going down hill steadily for as long as she could remember. Though Val's death had been like a beating, seeing Aunt Sarah, a ghost from the past, had pushed him over the edge. She pictured Letty; and her eyes welled with tears. She hung her head, unable to pursue the thought.

Once again, she grabbed the telescope, the view swimming before her eyes. She blinked hard. Roger would be home soon—her little boy, her darling. Without him and Stan, she'd still be in bed, covers to her chin, bawling her eyes out. Life went on, and they needed her, almost as much as she needed them.

She chuckled, wondering at the power of love and circumstance. Attitude was everything—acceptance and tolerance keen bedfellows. With her own personal transformation, both man and boy had magically changed from her worst irritations into her dearest loves. Yet it wasn't enough to take away the pain.

She eyed the stain across her blouse, resisting the urge to scream. She was leaking again and her breasts ached. Was Penny still alive? She'd been weaning her slowly; but now it seemed so foolish, helping her take that little step away from babyhood, when she might never see her again. How blind people were, taking each precious minute for granted, shrugging it away as if it were of no significance; when they should be holding on, begging for more. She exhaled slowly: it came out as a sob.

A gust blew in the wide-open windows. Maybe it would rain. She moved slowly, tiredly to the seat cushion, her joints aching; and lay down, facing the ceiling, seeing a thin arching crack in the shape of a crescent moon—another repair to add to her growing list.

She closed her eyes against a tear that started to fall. It had been thirty–seven hours since Penny's abduction. It had been a lifetime. She'd called in sick, as had Stan; though she'd sent Roger to camp, ignoring his rhetoric.

The police had found no trace of Penny; and the CIA had disappeared. Now, what was she supposed to do? How was she supposed to make it through another day, never mind the rest of her life? She pictured her baby in bed sleeping soundly, her face soft with innocence. She pictured chubby arms and legs flailing and a toothless grin, tears filling her eyes.

"Here you go," Stan said, moving into the room, holding a glass of red wine and a platter of nachos, paint spattered across the bridge of his nose. He'd been painting a table in the carriage shed—a present for Roger, who's birthday was in a few weeks.

"What's this?" she asked, eying the food and drink, feeling like she was going to be sick. "I didn't ask for that," she said, trying to hold her breath against the acrid smell of tomatoes and peppers. If she didn't know better, she'd think she was pregnant.

He shot her a dark look. "I was just trying to help."

"Aw, Stan," she said and took the glass. He moved quickly, setting up a tray table, putting the platter on it, a little too peppy and gleeful by her estimation.

She sipped the wine, feeling the burn of it down her throat, and then simply watched him, wondering what the hell he was thinking. Her child had been abducted, for God's sake, and he was playing waiter? He had to be a moron.

Yet he was studying her, too.

"I know you're not hungry, Meg," he said softly, "but you've got to eat something. Just nibble for a while. It'll make you feel better." He looked tired, the lines on his face deeper than usual.

"Fine," she said, then took another sip, her eyes brimming as she set the glass down. "I can't," she said, the smell of food too sour, too pungent. She started to retch, then leaned over, gripping her middle.

He came quickly and pulled her into his arms. She sighed, instantly relaxed, and snuggled against his shoulder. Then he sat, cradling her, stroking her hair.

"Aw, Meg," he said. "We'll hear soon . . . something's got to give. It's only been a day."

"What am I supposed to do?" she sobbed, grateful for his devotion. Never again would she take it for granted. She took a deep breath: her stomach was starting to settle.

"I don't know," he said, and kissed the top of her head. "I've left two messages with Floyd; but he's not returning my calls. The cops say they're doing the best they can; and the Feds seemed to have disappeared. All we can do is wait."

"It's so hard," she wailed. He mumbled something that sounded like ascent, and rocked her slightly, bringing comfort. She lifted her gaze and really looked at him, seeing the strength on his swarthy face, the kindness in his eyes. She'd never forget the wild look on his face when he and his brother had burst into the classroom on the heels of the cops; or the way he'd come to her, arms out, and held her hand while the cops had grilled her; his soft murmurs under his breath, utterly reassuring.

"I love you, Stan," she whispered, resting her head against his shoulder.

He looked at her for a long moment, his eyes filling. "I love you, too, Meg, " he said at last. "I have for a long time."

His lips were gentle at first, gentle and soft, so soft compared with the slight razor stubble around his face. She opened her lips, wanting more, giving generously. He pulled her closer, his kiss deepening, his hands in her hair, on her backsides. With a small cry, she even moved closer, submitting to the joy of it; stroking his neck, his face, his ears, wanting to erase the pain of losing her child, even for a moment. Her hands spanned his chest. She wanted all of him.

The red light on the intercom system near the door started to flash; but she paid no attention. They'd installed the system months ago, a concession to living in the sprawling house, with the front door seemingly miles away from every room. The selection box was outside, beside the front door, with a button for each apartment, beside which were the occupant's last names.

She kissed him again, moaning in pleasure; knowing by his moans that she was pleasing him, too.

The light continued to flash.

He fumbled with her shirt buttons, his hands

trembling. Then he had it off, and his hands were on her, touching, kneading. She slipped off her sandals and her shorts; while he stripped off his T-shirt. With one steady hand, she unzipped his jean.

She was breathing heavily: they both were. His kisses grew deeper, more insistent. She traced the sides of his face, breathing in his scent, wanting more.

Someone pounded on the front door; they were yelling loudly.

"Who the hell is that?" she said, moving away from him, holding onto his arms, unwilling to let go.

"I gotta see," he said, then slid her onto the cushion and stumbled to the window, the front of his pants distended.

"Shit," he muttered, turning back to her. "I think it's Floyd."

"Floyd?" she cried, and started gathering her clothes. "Does he have Penny?" Her heart pounded.

"I don't know," he said, craning his neck to look down through the trees. "I can't see."

"I know you're in there," called an aggrieved voice. "Put some clothes on, will ya, and let us in."

Us?

Megan buttoned her shirt, her fingers clumsy; and stuffed her feet into sandals, snagging the opposite feet, wanting to shriek in frustration.

"Damn," Stan muttered. "Floyd, is that you?" he called down. He zipped up his jeans, his expression pained.

"Yeah, bud," came the terse reply. "I got your messages . . . every one of them. Now get your ass down here!"

"I'll see you down there," Stan said over his shoulder, heading for the stairs, his chest naked. "Come as soon as you can," he called out.

ঙঙঙঙঙ

He sprang for the stairs, and took them two at a time; then sped through the lobby and flung open the door, seeing by a flash of Megan's legs, that she followed close behind.

"Floyd," he said, holding out a hand automatically. The skinny, pimply man, dressed in expensive tennis clothes stood at the threshold grinning.

"Buddy, Pal," he said, clasping his hand.

"Where is she?" Stan asked, yanking him in, then striding outside, leaving him stumbling awkwardly into the room. He had no time for niceties.

"You're Floyd Mello?" Megan asked, staring at the man her father had hired, who'd not returned even one of her phone calls. He looked like a joke; though something in his bloodshot blue eyes caught her attention. Was it elation?

"In person," he said, with a beatific grin. If he had a hat on, she imagined he would have doffed it.

ঙঙঙঙঙ

Stan jumped down the steps, seeing a flash of

pink coming up the walkway; then could only stare.

"Hi Stan," his stepmother trilled. Dressed in pink from her halter-top mini-dress to her four-inch sandals and pink-tipped toes, she looked all of fifteen. In her arms was a squirming baby, also in pink.

"Penny?" He stepped closer, his smile broadening as the baby held out a chubby waving arm, her dimpled face creasing in a toothless grin. He took the baby, laughing aloud, remembering Trisha's words—that she loved children and mourned the lack of them.

"What's going on?" he asked, cradling the child, unable to keep from smiling.

She jerked her head at the house. "Floyd had her all along . . . well, at least I did . . . and I was happy to have her. She's such a darling. Floyd knew she'd be safe with me." She shook her head, as she smoothed the baby's dress. "That dealer . . . he thought a wad of cash could buy old Floyd." She grinned out of the side of her mouth. "Floyd sure knows how to play 'em, Stanley. He promised to dump Penny in the river, make her disappear, make Megan suffer. Then he was going after the other kid."

"Roger?" he asked.

"Floyd's a loyal friend," she said with a nod. "And a fine actor." She kissed the top of Penny's head as she mounted the steps, her smile teasing.

ଔଔଔଔଔ

Megan caught her breath as Stan entered the lobby with Penny. She hurled herself at him and grabbed her baby, her sobs turning into soft crooning sounds as she cradled her. Tears streamed down her face as she took inventory of each chubby limb, each scented crease. Penny gurgled and kicked in glee.

"Trish?" Megan managed to get out, seeing her dearest confidant standing beside Stan. In the past few years, Trish had dispensed gentle advice along with a flattering cut. It was as if she'd known her forever; though she only saw her every few months. "Why are you here?" she asked, looking into her laughing bright eyes.

"You know my stepmother?" Stan asked, looking baffled and miffed, as if his most imitate secret had been revealed.

"Trish Z?" she said under her breath, looking from him to Trish. "But you're from Nashua," she said, shaking her head.

"Originally," Stan said, looking worried. "She's lived in Lowell for more than a decade."

Megan stared at him, the facts clicking in. He was the stubborn stepson Trish had often described—as judgmental and unforgiving as his aging, grief-stricken father. They had no idea what this gentle woman had endured. Trish dressed flashy, but that was her way. They could all take a few lessons from her in being uninhibited. So she'd made a mistake several years ago. Who hasn't from time to time?

She studied Stan, wondering if people ever really knew each other; if the barriers people erected against pain weren't as destructive as outright war.

"Of course," Trish said with a giggle as she flung her arm around Megan and Penny. "Meg's my best customer; and I just love her kids."

"She's your hairdresser?" Stan asked, looking at Trish as if he'd never seen her before.

"The best cut in the City of Lowell." Megan said, laughing through her tears as she smiled tenderly at her friend. "I had no idea this was the stepson you've been complaining about." She eyed Stan, who was shaking his head.

Floyd rolled his eyes, backed away slightly, and made a throat-cutting gesture under his chin. "Not my department," he muttered. "You people need to figure this out for yourself."

Megan smirked as she turned to Stan. "What are you gonna say about this poor woman, now? Saving Penny like that . . . and putting up with you father? I've never met the man, but you've got to admit, she must be a veritable saint?" She winked at Trish.

"I hear ya," Stan said, looking sheepish. Then a smile curled his lips as he looked at Trish. "And I'm sorry, Trisha; I really am."

Sorry? Megan looked from one to the other. Stan was actually apologizing.

Trish patted his arm and smiled brightly, making her laugh. "It's a good thing, kiddo," Trish said. "You're gonna be seeing a whole lot more of me, now that I've developed an addiction for this little tyke." She caressed Penny's cheek. "Maybe her mommy will let me do a little baby-sitting . . . give the two of you some alone time."

"That would be great," Stan said, and slung his arm around Megan's shoulders.

She nestled against him, feeling cherished and loved. For the first time, she had everything she'd ever wanted. She looked around the lobby, the dream of a lifetime, a gift from an old woman who still had a lot of life left in her. She studied her baby and her friend, people she adored, who needed her and loved her back. Even Floyd was part of her circle—a guardian sent by Pa to keep her safe. In a little while, Roger would be home. Though he'd come to her through painful circumstances, he completed her family picture. And then there was Stan … always Stan . . . forever Stan.

"Are you gonna marry her or what," Trish asked, shooting Stan a stern look. "You're a damn fool if you don't. She's been pining over you for years."

"Trish!" Megan gaped at her.

"Megan." Stan said her name like prayer. "I do want to . . .."

"Let me say something first," she said, seeing only him.

"Okay," he said slowly, looking anxious.

"I'm all right on my own, Stan," she said softly, gratified by the instant surprise on his face. He was shaking his head slightly, making her want to laugh.

But she didn't. Instead, she looked deep in his eyes, wanting to be as clear as possible.

"I don't really *need* you or any other man for *anything*," she said, widening her eyes. "You do realize that?"

"But . . . I . . .." Was he starting to pout?

She placed a finger on his lips, smiling gently. "My life is so much better, Stanley Zambinsky, now that I have you." Tears filled her eyes; and she could see in his eyes that he was really listening. "I can certainly live without you, darlin'; but I don't want to, and thank God, I don't have to."

He smiled then, this love of her life—whom she'd practically had to conk over the head to get his attention. He pulled her close, now grinning. There was a bratty look on his face that made him look something like Roger.

"You'll be marrying me soon," he said, talking out of the side of his mouth. "No shacking-it for us, Megan Rosswell. Your father would haunt me forever. We have to make it legal—for the kids' sake, if not for our own. I can't be living in a different place."

"You got that right," she said, laughing with the joy of it. She squeezed him back hard, making his eyes widen. "You're gonna be living here now, Stan, whether you like it or not. So you'd better get used to it."

Printed in the United States
126151LV00001BA/1/P